KINCAID
and the
Miners & Poachers

CURTIS D. CARNEY

KINCAID

and the

Miners & Poachers

CURTIS D. CARNEY

***

Print Edition ISBN 978-0-9861363-9-9
Nook Edition ISBN 978-1-7359128-0-6
Kindle Edition ISBN 978-1-7359128-1-3

Published by:

Insight Press Books, LLC.

Spokane, Washington

Visit us on the web at:

www.insightpressbooks.com

Designed and printed by:

Gorham Printing, Centralia, Washington, USA

Prologue

Since the first gold rush of 1896 in the Bonanza Creek area of the Klondike, individuals and companies, big and small, have traveled to Alaska searching for gold, and this migration has not stopped even to this present day. All types of gold mining operations were put to the test, such as panning, hydraulic mining, sluice mining, and actually sometimes just digging into the dirt and rock with a shovel.

Another activity that has drawn many active seekers of wealth to the Alaskan Territory is the game hunter. Leather around the world has always been in large demand by almost all countries on every continent. Even before Russia sold Alaska to the United States, in 1867, uncontrolled hunting for almost anything that would produce fur or leather was hunted extensively by many countries.

The greater part of the Alaska Territory had little or no enforcement of the laws, sketchy at best, throughout the entire territory. There were local deputy sheriffs in some of the boroughs, like Wrangell, but their authority extended only to the outskirts of the borough, leaving the rest of the Alaska Territory to be used and abused by men and companies to get rich quick by whatever means.

Cast of Characters

MAIN CHARACTERS:

Charles Weber...Captain of the Blue Sea, Braddock Shipping

Eddie Beck...Skipper of the boat Misty Charters

Ferrell Jones...Mining boss of Stone Mountain Mining

Fisher Minnow...Helps Kelly

Henry Wilson...Mining boss of Twin Forks Mining and Dredging Company

James Kincaid...Manager of Department of Agriculture, Wrangell District

Janet Moore...Works for Mrs. Mackly

Jeffery Maxwell...Works for Shane Keller at Wrangell Livery Stable

Jesse Holmes...Bookkeeper for Twin Forks Mining and Dredging Company

Kelly O'Brien...Works for James Kincaid, Natural Resource Manager, Wrangell District

Moaka...Works for James Kincaid, Indian Liaison Representative, Wrangell District

Mrs. Mackly...Owner of Parker Boarding House in Wrangell

Nancy O'Brien...Wife of Kelly O'Brien, school teacher

Oliver Marlin...Deputy Sheriff of Wrangell

Payuk...Tlingit Indian who helps Kelly and works for James Kincaid on part-time basis

Sara Keller...Secretary for James Kincaid, wife of Shane Keller

Shane Keller...Owner of Wrangell Livery Stable

Suzette....James Kincaid's wife, schoolteacher

OTHER CHARACTERS:

Arnold Smith...Fisherman in sacred stream

Ben Shaper...Fisherman in sacred stream

Doctor Bonds...Medical doctor for Wrangell

Fred Bingham...Smithy, works for Shane Keller

Harry Brooks...Fisherman in sacred stream

Hartford Harrison...Chief Mate on the Blue Sea

Keith Mason...Bank president

Kiviaq...Leader of Tlingit warriors

Kroviq...Tlingit warrior

Mike...Seaman on the Blue Sea

Neil Baxter...Landowner

Paul...Seaman on the Blue Sea

Sadie...James and Suzette's daughter

Sam Boren...Owner of Wrangell Mercantile

Saupeteese...Tlingit warrior

Sidney...Kelly and Nancy's son

Stan...Seaman on the Blue Sea

Strickland...Wagon driver

Thomas...James and Suzette's son

Tom Marks...Assistant to Keith Mason

Tom Mason...Beaver trapper

Wilbur Johnson...Legal representative for Department of Agriculture

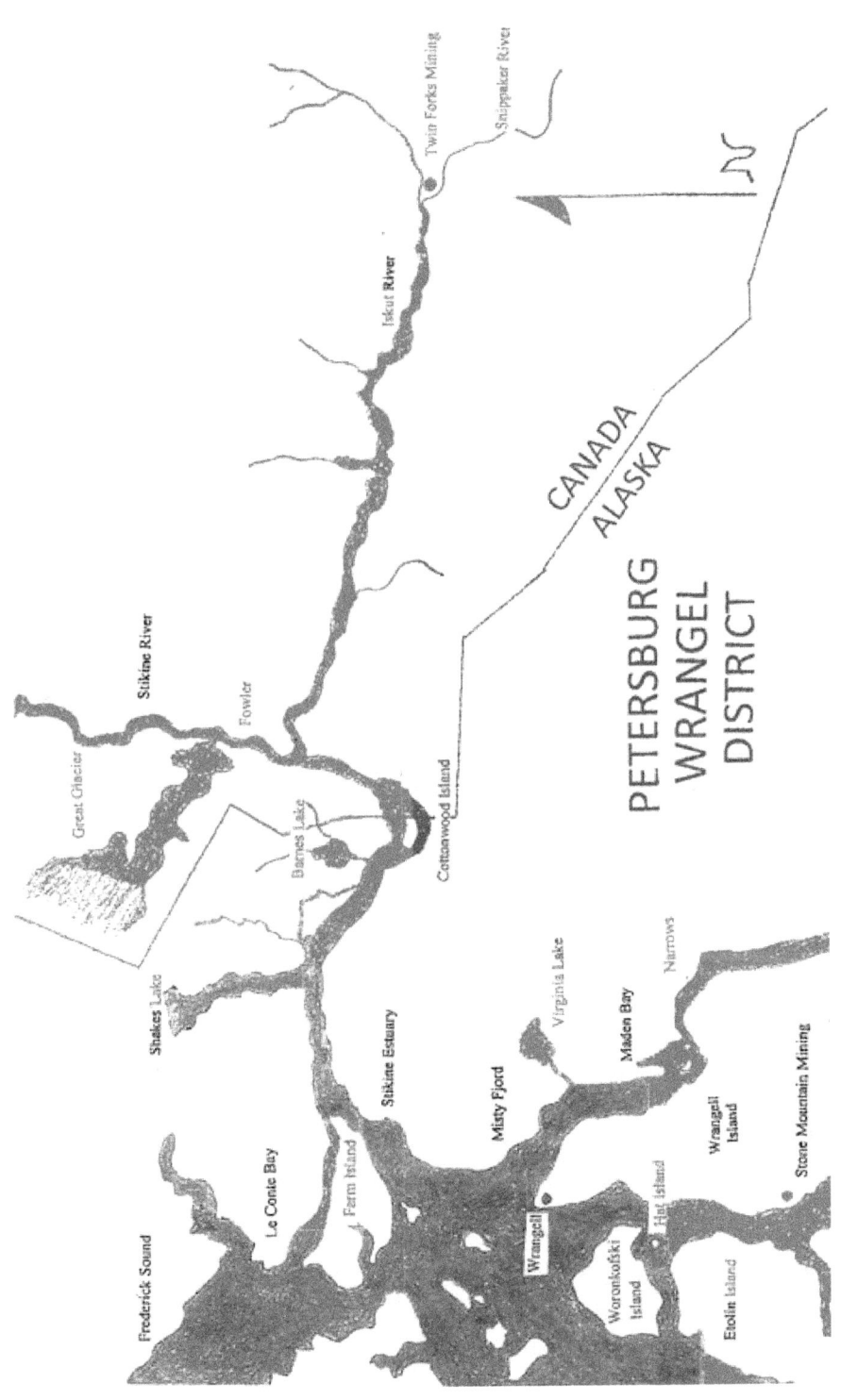

PETERSBURG
WRANGEL
DISTRICT

CANADA
ALASKA

Twin Forks Mining

Snippaker River

Iskut River

Stikine River

Fowler

Great Glacier

Barnes Lake

Cottonwood Island

Shakes Lake

Stikine Estuary

Virginia Lake

Misty Fjord

Maiden Bay

Narrows

Le Conte Bay

Ferm Island

Frederick Sound

Wrangell

Wrangell Island

Stone Mountain Mining

Woronkofski Island

Hat Island

Etolin Island

CHAPTER ONE

Kelly eased his tall frame forward in the saddle as he grasped the leather-covered horn, stood his long frame up in the stirrups, removed his brown felt cowboy hat, and combed his short, dark hair back. As he settled back down in the padded leather saddle, he commented to Payuk, "Coming up on this ridge sure gives us a bird's eye view of the entire river canyon. I wonder how far the Iskut River runs to the east."

Payuk answered, "Before we left Wrangell I asked several elders if they had ever been to the Snippaker River tributary that cut into the Iskut. One had, but he said it was many years gone by since he had been there." Pausing to scratch his head through his thick black hair, he continued, "But he did say it was very rough country and the best way to travel up the Iskut canyon was to stay close to the river." Payuk was a full-blood Tlingit who was shorter than Kelly, with a strong-built body and straight black hair. He was helping Kelly on this project that Kincaid had sent them on. Payuk had helped Moaka quite a bit in the past and Kincaid liked the way Payuk worked with his other employees of the Department of Agriculture.

"Huh," Kelly scoffed. "Well we sure the hell aren't close to the river being on this ridge. I just needed to see more of where I was going. Now I have a better idea of how things lie. Ever since the *Misty Charters* dropped us off, we've been climbing." Pausing, Kelly turned in his saddle to face Payuk and causally reflected, "You know, it was real nice of Captain Daniels to leave Eddie the *Misty Charters*. Eddie sure takes good care of it and I think Eddie is only about twenty-two years old."

"I think," Payuk added, "Daniels taught him right when Eddie was a deckhand for him. By the way, what is Eddie's last name?"

Smiling, Kelly said, "His last name is Beck."

Turning back, Kelly tightened the lead on the packhorse he was leading and nudged Peanut, his buckskin horse, slowly ahead. Hailing back to Payuk, "Watch where you are going; the game trail leading down the slope is not very wide—and keep your packhorse tight."

Reining up Peanut, Kelly waved his right arm out across the valley far below, and admired the scenery along the Iskut River canyon. "Look Payuk, did you ever see any prettier sight than that river valley below? The trees, meadows, rock outcrops, and river just seem to blend together."

Hearing some small rocks rolling down the slope above them, Kelly quickly turned just in time to see Payuk's horse lose his footing as he shied away from the small rocks rolling toward him. Kelly screamed at Payuk, "Jump!" Payuk was trying to control his horse's rearing, but the animal whinnied loudly and fell when he lost his footing on the game trail. Payuk rolled backward off the back of the horse to keep from getting rolled on as the horse tumbled down the slope uncontrollably. The animal somersaulted head over heels over brush and fallen dead timber, and finally came to rest against a tree about fifty feet below the game trail.

Kelly watched the horse as he quickly slid off Peanut and squeezed by his packhorse to see if Payuk was alright as he lay half on and off the game trail.

"That crazy horse," Payuk yelled. "Shane Keller told me he would spook some, and I should have listened and taken the roan instead."

"Are you OK?" Kelly asked as he was helping Payuk to his feet. "Here..." Kelly handed Payuk back his pistol that had fallen out of its holster.

Both men looked down the slope to check on the fallen horse. Looking closer, Payuk commented, "He is not dead, but he is not trying to get up. That is a bad sign." Payuk shook his head.

Leaving Peanut and both packhorses on the game trail, Kelly and Payuk carefully slid down the steep slope to the downed horse.

As Payuk neared the horse he stopped and touched Kelly's arm. "Let me take care of this. See the right front leg? It is really torn up, probably broken in several places. You know what has to happen." Payuk sighed deeply and half-jokingly said, "When I take care of business, do you want to have a couple of horse steaks for supper?"

Kelly quickly glanced at Payuk to see if he was joking, and realizing Payuk was serious, Kelly nodded. "Sure, why not."

Making his way back up the steep slope, Kelly yelled down to Payuk, "I'll throw down a length of rope so I can pull up your saddle and tack."

Payuk motioned OK, and then a single shot rang out that filled the canyon with rumbling echoes from the gunshot, and Payuk returned to the game trail with four large horse steaks that were wrapped in a cloth.

The saddle and tack loaded on Payuk's packhorse, Kelly suggested, "We'll make our way down to the river for the night and reorganize the supplies, then tomorrow we will build a travois for the supplies." Hesitating, Kelly asked, "Did you wrap those steaks in anything or just stick them in your saddlebags?"

Smiling, Payuk responded, "Yes, the meat may not be cold, but it will be clean."

Both men laughed as they led the horses down the game trail and then rode double on Peanut to the river's edge.

Reaching the river that was running high on its banks because of spring run-off, Kelly looked up into the clear skies and suggested,

"Let's not set up the tent tonight. I don't think it will rain before morning."

"Good idea. I hate to set up that crazy tent. It is not hard to set up, but it just takes a lot of time. Besides, we each have good bedrolls to curl up in."

Getting the gear off the packhorses and unsaddling Peanut, Kelly hobbled all three horses, and both men worked to set up camp.

Piling a few small sticks on the grass, Kelly got the fire started as Payuk cut some extra fat from the meat.

Looking surprised, Kelly jokingly exclaimed, "Holy cow, Payuk—you think you have enough horse steaks?"

"Yes, there will be some left to feed the animals. Look here, Kelly," Payuk said as he showed Kelly the rock he had used as a cutting table for the meat.

"By the damn," Kelly declared, "those ants did not waste much time going after the blood." Returning to his fire, Kelly explained, "You know, Payuk, ants talk to each other."

Payuk stopped in mid step and questioned, "How do they do that?"

Kelly smiled. "I learned about that and much more in college when I got my agriculture degree. I think that's why Kincaid hired me—because of my education. Anyway, the ants talk to each other by scent. If they find something to eat, they will lay a scent trail back to the ant hill and then other ants can follow the scent back to the food the first ant found."

Payuk shook his head. "Just like a bear: he can follow his own scent back to a kill."

Smiling, Kelly replied, "Well, something like that."

"Here." Payuk handed Kelly the metal grate Kelly had laid out to cook the four horse steaks on. "Do we want some mushrooms to go with the steak? If we do, I'll get some water boiling."

Thinking for a moment, Kelly responded, "Sure, sounds good. Are they the ones we gathered yesterday?"

"Yes," Payuk answered. "They are called Yellow Foot mushrooms."

"Payuk," Kelly whispered low, "where is your rifle? Get it right now. We're going to have company and I don't know what kind. Look at the horses."

Moving slowly toward his rifle, which was lying across his saddle, Payuk glanced toward the horses that were both looking in the same direction with ears pointed.

"I can't see anything, Payuk, because of the fire's reflection, but can you see anything in the darkness of the trees? Let's back away from the fire just a bit. No sense making a target of ourselves or an easy run for a bear or wolf."

Waa sa iyatee," sounded from the darkness of the trees.

Payuk smiled and instantly returned the call from the visitors in the darkness with "*Sh tug-a xat ditee ixw siteeni.*"

Just as suddenly as they came, they appeared in the firelight.

"What are you guys doing wandering around out here?" Payuk inquired.

Laughing, the three Tlingit men asked, "What are you two doing out here?" The older native shuddered.

Quickly, Payuk introduced two of the men, Saupeteese and Kiviaq, as members of his extended clan. The other man, Kroviq, was introduced to both Kelly and Payuk by Kiviaq, seemingly the leader of the three.

Kelly quickly motioned with his hand to come and sit by the fire as he said, "The chill of the evening has come down from the mountaintops."

Kiviaq held his hand up as if signaling. "We have to gather our horses, then return."

"Good," Kelly returned. "We have plenty of good horse steaks to share."

Returning to the fire, Kiviaq, Saupeteese, and Kroviq comforted themselves.

Kiviaq asked, "Where did you get the metal stove?" He pointed toward the grate the steaks were cooking on, and the pot of boiling water for the mushrooms was sitting on. The grate was being supported by four rocks above the small fire.

Payuk laughed and pointed toward Kelly. "That is a metal cooking grate that Kelly had made at the smithy in Wrangell."

"How much cost?" asked Kiviaq.

Shrugging, Kelly answered, "The smithy works for Shane Keller in Wrangell. He shoes animals, repairs wagons, and most anything that needs repair. He is a good hand and he won't charge you much. I can't remember how much he charged, but it wasn't much. I've even known him to except game as payment, course with Shane's permission," and everyone laughed.

After the steaks and mushrooms were enjoyed, the cooking grate was removed and a larger fire was stoked up. Leaning back against his saddle, Kelly reflected, "To answer your question about what Payuk and I are doing here, we are trying to find where the Snippaker River runs into the Iskut River. I can't imagine it will be much farther upstream from here." Kelly pointed toward the river they were camped near. "Kincaid sent Payuk and me up here to check out the mining operation. It may be an illegal operation of what they call hydraulic mining. That means they are using water to wash dirt into sluice boxes for the gold. By the maps, the locations of the mines are in British Columbia, Canada. What that means to Payuk and me is that we really can't do anything about anything except report back to Kincaid on what we have found and seen."

Kiviaq drew a deep breath and explained, "The Snippaker is about fourteen more miles from here. The area around where the two rivers come together is very open and a large mining operation is in progress on the side hills on both sides of the rivers."

Suddenly Saupeteese spoke up. "They make fishing no good. Make water dirty. Fill river with mud. They say someone say OK to mine on Tlingit streams."

Quickly Kiviaq motioned to Saupeteese. "Be quiet. Kelly and Payuk will see when they get there. Let them make their own decision." Pausing, Kiviaq continued, "The mines drain dirt into the Snippaker and Iskut. You will see tomorrow or the next day. The dirt up and downriver, even this far down, sinks to the bottom of the river, clogging the rocky bottom that does not allow for fish spawning."

Kelly nodded his head and quickly rose to stand. "Kiviaq, where did you learn to speak English so well?"

Smiling, Kiviaq quickly answered, "From Mrs. Kincaid. She would work with the Tlingit for learning English a lot of the time. I don't think she does it so much anymore for the adults because a lot of Tlingit speak English and they help each other. The reason we needed to speak English is because the people from the lower forty-eight could not learn to speak Tlingit easily, so we learned English to be able to work with and for them. Most Tlingit can speak some English."

Kelly stretched his arms into the air. "I think I'll check the horses, take a leak, and turn in."

"Before you go, Kelly, we have noticed you have only three horses."

Payuk grunted. "Where do you think those horse steaks came from. We had to put a horse down today because of a fall."

Kiviaq nodded. "We have an extra horse if you would like to use him for riding, and he is a tame horse."

Payuk quickly looked at Kelly as Kelly shrugged his shoulders OK, and Payuk answered, "Yes, we will accept your offer of a gift. We will return the horse to your lodge when we return to Wrangell."

Kiviaq raised his hand. "Then it is done."

Next morning as the sun was just peeking over the mountain on the east end of the canyon, Kelly and Kiviaq were getting the coffee brewing and starting to make biscuits, Payuk and Saupeteese were packing and saddling the horses, while Kroviq was gathering more small sticks for a cooking fire that Kelly had lit earlier.

Payuk approached Kiviaq as the biscuit batter was about mixed with water and flour, and handed Kiviaq a handful of berries to put into the biscuit mix.

Looking surprised, Kelly quickly inquired, "From the Steak and Stack Café?"

"Yes," Payuk answered. "They make the biscuits taste better."

"You're right there," Kelly responded.

Breakfast finished, the campsite cleaned up, and the horses all saddled and packed, Kiviaq mentioned to Kelly as he swung his horse around to face Kelly, "Where you are going is dangerous. They want no one around the mining area. These men are mining and washing the ground away. The dirt, brush, and trees are all washed into the rivers: both the Iskut and the Snippaker. They will not listen

16

that the streams are being destroyed or too much game is being killed." Looking at Kelly and Payuk, Kiviaq softly warned, "Go cautiously, my friends."

Parting from Kiviaq, Kroviq, and Saupeteese, Kelly and Payuk slowly rode their horses to river's edge. Dismounting, Kelly said, "Let's walk along the river for a while. Have you noticed, Payuk, that there is a well-worn wagon trail along the river? It looks as though many heavy wagons have used this trail to travel up and down the river. I want us both to look for debris and silt in the river as we go upstream. I want to know about how far down the debris and silt are being washed downriver."

Slowly making their way up the Iskut River, Payuk pointed and Kelly looked the way Payuk was pointing.

To Kelly's surprise, there was a rather new fish trap that had been pulled out of the river, pulled back away from the river, and destroyed. Fortunately, it was on the same side of the river as Kelly and Payuk were because the river at this point was narrow, deep, and running swift. Leading the horses over to the fish trap, Kelly observed, "This is not old at all. The wood has not even changed color as of yet. I wonder who did this. Payuk, it looks like something your people might have made."

Dropping the reins of his horse to the ground, Payuk slowly walked around the destroyed fish trap. "Look, Kelly," Payuk said, pointing to a small board on the fish trap. "It has the mark of the kwaan that built and put the trap in the river." Squinting, Payuk slowly spoke. "I believe it is from the tribe of the inland Tlingit Kwaan. I can't read the rest of the writings. This is their territory."

Shaking his head, Kelly muttered, "Why in the hell would anybody take the fish trap out of the river and destroy the structure? If it is the territory of this kwaan, what was the Shtax'heen Kwaan doing

17

around here. I thought the tribes pretty much stayed out of other tribes' areas."

"They do," answered Payuk, "but sometimes they must travel through other tribe's territories to get where they want to go, which is permissible."

Kelly patted Peanut on the neck and casually commented to Payuk, "I'll bet I know who destroyed the fish trap and so do you. I don't think it would do us a lot of good at this point to accuse anybody, but I'll lay you five to one I know who did this."

Leading the horses back to the edge of the river, Kelly motioned and said, "Look at that current, Payuk. Here the river is narrow, swift, and deep, but back down the river a piece, the river is much wider, much shallower, and flowing much slower." Kelly shook his head as he mounted Peanut. "Let out play in the lead line of your packhorse," Kelly advised. "We'll never get there if we don't keep moving."

CHAPTER TWO

Coming to a flat spot along the river, Kelly suggested, "Payuk, let's make camp for the night. The sun just dropped over the ridge of the canyon and darkness and the night chill will be on us soon. I don't know how close we are, but I think we are pretty close. What do you think?"

"We might be too close if they have a lookout on a ridge. From a good position, with glasses, the lookout could see for a long ways in both directions."

"Well, we are here so let's make camp. Let's set up over by those quaking aspen. They will give us some protection from the night air."

Unsaddling the horses and unpacking the packhorses, Payuk began setting up camp as Kelly hobbled the horses so they could graze close by.

"Do we want to build a fire tonight?" asked Payuk. "Tent?"

"Sure, why not," Kelly advised. "If they know we are here already, it will not hurt anything; if they don't, it's not that big a thing. No tent."

After a supper of salt pork and fried potatoes, both men settled down to enjoy the small fire. "Payuk, when we make contact with these miners, we'll tell them we are from the Wrangell Department of Agriculture, and are just doing the British Columbian officials a favor by routinely checking some of the mining permits in this area. Also, we are helping them because it is so far removed from any of their established offices." Kelly pointed, "Keep your side arm on at all times." Smiling, Kelly continued, "You never know."

"Are you going to keep wearing your green Department of Agriculture shirt?" Payuk inquired.

"Yes. Kincaid said he wanted you to wear one. Did the order come in from Seattle yet? Sara should have ordered you two of them. Although you are not officially employed by the Department, you help out a lot."

"I don't think they have got here yet. Sara would have let me know."

"Well, Mother Nature is calling. I'm going back over farther into the trees," Kelly said as he motioned to the trees. "I will return soon."

Walking back into the darkness of the trees, he could see Payuk kneeling next to the fire, laying larger pieces of wood for the night fire as the flames were reaching skyward.

Kelly smiled as he finished his nature call, and thought, *Nancy hates to go visit Mother Nature in the wild. Nancy and I've been married now for about seven years. I got a great job at the Department with Kincaid, she loves teaching school, and we have a five-year-old son, Sidney John.*

Being jerked from his daydreaming, Kelly quickly moved through the trees to see Payuk being shoved around by two men with rifles.

"Hell, Mike, this guy is nothing but a stupid Indian. What are you doing out here around our mining claim?"

Still lying on the ground propped up on one elbow, where the two men had shoved him, Payuk stammered, "We come here to check mining permits for people in British Columbia."

As one man kicked Payuk in the ribs, the other man grabbed him and scolded, "The boss said don't make a problem. Just see who they are." And turning his attention back to Payuk, the man demanded, "Where is the other guy? Our look-out said there were two of you; where is the other Indian?"

20

As Kelly walked from the shadows of the trees toward the fire, he pulled his .38 handgun out and challenged, "You guys want to take me on? I'm no stupid Indian as you say, but come ahead; I've got this .38 pointed right at your guts. Now, throw those rifles into the dark, help Payuk up, and back away."

One man raised his hands and begged, "Look, mister, you can put that gun away. We aren't looking for any trouble. The boss just told us to come over here and check you guys out and find out what you're doing here."

"Beating up on a person does not seem like just finding out who we are. Who is this boss you're talking about?"

"The boss of the mining operation around here is Henry Wilson and he does not like strangers poking around here asking questions."

"Well, you go tell your boss," Kelly explained, "that my name is Kelly O'Brien and I'm a representative from the Department of Agriculture, USA, and I'm representing the government of British Columbia, Canada. We are here to check your mining claim rights and mining operation...also, tell your boss that we will see him in the morning. Now get out of here and leave the rifles behind. You will get them back tomorrow. Before you leave, I want to know how far the Snippaker River is from here."

The large man nodded. "You are just about there, maybe another mile further upstream."

Next morning, Kelly and Payuk had a quick breakfast of coffee and corn dodgers. Kelly suggested, "Let's leave the camp as is and we can return later today." Pausing, he continued, "Let's saddle the horses and lead the packhorses. I don't want to leave the packhorses tethered and alone, not being watched for that long a time. No telling when a bear will come along."

Putting the fire out, Kelly and Payuk mounted with the packhorses being led behind them. The rifles of the two men of last night were tied on Kelly's saddle behind the cantle.

Shifting in his saddle to center it on Peanut, Kelly quietly said, · "Well, let's go and see how much trouble we can get into." Riding a short distance upriver, the area cleared out without any trees in a large area just as Kiviaq had told him it would be. Pointing across the river and to the steep walls of the canyon that had been made by hydraulic mining, Kelly shook his head. "Wow! No wonder the Tlingit are so upset. This outfit is washing half the mountain down into the streams and rivers. No wonder trees are not growing around here or spawning cannot be done in the rivers or streams. Payuk, I'm sure this type of mining is just about gone in the lower forty-eight. It just is too damaging to the landscape and environment."

Looking across the Snippaker River, Payuk commented, "River is shallow. Good crossing to mining camp although here is a small bridge."

"Yeah, Payuk, let's cross here. The main camp buildings seem to be situated in the fork of the Snippaker and Iskut Rivers."

Kelly and Payuk slowly rode their horses across the Snippaker River as they led the packhorses. Getting to the other side of the narrow river, Kelly reined Peanut toward the mining camp buildings. The camp buildings, as Kelly was not surprised to see, were built of cedar logs with cedar shingles. Reining up Peanut, Kelly commented to Payuk, "Look at those structures. They appear to be built quite good and to last."

Nodding, Payuk advised, "They look to be several years old, but have been well maintained."

Nudging Peanut forward with a small amount of pressure to his ribs, Kelly signed and instructed, "Now remember, we are here to

22

check mining claims. Never mind right now that Kincaid mentioned illegal killing of game. We can check that out as time goes on."

Nodding, Payuk reassured him, "Yes, it would not be wise to start asking questions about game hunting until we have checked everything out."

Arriving at the largest building, Kelly and Payuk tied their horses at the hitching rail, when suddenly there was a huge explosion heard coming from somewhere not far up the Iskut River, and the horses were instantly spooked with snorting and wild eyes.

Kelly and Payuk looked at each other and Kelly cautiously asked, "What the hell was that?"

Suddenly from behind them, a voice bellowed out as a large man with wide shoulders and simple canvas clothing came out the door of the building where Kelly and Payuk had stopped. "That was dynamite exploding. Isn't it a sweet sound? Better control those horses. If you stay around here long enough they will get used to the noise of making money like everything else around here."

Checking that the horses were still securely tied to the hitch rail, Kelly looked up at the large man and said, "I'm Kelly O'Brien from the Department of Agriculture, USA." He pointed to Payuk. "Payuk is my assistant and also works for the Department of Agriculture. Our office in Wrangell, Alaska, was asked by the government of British Columbia to check out the mining permits in this area because it is so far from their nearest office in British Columbia." Pausing for just an instant, Kelly continued, "Who am I talking with?"

"I'm Henry Wilson, the boss of this outfit, and it's called Twin Forks Mining and Dredging Company." Henry Wilson was a large man with graying brown hair. He carried a knife on his right side, hooked to his black belt that kept his flannel shirt tucked into his canvas trousers. "Do you have any identification to prove who you are and what you are doing here on my project?"

"Yes, we do," answered Kelly as he stepped back to his saddlebags for a leather folder. "If we can go inside, I will show you the paperwork we have from the British Columbia Mining Office in Victoria and from our office in Wrangell."

Waving his hand in the air, Wilson said, "Well, come on in. We might as well get this over with."

As the three men went inside the large room with a lot of tables with drawings, small piles of rocks, pencils, and drawing paper strewn about on them, Henry Wilson explained, "These tables represent locations of drilling, explosion locations, hydraulic areas, and sluice boxes. It is quite a complicated operation, and I'm sure you don't understand, but that is not important. Let me see your paperwork from Victoria Mining Office in Victoria."

Kelly slowly loosened the leather binding on his leather satchel as he commented, "It sure looks like you have to destroy a lot of timber ground to get the gold." He waved his hand toward the outside.

"What do you expect," Henry sneered. "The gold does not lay on top of the ground."

Hearing someone snicker behind them, Kelly and Payuk quickly turned to see a man sitting behind a small desk writing something.

Handing the paperwork to Henry Wilson, Kelly explained, "These forms are for me to fill out once I've asked you the questions."

"Jesse," Henry commanded, "get over here and go through this paperwork with these two greenhorns." He waved his hand toward the man, who came over from his desk. "Jesse Holmes is our bookkeeper. He will go through these papers with you. Jesse, you be sure this stuff is in order. I want to review it when you get it all done. Now I've got to go check out that last blow."

24

Jesse smiled at Kelly and Payuk and pointed to a clean tabletop next to one of the windows and advised, "Let's move over there. There will be better light. On the way, grab a chair to sit on." Jesse seemed to be a mild-mannered man of slight build, clean clothes, and longer black hair that was combed back.

Before Kelly had a chance to ask any questions, Jesse informed Kelly and Payuk, "Let me read through some of this stuff before we start writing anything down on paper." Pausing for a minute, Jesse motioned to the outside. "Why don't you gents go outside and have a look around. Stay pretty close to this building and everything should be just fine."

"That's a great idea, Jesse. Payuk and I will be around close when you may want us back in here. How long will it be, you think?"

"It should not be long," Jesse responded.

Payuk gently slid back the wooden bolt on the door and slowly opened the door as he and Kelly walked to the wooden porch of the building. "Look at this, Kelly," Payuk said, amazed. "Have you ever seen anything like this before?" And before Kelly could answer, Payuk continued, "The elders of our kwaan have spoken of such things, but few of our people have ever seen this up close." Shaking his head, Payuk was perplexed. "Why would anyone destroy the homes of animals, fish, and people, and the growth of plants and trees in such a way?"

Kelly sighed deeply as he stepped off the porch and loosened the cinch on Peanut and Payuk did the same for his mount.

"Payuk, I can see why the government outlawed this type of mining. It is very destructive to the landscape. They use dynamite to loosen the hard soil, then the whole mountain is washed right into the rivers as the dirt, rock, and silt is washed through the sluice boxes for the gold. Then all the dirt, rocks, and silt are discarded into the rivers, streams, and waterways to do damage to the wildlife and fish, not to mention the sandbars that build up in the river channel."

Kelly walked a short distance to be able to see up the Iskut River. "Come here, Payuk. Look at what's happening to the canyon where they have been blasting and using that pressure hose to blow the loosened soil into sluice boxes. They have blasted and washed the south side of the canyon wall to the point of creating a massive cliff instead of the natural slope of the canyon wall. James was right; this hydraulic mining is a disaster for the landscape, environments, fish, and animals."

"Hey, you guys..."

Turning, Kelly waved and responded, "OK, Jesse, we are on the way."

Getting inside and finding a chair around the table that he chose to work on, Jesse started explaining, "First of all the British Columbian Mining Council (BCMC) wants a lot of information, besides what the Mining Council in Victoria wanted. The information they are wanting is contained in the permit agreement for this mine." Shifting through many sheets of information, and handing them to Kelly for his viewing, Jesse advised, "It will take me some time to fill in the blanks on the forms the BCMC wants."

"How much time will it take for you to fill in the information for the British Columbian Mining Council and the Victoria Mining Office?" Kelly asked as he handed Payuk the paperwork for Payuk to read over.

Laughing, Jesse pointed to Payuk. "I didn't know Indians could read information of such difficulty."

Payuk started to respond, but Kelly spoke over him. "Of course he can, Jesse. He has a full high school education."

Shaking his head, Jesse said, "Well, that is something I never heard of before for an Indian, especially this far north."

"OK, Jesse, how long to finish the forms?" Kelly asked.

Nodding his head and looking at the forms from BCMC, Jesse cautiously answered, "About four or five hours. I will not be able to start on them until tomorrow, and I can't work on them all the time. I have to keep track of a lot of stuff around here for Henry. He gets really pissed if things aren't done when they are supposed to be. You understand, Kelly?"

Suddenly the door slammed open, and the men at the work table quickly became alarmed. The man that stood in the doorway had a rifle in his hands, seemingly ready to shoot. Screaming at the top of his lungs, the dirty, rugged-looking man pointed the rifle at Kelly. "Are you the asses from that office in Wrangell?"

Instantly, Jesse stood up and commanded, "Get out of here, Simmons."

Moving out of the doorway into the large room, Simmons screamed again, "Answer my question, you murderers."

Quickly, Jesse affirmed, "Yes, Simmons, they are from Wrangell. What of it?"

With the speed of lightning, Simmons shouldered the rifle and shot toward Payuk as he screamed again, "You people shot and killed my brother, and now it is my turn."

Kicking back in the chair, Kelly drew his .38 and fired two quick rounds into the chest of the man named Simmons before he could lever another round into the rifle chamber.

Simmons let the rifle fall to the wooden floor and with pain cringing his face followed the rifle to the floor. He lay dead with two .38 slugs in his chest.

Stillness filled the room as the smoke and stink of gunpowder smoke drifted out the half-open door and open windows. The heavy wooden front door moved slightly with a squeak and suddenly Henry Wilson barged through the doorway, yelling, "What the hell is happening in here!" Upon seeing Simmons lying on the floor with blood still oozing from his body, he quickly knelt down and realized Simmons was dead. "Who did this?" he screamed.

Quickly, Jesse said loudly, "Simmons came in here wanting to kill the men from Wrangell because someone from the Wrangell office killed his brother."

At the same time, Kelly jumped over to see how Payuk was doing as Payuk lay on the wooden floor grabbing his arm and moaning. Kelly slowly rolled Payuk over to check the wound as Henry came over to look at the wound.

Waving his hand into the air, as if nothing was wrong, Henry instructed, "Jesse, get Bingman over here to take a look at the wound in this Indian's arm."

As Kelly stood up, he emphatically remarked to Henry Wilson, "We did nothing to promote this shooting." Hastily pointing to the man on the floor, "That man, Simmons, I think Jesse called him, came in this room as we were working on paperwork. He was waving a rifle around, threatening to kill Payuk and me, and he damned near did."

Sighing deeply, Henry Wilson explained, "When Bingman gets here he will take care of the Indian. How much longer are you going to be sticking around here?" He looked at Kelly.

Shrugging, Kelly looked to Jesse...

Jesse quickly explained to Henry Wilson, "I'll need about two more days to check out this paperwork from BCMC and get the Wrangell forms filed out." He motioned toward the desk.

Bingman came running through the open door into the room, and instantly stopped when he saw Simmons lying on the wooden floor. "I hope you did not bring me over for him." He pointed at Simmons.

"No, Bingman," Jesse said as he pointed to Payuk, who was taking off his shirt for Bingman to look at the wound.

Stepping toward Payuk, Bingman held Payuk's arm out straight and asked, "Does that hurt any?"

Shaking his head, Payuk replied, "No, I think the bullet just grazed my shoulder."

Bingman continued to ask Payuk questions about the wound as he bandaged it up. "There," Bingman stated, "that will be OK in a day or so. You are lucky; the bullet just barely broke the skin."

Running out of patience, Henry raised his voice. "Well, for hell sakes, Jesse, hurry it up with that paperwork. I don't want these guys wandering around here forever." Turning to look back at Kelly, Henry asked, "Are you going to stay in our bunk houses and eat at our mess hall?"

Shaking his head, Kelly stated, "We would like to eat in your mess hall when we are close around, but we will probably set camp up a short distance away." Pausing, Kelly asked, "At night, can we picket our horses in your corrals?"

Henry nodded. "Yeah, that will be fine. We don't have any grain or hay to feed them. In the daytime one of my men herds our horses out for them to graze."

"That will be fine," Kelly agreed. "We'll put them in and take them out of the corral as we need them, and thanks."

Outside the office, Kelly started to untie the horses when he grunted to Payuk in low tones, "Look at all the horses they have, and the two large freight wagons."

Nodding, Payuk grunted, "Yes, I see."

Untying the horses from the hitching rail, Kelly motioned, "Let's go over there and see if we can set up camp. It looks like a good spot."

Walking and leading the horses, Payuk commented, "I wonder—"

Suddenly a large explosion was heard and the noise echoed up and down the canyon walls. The horses quickly threw their heads into the air and reared slightly.

"Easy, easy..." Both men quietly spoke to the horses and patted their necks until they settled down. Kelly said, "I guess they will get used to that noise," as he motioned to the other horses in the corral.

"As I was going to say before the blast," Payuk continued, "in the trees up the hill, to our left, there seems to be a lot of skinning racks and kenching tables with a couple men working on some skins. Kincaid might have been right about the poaching also."

"Don't look over there, Payuk," Kelly cautioned. "We are probably being watched pretty close."

Walking a bit farther, Kelly stopped and asked, "Will this do, Payuk? We have water right here," as he motioned toward a small creek. "Plenty of firewood all around, and a good flat area with two trees not far apart for the tent rope to anchor."

Suddenly another loud explosion was echoed up and down the canyon walls, alerting all living things in the area that danger was around them.

CHAPTER THREE

James Kincaid leaned on one of the corral rails as Shane Keller approached him. "When did you get back from Seattle?"

James smiled. "On the ferry, last night." Sighing heavily, James continued, "I'm getting pretty tired of traveling back and forth between Juneau and here, Ketchikan and here, and Seattle and here. Even the trips to Petersburg get long. You know, Shane, I long to be tramping around in the wild. It seemed so easy, now that I think about it."

Laughing and shaking his head, Shane explained, "That Thomas, your son, comes down here when he can and wants to ride a horse, and Kalli, Moaka's son, sometimes comes with him, but Kalli is more likely to be out killing frogs or something. Thomas sure loves horses. He is about ten or eleven now, isn't he?"

"He is eleven this year. Yeah, he talks a lot about riding that little pony around in the breaking corral when he comes home. I'm glad you watch after him, Shane. Suzette and I really appreciate you letting him ride that little pony. You have a clean livery stable and Wrangell would be in bad shape without a good livery."

"Thanks, James, but are you ever going to get another horse?"

"Well, Shane, you know I never had a horse of my own. You just kept that roan for me to ride. He got pretty old. I rather hated to see you take him back down to the Seattle lots. They probably fed him to the pigs."

Shane explained, "Yeah, when you take an old horse back to them, they only have one thing to do with them, but he served you well, James."

Laughing, James slapped his hand on the railing. "Yes, by the damn, he was a good, strong horse."

"Have you heard anything from Kelly or Payuk lately?"

"No, Shane. There was no communication that Sara had from them." He paused. "They were only supposed to check things out and get back here. Knowing Kelly, he would not come back until he could give me a full accounting of what he and Payuk found." Shrugging, he added, "Course, Payuk would be the same way."

As Shane leaned on the railing, he asked, "How long has it been since Tess passed away?" Pushing some dirt into a pile with his boot toe, Shane continued, "I heard that Moaka may take Kalli and his young daughter back to Teshpuk to raise them as Inuit rather than white."

Sighing deeply and then exhaling, James said, "Yeah, Shane, I know he has mentioned it several times since Tess passed, but I never thought he would do such a thing. Tess and he were so happy here, but with Tess gone and two kids to raise, he thinks he might be doing the best thing for the children and himself. He has never asked my opinion. Kalli is twelve, a year older than Thomas, and Kasha is four. And Tess died in 1910 from some infection that Doc Bonds could not stop." Shaking his head, James turned to look up into the sky. "That was a sad day in Wrangell. Everybody just loved Tess...not a mean bone in her whole body."

"You have another little one, don't you, James?" Shane asked.

"Yeah, her name is Sadie...she is three years old. You and Sara have a daughter? I think you said she lives in Seattle."

"Yes, she and her husband and our two grandkids are doing just fine." Shane emphasized, "Sara and I wish they would get up here to Wrangell more often to visit, but I guess they are busy."

James took his foot off from the bottom corral railing and turned. "Be seeing you Shane. I've got to go back to the office and see if the mayor may want a meeting tomorrow morning."

James slowly walked up the street from Keller's livery stable to his office some four blocks away, stopping from time to time just to look at the changes that had happened in Wrangell in the last few years. New stores started up, new boardwalks, and more homes being built, which meant more people.

James opened the door to the Department of Agriculture and saw Sara, Shane Keller's wife, sitting at her desk busily turning sheets of paper. "What are you doing, Sara?"

"Oh! James, you startled me. Ever since Kelly fixed that front door it does not squeak anymore or not as much."

"Where is Moaka?" James asked.

"Early this morning he got a horse from the livery and went to check some streams on south Wrangell Island to see how bad the erosion was or some kind of stream stoppage that was reported on Terrace Point. One man came in here two days ago complaining that someone had stopped a stream up for water for a sluice box operation, and it overflowed into another man's property. Since last year there have been two new places established in that area. You remember last year it about washed that place away during spring thaw. I think he is about finished with the report you wanted him to do on some research. You know Moaka—he's very complete."

Clearing his throat, James slid a nearby wooden chair over in front of Sara's desk and casually commented, "Sara, I want to ask you something. I have asked your advice before and you have never steered me wrong yet." And smiling, he continued, "So with knowing that, I want your counsel on a decision I think I'm going to have to make."

Not letting James continue, Sara jokingly stated, "I hope this is not a hard question."

Leaning back in his chair and crossing his arms, James asked, "Has Moaka mentioned anything to you about going back to Teshpuk?"

"Oh, James," Sara said earnestly as she turned to face him. "He wants to go to Teshpuk so bad, but he does not want to leave you. You know he would do anything for you."

"I know, I know, he is very loyal to me, sometimes too much so. He is always thinking of my needs other than his own. It has always been his way. What do you think of him taking those kids and moving back to Teshpuk?"

"Shane and I have talked about this, privately, of course, and we seem to agree that if Moaka wants to raise the children Inuit, that should be his own prerogative. The First Nations cultural pull is very strong."

Leaning forward a bit, James squinted slightly. "Are you saying that I must cut him loose if he is to go?"

Sara, looked straight into James's eyes and sternly advised, "You are the only one that can tell him he can go...he would not listen to anybody else."

"OK. So if Moaka goes, who—"

"Payuk, of course." Smiling at James, Sara said, "You were going to ask who was going to take Moaka's place."

James shook his head and exclaimed, "Sara, you have worked here too long. You are absolutely right. Don't breathe a word of this. Let me work out the Moaka situation first." Getting up from the wooden chair, James replaced it and instructed, "Close up when you get done. If the mayor comes over for a meeting tomorrow, tell him I'll get back with him. I might ride down and see how Moaka is doing at Terrace Point. I'll see you in the morning. I've got to think about this Moaka thing some more." Shaking his head, James opened the heavy wooden front door. "He has been with me for a long time, through many an ordeal."

Standing on the steps of the Department office, James could feel the weather warming up as he began to walk toward home. The sea breeze still blew in from the west, but it was warmer and not as wet.

Seeing Deputy Sheriff Marlin coming out of his office, James hailed, "Hold up one minute, Marlin."

Turning out the lights and closing the door, Deputy Sheriff Marlin responded, "Sure, what can I do for you, James?"

Approaching Marlin, James asked, "Have you heard anything about the Alaska Native Brotherhood?"

Deputy Sheriff Marlin looked surprised. "How do you know about that? I just got a letter from Juneau mentioning that very topic. They did not seem to be up and ready to do anything special about the law or whatever it will be. They just mentioned to file the letter and keep it in mind if anything comes up. It has to do with racism against the Native Americans. I guess there are two guys over in Sika that are pushing this thing."

Nodding, James added, "Yeah, the Department is talking about it some in Seattle. I reckon those same guys were in Seattle some time back. Anyway, I was just checking with you. Will you let me know if you hear anything else about the law or whatever it turns out to become."

"Sure, James. Oh, by the way, welcome back."

Touching his hat brim, James said, "Thanks, it is good to be back."

Looking west over the bay and ocean as he walked home, James could feel the light breeze coming in from the ocean and it felt good, knowing that the warmer breeze would melt snow on the mainland high points. Shrugging, he knew the low valleys were already melted out with plenty of water draining toward the Stikine River.

Walking around the back of his home that faced east and sat just below Turner Hill, James saw Bray standing and waiting for him. "Crazy dog," James muttered. "He still hears well."

Bray pulled on the long chain that secured him as James approached him to set him free. "There you go, boy. Let's go for a run on the beach."

Instead of taking off at a full gallop, Bray walked beside James, content to be let free of his chain and being with James. Arriving on the shore, James found an old washed-up log and sat to enjoy the sight. Petting Bray, James said quietly, "How you feeling, old boy? You're about to the end of your line and you have had a great life. Remember all the polar bears we used to chase, all the nights out together fighting off wolves, and beating Moaka's lead dog and team every time?" James paused. "Yeah, Anore was a great dog. As Moaka is a great friend."

James rose off the log and Bray walked to the water's edge and lapped up some water, shaking his head so the water came out both sides of his mouth. James laughed. "Don't like the saltwater, huh?"

Arriving back home, James let Bray in the house, and Bray lay on his pad that was located by the back door, where Suzette had designated Bray's place when he was in the house.

Going into the living room, James scooped up the paper and headed for his chair. Turning on the lights over his chair, he sighed and thought about Moaka. *A lot of time has passed since I first met Moaka in Nome so many years ago. So Sara thinks I should tell him to go.* Shaking his head, he had just returned to his paper when he heard the back door slam and Bray yelp.

"What are you doing to that dog?" shouted James.

"Nothing," came the reply. "He lies right in the middle of the doorway." Thomas headed for his room with his school satchel.

"Come in here, Thomas," James directed. "I want to talk to you for a minute."

Abruptly Thomas was sitting on the hassock in front of James. "What do you want, Dad?"

"Now, Thomas, I want you to think carefully before you answer my question. Your answer could mean a lot to me." Taking a deep breath, James asked, "Has Kalli ever mentioned to you about him moving to Teshpuk?"

Straightening up on the hassock, Thomas cheerfully responded, "Sure, all the time. He said his dad wants to go there, but his job is getting in the way. I thought you knew that."

"Well, son, thanks. You have made a difficult task easier for me. Now, go haul the wood in and get in the kindling for tomorrow morning." Pausing for a moment, he continued, "And quit stepping on Bray. He is an old dog and he hurts easy."

Just barely beginning to reading the paper again, James heard the back door open as Suzette say to Sadie, "Go see Daddy—he's in the living room."

Quickly putting the paper down, James exclaimed, "There's my little girl," as he grabbed her and set her on his lap. "What did you do today?"

In her tiny voice, she answered, "Color."

"James, get a fire started," Suzette said as she walked into the living room. "It is chilly in here. Did Moaka get back yet?"

Setting Sadie down, James replied, "No, not yet." James gathered some old newspaper and kindling and built a small fire in the cast iron stove. Watching the fire light, he added a couple of large pieces of wood to bank the fire.

After supper, Suzette and James were sitting in the living room. James was finishing the paper and Suzette was working on something for school the next day. James laid the paper down on his lap, cleared his throat, and asked Suzette, "Has Kalli mentioned he may move to Teshpuk?"

Suzette stopped her writing. She glanced up at James and answered, "As far as I know he has only talked about it to his friends. I don't think anybody believes him."

"Thomas said he talked to him about going to Teshpuk," replied James.

"Thomas," James called, "come in here for a minute." Seeing Thomas coming into the living room, James asked, "Did Kalli talk to you about going to Teshpuk?"

"Yes. Everybody knows it."

"Who is everybody?"

Thomas shrugged his shoulders. "I don't know, his friends maybe."

"OK, Thomas, that's all I wanted, just to check one more time." Waving his hand toward Thomas's bedroom, he said, "You can go back in your room."

* * *

As James walked into the office the next morning, Deputy Sheriff Marlin was waiting for him in the large waiting room, sitting beside a small fire in the cast iron stove.

"It was cool in here this morning," said Marlin, waving his hand in the air, "so Sara and I decided that we would build a fire."

"You guys are a little early this morning. What is the occasion?"

38

"Mr. Kincaid," Sara explained, "I need to take off a little early today, if possible, so I came in early. Deputy Sheriff Marlin saw me come in this morning and he kinda followed me into the office."

"Yeah, James. I need to have a discussion with you about a complaint that Shane Keller has filed."

Motioning with his hand, James said, "Come on in." He walked toward his office and asked, "Sara, is there any coffee yet?"

"Sure, Mr. Kincaid. Do you want a cup? Also, do you, Deputy Sheriff Marlin?"

"Yes, that will be fine, Sara."

Settling himself behind his desk, James motioned for Deputy Sheriff Marlin to have a seat. "Now, Oliver, what can I do for you this early morning?"

"Well, James, I would not have bothered you with this issue today, but I have to go to Petersburg as a witness, and I'll probably be gone for a day or two at least."

"Here, you two guys," Sara said as she came into James's office. "Here is your coffee. Let me know if you need any more."

Both men nodded and thanked Sara as she returned to her desk.

"Anyway, James, Shane Keller came to me yesterday and filed a complaint on the Twin Forks Mining and Dredging Company out of Seattle. Apparently that company leased four horses from the livery and Keller wants to know how he can get in touch with them. He leased them for a month and it has been over two months since he heard anything from them." Pausing, Deputy Sheriff Marlin stood and went to the map table as he waved James over to look at a location.

As Deputy Sheriff Marlin turned on the light over the map table, he pointed to the junction where the Snippaker River runs into the Iskut River. "That location is in British Columbia, and I can't do a thing about it until they come back into the Alaska Territory; even then an arrest would be thin as hell. You know I don't have a lot of jurisdiction away from Wrangell."

James eased over to where Deputy Sheriff Marlin was pointing. Shaking his head, James cursed. "Damn it, Oliver. I sent Kelly and Payuk to that very location to check that mining company's mining claim and maybe check for some poaching for skins. Apparently the British Columbia Mining Office in Victoria wrote a letter to the Agriculture Department in Seattle and asked if we would check out some mining permits in their Providence of British Columbia that are almost inaccessible to them because of the distance."

Letting James finish, Deputy Sheriff Marlin emphasized, "Don't you have a contact with the Mounties in Telegraph Creek? They maybe could help us out if we got in trouble trying to arrest someone in British Columbia."

Thinking for a minute, James commented, "Yeah, maybe I could write a letter to Jacob Perkins. He is the head Mountie around Telegraph Creek." Smiling, James continued, "He has some fancy title, but hell I don't remember what it is. I'll have Sara dig it out of the files. I could write him a letter and at least request some authority in the matter with this Twin Forks Mining and Dredging Company."

"Well, James, I've got to go. I've got to catch the ferry to Petersburg in about an hour and I've got some paperwork to get together. I'll see you when I get back." Standing to leave, Deputy Sheriff Marlin advised, "Be sure to mention to Shane Keller that I talked to you about his complaint."

James smiled. "OK, I will, Oliver. Have a good trip."

Shaking his head, Deputy Sheriff Marlin looked back at James. "Don't call me that in public."

As Deputy Sheriff Marlin was leaving the Department of Agriculture office, Sara waved and wished him good travels to Petersburg.

"Sara," James called, "did you see anything of Moaka this morning?"

"No, not yet," was Sara's reply.

"Did you say he was just going down to Terrace Point to check on erosion or something?"

"Yes."

"He should have been back by now. He left yesterday morning, right?" James asked.

"Yes."

"Well, hell. I guess I should take a ride down there. It's about twenty miles or so along the coast. Only thing is that old wagon road is rough as hell. I should be back in a couple of days."

CHAPTER FOUR

Getting the eight-by-twelve-foot tent set up, Kelly and Payuk cut small pine boughs to lie under their canvas mats for sleeping. Getting their bedrolls laid out on the sleep canvas, they started hauling extra clothes and gear into the tent. While Kelly set up the fire tripod and got a cast iron cooking grate out from the gear, Payuk started gathering firewood for cooking and for the night. Both men met at the fire circle that Payuk had made, and they got the large game bag from the tent and stuffed all the food in it. Kelly threw a rope over a high tree limb, and they hoisted the game bag of food high into the air away from animals.

Both men looked up at the food bag swinging slightly and Kelly commented, "That ought to do it," as he tied the rope off.

Meanwhile the four horses grazed on new grass near the campsite.

As Payuk started gathering firewood again, he was surprised to discover early spring berries. "Hey, Kelly, come over here and let's pick some berries before it gets dark."

"Dark?" declared Kelly. "It is still the middle of the day."

"Yes, I know, but if we pick them now we will be able to see more."

"OK, I'll be there in a minute."

With the camp set up and the berries picked, Kelly nonchalantly mentioned, "Let's take a ride around the area a bit. No telling what we might find out. We'll drop off the packhorses in the corral before we go for the ride."

With creaking leather, Kelly and Payuk dismounted as they topped over a high ridge that oversaw the entire mining operation in the valley below. Kelly took the glasses from his saddlebags, and jokingly commented to Payuk, "Sit here, this looks like a comfortable rock."

"What are you looking for, Kelly?"

Slowly moving the glasses from left to right, then back again, Kelly answered, "I don't know. I guess anything that does not fit the landscape." Handing the glasses to Payuk, he said, "Here—you look; I've got to take a leak."

Returning to the comfortable rock, Kelly asked, "You see anything?"

Shrugging, Payuk handed the glasses back to Kelly as he pointed. "Look over there beyond those cedars. There seems to be a clearing on that side hill with some of this red dirt showing through."

Taking the glasses from Payuk, Kelly looked in the direction that Payuk was pointing. "Why would there be digging way up there, Payuk?" Lowering the glasses from his eyes, Kelly pondered for a moment and then commented, "It looked like they were burying something. Oh, it is probably only their trash and garbage."

Holding the glasses up to his eyes again, Kelly remarked, "I see where three fish traps have been removed and dragged out of the Iskut River. They must have taken them out to do some more hydraulic mining farther upstream in the river." Moving the glasses around, Kelly scanned the area below. Suddenly he grabbed Payuk's shirt, then quickly handed the glasses to Payuk and exclaimed, "Look at that area where the digging was happening and tell me what you see!"

Describing very slowly what he was seeing, Payuk advised Kelly, "I see four men leading horses with what looks like carcasses of skinned animals." Squinting, he went on, "I don't see any antlers on the skinned animals. They are stopping by the place where that digging was being done."

43

Shaking with anticipation, Kelly said, "Give me those glasses."

Handing the glasses to Kelly, Payuk added, "I think they are burying the carcasses to hide their poaching. What I saw was about six or eight deer or elk, all skinned out."

"That's right, Payuk," Kelly confirmed, "They are now untying the meat and letting it far on the ground. Well hell Payuk, two guys are starting to dig holes." Handing the glasses back to Payuk, here take a look. Kincaid was right about the poaching, now what are we going to do about it."

With the glasses still at his face, Payuk advise, "Didn't Kincaid say not to make any problems and just report back to him."

"What are they doing now Payuk?"

"They are still digging holes to put the skinned animals in to hide them. I guess they are burying them to hide the bones also."

"OK, Payuk, give me those glasses. We have seen enough. I want to take a closer look. So far I think they are breaking the law with this hydraulic mining, they have destroyed fish trap of the Tlingit, and now we have proof of poaching." Snorting, Kelly threw his hands in the air. "And hell, I even killed a man, and we have only been here for one day."

Putting the glasses back in the saddlebag, both men mounted. Kelly pointed out the direction he was going to skirt around the mining area and come back down on the opposite side of the canyon above the animal burying grounds.

Reining in their mounts at the edge of Snippaker River just upstream of their camp, Kelly observed, "Not much of a river," as he dismounted.

Letting the horses drink, Payuk looked at where they had come from and commented to Kelly, "Look at the ridge we just came off— as we came down the steep slope I noticed many game trails that crisscrossed all the way down the slope." Gently pulling up on his horse's reins to stop the animal from drinking, he added, "There is much game in this area; probably because not many ever come this far upstream on the Iskut River."

Remounting, Kelly nodded. "Let's swing over to the right and cut back left and come in above the diggers."

Letting the horses pick their way up the thickly foliaged slope, Kelly finally told Payuk, "Let's dismount and leave the horses here, and walk over closer to them so we won't be seen or heard."

Suddenly another loud explosion rocked the canyon walls.

"Damn that's loud, but not as loud as when we were down in the valley by the camp," Kelly said.

Payuk took their horses and tethered them to a small tree. He mentioned to Kelly, "If something does spook them, they will be able to strip away from that small tree."

Shaking his head, Kelly retorted, "I hope we don't have to go chasing our horses all over the place." He added, "Let's leave the rifles in the saddle scabbards; we should not need them. We have our side arms."

Slowly making their way through the underbrush and stands of cedar, cottonwood, and aspen, Kelly finally stopped and knelt down as Payuk come beside him and knelt down. Whispering, Kelly explained, "It looks like they are burying the whole carcass to get rid of the bones, like you said, Payuk."

"Look closely, Kelly. The horns and hooves have been removed. We've both seen that happening before. That pretty much solidifies the idea that they are poaching and sending out the skins, horns, and hooves, but to who?"

"I'll bet," Kelly said, "they must be hauling everything out on those freight wagons that we saw that made that well-used trail down the Iskut. Remember I mentioned coming up here that there was a well-worn wagon trail next to the river or at least close to the river. They could not boat the skins and stuff out because the river is just too rough in many places with falls and rapids. They probably pick up supplies from a Stikine riverboat and drop off the booty and gold to be shipped back to Seattle."

"They probably use the wagons to haul out the choice skin samples," Payuk added.

"Yeah, you are right, Payuk," Kelly agreed. "They really don't have any other way. No wonder they have so many horses."

Kneeling and watching the men dig holes and roll skinned carcasses into them, and then cover with dirt, Kelly sighed. "OK, I've seen enough. Have you seen enough, Payuk?"

"Yes. It is starting to get dark in the trees, Kelly. We need to get back to camp and get ready to go to supper at their mess hall."

"You're right, Payuk, let's ease out of here real slow."

As Kelly and Payuk were quietly making their way back to their horses, suddenly Payuk groaned with pain.

Kelly snapped around to see Payuk lying on the ground holding up his foot with a spring trap clamped around his boot. Payuk quickly whispered, "Help me get this thing off my boot. It is a good thing I have these heavy boots on, they saved my foot from getting hurt."

Quickly leaning down and putting Payuk's foot on the ground, Kelly pushed down on both sides of the trap to release Payuk's foot. As Kelly was kneeling down, he held the trap up and commented, "Someone is trapping rabbits. Can you stand, Payuk?"

Slowly getting to his feet, Payuk sighed deeply as he stood on the foot that had been in the trap. "Yes, it feels fine."

"OK, Payuk, good. Now I'm going to reset this trap so the owner of the trap will never know it has been tampered with. I don't want anybody to know we were even in this area."

After Kelly reset the trap, Payuk helped to cover the trap with small leaves, and added, "Yeah, it appears that someone around here likes rabbit for dinner."

Back at camp, Kelly and Payuk unsaddled the horses and stood the saddles up with the horse blankets covering the saddles. In case it rained during the night, the saddles would not get as wet.

"Before we go, Payuk, I want to get some beans soaking in the cast iron pot. If you'll get the beans, I'll grab the pot." Hanging the pot on the rod dangling from the tripod hook, Kelly filled the pot with water while Payuk poured some beans in the water to soak.

"That should do it, Payuk." Kelly placed the lid on the pot. "When we get back I'll start a fire under the pot and by morning the beans will be done. I know that we will be eating most of our meals with the mining crew, but I like to have beans available when I want." Making their way back to the mess hall, leading their mounts to put in the corral for the night, Kelly commented, "I'm sure hungry."

"Me too, Kelly."

Walking into the mess hall, Kelly was surprised that so many tables were placed so men could sit and eat their meals. Half mumbling back to Payuk, he said, "I think we go get in line and we will be served as we walk in the line."

Kelly and Payuk carried their tins filled with sliced elk, fried potatoes, beans, biscuits, and gravy to an open table and slid down on the benches. Looking down at the food, Payuk commented, "A lot to eat."

"Well, Payuk," Kelly responded, "You did not have to take everything."

"Yes, but all looks so good."

As Kelly was eating he saw Henry Wilson coming up behind Payuk. Henry was dressed in clean clothes, his graying brown hair was combed, and he had a clean shave. "How is the meal, you two?"

Payuk quickly jerked around to face Henry. "Good, Mr. Wilson. I won't be hungry for a while."

Henry nodded toward Kelly. "I saw you guys heading up the Snippaker. Did you find anything of interest?"

Kelly shook his head, "Nah, wasn't really looking for anything. We were just riding around checking out the Snippaker."

"Well, good," Henry replied. "Jesse said he should be finished with the paperwork tomorrow, so you guys can plan to be on your way day after tomorrow."

As Henry started to walk away, Kelly asked, "When is breakfast served?"

Smiling, Henry advised, "Starts about five in the morning."

Finishing the meal, Kelly and Payuk left the mess hall too full of food. "I feel like I won't need to eat for a week, Payuk."

"Me too," Payuk agreed.

Back at camp, Kelly started the fire under the bean pot and set the coffeepot next to the fire as both men settled down to enjoy the cool evening air coming down off the mountain and a warm fire.

Both men sat silently watching the flames curve around the bottom of the cast iron pot, then reach up into the darkness. Kelly raised up from his laid-back position. "You know, Payuk, what I would like to do?"

Sitting and staring into the fire in a state of stupor, Payuk was disturbed by Kelly's question. "I don't know...go swimming in the Snippaker River or some stupid thing," he answered sarcastically. "I'm going to bed."

48

Raising his hands in the air, Kelly exclaimed, "No, no, listen. Sometime tonight I want us to go check out some of those outbuildings behind the mess hall. I got an idea that some furs are stored in those buildings, waiting for another trip to the Stikine River. I don't know where they keep the gold, but I don't care about that. I just want to prove to myself that they are poaching and shipping furs and body parts."

Kelly had stoked the fire several times and finally checked his pocket watch: 1:00 a.m. Standing and stretching, Kelly walked over to the tent and called to Payuk, "Get up! It is time to check out those other buildings. All the lights are off in the camp except a few lanterns, and I'll bet that the night guard is keeping himself somewhere close to the fire."

Payuk was rubbing his eyes as he walked out of the tent to the fire to warm up from the chilly night air. "It is cold out here. Remember what Kincaid told you, don't be making any problems."

"Oh, Payuk, come on. We aren't going to make any problems. We'll just sneak around the back side of the camp and take a look in those buildings. They don't have any dogs, so that won't be a problem. I've also got Wilson's quarters located. I saw him coming out of that small building next to the main office. I don't know that we need to know that now, but it might be of some value later."

"OK, Kelly, let me have a cup of coffee and then we will go. You sound just like Kincaid. He always wants to know everything no matter what the danger."

Shivering slightly from the cool night air drifting down from the mountaintops, Kelly pushed aside a small bush and whispered to Payuk, "Here is the first building I want to check out." And pointing to his left, "There are two more over there we need to check also."

Keeping a low silhouette, Kelly and Payuk moved toward the back of the first building. Getting to the building, both men stood up with their backs to the building wall. Reaching over, Kelly tried the door and it was unlocked. He slowly eased the door open slightly. The inside of the building was pitch black and neither man was able to see anything inside.

Just barely able to see Payuk by a waning moon, Kelly placed his finger to his lips, for being quiet. Slowly the men went inside. Crawling on the wooden floor, Kelly bumped into something. Payuk crawled up beside Kelly and whispered, "Are they hides?"

"I don't know yet," Kelly whispered back.

Using his knife, Kelly slit the burlap wrapping slightly and felt inside. Smiling to himself in the darkness, he whispered, "Yes." Moving aside a bit, Kelly whispered to Payuk, "Here—you feel," and guided Payuk's hand to the slit in the burlap covering.

Payuk felt inside the burlap and whispered back to Kelly, "Yeah, this bag is kenched hides. I can feel the hair and salt."

Crawling backward outside, Kelly silently closed the door. "Let's take a look into those other two buildings."

"Kelly," Payuk snorted, stressed. "We're going to get caught if we keep fooling around."

"Shhh..." Kelly whispered. "The watchman is making his rounds. I just saw his shadow around the corner. Sit tight; he won't come back here."

They heard the watchman curse as a rock hit one of the buildings. "Damn skunks, they're all over the place at night."

Soon all was quiet again as the watchman went back toward the fire.

After checking the other two buildings, Kelly and Payuk discovered that all three buildings held bundles of salted-down skins ready to be hauled down to the Stikine River in freight wagons for shipment on a boat, probably to Seattle.

Arriving back to camp, the fire had burned down and Kelly had to refresh his wood under the beans. Grabbing the big metal spoon that hung on the tripod, Kelly removed the lid from the pot of beans and stirred the contents. Once the stirring was finished, he dipped a small sample out and tasted the beans.

Payuk asked, "Are they done yet?"

Chewing and swallowing the beans, Kelly answered, "Yes, just about. They sure are good. Those spices from the cook at the Steak and Stack in Wrangell give the beans a good flavor."

Offering some to Payuk, Payuk declined. "No, I'm going back to bed. You can stay up all night if you want."

Next morning, as light was just breaking over the east mountains, Kelly and Payuk showed up for breakfast at 5:00 a.m. sharp. The morning meal consisted of pancakes, sliced venison, biscuits, gravy, fried potatoes, jam, dried fruit, and coffee.

Payuk looked at all the food and commented to Kelly, "I'm not going to take everything this morning because I get too full."

"Yeah, me neither," Kelly assured him.

As Henry Wilson came toward the table where Kelly and Payuk were sitting, he inquired, "Well, where are you guys going today? Remember, Jesse will have that paperwork done today so you can start back tomorrow morning right after breakfast. We would not want you two to get lost in these mountains."

Kelly nodded. "I think we will go farther up the Snippaker than we did yesterday. We'll just be looking around at the lay of the land with nothing in particular in mind. And we might do a bit of fishing."

"Well, good," Henry replied. "Be careful in these mountains, there are a lot of dangers."

Payuk nodded his head. "Good advice, Mr. Wilson. We will be careful."

When Kelly and Payuk had left the mess hall, Henry Wilson motioned for Jesse to come and sit down at his table.

"What can I do for you, Henry?" Jesse asked as he sat across the table from Henry.

As Henry pointed, he said, "Get hold of Chapman. He is the lookout for the day, and tell him to keep an eye on those two from the ridge. No telling where they may go or end up, and I don't want them going up the Iskut any farther than the office around here. If they start up toward the Iskut, he is to fire three shots and I'll have the boys take care of it from down here."

"OK, Henry. By the way, I'll have all those forms filled out today." Pausing, Jesse added, "All those papers are from the British Columbia Mining Office in Victoria. None of them are from Alaska. It looks like these guys are just doing the Canadians a favor." Jesse combed his dark hair back. "They probably don't know a damn thing about mining, which is a good thing. The office in Victoria wants to know a lot of information that we don't want them to know about. They prescribe that only ten percent of the mining is accomplished by the hydraulic method. Hell, we do all our mining hydraulic. There were some other items that had to be doctored up a bit, but I think there will be no more questions."

Henry Wilson chuckled. "That's good, let's keep them in the dark."

CHAPTER FIVE

After going to the corral, Kelly and Payuk roped their riding horses and led them back to their camp area where the saddles were. "Grab the rifles, Payuk, and I'll get some fishing gear."

Putting the rifles in their scabbards, Payuk glanced at Kelly. "What are you doing?"

"Just having a quick taste of my beans before we go," Kelly said. "Damn, those are good!" He covered the iron pot and hung up the metal spoon on the tripod.

"Are they still warm from last night? We ought to pick some mushrooms and add to the beans," Payuk added.

"Sure, Payuk, that old iron cooking pot takes a long time to cool down, especially when there is hot food in it, and yeah, you're right. If we have time, we'll pick some mushrooms."

Pausing for a second, Kelly continued, "Payuk, we might be gone most of the day, let's put some grub in our saddlebags just in case we might get hungry. Let's get the wrapped-up cured meat, some corn dodgers, and some of that dried fruit."

The extra food put in the saddlebags, Payuk said, "I haven't asked where we are going today. I guess you will tell me pretty soon."

"You're right, Payuk. I was just thinking ahead of myself. Come over here." Kelly motioned for him to come to a little clear area next to the fire pit. With a stick, Kelly drew on the dirt a drawing of the Iskut River running to the east and the Snippaker River branching off to the southeast. Using the stick, Kelly pointed and said, "This is the mining camp. I would like to circle wide up and around Snippaker, and cross over that ridgeline to the left." He drew the ridgeline in the dirt. "That way we will get a good view of the Iskut and see just how far—"

Suddenly another loud explosion rattled the canyon.

"Damn, that's loud. To continue, I want to see just how far they have gone up the Iskut with the mining operation."

Smiling, Payuk declared, "We, you and I, are just like Kincaid and Moaka. Moaka used to talk about Kincaid always having a plan, but he would never tell Moaka about it until they were doing it. Moaka said it used to drive him crazy until he got used to how Kincaid thought." Shaking his head, Payuk stammered, "Uh, sometimes I feel the same way."

"I'm sorry, Payuk, but I just think of stuff and put it together quickly to see if it fits for a plan."

"Oh, I know you do. A lot of time I watch you, and I can actually see the wheels of your brain turning."

Both men laughed as Kelly asked, "Are we ready?"

Nodding his head, Payuk answered, "I sure hope so. We have a long, hard way to go if we go where you want."

The leather squeaked as the men mounted and then started up the Snippaker. Payuk reminded Kelly, "Don't forget about the lookout they may have posted. No telling where he may be located. He will be able to see a lot of country all around."

Raising his hand, as if understanding, Kelly urged Peanut on.

With Kelly in the lead, they nudged their horses up the small canyon where the Snippaker drained into the Iskut.

Both men looked to both sides of the canyon walls and were amazed at the beauty of the area. Payuk hailed Kelly, "Let's stop for a bit because I want to look around."

Dismounting, Kelly dropped his reins on the ground and walked back to Payuk. "Beautiful country, isn't it? I can't believe there are so many shades of green."

Sighing deeply, Payuk slowly shook his head. "My people have been hunting and fishing these mountains and valleys for thousands of years. No one really knows how long, but the stories of the elders go back many, many generations. My people believe that these waters," he pointed to the smaller and shallower Snippaker River, "are lost when they bleed into the ocean and then they are lost to us for hunting and fishing forever. That is why my people try and protect these waters for the fish, bear, and all other animals. The raven flies high into the air and when things are not right, he will tell the tribal elders. The raven is the beginning of the light to the universe and cleverly deceives by many adventures; he is a trickster. These mountains that you come into and live in, Kelly, are our home. This is not your home, it is just a place that you are now. With the Tlingit, we have always been here." Pausing for a moment, Payuk asked, "Do you understand, Kelly?"

"Wow!" Kelly exclaimed. "You are right, Payuk. Sure is something to think about."

"Kelly, I know you look upon the Tlingit with favor, and that is why you are my friend. Also, Moaka thinks of Kincaid as his friend for the same reason. Moaka would do anything for Kincaid...even risk his life."

Grunting quietly, Kelly answered, "Yes, friendship and trust can be the greatest thing between men."

"I guess I am through looking for now, Kelly. Lead the way."

Following the Snippaker River farther up the canyon, Kelly reined up Peanut and advised Payuk as he pointed, "Let's cut over to the left and go up the slope in that direction."

Nodding, Payuk answered, "OK, I'll follow a ways back."

Half reining and half letting the horses have their head, they slowly made their way up the slope of the mountain as the horses weaved between cedar and hemlock trees and lower brush like willow and wild berry shrubs.

Coming to a small clearing, Kelly dismounted Peanut and let the reins fall to the ground as Payuk also dismounted, and they let their horses graze on the new grasses in the trees so a lookout would have more trouble seeing them.

Kelly sat on a fallen tree as Payuk joined him. Kelly leaned back slightly and folded his arms over his chest and coolly commented, "There is something calming about watching a horse graze. They seem to go at it so peacefully and seem to have a rhythm to the motion of taking a bite and chewing the grass to the back teeth. When I was in college, I learned a lot about horses and stock in general. Payuk, did you know that a cow has two stomachs? The first time they eat, the food goes into the first stomach, then they belch it back up and finish chewing it, then it goes into the second stomach for digestion. Or did you know that a horse will eat its own crap if he gets hungry enough? A horse only digests about fifty percent of its food."

Payuk was looking up into the trees and around the mountains that he could see, as he remarked, "That is interesting, Kelly, but why do I need to know that stuff? Tlingit boys are taught about hunting, fishing, basket weaving for fish traps, what to eat and what not to eat, and how to get along with the family."

"Well, Payuk, you learned to speak English well enough to get along with the whites that were moving into Alaska. It is the same with the knowledge I just told you about; it is knowledge needed to be a successful rancher or animal doctor."

Payuk glanced at Kelly and asked, "Are you neither of those things you mentioned?"

Smiling, Kelly responded, "You got me there, Payuk, but I could have been. Instead I came to Alaska to be your friend."

Payuk jokingly gave Kelly a small shove on his shoulder. "That's not true."

"You're right, Payuk, but it worked out that way. Let's push on up to the top and see what's over the ridge."

The ridgeline was covered with tall spruce and cedar and the pair had to find a place to see down in the valley. Getting the glasses from his saddlebag, Kelly scanned up and down the valley.

"See anything, Kelly?"

"No," Kelly answered, "just trees and more trees. We need to go into the valley and up the other side to the next ridgeline. It is a ways, but we can still make it back to camp for supper so no one will be suspicious about where we have been."

Mounting and reining the horses some and letting them have their head, Kelly and Payuk made good time to the narrow valley floor.

A narrow stream was flowing as the water chattered over the rocks, making a rhythmic sound. Letting the horses drink and graze, Kelly and Payuk filled their canteens with fresh water.

Looking up to the top of the next ridgeline, Kelly observed as he pointed, "This one is not as high as the other one. It should not take us long to reach the crest."

Letting the horses find their way with minimal reining up the steep slope, Kelly dismounted just before reaching the crest. "Let's walk the rest of the way—"

Suddenly there was rapid-fire shooting heard coming from just over the ridge. Pulling Peanut to the top of the ridge, Kelly grabbed the glasses from his saddlebags and ran to a vantage point to look down in the valley floor to see at least twenty head of elk being slaughtered. Handing Payuk the glasses, Kelly exclaimed, "Look at that!"

Soon the shooting ceased as the last elk lay on the ground. "This is what our elders said would happen," Payuk said as he shook his head, "and sorrowfully admitted."

Quickly the shooters ran to the elk and started skinning as fast as they could. Kelly saw through his glass that they cut off all hooves and horns, and were careful when skinning not to damage the hides. Soon after, other men came and started burying the carcasses. "Look, Payuk." Kelly handed him the glasses. "They are using the same procedure as we discovered before. Kill, skin, and bury the carcasses."

Taking the glasses down from his face, Payuk asked Kelly, "Why do men do these things? Let's get out of here and get back to camp."

"No, wait!" Kelly urged. "I really want to watch for a while to make sure I know what I'm going to tell Kincaid."

While Kelly continued to watch the skinning and burying, Payuk checked the horses for tight cinch straps, and tied down the saddlebags on his horse and Peanut. "See anything different than before?" Payuk questioned.

Shaking his head, Kelly commented, "They are even taking the hide off from the legs of the animals." Adjusting his position, Kelly continued, "They have some kind of small saw that they are using to cut the feet and antlers off." Removing the glasses from his eyes, Kelly lay back against a large rock and casually asked Payuk, "I wonder how many skins, hooves, and antlers they take down to the Stikine River for shipment. I wonder if the boat is marked with Canadian markings so they do not have to worry about being boarded and searched going out of Alaskan waters."

"You do a lot of wondering, Kelly. Let's get out of here before someone finds us up here spying on them."

Putting the glasses back in the saddlebag and fastening it up, Kelly stepped in the stirrup and threw a leg over and pulled on Peanut's reins to stop the horse from moving. Kelly leaned up on his saddle horn, and sighed. "Payuk, how could we find out how many skins they are trying to ship?"

"Kelly," Payuk shook his head, "like I've heard you say, you are playing with fire. Remember what Kincaid told you."

"Yeah, yeah, I know, Payuk."

Arriving back at camp before supper in the mess hall, Payuk and Kelly lowered the food bag and placed the food they'd taken with them into the bag and hoisted the game bag up again and tied it off for the night.

Lifting the lid off his cast iron pot, Kelly said, "Well, they aren't warm anymore, but we'll take them with us when we leave tomorrow. Damn it, maybe we can eat some of them tomorrow night."

CHAPTER SIX

James walked up to the large corral railings and hailed, "Jeffery, where is your boss?"

Quickly rising up from fixing a corral post, Jeffery Maxwell answered, "Oh hi, Mr. Kincaid. He took that new bay we got for a short ride. I guess he thought she needed some settling down."

"Jeffery, I need a horse for a couple of days or so. Make sure the saddle has a rifle scabbard hooked on."

"Yes sir, Mr. Kincaid. I'll get the horse saddled with a scabbard right now. I really don't know when Mr. Keller will be back."

As James crawled through the second and third rail of the corral, he pointed to the roan. "I'll take that one, Jeffery."

"Yes sir, Mr. Kincaid. I'll always remember that big roan you rode for many years. He was a great horse."

Riding up to the Department of Agriculture, James dismounted and tied the roan off on the porch post. Going inside he informed Sara that he was riding down to Terrace Point to see what was holding up Moaka. Getting his saddlebags, sidearm .38 and belt, Model 94 Winchester rifle, and slicker, James said good-bye to Sara and rode home to pick up some food supplies.

Just before leaving his house, James wrote Suzette a quick note to let her know that he was going down to Terrace Point and would probably be back in a couple of days.

James rode the roan south out of Wrangell along the coast on the old wagon trail that was pretty much overgrown because the logging on the west coast of Wrangell Island had been finished up for the time being. He marveled at the calmness of the ocean surface off to his right to the west, with a very little breeze and springtime warm sunshine. Looking down at the horse's reddish mane, James patted the roan on the neck, and muttered, "I don't even know your name, horse. I guess I'll call you..." He thought for a minute. "Red. Yeah, that's a good name for a roan horse, Red."

Letting Red have his head as the horse followed the wagon trail, James thought, *Kelly and Payuk were to check on mining claims up on the Iskut River.* He was uneasy with what Deputy Sheriff Marlin had told him about Keller making a complaint about the very people he sent Kelly and Payuk to check on. Sighing deeply, James muttered, "Red, you're lucky you are a horse; you do not have many problems, just food, water, and rest." His mind returned to Kelly and Payuk. *I know both men are competent employees, but we all make stupid mistakes.*

Seeing someone coming toward him on the wagon trail, James held up Red and waited for the single rider's approach.

As the rider approached he waved at James. "Hey, Kincaid, what are you doing down here?" He stopped his horse even with Red.

"Hi, Mason. I would ask you the same question. There's not many beaver down here."

"You're right, Kincaid, but I'm not after beaver on this trip. I was down in Hoqur Cove. I was helping a friend of mine dig for a little gold." Pausing, Mason continued, "We never found any to amount to much so I decided to come on back to Wrangell and outfit out for some good beaver trapping areas."

Raising his hand, as if saying wait, "Tom, before I forget, you have a bunch of mail in the post office from your two daughters in Seattle. They probably want to know if you are still alive or have got eaten by a bear..." Both men laughed.

Nodding, Mason asked, "I guess you have heard about the problems at Terrace Point. A couple of guys even got shot yesterday,

61

not shot dead, but wounded pretty bad. I don't believe anybody is going to die, but they will be limping around for a while."

Sighing deeply, James asked, "So what in the world happened down there? Moaka went down there day before yesterday morning when I was still coming back from Seattle. He had gotten a complaint about someone damming up a stream and it was flowing over onto someone's place."

"Kincaid, I don't know a thing about the situation. I damn sure did not want to get involved so I pushed on after a night's sleep in the area. I do know that two guys got shot, and there is an argument about water usage."

James stood in his stirrups and stretched his legs and advised Mason, "Get your mail. I've got to be on my way."

"OK, Kincaid, thanks for the message; be careful at Terrace Point. Some people are just crazy with what they want."

Looking back at Mason, who was leading a packhorse, James shook his head and thought, *Tom Mason, what a strange person. Lives in a tent outside of Wrangell and sends almost every dime he makes beaver trapping and selling skins to those two daughters in Seattle that are going to some finishing school for girls.*

Following the wagon trail a short way above the coastline, James smelled smoke. Reining in Red, he soon saw a small tent pitched down next to the waterline. Dismounting and leading Red toward the small tent, he saw that the camp had a smoldering fire and appeared to be deserted. The small tent was pitched on flat ground with some firewood stacked nearby. Stopping, James hailed, "Hello, the camp. Is there anybody here?"

Instantly a very small brown and white dog came charging out of the tent yapping so loudly and quickly that it spooked Red, and the horse tried to shy away from the nuisance dog's shrill barking.

Calming Red, James pushed the dog away with his foot, and the small dog backed away but continued the irritating barking. "Hello, the camp," James repeated.

Slowly the tent flap opened and a young girl came creeping out slowly, carrying a single-shot, break-open shotgun. "You don't have to kick him. He will stop barking when he knows you will not do any harm. What do you want?"

Astonished, James quickly looked the young girl over. She was dressed in a dark, ragged shirt with leather pants, and her shoes were about worn out. Her blond hair needed combing, and her face was dirty. She was tall and slender with a nice-looking face. Shaking his head, James asked, "What are you doing here?"

"My father and I came over here for fishing and hunting and he was killed a while back by a bear that raided our camp one night. Runback," she pointed to the dog, "and I have been here ever since. We have plenty to eat—fish, berries, and squirrels. My dad taught me to live out in the wild."

James shook his head. "Well, you can't stay here. Where did you come from?"

Calmly the young girl said, "Change Island."

"Change Island!" James exclaimed. "There is nothing there; what did you do there?"

"My father and I cut wood for some folks and dried hides for sale in one small village."

"What is your name?"

"My name is Janet Moore. My father was Frank Moore. He was a miner until he got hurt mining, then we had to do other stuff to live. That's my boat over there." She pointed to the water's edge. "It is a good, heavy wooden boat and does not leak hardly any. It has three flat seats and two oars."

Dropping his reins to the ground, James walked over to the boat and stated, "Your boat needs some repairs." Looking up and down the shoreline, James explained, "Well, you can't stay here. You may have food now, but when winter comes on you will have a hard time surviving out here. Where were you and your father going?"

"We were not going anywhere. One place is as good as another."

"How old are you, Janet?"

"I am eighteen. I was quite young when my mother died so my father raised me."

"Miss Moore, my name is James Kincaid, and I work for the Department of Agriculture." He walked back to Red and opened one of the saddlebags and removed a tablet. Writing something on the tablet, he tore the sheet from the pad and handed it to Janet. "Here—I want you to take this to Mrs. Mackly in Wrangell. She owns the Parker Boarding House. Ask her to put you to work for room and board for a while until I get back to Wrangell."

"Where is Wrangell?"

Sniffing, James pointed to the north. "Just stay along the shoreline till you get to a town and then look up Mrs. Mackly. Everybody knows her so you won't have any problem finding her. It will take you about two, maybe three, days of rowing that heavy boat, but you'll eventually get there."

Setting the shotgun against a fallen tree, Janet read the note.

"Can you read?" James asked.

"Sure, and I can do my sums. My dad made sure of that."

"Does anybody stop and see you from time to time? It is a good idea to keep the shotgun handy for bears and the like, but you don't have to point it at everyone that may come and visit." Pausing, James continued, "If a bear does come around, you can just fire a shot into the air and most bears will run for cover."

"There was a man that was riding a horse and had a packhorse that went by earlier this morning," Janet explained. "But he didn't stop, just looked and kept going."

Sighing, James put the tablet back in his saddlebag and instructed Janet, "Tomorrow morning early get your camp picked up and put it in your boat and start rowing for Wrangell." James mounted Red. "Like I said, it will probably take you the better part of two days or more."

Riding toward Terrace Point, James smiled as he mentally reviewed what had just happened. *That poor girl was left to her own being by her father being killed, although it sounded like her father did well by her by teaching her to read and do the sums...that's something.*

CHAPTER SEVEN

By the time Kelly and Payuk arrived at the mess hall just a little after 5:00 a.m. almost the entire crew was inside chowing down on the victuals. Getting in line with a metal tray, they filled their trays with spiced venison, fried potatoes, meat gravy, biscuits and jam, and filled their cups with hot coffee.

Making their way to an empty table, both men settled down to enjoy their last breakfast with the miners. All the men who worked for Henry Wilson were friendly, knowing that Kelly and Payuk meant them no harm.

"Payuk, here comes Wilson," Kelly murmured low.

"Good morning, gents. You'll be glad you can see Jesse when you get finished with breakfast and get your paperwork for the British Columbian Mining Council. I checked the paperwork over yesterday when Jesse finished, and all is in order according to our contract."

Kelly stood and shook hands with Wilson and cordially commented, "It has been a pleasure being here, Mr. Wilson. Payuk and I don't know much about the laws, but we have learned a lot about hydraulic mining, and I want to thank you for that knowledge."

Listening to Kelly talk to Wilson, it was all he could do to keep from smiling. Inside himself, Payuk was laughing his ass off...Kelly was the biggest bullshitter. No wonder Kincaid trusted him to get out of tight spots. Payuk stood to shake hands with Mr. Wilson and said, "We wish you good luck in your mining project."

Taking a deep breath, Henry responded, "Well, that's alright, young feller. Everyone has to learn. Motioning toward their breakfast, Henry commented again, "When you guys are finished here, see Jesse for the papers, and then you can be on your way downriver."

Kelly and Payuk nodded and replied together as Henry turned to go away, "Thanks, Mr. Wilson."

Finishing their breakfast, Kelly and Payuk retired to the main office where Jesse was waiting for them. "Come on in," Jesse hailed as Kelly opened the door.

Seeing a stack of papers tied together with string and with a cloth wrapped around the papers to keep them clean from trail dust, Kelly remarked in astonishment, "Wow, what happened to the few forms I gave you?"

With a soft laugh, Jesse answered, "Well, I had to answer all the questions." Pausing, he began again, explaining, "There is something else I would like to speak with you about." Getting up from his desk chair, Jesse walked over to the door and opened it slightly to check and see that no one was outside near the office. Returning to his chair, he asked Kelly and Payuk, "Will you please sit down while I explain my concerns? I won't take much of your time."

Both Kelly and Payuk grabbed a chair and sat close to Jesse. "OK, shoot, Jesse...we are listening," Kelly offered.

"First off, I have a brother that works for the Department of Agriculture in Portland. He has worked for them for many years, ever since he graduated from college. We are real close and we see each other two or three times a year or when we can with our families. We don't really talk much about my job because he knows who I work for, and he disagrees with Twin Forks's opinions on hydraulic mining. This job pays me a lot of money so I would not want to jeopardize my position with Twin Forks unless I had something else to go to. I hope you can understand."

Kelly and Payuk nodded as Kelly responded, "Yes, Jesse, we understand. What is it you want to tell us?"

Pointing to the stack of papers that Kelly and Payuk were to take back, Jesse sternly stated, "They are a pack of lies. I did not answer the questions truthfully. I answered them according to what I knew Henry Wilson would approve for you to take with you. I really don't know who approved the contract for Twin Forks Mining, but to be sure it was not the Victoria Mining Office or the British Columbian Mining Council. I really don't know how far these reports will go up the line, but if they get to those two organizations...heads are going to roll."

Shifting in his chair, Payuk asked, "Can't you just quit and go somewhere else for a job?"

"My brother has always told me to get out of this mining business and he would get me a job in the Department, but up till now I didn't feel threatened. It may be time for me to reevaluate my position here at Twin Forks."

"What do you want us to do, Jesse?" Kelly asked sympathetically.

"Well, I don't rightly know, but maybe if you have to take measures to shut this mining operation down..." Shaking his head, Jesse solemnly proposed, "I could be an inside man for you as long as it would be understood that I walk free when it is all over with."

Breathing deeply, Kelly admitted, "I can't guarantee you that, but I know a man who can and will, especially when Payuk and I vouch for you."

"Who would that be, Kelly?" Jesse asked.

"His name is James Kincaid in Wrangell, Alaska. He is the he-bull for the Department of Agriculture in this area. He is also the game warden for this area. He does not have a lot of jurisdiction right here where the mine is, but he knows and has worked with the Mounties out of Telegraph Creek, British Columbia, and I know they would readily cooperate with the Department and especially Kincaid." Pausing, Kelly then questioned, "Jesse, you made a comment about 'if' we would strive to shut down this mining operation. I'm here to tell you that is exactly what will happen; and Katie-bar-the-door if anybody gets in the way."

Smiling at Kelly and Payuk, Jesse stressed, "Henry Wilson will have the full support of Twin Forks Mining and they will not go down easy. These big companies are in some kind of litigation all the time. Remember, Twin Forks Mining has a contract to be here, regardless of who signed the contract at its origin."

"Jesse," Kelly emphasized, "you let people like Kincaid worry about things like that. I want you to just keep your nose clean until time to make our move. I can't tell you when that will be, but it will be sooner rather than later. By the way, when do you figure the freight wagons will make a trip to the Stikine River?"

"Why in the hell do you want to know that?" Jesse asked.

Kelly shrugged. "I don't know, just some information."

"Well..." Jesse thought for a moment. "They should be leaving here soon." He didn't know that Kelly and Payuk knew about the skins and body parts. "Maybe tomorrow, I'm not sure." Jesse shook his head. "They usually have only one driver for each rig. No one expects problems, nor has anybody had any problems, going down to the Stikine River."

"Thanks, Jesse; you have been a real help," Kelly said in a friendly way.

Nodding, Jesse stood and motioned Kelly and Payuk to stand. "OK, you guys get out of here and get down the river. I'll wait for your contact." Jesse extended his hand in friendship to Kelly and Payuk.

Picking up the horses at the corral, Kelly and Payuk led them to the camp area and let the horses graze as Kelly and Payuk tore down the tent, cleaned the fire pit, and stacked up the extra firewood. They saddled the riding horses, loaded the packhorses with all the supplies, and took one last slow look around the mining camp.

"Payuk," Kelly advised, "Take a good look around the entire camp. We want to know where Wilson, Jesse, and the crew sleep because that might be important when we come back. I want to ride out of here real slow, taking account of everything we are seeing."

Slowly following the Iskut River downstream, Kelly and Payuk let Peanut and Payuk's riding horse have their head to follow the wagon trail as they crossed the small bridge over the Snippaker River. When they were out of sight of the mining camp, Kelly pulled up on Peanut's reins and they stopped to look back. "Payuk, I wonder when they plan on shipping those skins and gold. There has to be a way to find out."

Crossing his arms on his saddle horn, Payuk shook his head and warned, "Do I see the wheels in your head turning, Kelly? Don't be so curious. Just report back to Kincaid and let him make the decisions."

"How long do you think it will take the two freight wagons to make the trip from the mining camp to the Stikine River?" Kelly asked.

"Kincaid said it was about forty miles from the Stikine River to the mining camp, so I figure about three days and they'll be unloading on the fourth morning."

Biting his lower lip and nodding his head, Kelly rose up in his stirrups to stretch his legs and responded, "I think you are right on with that time frame." Sitting quiet a moment or two, he then cautiously remarked, "We need to let the wagons be almost to the Stikine River before we take them."

"Take them where!" Payuk exclaimed. "Kelly, you can't capture those wagons. That would be theft, and besides that, what are you going to do with them?"

"We, Payuk, you and I, are going to set a plan to get those freight wagons to Wrangell."

Shaking his head in disbelief, Payuk remarked, "Kelly you are going to get us killed or put into jail, and I don't like either idea. Why can't you just do as Kincaid told you to do?"

"Payuk, listen...this may be our only chance of capturing the goods coming right from the mining claim. By doing this we have the riverboat, its captain, men that work for the mine, the poached skins, and the gold. I guess there will be gold, but Kincaid will probably put that in the care of the bank in Wrangell. You and I have seen how the poached skins are taken, and that is also very important."

Sighing and changing his position in the saddle, Payuk agreed. "You are right, Kelly, but how in the world are we going to pull all this together with just the two of us?"

"Let's ride a ways farther to be sure we are not in sight of the lookout." Urging Peanut forward and leading his packhorse, Kelly led the way downriver for another four or five miles.

"Oh, look!" Payuk exclaimed. "Look at the mother fox leading her three pups away from the river. They must have come down for a drink and we showed up. Aren't those little ones cute? Tlingit will not keep animals in cages like the white man does. If we want to see wildlife, we go where they live and grow." As they were stopped along on the wagon trail, Payuk told Kelly, "Let's sit for a minute. I want to watch the little ones play."

71

"Sure, Payuk. I like to watch the animals in their natural habitat."

Soon the mother fox led her pups up into the brush away from the intruders.

"OK, Kelly, let's go."

A short while after seeing the foxes, Kelly held up Peanut and dismounted. "Let's stop for a while and talk about what we need to do."

Letting the horses graze, Kelly and Payuk sat on a large, flat rock that overlooked the river. Watching the river flow past them, and looking around the general area, Kelly mentioned, "What a place, Payuk. This would be a great place to live if it did not have ten feet of snow every year...probably more than that. Look at the mountains, the trees, the river, and the sky; what a place."

"Yes, Kelly, I like places like this. It is Tlingit land. Not that we own it, but rather we and our northern brothers, the Tahltan, have lived here for many generations."

Breaking a small stick and tossing the small end away, Kelly advised, "OK, this is my plan. I really need you to have input on this so speak up if you see something that is not right." Moving down to a dirt area, Kelly used his stick and drew a rough print of what he thought should happen.

During Kelly's explanation of the series of events, Payuk would add certain pieces of advice to the conversation that were useful to the completion of the takeover of the freight wagons and getting them on board the riverboat. Finally, after much give and take from both men, the plan was set.

Standing and looking down at the drawing they had made in the dirt, Payuk shook his head. "There have to be a lot of things go right for this thing to work."

Standing alongside of Payuk, Kelly scratched out the drawing in the dirt with his boot, and jokingly commented, "Never can tell who may see that."

"Huh," Payuk said, smiling. "No one could make anything out of those chicken scratches."

Rounding up the horses that had been grazing, Kelly and Payuk led them to a small stream that was slowly making its way toward the Iskut River, for a drink before heading out again. "Are all our canteens filled with water?" asked Payuk.

"Yes, all of mine are," Kelly said, checking the three canteens that hung on his packhorse.

"I have four full ones," answered Payuk. "There may be little ponds on top."

After remounting and riding easy for a ways, Kelly advised, "Payuk, let's speed up just a bit. I want to get down this river and spend the night farther downstream. We've got about forty miles to the Stikine River."

The shadows were starting to grow longer as the sun began dropping over the west mountain ridge; they began to see game coming out of hiding to drink and forage for food before nightfall.

The sun was starting to drop over the ridge, and the valley began to take on a darker tone as the light was decreasing. Stopping, Kelly pointed to a spot in the trees that looked like a good camp spot for the night. "Let's go over there and spend the night up next to the trees. They'll give us good cover from any wind or rain that might fall."

"No rain tonight, Kelly; the sky is clear and the wind is calm."

Smirking, Kelly jokingly asked, "What are you, the weather man?"

"Tlingit knows how to read the weather."

Moving to the location for the night's camp, Kelly said, "I'll get the hitch rail pole for the horses."

The packhorses unloaded and the saddles off the other horses, Payuk led the horses to water not far from the camp area as Kelly used a small rope to tie the horse hitching rail pole up between the trees. Bringing the horses back, Payuk made a hackamore halter for each horse, removed the straight bit bridle, and mounted hackamore halter onto each horse. Each horse's hackamore had an extension rope of eight or so feet to tie the horses for the night to the hitching rail.

Kelly got both the bedrolls and laid them in front of the hitching rail and began gathering small pine and fir boughs to put the bedrolls on to keep the them off the ground. Making two places in front of the horses with the boughs, Kelly unrolled the bedrolls.

Payuk gathered some small twigs for a fire as Kelly gathered larger wood for a night fire.

Looking up into the sky, Kelly commented, "Boy it gets dark quickly when that sun goes behind that mountain, and it's starting to get cooler." Getting the tripod set up over where Payuk was building a small fire, Kelly got his pot of beans and hung them over the fire, close to the flames.

Sitting on the edge of their bedrolls, Kelly looked back at the horses that were secured for the night. "We'll hear the horses jumping around if anything comes around, and just in case, I'm going to keep my rifle handy."

Payuk looked at Kelly's new 30-06 rifle and asked, "When did you get the new rifle and get rid of that old Krag you used to carry. That old Kraig must have been getting pretty old." He jokingly made fun of Kelly's old rifle.

"You don't be worrying about that Krag. I've still got it put away. It shot farther than your rifle with a one-hundred-and-sixty grain bullet, and that is a lot of impacting power. Course, this Springfield 30-06 is a little better rifle. It is lighter and actually is easier to handle and shoot. It also has a little more punch with a one-hundred-and-eighty grain bullet. I prefer the bolt action to the lever action. I bought this rifle last year when Nancy and I took a trip to Seattle." Looking toward the coffeepot, he said, "If there's water in that coffeepot I'll make coffee for after supper."

Digging around in the food bags, Payuk asked, "What do we want to eat tonight?"

Sniffing, Kelly sighed. "I don't know. I think we have got some dried salmon left and these beans will be ready pretty quick." Kelly stood up and leaned forward to dip a sample with the metal spoon. Whistling, Kelly exclaimed, "Those are just about ready to eat. Where are the metal plates?"

Payuk dug in the supplies bag and dug out two metal plates, then dug into the food bag and got several pieces of dried fish.

Their supper of beans and dried salmon finished, each man had a cup of coffee.

Both men sat quietly on the end of their bedrolls next to the fire and enjoyed the quiet night. Finally Kelly commented, "That damn Kincaid. He sure knows his business. He suspected this mining outfit was poaching. I'm not sure how he knew or suspected that, but he was right on."

Smiling, Payuk retorted, "That is not always the case."

As Payuk kept smiling, Kelly snorted, "What are you smiling at?"

"You remember Skipper Daniels?" Payuk asked.

Kelly nodded. "Sure. What are you laughing at?"

75

"Well, Skipper Daniels had Kincaid's number right off. What I mean is Skipper Daniels had Kincaid going on a matter. It seems every time Kincaid took Skipper Daniels's boat anywhere, Bray would always disappear up into the wheelhouse. Kincaid always wondered if it could be that the wheelhouse was warmer, so one day when all the horses and gear was loaded, going wherever, Kincaid climbed the ladder to the wheelhouse, unbeknown to Skipper Daniels, and caught Skipper Daniels giving Bray pieces of meat for a snack. Kincaid was furious. He kicked Bray out of the wheelhouse and scolded Skipper Daniels for making Bray fat. All that time, Skipper Daniels was having the time of his life because he had pulled one over on Kincaid.

"It was really kind of funny because Bray would climb the metal ladder to the wheelhouse; you know, it was the kind of ladder that had flat pieces of metal instead of bars for steps that made it easy for Bray to climb to the wheelhouse. When Bray left the wheelhouse he would jump down on the bait box that was just forward of the wheelhouse, then onto the deck of the boat.

"After a while, Kincaid never seemed to care. He and Skipper Daniels were good friends."

Leaning forward to put a larger piece of wood onto the fire, Payuk smiled and laughed.

"Now what are you laughing at?" Kelly demanded.

"Hmm. Another good story before you were around. Moaka always had a thing about keeping truth. It must have been something to do with the Inuit teachings, course no one likes a liar or a cheat. Anyway, Kincaid and Moaka were having a hard time with two local bosses that owned...too far back, I can't remember, maybe a fishery and a logging camp, whatever, it does not make any difference for the story. The employees of these outfits would come into Wrangell and get drunk and start fighting among each other and Deputy Sheriff Marlin was getting tired of breaking up fights and hauling workers into jail. When they sobered up, the city would feed them breakfast and let them go with a small fine." Smiling and nodding, Payuk continued, "That does not sound too bad, but it was getting to be a lot of the time, and the city was starting to complain about having to buy breakfast for a bunch of drunks because they had been locked up all night. So Deputy Sheriff Marlin went to Kincaid and complained, hopeful Kincaid could help out."

Pausing for a moment to take a drink of coffee, Payuk continued, "Kincaid talked with Moaka and me to check and see if the Tlingit or Tahltan were having any problems with either crews or outfits, and we were not. Kincaid talked with several other parties that were uninvolved in the dispute and nobody seemed to have a problem except the two crazy bosses that were fighting all the time."

"Is this story going to take all night?" Kelly pursued.

Smiling, Payuk held up his hands and quickly stated, "Hold on, Kelly, it gets better. Anyway," Payuk continued, "Kincaid went to see both of these company bosses with Moaka in tow. Kincaid made them agree to come to a meeting at the conference room in back of the mayor's office on a certain date. By and by, the date came and all parties showed up. One of the bosses wanted to accept the deal that Kincaid had proposed, but the other one was hemming and hawing around about rights, contracts, and workers keeping busy. Kincaid tried several options to his proposal, but this one boss would not give and he wanted to take everything he could. This went on for an hour or so and you could see Kincaid was about to throw in the towel for the meeting." Pausing, Payuk added, "This part I will never forget. Suddenly Moaka jumped up on the long table and kicked the boss over backward that was not agreeing to anything. His back was

77

on the floor, and Moaka was instantly sitting on top of him with his eight-inch knife pulled, and was poking this guy in the neck. Moaka's left hand had a handful of the man's hair and he jerked the man's head sideways and actually brought a blood spot on the tip of his knife. Before anybody could do anything, Moaka screamed in the man's face, 'Say yes to Kincaid—be of blade of truth. No do, and blade of truth slit throat.'"

Smiling, Payuk swore, "Believe me, Kelly, I was no more than from here to that rock from the whole action. The poor man was almost crying for Moaka to let him up. And he did agree to the proposal Kincaid had made. It was really something to see."

"What did Sid Bonner say about all that?"

"I don't know, but nothing ever happened to Moaka. My guess is that Kincaid stuck up for him. You may not know it, but your boss believes in getting to the truth of the matter, regardless what it takes."

Kelly nodded and smiled. "Yes, I know that, Payuk. I learned that when I went up to Telegraph Creek to help the Mounties. I remember one time when someone shot into James and Jacob Perkins's campsite, the Mountie we were helping, and James and Bray took out after him. James grabbed a handful of red mane and was up onto the roan with no bridle or saddle, and Bray took off at a fast run. Finally James brought back the guy—who was shot dead. I remember Perkins had a fit. He asked James why in the world he had to kill the guy. James just looked at him and said, 'Anybody that shoots at me will get the same in return, only I shoot straight and a lot of people don't.'"

Tossing the rest of his cold coffee out on the ground, Payuk put a large log on the fire for the night and announced, "Enough stories. I enjoyed them all," as he rolled into his bedroll.

CHAPTER EIGHT

The light was starting to disappear from the sky when James neared Terrace Point. James thought, *Terrace Point is not really a place, it's more like an area, and I've not been down in this area for some time.* Dismounting, James was undecided what to do right then. "Well, Red, do we want to ride around here looking for Moaka now or wait until morning?"

Suddenly the evening calmness was broken by two quick gunshots from a rifle. James stood still, wanting to listen to see if he could tell where the two shots were fired from. Remounting, James urged Red forward slowly up the wagon trail and then winding up the slope of the mountain away from the trail.

Another single shot. "OK, Red, I got where it's coming from. Let's pick up the pace a little." As James nudged Red's sides, the horse began to walk faster up the slope.

Red slowed to a walk as James pulled gently on the reins and then Red stopped. Sliding the rifle from its scabbard, James dismounted and tied Red off on a tree limb. Quietly levering a round into the chamber of his Winchester, James proceeded forward slowly at a crouched walk. He tried to walk as quietly as possible through the timber and pine-needle forest floor when he heard a loud voice coming from just up ahead.

Another single round from a rifle echoed through the trees and the bullet sounded like it ricocheted off from a rock.

James stopped to survey the area ahead of him. Suddenly he saw movement from a person on the downhill side of a large rock. Looking closely, he could not believe his eyes. It was Moaka crouching down behind the large rock with his rifle poised to fire, but at the same time not firing. James quickly looked up the slope to a small structure, maybe a cabin, where the firing was coming from.

"Moaka, cover me, I'm coming over there."

"Kincaid! Come on, I cover." Moaka quickly fired three shots up the hill at some structure to give James covering fire.

Sliding on the wet grass, James stopped beside Moaka behind the large hunk of granite. "Why are you being fired on, Moaka?" James quickly asked.

Pointing up the hill, Moaka sternly replied, "He think I miner."

"Who is up there?" James asked.

"Man who own cabin."

"Do you know his name?" James inquired.

"No name."

"Have you tried to talk to him to see what his problem is?" James probed.

"Talk yesterday, now he think I miner."

Suddenly another shot echoed through the forest and another round ricocheted off the large boulder of granite that James and Moaka were hiding behind.

"Well, this has got to stop," blurted James. "Moaka, I want you to slide over to the other side of this boulder and get behind that large rock over there." James pointed to the place. "When you get there, I'm going to yell at this guy to stop firing so I can identify myself. How come you don't have your Department shirt on?"

"Get dirty."

Seeing Moaka settled behind the other boulder, James stood up just so his head was above the top of the rock and hailed, "Who is up there in the cabin?"

"Who the hell wants to know?" Came the quick reply.

"This is James Kincaid from the Department of Agriculture in Wrangell."

"The same guy who used to work for Sid Bonner?"

"Yes, the same."

"Who is that idiot with you? He's one of those miner guys trying to wash me and my cabin off this mountain."

Breathing deeply, James hailed back, "We need to talk. I'm sure we can work out some viable solutions to both parties' satisfaction."

"Don't be too damn sure," came the man in the cabin's reply.

"Listen—to whom am I talking?" yelled James.

"My name is Neil Baxter. And I never cared much for Sid Bonner because he spoke against me for Benny Wilkins. Now what the hell do you want?"

Taking a deep breath, James dropped his head down on his rifle barrel and thought, *Neil Baxter. I knew he was still around, but never heard much of him. Baxter was never a model citizen, in and out of scrapes all the time.* Slowly shaking his head, James remembered, *That Baxter sued Benny Wilkins for back pay, but when the judge heard all the evidence, like Baxter had a drinking problem and never showed up for work all the time, the judge ruled that Wilkins never owed Baxter any back pay. Baxter soon left Wrangell and in a year he returned with a pocket full of money. Everybody knew he could not have earned that much money in one year legally, but where was the proof; so it passed.*

"I remember you, Mr. Baxter, but let's forget about the past and deal with the situation as it is right now. Maybe I can help you and the miners."

"You got that big dog with you?" Neil Baxter inquired. "I hated that big dog; he always looked like he would tear a leg off from someone."

Smiling, James yelled back, "No, I left him home this time. It's just Moaka and me here now."

"Moaka...is that the Indian's name I talked to yesterday?"

"He's no Indian, but yes, you talked with him, and he does not work for the miners. In case you have forgotten, he works for the Department of Agriculture the same as I do."

"That doesn't change anything," Baxter hollered back. "My rights are still being run over."

James stood up and called, "Mr. Baxter, why don't you come down here or we can come up there. Let's stop all this yelling back and forth."

"I want you to come up here and take a look at what is happening with my property," Baxter urged.

"Sure thing, Mr. Baxter. We will be carrying our rifles, but we mean you no harm."

Waving Moaka over to him, James instructed, "Let me go first, but keep close behind me all the way up to the cabin. No telling what this idiot will try. Do you remember the problems he caused a few years back? Sid Bonner was glad to see that guy go, wherever he went for a year or so."

James and Moaka slowly made their way up the slope for about one hundred yards and finally arrived at a small cabin that looked like it had been hastily built. The chink had fallen out between some of the log cracks, and the roof appeared to be in bad repair. The door was open slightly, but James could see no one at the small window or at the door.

"OK, Mr. Baxter, we are here," James announced.

Finally the door opened all the way and a small man with filthy clothes on, and in bad need of a shave and haircut, stepped onto a small wooden platform. He spoke sarcastically, "Yeah, you're Kincaid. I'd recognize you anywhere."

"OK, Mr. Baxter, we are here to look at your problem and talk about what can be done. Can you show us what the miners are doing to your property?"

Baxter waved his rifle in the air and pointed. "Come on, and I'll show you."

James and Moaka plodded along behind Baxter for a distance, until James started to see what Baxter was talking about. "Wait, Mr. Baxter," James stated. "I can see that some of the sluicing tailings is in fact running onto your property and it is coming near your cabin. Have you approached the mining people and asked them not to load your land with sluice tailings or at least redirect the tailings away from your land?"

"Yes I did...those assholes. They wouldn't even listen to me. The foreman told me to file my complaint with the Alaska Mining Council in Juneau. Hell, I'm not even sure there is a Mining Council in Juneau."

"There is a place in Governor Walter Clark's office where you can file complaints about mining claims and mining issues," James explained.

"Well, I'm not going all the way to Juneau when I can handle the situation here all by myself. I shot two of their men yesterday in the legs. I did not want to kill anybody, but by hell they have to understand that I won't tolerate that outfit dumping on me."

"What are they mining for, Mr. Baxter?"

"I'll be damned if I know, but I think it is gold."

Shaking his head, James muttered to Moaka, "I've never heard of anybody getting any gold from around here, have you?"

"No, Kincaid. No gold here."

"What did he say?" Baxter butted into the conversation.

"He said he never heard of anybody getting any gold around here," James explained.

In an aggressive tone, Baxter stammered, "Well, so what are you going to do about this, Kincaid?"

Nodding and glancing at Moaka, then looking into Baxter's stern gray eyes, James answered, "Well, Mr. Baxter, tomorrow Moaka and I are going to go see these miners. Is there a person I should be looking for? Or what's the foreman's name?"

"The boss's name is Ferrell Jones, but I don't know the foreman's name. Ferrell Jones is a big, fat guy, about thirty years old. He has brown hair and wears overalls. Hell, you can't miss him. He's the one that will be giving the orders."

"OK, Mr. Baxter, don't be shooting any more folks until we get back with you sometime tomorrow. It is getting late so Moaka and I will be on our way."

"They start early in the morning, so you won't have to wait on them."

As James and Moaka started walking back down the slope that was covered with low brush, cedar trees, and willows, the sun was starting to dip below the water. "It will be dark soon, Moaka, where is your horse?"

"Close big rock."

"OK, Moaka, you get your horse, and I'll get mine, and I'll follow you to your camp."

Arriving at Moaka's camp, James smiled. "You brought a packhorse." It was just what he would have expected from Moaka. He always came prepared. He chose a spot close to the water, backed up into the treeline for protection against the wind, and a nice flat spot for the fire, bedroll, and maybe the tent. Dismounting and unsaddling Red, James stood his saddle on end and covered it with the heavy wool horse blanket to keep it dry if it rained during the night. Putting a hackamore bridle on Red, he let the horse graze a short time before dark.

Moaka performed the same tasks with his horses and they met at the fire pit Moaka had made yesterday. He had his metal tripod standing over the fire pit with a metal pot with a lid hanging from the tripod.

"I see you brought the tent. Are we going to set it up?"

"No rain."

"What's in the pot, Moaka?"

"Good stew, Steak and Stack. Pot close full."

"Yeah that café does a good job."

"What bring eat, Kincaid?"

"Just a minute, Moaka. I need to unroll this bedroll, but before I do, help me gather some boughs for my bed."

Both men gathered boughs for Kincaid's bed and then James unrolled his bedroll with cans of food rolled up inside. "Well, Moaka, I've got two cans of canned beans, two cans of canned peaches, a large piece of salt pork, and coffee, sugar, and salt."

"Where stool, Kincaid?"

"Oh, I don't know. I really did not think I was going to be down here that long." Looking around at the camp, James commented, "You get a fire going and I'll round up the horses and get them secured for the night. Have you seen any bears around the area?"

"No bear."

Waiting for the stew that Moaka had brought from Wrangell, James made biscuits from white flour, water, salt, lard, and sugar. "Moaka, did you bring any baking soda?"

"No baking soda."

86

"OK, Moaka, that will be fine. Only thing is, the baking soda helps to make the biscuits fatter."

Hearing no further response from Moaka, James mixed the ingredients for the biscuits.

Having a supper of stew, biscuits, jam, and coffee, James and Moaka settled next to the fire before going to bed.

James looked across the fire flames at Moaka. He was arguing within himself about talking to Moaka about going to Teshpuk. Finally James cleared his throat and asked, "Moaka, I remember you talked about going to Teshpuk after Tess passed to raise Kalli and Kasha being Inuit. Are you still planning on doing that?"

"I think."

"Moaka, you have been a good and loyal friend to me and Suzette for many years. We have let our teams run for miles together and can tell many stories of polar bears and feats of danger we experienced. Wherever you go, you know our friendship will never change. I don't know your schedule for leaving, but if it's about still working for the Department of Agriculture, you can leave anytime you want...even as early as this month if you want. Once, when I was in the home office in Seattle, I spoke with Sid Bonner about you leaving and going back to Teshpuk. He was surprised you were leaving, but he just mentioned if you wanted to go, that was pretty much it."

"No want leave job and Kincaid and Suzette."

"Another thing that Sid Bonner mentioned was that maybe he could make a contract with you for sightings of wildlife between Teshpuk and Barrow, and between Teshpuk and the coast. You would have to take counts of animals or any event that could affect the wildlife, and make a report back to this office. Sara would set them up in a report to Sid Bonner in the Seattle office. The report also could include migrations, whether it is birds or animals, and poaching. Pausing for a second, James continued, "Just think, Moaka, if you moved up there you would still be working for the Department of Agriculture and Sara would be putting your facts and numbers into a report and sending them to Seattle. Now how does that sound?"

Moaka looked skyward. He stood up and walked over to the horses, and asked, "Make decision now?"

"No, no, Moaka," James stressed. "If you really want to go back to Teshpuk and take the kids, you do not have to make the decision tonight, but if you are going to leave this year, you know it should be soon to be able to get settled up there before colder weather sets in."

Walking back to the fire, Moaka leaned down and set a small log on the fire as the flames and sparks leaped upward to surround the metal pot that was hanging from the metal tripod.

"I think long time."

"I know you have been thinking about this for some time, but I think it is about time you made up your mind to stay or go. You need to settle it in your mind and in the minds of your children."

"Could live in Barrow?"

"What!" James exclaimed, "and not live in Teshpuk?"

"School better Barrow. Want Kalli and Kasha to live Inuit...Tess want they know speak good English."

Shaking his head, James smiled. "Moaka, you just wrote your own ticket if you want to live in Barrow. Sid Bonner even suggested that if you could live in Barrow it would make it a lot easier to have communication with you. You would still have to go back and forth between Barrow and Teshpuk and the coast for animal sighting and whatever you see along the way."

As James was speaking, Moaka turned his back to the fire, and asked, "Can let know tomorrow?"

"Of course, Moaka. Your decision does not have to come that early."

"Talk in morning."

Suddenly Moaka looked toward the horses as they all looked toward the water's edge. "Kincaid, where rifle?"

"What?"

"Where rifle, Kincaid?"

Quickly getting up, James also saw the horses heads all turned toward the shore. Stepping back to get his rifle that was set against his saddle, James muttered, "I don't see anything, do you?"

"Shhh." Moaka put his finger to his lips. "Move from fire."

Both men slipped quietly into the shadows as they both heard noise coming from the shore. They were silently waiting for another sound or movement from the shore...and suddenly a small, white-and-brown dog came charging into camp, yapping loudly as he nearly ran into the fire.

Instantly, Moaka shouldered his rifle and was going to shoot when James yelled, "Don't shoot, Moaka."

Shaking his head in disbelief, James recognized the dog. "Janet, Janet Moore—are you there?"

The call from the night was, "Yes, Mr. Kincaid. I am coming."

"Miss Moore, will you please come and get this yapping dog before it wakes the dead?"

Coming into the light of the fire, Janet coached Runback to come to her, and the dog stopped making a fuss.

Looking at the young girl, James could see no difference in the way she looked from earlier today. Her blonde hair was uncombed; she had dirty, raggedy clothes on, with shoes that were about worn out. "What in the world are you doing here?" James asked. "I thought I sent you to Wrangell to see Mrs. Mackly. And how did you ever find me here?"

"I could not go to see anybody looking like this," she said as she pointed at herself. "Mrs. Mackly would have probably thrown me out the back door. As far as finding you here, I just followed the shoreline and I happened to see your fire, and I came close and saw you at the fire. I know this part of the shore area pretty good. My father and I hunted and trapped along here."

Taking a deep breath, James pointed to Moaka. "This is Moaka. He works with me at the Department of Agriculture. Moaka, this Janet Moore."

Moaka nodded and walked over and leaned his rifle against his saddle, then looked at the girl. "Hungry?"

"Oh, yes—and Runback is hungry too. Could you spare some food for me and him? I never stopped oaring to eat anything we had in the boat."

"Miss Moore, I want you to get your bedroll from the boat or anything else you need for the night, and don't forget that shotgun...don't leave it out in the boat. Moaka will find you and your dog something to eat, and I will lay some boughs down for your bed. Now go."

Seeing Janet return with the shotgun and one torn blanket, James straightened up from putting boughs down for Janet's bed and, frustrated, said, "Lay your one blanket here, and I'll get you a couple more."

Hearing Moaka hitting a tin pan with a spoon, Janet almost rushed to his side for a meal of stew and leftover biscuits. Janet took the pan and began eating as Moaka commented, "Here pork for dog."

Sitting on the ground and petting Runback while he was eating his pork, Janet was smiling at Kincaid. "I like you, Mr. Kincaid. You and Moaka are nice people. Runback and I do not fear you."

Handing Janet some soap, James instructed, "As soon as you finish eating, Miss Moore, I want you to go down to the shore and wash your face and hands and go to bed. You will sleep warm with the extra blankets I've given you."

"Missy, how old?"

Smiling at Moaka, Janet replied, "I'm eighteen." Sensing Moaka wanted to ask more questions, Janet began to tell him her life story about her and her dad's mining, hunting for skins, and living alone with Runback. When she finished, she reminded Moaka, "My name is Janet Moore."

Shaking his head, Moaka's only reply was "No easy."

As Janet handed Moaka the plates and spoon, James advised, "OK, Miss Moore, to the wash and then to bed."

Next morning early, as the sun's rays were spreading out across the ocean, it was still not light all the way as the mountain and trees were standing in the way of early sunshine.

"Damn, it's cold, Moaka. Let's get the fire going. You get the small stuff, and I'll get the cooking wood."

"OK, young lady, let's roll out of there." James spoke loudly to where he thought Janet was still lying in bed.

"Huh, you guys don't get up very early," Janet said as she came up from the shoreline holding four large trout.

Instantly Moaka jumped up and took the fish from her. He walked a short distance back to the shoreline and gutted and cleaned the fish in the water so the fish guts would not attract any unwanted creatures.

"Good fishing, Miss Moore," James congratulated, "the fish will be good for breakfast with a few biscuits and jam."

"Runabout!" Janet called, and the little dog came charging through the underbrush and ran to Janet. "He is such a good boy," Janet stressed. "He minds well and does not require a lot of food, and he will eat most anything."

Placing the four fish, with heads and tails removed, in the large, black skillet with a large spoonful of grease, Moaka announced, "Fish done soon. Where biscuits, Kincaid?"

Finishing the mixing of the ingredients for the biscuits, James placed the iron griddle on the fire to get warmed up. He waited for a few minutes as Moaka tended the fish and Janet played with Runback. Dipping the large spoon into the biscuit mix, James asked, as he slapped a pile of dough on the griddle and smoothed it out, "Are the fish cooked yet, Moaka, because the biscuits will be done soon."

Janet pointed to the fire and almost squealed, "Look at that good food, Runback. Breakfast will be extra good this morning."

All the fish eaten and the biscuits finished, save two, by Runback, Janet asked, "What are we going to do today, Mr. Kincaid?"

Quickly James answered, "Moaka and I are going to see some people about mining claims and you, young lady, are going to stay here as camp watch. We will be leaving a horse here. It is Moaka's packhorse. Be assured he is not a riding horse. Just make sure no animals come around that probably smelled our breakfast." Pausing, James was persistent, "If you have to fire to run a bear off or something, fire into the air, and that should take care of the problem. Moaka and I will not be too far away, so if we hear a shot we can come right back in no time at all."

Excitedly, Janet emphasized, "What if the bear will not stop?"

Breathing deeply, James quickly remembered that Janet's father was killed by a bear, "Well then, drop him where he stands. We'll clean him up, you'll have a bear rug, and we'll have bear meat for supper."

Saddling the horses, both men inserted their rifles in the saddle scabbards and wore their side arms.

"Miss Moore, I want you to keep the camp clean. I need you to take the skillet, grill, and tin plates and eating ware to the shoreline and clean them. Make sure the skillet and grill get dried so they don't rust so much."

"Yes, Mr. Kincaid, I will do what you say. I hope you have good luck mining."

. . .

Riding away from camp, James told Moaka to lead the way because he knew where everything was located and where they needed to go to see the mining operation.

James asked, "Was the name of the guy we are looking for Ferrell Jones?"

"Yes," Moaka replied.

Stopping on a small flat place on the slope up to the mining operation, Moaka reined up on his horse and dismounted, explaining, "Jones no good. He no care for other people. He no care for animals. I see him kill two female deer, one with baby."

"Should we arrest him for poaching?" inquired James, as he dismounted.

"No. Men eat deer. Better kill buck."

Shaking his head, James commented, "Yes, I agree with you, Moaka, but if it is for day-to-day subsistence...for only two deer, male or female, I don't know if the charge of poaching would stick."

Seeing James starting to get on his roan, Moaka muttered, "Kincaid, want talk."

Releasing the saddle horn, James stepped back and asked, "What about, Moaka?" as if James didn't know.

"I like live in Barrow. Better for Kalli and Kasha school. I make trip Teshpuk and north to coast for animal count. Maybe see something else report. Will Kincaid come see me in Barrow? How often do you want me to come see you in Wrangell?"

Nodding his head, James smiled and said to Moaka, "Sid Bonner wants it that way and you know why. Sure, there will be a time when you can come to Wrangell and I may go to Barrow. This should not bother you or me because we know the country up there and here. I want you to stop worrying about the job here. When you leave I will hire another person for your position for Native American Liaison. You will be hard to replace, but I think I can do it alright. Just think, Moaka, you will be able to build yourself another dog team."

Looking west out across the shiny ocean through the trees, Moaka turned to James. "Kincaid, I miss you and Suzette. Tess love both you."

Waving his hand at Moaka, James reassured him, "Oh, Moaka, don't be that way, you will still be working for the Department of Agriculture, only in Barrow."

"How much pay, Kincaid?"

"Sid Bonner said you will be under contract and he is willing to pay you most of what you make now. You will use vouchers to buy things for the job in Barrow or Wrangell. Even buy your dogs and sled with a voucher. Sid also suggested you have your paycheck sent to Nome. Nome has a larger bank there that can keep your money for you."

"When can leave, Kincaid?"

"Sid Bonner said to tell you that he will have to make the administrative arrangements before you can be transferred to Barrow on a contract status. I'll write a letter to Sid Bonner when we get back. It is early in the season, so we have some time before the ice closes Barrow up for the winter for boat navigation."

Smiling, Moaka shook his head. "Kincaid good friend."

Taking a deep breath, James said, "OK, Moaka, where is this mining operation's location?"

CHAPTER NINE

The sun was peeking over the east mountain ridge and dew was still on the grasses when Payuk awoke, sat up in his bedroll, yawned, and stretched his arms out to full length. The fire was out, Kelly was still asleep, and the horses were standing quiet. One of the horses had dropped a load that made the entire camp smell awful.

"Get up, Kelly. I think you need to clean up some crap that Peanut dropped down last night." Kelly, with his head covered up, didn't move so Payuk spoke louder, "Get up, Kelly. The sun is nice and warm."

Slowly pushing the bedroll from his head, Kelly said, "What is that smell?"

Laughing, Payuk repeated, "I think your horses dropped a load last night."

Sitting up and pushing his bedroll down farther, Kelly shook his head. "Holy cow, does that stink." Looking back at Peanut, he said, "What in the world have you been eating, Peanut?" Taking his boots from under the foot of his bedroll, Kelly pulled his socks up and looked inside his boots for any unwanted strangers then slipped his boots on. Standing up, he straightened his trousers.

Walking over to where the gear was stored, Kelly looked back at Payuk. "Where is that shovel?"

"Oh," Payuk remembered, "I put it next to that tree." He pointed and said, "I used it last evening."

Kelly pushed Peanut's rear over just a bit so he could pick up the last night droppings of Peanut. "Damn, that smells terrible." He carried the horse crap away from the camp and threw it into the air to broadcast it. Coming back to camp, Kelly stood the shovel back where Payuk had put it and untied the horses from the hitching rail.

He led them down to water in the small stream. As the horses drank their fill, Kelly stretched and reflected, "What a wonderful morning, Payuk."

"Yes, I slept very well last night. We must have had no visitors during the night."

"Was there a moon out last night?" Kelly asked.

"I don't know."

Taking the horses away from the water, Kelly let them freely graze next to the camp area with the hackamore halters still on. "What's for breakfast, Payuk?"

"We can make biscuits, make gravy, and chop up dried elk and put it in the gravy to spread over the biscuits. Course we got coffee...Oh, and of course we have your beans if you want them."

Returning to the camp, Kelly started the fire for the biscuits and gravy, while Payuk got the flour for the biscuits. "I don't think we need the beans this morning. It sounds like we'll have plenty to eat."

Finishing breakfast, both men enjoyed a fresh cup of coffee before breaking down camp.

"You don't smoke, do you, Payuk?"

"No, I learned early on that tobacco was not good for the soul. My people, before they had tobacco, had a tobacco substance they chewed. It was a mixture of crushed clam shells, ground up tree bark, and the nicotine ground up. They made it into a paste and let it harden into a pill sort of thing and then they would suck on it. I tried one of these things and it tasted terrible. Some of the elders wanted to keep doing things the old way, so there was still some of that kind of stuff around for a while. The Tlingit got tobacco in about late 1880s then passed it on the Tahltans in the north. As a matter of fact, you can still get that old tobacco substitute in any Indian village." He paused.

"Why don't you smoke, Kelly?"

"Wow! Of course not, if my mother would have heard of anybody smoking in the family, there would have been hell to pay." Throwing out the rest of his second cup of coffee, Kelly advised, "OK, let's get down the trail."

Getting the horses saddled, bedrolls rolled and packed, packhorses packed, and the fire put out, they were ready to proceed toward the Stikine River.

As Kelly mounted Peanut, grasping the packhorse's lead, he reminded Payuk, "Remember the drawing. I want to be about five miles or closer to the Stikine before we stop. There should not be a problem with time. We just need to get set up to take those freight wagons."

Payuk motioned that he understood and followed Kelly down the wagon trail. As Kelly and Payuk followed the Iskut River downstream, Kelly marveled at the tall mountains and all the small streams that flowed into the main river. Every so often they would cross a small stream that had been well worn down to the stream's bedrock bottom by the freight wagon wheels and horses wading across the stream.

Reining up Peanut at a small stream they had to cross, Kelly remarked, "Let's let the horses water up and let's get out of these saddles and walk around a bit." Laughing lightly, he explained to Payuk, "Even when I was a kid on my dad's ranch in Pennsylvania, I never could get used to being in a saddle for very long at a time without dismounting and walking around to ease my butt."

"Rather walk?" Payuk nonchalantly asked.

"No, damn it. I just need a break from having my legs spread apart and sitting in the same position."

Payuk spread his arms and took a deep breath. "I love this place. It is quiet of boats, beautiful because of the trees and bushes, and has clear running water in the small streams."

"OK, dreamer, let's go," Kelly said as he grasped his packhorse's lead and mounted Peanut. "I want to go another ways and then get on some high ground to see if we can see the Stikine River. Once we can see the river we'll know that is about the right place to take those freight wagons."

"Why did you call me a dreamer?"

Shrugging, Kelly clarified. "To be a dreamer, someone has to take the very best of everything from all situations, and Payuk, you try and do that. That is one thing I like about you."

"I like being called a dreamer!" Payuk exclaimed. "It makes me feel better and good. My people like to follow their dreams."

Gently tapping Peanut's sides with his heels, Kelly responded, "OK, dreamer, let's go."

After riding for couple of hours at a good pace, Kelly pointed upward. "Let's go up there on the clear ridgeline and see what we can see."

Reaching the ridgeline, Kelly pulled up on Peanut's reins. "Look at that, Payuk. I'll bet we aren't more than three miles from the Stikine River."

Payuk dismounted and walked to the edge of a rock outcrop and waved his right hand toward upriver of the Iskut. "We can see for miles this way. Also, we can see where the Stikine River and the mouth of the Iskut come together. That is where the riverboat will moor for the freight wagons."

Dismounting, Kelly agreed. "That's right, Payuk, we have an excellent observation point in both directions. This is just perfect. When we see the freight wagons coming down the canyon, we will have plenty of time to get into position on the valley floor to take the skins and anything else that is on those wagons."

"When do you think the wagons will get here?" Payuk inquired.

Slowly moving his head back and forth as he looked down at the ground and then looked up at Payuk, he said, "I sure don't know. We don't know when they sent them for one thing and the other thing is we don't know how fast those freight wagons would travel over that rough wagon trail." Walking to the end of the rock outcropping, Kelly instructed Payuk, "Well, this is the place. Like we planned, you need to go down and get a place ready for us and the horses to hide close to the trail, so when they get at our position all we have to do is jump out of the ambush spot on our horses and let our intentions be known. I'll take the front wagon and you can handle the second wagon." Kelly stressed, "If you have to shoot, shoot for the legs or arms, which will normally put most people out of commission. But, most of all we have to stop those wagons and take control."

"Will we leave the packhorses in the thick when we go out to stop the wagons?"

"Yes, Payuk. We can always grab them before moving on. The way I got it figured, the most dangerous time is when they first see us and what their reaction will be. If they throw their hands in the air that will be great, but if we have to shoot them, so be it."

"I'll go down to the valley floor and try to find a good place for us to wait along the wagon trail. I'll try to mark a good path for us to follow down the slope so we don't get all messed up with all kinds of underbrush. Also, I'll make a rail so we can secure the packhorses. Is there anything else I need to do?"

"No, Payuk. I think that will do." Looking around, Kelly remarked, "We have only about four hours of daylight left. Try and be back up here before dark or shortly thereafter."

"I'll do what I can, Kelly." Payuk grabbed an axe, a large knife, and some small rope. He mounted his horse and then disappeared down the tree- and brush-covered slope.

When Payuk disappeared down the slope, Kelly began to unload the packhorses. Loosening the bindings, he took the gear from one side of the cross buck and laid it on the ground and then walked around to the other side and loosened the bindings and removed the gear from that side of the cross buck and laid it on the ground. Doing the same for Payuk's packhorse, Kelly staged the gear close together for easy and quick reloading onto the cross bucks. After loosening the cinch straps for the cross bucks for each horse, Kelly started setting up a cold camp for the night.

Glancing up the canyon once in a while just to check for freight wagons, Kelly knew they were not due yet, but just checking made him feel better.

Trying not to unpack the gear, Kelly dug out the berries, salt pork, and dried salmon. He did not want to build a fire on the ridge for someone to see and know they were there.

Soon Payuk returned from building a shelter for the ambush. "I made a good place, right next to the wagon trail. They will never see us until we ride out and point the rifles right up their noses." Laughing, Payuk stammered and explained, "I've always wanted to say that."

"Say what?" Kelly asked.

"Pointing rifles right up their noses."

Smiling, Kelly casually commented, "I'm glad you got it off your chest. Now let's get supper over with. We are having berries, salt pork, and salmon." Looking around the top of the ridge, Kelly said, "I wonder if we could have a small fire for coffee?"

"Why not, Kelly. Who is going to see it right now?"

"You're right, Payuk. Get the coffeepot and makings and I'll slice the pork."

Finishing a late supper, with a freshly boiled cup of coffee, Payuk reflected, "I would like to go over the plan one more time for when the freight wagons get here."

"That's a good idea, Payuk." Kelly stood from the short log he was sitting on and picked up a small stick and drew the layout of the ridge and wagon trail. Kelly explained some movements that were to happen, as Payuk asked questions.

Finishing the back and forth conversation, Kelly smiled and advised, "It will be fine, Payuk. I don't think that we will even have to fire a round. These drivers are not gunmen, they probably only have a rifle sitting beside them. Their job is to drive the teams down to the boat...that's it."

Nodding his head, Payuk slowly commented, "Sure looks simple; I hope it works. Put out the fire when you're ready. I'm going to bed."

Next morning, Kelly awoke as the northeastern sky was just starting to light. As he pushed his bedroll down, the cold morning air penetrated into his body. Shivering, he muttered, "Damn, it's cold." Quickly checking his boots for strangers, he pulled his cowboy boots on and stood. Taking his jacket from a tree limb, Kelly shook it, then swiftly slid into it. Checking the horses, he gave each horse a small drink of water as he used one canteen full for all four horses.

"Why are you up so early, Kelly?"

"I want to be ready; I figure the freight wagons will be coming along soon, maybe this morning."

Light was increasing as Kelly walked to the rock ridge with the glasses and peered down the canyon for possibly a riverboat, and then looked up the Iskut River for the freight wagons.

"See anything, Kelly?"

Sighing, Kelly meekly replied, "Nah, they should not be here yet. I was just looking. Let's get breakfast over with and get the gear packed so we can move promptly down the slope. When we do spot the freight wagons, I want to get down the slope and get positioned in the ambush shelter way ahead of them getting to our position."

Building a small fire, with very little smoke, on the side of the ridge away from the Iskut River canyon, Payuk and Kelly warmed up some salt pork and made biscuits and coffee. Finishing breakfast off with biscuits and jam, Payuk and Kelly poured a tin cup of coffee and went to sit on the rock outcrop on the ridge to wait for the sighting of the freight wagons.

"What if they don't come today?"

Kelly shrugged his shoulders. "I don't know. I guess we wait another day. Sooner or later they will come down that canyon." He pointed his cup upriver. "It is the only way to get stuff in or out of here."

"Do we want to pack everything up and put it on the packhorses?" Payuk asked. "Oh, by the way, you need to change your Department of Agriculture shirt to the other one that does not say who you are."

"I hate to have the horses loaded with pack and standing around," Kelly stressed. "It is hard on them. I've learned they need to be walking or moving some to breathe right. I don't know if that's true, but it makes sense to me...I think we will have time to load and get down to the ambush shelter in time."

"It will take us about ten minutes to get to the ambush shelter," Payuk explained.

"Good, Payuk. Let's just get everything packed and ready to hook onto the cross bucks."

The four bundles of gear sitting on the grass, the fire out, and the horses saddled with the cinches loosened, Kelly and Payuk scanned the canyon, looking downstream toward the Stikine River for the riverboat and upstream for the freight wagons.

Sitting in the shade of a large fir tree, Payuk yawned. "This sitting around waiting is boring and makes me more tired than if working."

"How long has Jeffery Maxwell worked for Shane Keller?" Kelly asked. "He seems to have a pretty good handle on that livery business."

"Long time. Maybe ten years—why are you asking?"

"Well, did you know Skipper Daniels?" Kelly asked. "He gave the *Misty Charters* to Eddie Maxwell, his deckhand for all those years. And I was just wondering if Shane Keller would ever give the Wrangell Livery to Jeffery Maxwell."

"I don't think so. You see Shane Keller has a wife, Sara, and a daughter in Seattle. I don't suppose his daughter would ever want the livery. For that matter, neither would Sara, but she would probably want to sell it, not give it away."

"Yeah, you're probably right, Payuk. I was just thinking."

"Do you think Moaka will ever leave Kincaid for Teshpuk?" Payuk asked.

Moving into the shade more as the sun was moving, Kelly shook his head. "That is a tough one. Moaka wants to take those kids to the far north, but he'll have a hard time leaving Kincaid. Those two guys have been through so much together. I know that Tess did not want to go north, but since she passed, Moaka has mentioned it several times, but nothing has ever come of it."

Casually, Kelly stood and took the glasses to the forward edge of the rock outcrop and sighted up the canyon. Staring intently, Kelly called, "Come here, Payuk. I want you to see something."

Payuk came to Kelly quickly and took the glasses that Kelly handed him. Looking up the canyon, he said, "Yes, I see the reflections. Those are our freight wagons."

Payuk handed the glasses back to Kelly and they both moved quickly to load the pack animals. Tightening the cinches on the riding horses and packhorses, Kelly looked around the camp, "I guess we haven't left anything?"

Kelly edged Peanut onward with a light touch of his heels to the horse's sides and Kelly's packhorse followed along behind. Looking back, Kelly saw Payuk coming along nicely as his packhorse was also following well.

Getting toward the bottom of the slope, Kelly waved Payuk to take the lead because he knew where the ambush shelter was located.

Not much farther on, Payuk waved Kelly to the left and as soon as Kelly had turned Peanut to the left he was surrounded by a large thicket with a small pole anchored between two trees to secure the packhorses.

Quickly dismounting, Kelly looked around in amazement. "Good job, Payuk. Now let's get the packhorses secured and wait for the freight wagons that will be passing this shelter right out there." Kelly pointed.

Holding onto Peanut's reins, Kelly peeked out of the shelter to see the freight wagons coming slowly down the wagon trail. Mounting Peanut, he said, "Payuk, they will be here in about ten minutes."

Checking his 30-06 rifle and .38 pistol for a full load, Kelly settled back in the saddle as he watched Payuk checking his weapons.

"Remember, Payuk, if you have to shoot, shoot to wound not kill, but if there is not time for decisions, shoot to kill. I'm sure Kincaid would approve of that. Have you got anything to say before we have to take these guys?"

"Be quiet, Kelly," Payuk sharply replied.

Surprised, Kelly looked back at Payuk. His head was bowed and his lips were moving.

He waited until Payuk looked up before continuing, "OK, Payuk, get ready. Lever a round in the chamber of that .94 and cock the hammer."

Suddenly Kelly yelled, "We are on the way!" and with that, he slammed his heels into Peanut's sides and the horse lunged forward out of the shelter, with Payuk right behind.

Kelly quickly rode to the front wagon while Payuk rode to the second. Both drivers made a motion to grab for rifles, but seeing a rifle pointed straight at them, they had better thoughts about trying to grab their weapons.

Almost simultaneously, Payuk and Kelly yelled to the drivers, "Get away from those rifles, tie the reins, and get down!"

Seeing the men obey their orders, Kelly slowly dismounted and ordered, "Both of you guys come over here to me."

As soon as they had approached Kelly, he told Payuk, "Check the wagons for any more weapons. OK, you two, clean out your pockets and lay the stuff on that log." Kelly was motioning toward it. "We don't aim to hurt you if you behave yourselves."

Payuk hailed to Kelly, "I can't find any more weapons on the wagons."

"All we had with us is rifles," spoke up one of the men. "We never figured to have to fight our way to the boat." One of the men pointed at Kelly. "You're the one that shot Simmons."

"Yes, and I'll shoot you also if you don't behave yourselves. Looking at Payuk, Kelly hailed, "Payuk, check under the seats for more gear we might want to look at."

Pointing to a place on the ground a few feet away, Kelly ordered, "Sit on the ground over there and don't move."

The older man complained, "You have no right to stop us. We are miners taking our freight to a boat on the Stikine River. What rights do you have taking our wagons? You are from Wrangell, Alaska, and this is in British Columbia. Just wait until the mining commission hears about this. You'll be sorry you ever bothered us."

Kelly yelled at the older man, "What is your name and the name of your partner?"

"My name is Strickland, and the boy's name is Minnow. Mr. Wilson is going to be mighty angry with you two. You," he pointed to Kelly, "Have already killed his best powder monkey."

"Well, Mr. Strickland, my name is O'Brien and his name is Payuk. We both work for the Department of Agriculture of the United States. I'm sorry to inform you that we do have authorization to be here enforcing the laws, by a letter that was written to our agency from the British Columbia government and British Columbian Mining Council."

"Let us go," Strickland yelled.

"Payuk, bring those rifles over here with the rest of their stuff on this log. Then get in our packs and get that small rope to tie these guys up for safe keeping." Kelly requested this as he kept a close eye on the two freight wagon drivers.

Noticing that Strickland was trying to shift around for some reason, Kelly scolded, "Sit still if you know what's good for you."

Kelly looked down at his rifle to check if the safety latch had been flipped over, when suddenly Strickland jerked a knife from his boot and made a wild throw at Kelly.

Jerking his rifle up as the knife hissed by his shoulder, Kelly fired one quick shot into the chest of Strickland. Running to Strickland's side, Kelly yelled, "I told you to behave yourselves and nothing would happen to you." Frustrated, Kelly kicked dirt on Strickland. "Why did you throw that knife at me!"

Payuk came running around the horses and stopped dead in his tracks when he saw what had happened. Kelly had shot him dead center. And the man lay in the freight wagon's dirt trail, dead.

Minnow quickly scooted backward on his butt, and begged, with his hands in the air, "Don't shoot me, mister. I didn't do anything."

"Shut up, Minnow, no one is going to kill you," Kelly assured him.

Payuk stood holding several lengths of rope and remarked jokingly, "Kelly, if you keep killing our prisoners we won't need any rope."

Still nervous, Kelly abruptly stated, "Get Minnow tied...no, wait...Get that shovel from our gear, and Minnow will bury Strickland right here and now." Kelly stared at Minnow. "Minnow, you got any knives or hidden weapons?"

"No sir, I don't, and I won't try anything funny, I promise," Minnow pleaded.

"How old are you, Minnow?" Kelly asked.

"I think I'm nineteen. I didn't go to school so I'm not sure."

"You are old enough to bury your partner." Kelly pointed to a spot away from the river and instructed, "Bury him right over there...nice and deep."

Payuk handed Minnow the shovel and helped him drag Strickland's body to the spot to be buried. He said to Kelly, "By the way, the freight wagons are loaded down with kenched skins. I did not find any gold."

Kelly addressed Minnow, "Have you ever made this trip down to meet the riverboat before with the freight wagons?"

"Yes sir, several times."

As Kelly watched Payuk walking toward him from Minnow, he said in a low voice, "That kid knows the routine from here on. I don't think we will have any problems with him until we get to the riverboat. He does not want to go the same way as his partner, Strickland."

"OK, Payuk, I need you to get me some rope for hackamores and lead lines for the freight horses. They will need water and some grazing. In the meantime, I'll start unharnessing the teams."

"Minnow," Kelly hollered, "when you get Strickland buried, come over and help me and Payuk with the teams."

Walking by Minnow, Payuk asked, "When is the riverboat supposed to be getting here?"

"I don't know, Payuk. They usually give us several long blows on their horn." And smiling, he continued, "You can hear that thing clear up the canyon for a long ways. We have had to wait a day or so sometimes for them to get here."

"Did you hear that, Kelly?" Payuk asked.

"Yes. I figured there had to be some kind of signal."

"Minnow," Kelly asked as he rose up from hooking up the harness, "what did you guys do to signal back?"

"Mr. Kelly, we just fired a couple of rounds into the air to let them know we were waiting or real close."

With the wagon team horses bridled with hackamores, Minnow, Kelly, and Payuk led them to a small adjacent stream for water that was coming down from the slope of the mountain. Leading them back to the camp area, Payuk told Minnow, "Just drop the leads," as Payuk and Kelly did, "and they will stay close and graze."

"OK," Kelly said, "I guess this will be camp for the night or somewhere close to here," and he waved his arms toward the mountain slope.

Payuk advised, "Let's used the ambush shelter to put the horses in for at least tonight. We can put up another hitching rail for the rest of the horses."

"Great, Payuk." Kelly's approval was evident. "Minnow, you help Payuk get the shelter ready for the horses and I'll unload the gear."

Moving up closer to the shelter for the campsite, Kelly unloaded the packhorses of the cross bucks and stood the riding saddles upright on end, covering them with the horse blankets. Clearing a small place for the fire, Kelly gathered some small sticks and built a fire for cooking supper and gathered a few bigger sticks and small dead logs for later on.

Soon Payuk and Minnow came out of the ambush shelter and Minnow proudly announced, "That Payuk is a good teacher about building shelters. I never would have guessed it was so easy."

"Kelly," Payuk said, "I'm going down to the edge of the river and try and catch some fish for supper."

No more had the words come out of Payuk's mouth than Minnow quickly asked, "Have you got any extra fishing gear? I would like to catch my own supper."

Looking surprised, Payuk nodded. "Yes, come with me. I think we will have supper soon."

"OK, you guys," Kelly added, "I'll get the coffee brewing while you're gone and set up my beans on the tripod."

Kelly smiled as he heard Payuk and Minnow yelling to each other about the fish they just had caught. Kelly thought, *That Minnow seems like a good kid. Young, short brown hair, medium height, and seems to be quick, although he never went to school.* He sighed. *Maybe he can really help us pull this thing off if we can get him off clean.*

Soon Payuk and Minnow returned to the camp with at least seven large trout. Minnow bragged, "I caught one more than Payuk, but his are bigger."

The fish cleaned and ready to cook, Payuk laid them across the grill to cook slowly over a low fire. "How are those beans doing, Kelly?" he asked.

"We better eat them tonight because they're starting to get old. Do you like beans Minnow? By the way, what's your full name?" Kelly inquired.

Smiling, Minnow requested, "You won't laugh, will you?" He looked from Kelly to Payuk. "My first name is Fisher, Fisher Minnow. I'm named after my grandfathers' first names."

"OK, Fisher, go get that rifle over there and give it to Payuk."

Fisher slowly stood and walked calmly to the rifle that was leaning against one of the nearby trees. Reaching down and picking the rifle up by the barrel, he grabbed the stock to take it to Payuk. Turning, he heard Kelly's hammer click back on his .38 and he instantly dropped the rifle to the ground. With wide eyes and a squeaky voice, he pleaded, "Mr. Kelly, I wasn't going to try anything!"

Easing his hammer down on the .38, Kelly smiled. "Thank you for reassuring me of the trust I have in you. Now pick up the rifle and stand it back where it was, and sit down here at the fire, for there is something I want to talk to you about."

"Is that coffee ready?" Payuk asked.

"Yes, I think it should be. Pour me a cup, and if Fisher wants one get him one also."

Payuk motioned toward Fisher, and Fisher nodded. "Yes, I drink coffee."

"OK, Fisher, this is the setup. Whenever the riverboat gets here, Payuk and I are going to drive the teams and freight wagons onto the riverboat ramp and into the boat."

"No one knows we are here," Payuk chimed in.

Nodding to Payuk's statement, Kelly continued, "I want you to tell us what happens next."

Shrugging, Fisher explained, "I don't know, we just unhooked the teams from both freight wagons and hooked them up to another two freight wagons that were loaded with supplies for the mine. Stuff like dynamite, food supplies, shoes that men ordered, clothes, cloth for mending, and, you know, just stuff."

"Did you have to talk to anyone in particular?" Kelly probed.

Shaking his head, he responded, "No and that's funny. A while ago Payuk mentioned he did not find any gold. Well, I'm here to tell you, I've made this trip about three times or so, and I've never seen any gold yet. I don't know what they do with it. What we do is drive the teams on with our freight wagons and drive the teams off with their freight wagons."

"Fisher, you have helped us a lot. Payuk, I, and you, if you are willing, are planning on taking the riverboat to Wrangell for evidence against the Twin Forks Mining and Dredging Company for game poaching and illegal hydraulic mining."

"I can help, Mr. Kelly. I really don't want to go back to the mines."

"If you give us a hand, Fisher, I can help you get your feet on the ground and get good employment. Have you ever been to Seattle?"

"No, Mr. Kelly. I was hired in Vancouver for this mining job. I really don't like this job, although it does pay more than some other jobs I've had."

"Well, if this plan works out, I know several people in Seattle that would hire you just on my or Kincaid's say so."

Shaking his head, Fisher responded, "That would be great, Mr. Kelly."

"Do you ever have to tell anybody what is in the freight wagons?" Payuk asked.

"No," Fisher replied, looking at Payuk.

"OK," stated Kelly. "So here we sit until we hear the horns blow from the riverboat. Then we signal back with two rounds to let the captain of the riverboat know we are close. Then we harness up the teams and start toward the Stikine River. Then what, Fisher?"

"If the boat ramps are not down, we wait for them to be placed and locked to the shoreline with ropes and poles, and they are hooked to stakes driven into the ground. I think that helps keep the boat still and makes a good ramp for the horses and freight wagons to enter the lower deck of the boat.

"I know that once they got there before we did, and they went upriver to kill time. Boy, was that captain angry about that. He didn't say anything to me, but he sure gave the other guy hell for being late."

"Was the other man Strickland?" Kelly asked.

"Nah, his name is Norman. He did not like to drive the teams so much, and he talked Wilson into making Strickland drive the other team. I like driving the teams down to the Stikine River and back up the Iskut. Sure beats that mining stuff...that is very hard work."

"Back to driving the teams," Kelly advised. "The ramps are anchored and we get the signal to board the riverboat with the teams and freight wagons. We just drive them right on in...right?" He looked at Fisher.

"Yes, Mr. Kelly, just drive them right on in."

"OK, we are in the riverboat. We unhook the teams from our wagons, and rehook them to the new wagons they have that are full of supplies for the mines. Then we just drive the teams out of the riverboat on the ramps, and up the road and don't look back." Stopping, Kelly quickly stated, "Of course we won't do the last one."

"One more thing," Fisher added, "We have to block the wagons we leave so they will not roll around in the lower deck."

"Is there any member of the riverboat crew on the lower deck when you drive the teams into the riverboat?" asked Payuk.

"Good question!" Kelly exclaimed.

"Yes, one man—and he tells us where to park the wagons."

"How many crew members are there on the riverboat?" Kelly probed.

Fisher shook his head. "I don't know. But if you, Mr. Kelly, or Payuk could get to the captain in the wheelhouse, I think your chances of getting to Wrangell would be better. If he resists, then you can stick that pistol in his neck."

"Well," Kelly summarized, "It could work if I can do it right, but like Fisher said, as a last resort I could stick this pistol in his neck." Kelly patted his .38 on his hip.

Supper finished and the cleanup chores being done, Kelly announced, "I'm taking four of the horses to water and let them graze for a while before dark. Payuk, you and Fisher can take care of the rest of them."

All the horses watered, let grazed, and secured in the shelter, Kelly let Payuk and Fisher gather around the fire before he instructed, "Fisher, I want you to ride under the tarp right behind my seat. I want to adjust the tarp so you can see what is going on and tell me what to do next if there is a problem."

"Yes sir, Mr. Kelly. I can do that."

"Build up the fire before you go to bed," Kelly said, and just before he went to sleep he heard Payuk and Fisher talking about family and what they liked and disliked. Thinking, *I hope nobody gets shot, I hope I can persuade the captain about Wrangell...I hope...*he drifted off.

Next thing Kelly knew, Payuk was kneeling close to him. "Be quiet, we have a bear coming around and it is spooking the horses."

Quickly sitting up and grabbing his boots from under his bedroll, he slipped them on. After a quick shake, he stood and made for his rifle. "Where is he?" Kelley asked as he came close to Payuk.

Sighing lightly, Payuk said, "Over there, I think." He pointed into the darkness. "Fisher is on the other side of the shelter, watching."

Payuk had thrown a large piece of wood on the fire and now it was starting to burn brightly.

Suddenly the darkness was pierced by the sound of grunting. "Hell!" Kelly exclaimed. "Sounds like a big old bear."

CHAPTER TEN

As Moaka led the way to the mining operation, he explained, "Ferrell Jones say he got map of claim. I no see map, but he say mining claim is legal."

Urging Red forward with light taps to the horse's sides, James muttered, "How far up do we go?"

"We almost there," Moaka quickly responded.

Seeing Moaka dismounting, James followed suit, as he could see the sluice tailings running in all directions down the hill.

"Kincaid, tie horse here, we walk up mountain."

James tied Red and hailed Moaka, "Wait a minute. Let's take a look at this situation." He pointed toward the sluice tailing. "Isn't there a ditch or wash that this stuff could be running into to control the direction of flow down the slope to the water's edge?"

"No see any, Kincaid."

Taking a deep breath, James started walking up the slope as he followed a larger flow of sluice tailing.

Stepping into a clearing, James was surprised to see such a large sluice operation. "Wow!" he exclaimed. "This is quite an operation, Moaka." James continued, "Look at that long sluice run, the large amount of water carrying the dirt and rock through the sluice trough, and the number of men working to keep the sluice trough full at the head of the sluice operation. See the length of the sluice trough already built, ready to move up into position when the men get the material pushed down into the trough, and then they have to redirect the water from the water coming down from the mountain side. What an operation."

"Want see Ferrell Jones?" Moaka asked.

"Yes."

"Look up top of sluice, he man with bucket."

Watching Ferrell Jones giving orders, James thought, *He could be a handful. Undoubtedly he knows what he's doing by the look of this operation.* "Well Moaka, let's walk up there and see what he has to say."

Finally Ferrell Jones noticed James and Moaka approaching him as they walked up the slope toward his position. Holding a bucket in one hand and pointing at James and Moaka with the other, Ferrell Jones bellowed, "Who are you guys?"

James walked ahead of Moaka and, turning slightly, said to him, "Keep walking and don't answer him till we get there."

Setting the bucket down, Ferrell Jones demanded again, "Who the hell are you people?" Then, seeing Moaka, he continued, "Hell, I ran you off the job yesterday. What do you want?"

Stopping in front of Ferrell Jones, James turned back to look down the length of the sluice trough and commented, "You have a large operation here for hand labor."

"We do just fine—who are you and what do you want?"

Clearing his throat, James questioned, "Is your name Ferrell Jones?"

"Yes." Ferrell Jones spoke in an unfriendly tone. "I'm the boss of Stone Mountain Mining."

"Can we have a word with you, Mr. Jones, away from all this noise of rocks and water treading down the sluice trough?"

"I guess." He spoke to one of the workers, "It is about time to put in the sluice trough extension."

"Yes sir, Mr. Jones. We'll get right on it," the worker responded.

Away from the constant noise of the sluice trough, James stopped and turned to Ferrell Jones. "Mr. Jones, I'm James Kincaid and this is Moaka."

Pushing his big heavy hand toward Moaka, like Moaka meant nothing to him, Ferrell Jones sarcastically remarked, "I run that Indian off the job yesterday."

James could feel his anger building within him, but he knew at this juncture of the meeting he had to be calm and listen to what this crude man had to say. "Anyway, Mr. Jones, Moaka and I work for the Department of Agriculture in Wrangell. My office has received several complaint calls about your sluice mining operation. Apparently your sluice operation is washing sluice tailings on other people's property."

"Well, Kincaid, like I told that idiot behind you, I have a permit for free flow all the way to the shoreline. It does not specify property lines or obstacles in the way of the sluice tailings."

Standing squarely in front of Ferrell Jones, James sternly announced, "Let me give you a piece of advice, Mr. Jones. "If you insult this man behind me one more time I will take this .38 you see on my right hip and stick it under your chin and blow your brains up into the trees for the squirrels to eat." James stepped closer to Ferrell Jones, looked eye-to-eye with him, and whispered in his face, "Jones, nod if you understand."

Ferrell Jones's eyes were wide, and he let his arms fall loosely to his sides as he answered, "Do I have a choice?"

Stepping back away from Jones, James remarked, "You insult this man, and you don't even know him or who he is or where he came from. For your information, Moaka is a giant among his Inuit people, not Indian. He is revered as a wise person in the clan, and you stand there and insult a person like that?"

"I didn't know he was some kind of chief," Jones pleaded.

"He is not a chief, but an important man with much knowledge. That is why he works for the Department of Agriculture because of this knowledge he has."

"I Inuit, no Indian," Moaka stressed.

"OK," Ferrell Jones conceded, "it is hard for me to tell the difference."

James smiled and advised, "Another piece of advice I have for you, Mr. Jones, is that Moaka and I are both representatives of the United States government. We have authority you can't even imagine over your sluice mining operation. If you keep insulting, screaming and hollering, and rejecting offers out of hand to work the problem out so both parties can walk away with pride, I personally will shut you down. I will bring marshals out of Seattle and Juneau to take care of business. I can have them here on this spot where we stand now in about one week, so make up your mind."

"How long have I got?" Jones asked.

James did a double-take. "How long have you got for what?" he snapped.

"How long have I got to make up my mind?" Jones tested.

Shaking his head, James stared at Ferrell Jones. "Are you deaf, Mr. Jones? I told you that I will close you down. That does not mean tomorrow, next week, or next month, that means right now. You have no time. Make your decision now so I can know what to do to your operation next."

With a sneer, Ferrell Jones said insultingly, "You government people think you run the whole world. Just wait till I get my lawyers up here from Seattle. Then we'll see who closes what down. My lawyer will probably have both of your jobs."

Standing toe-to-toe with this big, fat guy in need of a shave and haircut, James quickly decided he might as well try and make a deal with him to solve problems for everyone around. "OK, Mr. Jones, you had your say, now I want to make an offer to you, if you will listen."

"Go ahead, for all the good it will do," Ferrell Jones defiantly answered.

James cleared his throat and began, "Yesterday I spoke with Mr. Neil Baxter. He's the man just below you off to the left some, who owns the small cabin. Have you met Mr. Baxter?"

"Oh yes, I've met that ass. He swears that his cabin is going to be washed away by the mine's sluice tailings."

James nodded. "Well, the sluice tailings are coming pretty close to his cabin, and the sluice tailings are actually trespassing on his ground."

Ferrell Jones threw his hands into the air. "Hell, those sluice tailings aren't going to wash his cabin away. That's nonsense; who would believe that?"

"The important thing is, Mr. Jones, Mr. Baxter believes it." Turning back to Moaka, James continued, "Moaka has also spoken with some other landowners around here, and they complained about the mess you are making with the sluice tailings by letting them run helter-skelter down the slope to the water's edge. Without any drain ditches or corridors for the sluice tailings to run in, on the way to the water's edge, it is making a mess of the forest floor, disturbing local wildlife, and destroying new growth."

Ferrell Jones's facial expression changed from nonchalance to concern as James continued to speak. "Well, my contract does not specify any route for my sluice tailings to follow down the slope. The contract just states 'free flow to water's edge.'"

James scratched the back of his head as he looked at Moaka. "Mr. Jones, I'll tell you what I would like you to do. But first, where is your base camp located?"

Turning half around, Jones pointed and said, "About fifty yards up the hill and to the right of that big fir tree. There is a large, flat spot with all our buildings up there."

"OK, Mr. Jones. I would like to meet you there tomorrow about ten a.m. with Mr. Baxter. I would like to see your mining lease and contract. Can I count on you to keep this agreement?" James asked.

Breathing deeply, Ferrell Jones reluctantly agreed. "OK, ten a.m. it is. I still don't see what it is going to solve."

Turning away from Jones, James and Moaka started walking down the slope to their horses, and they noticed all the different paths the sluice tailings were taking down the mountain slope.

Getting to their horses, James mounted and gave instructions, "Now we need to go see Neil Baxter. It won't be much of a meeting if everybody involved is not there."

Seeing Kincaid guiding his horse in the wrong direction, Moaka laughed. "Kincaid go wrong way."

Pulling up on Red's reins, James turned in his saddle. "OK, smarty, you lead."

Arriving at the cabin, James and Moaka dismounted and Moaka walked up to the cabin door and knocked. There was no reply within so Moaka knocked again. Finally there were sounds coming from inside the cabin.

The door slowly opened as a voice from inside called, "Who is there?"

"Mr. Baxter," James called, "It is Moaka and James Kincaid from the Department of Agriculture. We would like to have a word with you if that is possible?"

"Sure thing." Neil Baxter stepped out onto the wooden deck in front of the cabin. "Now what can I do for you? Did you convince Ferrell Jones to stop with all the sluice tailings running all over the slope, messing everything up?"

Moaka and James sat on the side of the wooden deck as they talked with Neil Baxter. "Not really, Mr. Baxter, but we did set up a meeting between you, him, and Moaka and me for ten a.m. tomorrow morning. Also, I want you to bring your squatter's rights forms with you, and he is going to bring his mining claim and contract with him from the Alaska Mining Council."

"I like this little cabin. I live here alone, minding my own business and visiting with a few folks around. I fish and hunt for food to put in my smoke house," he motioned behind the house, "for the winter food supply. I was away from Wrangell more than a year and I worked on a large fishing trawler. I never left the boat for the whole time. I wanted to save the good money I was making for retirement." Pausing, Neil Baxter continued, "Course I sell a few pelts of beaver and rabbit for extra cash, but all in all I like what I'm doing here. That is why I'm so upset with this mining outfit, they are ruining what I have worked hard to establish for myself." With frustration, Neil Baxter said, "I don't think I'm asking too much of the mining outfit to channel their sluice tailings."

"Sluice tailings make mess on ground," Moaka spoke up.

"You're right, Moaka, and it has to stop," agreed Neil Baxter.

James was sitting on the wooden porch deck, and as he stood up, he advised, "We have to be on our way, Mr. Baxter. I hope to see you tomorrow at the mining camp at about ten a.m."

"I'll be there, Kincaid, don't worry about that."

Leading their horses away from Baxter's cabin, James asked Moaka, "Would these other people you talked to before about the sluice tailings, would they be interested in sitting in on this meeting tomorrow?"

"Yes, Kincaid, they would come."

"For the rest of the day, why don't you try and contact those folks and let them know about the meeting. Make sure they understand where and when. Also, ask them not to bring guns." Smiling, James expressed further, "Tell them it is going to be a friendly meeting."

"Say Kincaid be there?"

"Yes, Moaka, that will be alright. Also let them know, if they don't know, that we are Department of Agriculture representatives."

As Moaka mounted, he said, "Be back to camp later."

"That will be fine, Moaka. I'm just going to wander around this area for a while to really get a feel for this sluice tailings situation." Watching Moaka ride slowly away from him, James thought, *The more people there, the better the chance of getting something productive accomplished.*

Leading Red and slowly walking up and down the slope, he crossed over several paths that the sluice tailings were taking. James shook his head. It did seem to make a mess of the ground and environment.

Breaking out into an opening, James could see the Pacific Ocean from his high vantage point. "What do you think, Red, pretty or not?"

Making his way back to camp, and before Janet heard him coming, James was surprised to see her sitting beside a small fire, drawing on flat rocks that she had gathered from the shoreline.

"What are you doing, Miss Moore?"

"Oh hi, Mr. Kincaid, I'm just amusing myself while you and Moaka have been gone. I caught several nice, big trout, and they are wrapped in wet leaves to keep them fresh."

"By the damn, Miss Moore, you know what to do out here. We'll have those trout for supper."

Showing James one of the rocks that she had drawn on, she explained, "My father was always gone a lot making money for us so he taught me to draw things in nature to keep me busy."

He took the flat rock from Janet. "What did you use for making the drawing?"

"Oh, that is easy." She lifted up a small stick with a burnt end. "Black from the burnt stick." Pausing, she explained, "I can do drawings in some colors. There are rocks you can grind up into a powder and make color for drawings."

"Huh," James grunted, "they call that black stuff charcoal, Miss Moore."

Holding the flat rock away from him, he studied the drawing of a fish jumping from the water. "This is very good, Miss Moore. I know many people that will pay money for drawing like this, especially on a natural flat rock." And seeing her facial expression of doubt, James strongly expressed, "I'm not kidding you, Miss Moore, this is really good."

Smiling, Janet asked, "Could I sell these in Wrangell to help me make a living?"

"Miss Moore, you could sell this kind of art anywhere in the world. You just have to get known. In other words, you have to start selling these pieces and people will know who you are and want more for themselves or for gifts for friends and relatives."

"I can draw people also, but I need better drawing stuff to do a proper face drawing."

Bending down James shook the coffeepot...

"Oh, Mr. Kincaid, I made some new coffee while you and Moaka were gone. I don't drink coffee, but the pot was about empty."

Hearing Moaka riding up, James decided to strip the saddle and bridle from Red and let him graze for a while.

Both men were finishing with their horses when James commented, "Miss Moore made some fresh coffee for us."

"Good, need coffee."

Pouring both his and Moaka's cups full of hot coffee, James inquired, "How did it go with the meetings of the other interested folks around here?"

Taking out a piece of paper from his coat pocket, Moaka said, "Five will come to meeting: Ted Wells, Roger Ray, Jud Dillan, Archie Bench, and Tim Cord."

"No guns, right Moaka?"

"No bring gun."

Sitting next to the fire, enjoying their coffee, Moaka stood up and walked over to a short stump and carried it over to where James was sitting on the ground. "Here, Kincaid, stool."

Janet laughed. "What is that for, Moaka?"

"Kincaid need stool. I cut today."

"You are right, Moaka." James stood up and then sat on his newly presented stool. Sitting on the stool for a moment, James commented, "Just like old times; thanks, Moaka."

"You two guys are crazy," Janet mused. "How long have you known each other?"

"It's not how long we have known each other, Miss Moore, but rather what we have been through together. Moaka and I first got together in Nome, Alaska, in 1899, and have been together ever since. We've had dog teams, fought polar bears, saved a lot of Northern Fur Seals, and captured game poachers. I guess the hardest task we have worked on is keeping the new people to Alaska—like fishermen, loggers, and hunters from the lower forty-eight—from upsetting the balance of the Tahltan and Tlingit tribes' sacred areas."

"I did not know the Indians had sacred areas," Janet expressed.

"I'm not going to explain it to you, Miss Moore, but I will leave that job to a man by the name of Payuk that lives in Wrangell. He is a Tlingit native who knows how to explain the sacred areas better than I can. Moaka and I both can tell you about such things, but Payuk does a better job."

"Let's have supper," Janet announced. "I'll get the fish."

Startled, Moaka looked at James. "What fish?"

"Oh, when you and I were running around today, Miss Moore caught us some fish for supper."

"Get grate," Moaka said.

"I'll get the flour and makin's for biscuits," James followed up.

Soon the three were enjoying fried trout, biscuits and jam, and berries for supper.

Finishing supper, and after all the tins were cleaned, James announced, "I think I'll take a little walk around the area just to settle my supper. Moaka, you might want to take a look at Miss Moore's drawings she has done today. I think you will like them."

Walking along the shoreline, James thought, *I somehow have got to get all these people around here to agree on not having the sluice tailings flooding the whole side of the mountain without causing the mining outfit to sacrifice too much. They probably do have a contract stating free flow of sluice tailings to water's edge. The Alaska Mining Council probably does not care because of the sparse population in the area. Nobody around here, including the mining company, has any equipment that could dig a trench down the slope for the sluice tailings to run in down to water's edge.*

Watching the sun getting close to dipping below the ocean surface, James headed back to camp. Smiling, he thought, *It could be interesting tomorrow.*

CHAPTER ELEVEN

Standing in the firelight trying to see into the darkness, Payuk and Kelly moved apart from each other. Both men were on high alert, looking for any movement in the darkness.

"Fisher," Kelly yelled, "you OK over there?"

"Yes sir, Mr. Kelly; I've got this rifle ready to go to work."

Suddenly Payuk saw two eyes shining in the firelight. "Kelly!" Payuk pointed with the end of his rifle. "Two eyes...in the firelight."

"Stand steady, Payuk; let him come on in if he's going to make his run."

Gripping his rifle firmly, Payuk licked his lips...abruptly the bear made his run and Payuk shouldered his rifle and shot once, levered another round and shot again. As the fire was burning brightly from the extra wood that was put on by Payuk, Payuk could see the dark mass lying motionless not more than twenty feet in front of him. Shaking his head and swallowing hard, Payuk thought, *Thank goodness for rifles.*

Slowly Kelly let his hammer down on his rifle. "Fisher, come on over here. It is over. Payuk took care of the bear."

Fisher was standing right behind Payuk, and he said jokingly, "You don't have to yell, Mr. Kelly, I'm right here. I was right behind Payuk if he missed."

Taking a deep breath, Kelly shook his head. "I'm glad that is over with. Those critters are very determined and vicious. In this country they are at the top of the food chain, and the only thing they fear is man. Let's settle down the horses and get back to bed. I wonder if that coffee is still hot."

Laughing, Payuk assured him, "It should be after sitting next to that big log I laid in the fire for more light."

"OK. Let's take care of the stock and settle them down, and then I'm going to have some coffee and go back to bed for whatever night is remaining."

Next morning, Kelly awoke with the odor of fresh coffee being brewed. Peeking out from his bedroll, he said, "What time is it?"

Fisher abruptly answered, "About seven o'clock. Payuk is skinning out that bear and cutting some steaks off for breakfast, and I am getting the biscuit mix made up."

"Yuck, I am getting tired of biscuits. I want some pancakes with berries in them, some fried salt pork, and fried potatoes."

"If we are here tomorrow morning, I'll make pancakes for you and fried potatoes," Payuk stressed, as he returned from cutting off three nice size steaks from the bear's rear haunches. "After breakfast, I'll cut some more steaks off just in case we are here longer than we think. Also, the bear's pelt is in excellent condition. I know a man that will make a nice winter coat of the hide."

Throwing his bedroll open, Kelly whined to Fisher, "See'en how you are up, would you please get me a cup of coffee."

Quickly Payuk mocked Kelly. "Look at you, you want servants now."

"Well," Kelly meekly answered, "He's up already and I'm still in bed."

"That's OK, Mr. Kelly, I don't mind."

Breakfast being finished, Payuk declared, "That was good meat."

"Yes, by the damn," Kelly agreed. "Some bear meat is tough and gamey, but I'm still looking for my pancakes and fried potatoes."

"Fisher, will you help me skin that beast out there?" Payuk asked. "I'll need some help rolling him over and over to get the skin off without putting too many holes in it."

"And as you guys are doing that, I'm going to saddle Peanut and take a ride up to that ridge," Kelly said as he pointed. "I should have a good advantage point to watch the river."

"What else do you want us to do while you are gone?" Payuk asked.

Kelly shrugged his shoulders. "I don't know...clean guns, check harness, keep camp ready to pack in a moment's notice, and...I don't know, just get ready to move fast when we have to."

"Mr. Kelly, we don't have to move too fast. Normally when they blow the horn signal they haven't even got the ramps out or the boat set in for us to drive the team on."

Nodding, Kelly reiterated, "Just keep things ready to go. I'll be back later, or sooner if I see the riverboat coming up the river."

Saddling Peanut, Kelly checked his 30-06 rifle and .38 for being loaded, placed his rifle in the saddle scabbard, and tied down his saddlebags. As he left, he said, "I'll be back later."

Urging Peanut up the steep slope, he stopped at a small opening where he could see

east up the Iskut River canyon toward the mining outfit. Kelly shook his head and thought, *What a wonderful country; no wonder the Native American tribes love this land. Yeah, this is their home.* Hanging onto the saddle as Peanut lunged from time to time while climbing the slope, eventually Kelly's legs took a toll. Dismounting and letting his legs rest, Kelly walked around for a bit while Peanut grazed on new grasses.

Looking down the slope, he could see their camp below. Payuk and Fisher were still working on the bear, probably still skinning and cutting some steaks.

Kelly yawned and patted Peanut on the neck as he watched the small estuary of the Iskut River. Somewhere close to that area the riverboat would make land and set up for the teams to be driven onto the riverboat.

"OK, Peanut," Kelly told his horse, "let's get to the top of the mountain and see if we can see any riverboats coming. Starting to mount Peanut, Kelly saw a small riverboat making the turn coming down the Stikine River. "Too small a riverboat for us, Peanut."

Soon Peanut had carried Kelly to the top of the mountain ridge. Very little timber grew on the rocky terrain other than small trees and brush.

Dismounting, Kelly let Peanut graze as Kelly walked around just getting the feel of the rocks and ground. Watching Peanut, Kelly spoke, "Not much to eat up here is there, boy?"

Taking his glasses from his saddlebag, he adjusted them to look down the Stikine River, hoping to see a large riverboat coming upstream to the Iskut River. Sighing and removing the glasses from his eyes, he said, "Not much chance."

Walking over to a small bush, Kelly relieved himself. He shrugged. "I guess we just wait, Peanut. I hope we don't have to wait too long."

. . .

"Here, Fisher," Payuk explained. "You have to hold the skin tight so I can slide my knife between the fat and the skin. I do not want to cut the hide." As Payuk continued to skin the bear, he said, "Tlingit have a special feeling for the bear as they do the wolf, the beaver, and the deer. Each animal has its own place in our society. Each one has made the Tlingit stronger. We appreciate the animals because they feed us, they cloth us, and they protect us."

"How do animals protect the Tlingit?" Fisher asked.

"In spirit they do this thing. It is like the raven, he is the organizer of life, and he is a trickster. He makes our tribe worthy of war,

131

peace, and friendship. There is much more to explain, but for now you know that much. Here turn this bear over a little, I'm through skinning on that side." He shook his head in approval. "This is going to be a fine gift to one of our elders." Pausing, Payuk looked at Fisher. "Do you believe it is good to give gifts to old people?"

As Payuk stood over the bear carcass he held up the bear's skin and yelled something in Tlingit.

Startled, Fisher quickly asked, "What was that about?"

"I was thanking the spirits for this bear. You have to understand that the bear lives for us to have. He is our spiritual brother."

Shaking his head, Fisher nonchalantly muttered, "Just a bear to me. He could have killed one of us, Payuk. What then?"

"We must be strong because the bear is strong. He makes us strong in surviving life."

"How do you know all this stuff, Payuk?" Fisher asked.

"It is my life as this ground is the home of the Tlingit."

Shaking his head, Fisher asked, "OK, what else is there to do?"

"While I cut off some more steaks and wrap them, you can check the harness or clean guns. You will find gun cleaning equipment in our gear."

"I guess I will clean guns, if that will be OK?"

"Sure. When I get these other steaks cut I will show you how to wrap them in wet grasses to keep them fresh and keep them from rotting very soon."

...

Yawning and standing, Kelly looked at Peanut. He was just as bored as Kelly was. Peanut had his head down and was half asleep. Kelly thought about clapping his hands real loud, but, shaking his head, he said to himself, "Better not do that, might scare the poor animal." One of the things Kelly learned early on in his life, being around horses: if you leave one alone for a while, he will lock his legs and go to sleep. If you want to scare the hell out of a horse just walk up to him real quiet and yell. That crazy horse will kick and buck all at the same time.

"Peanut, wake up," Kelly spoke softly.

Sure enough, Peanut unlocked his legs and shook his head. He had taken a nap.

Walking to the edge of the rocks, Kelly lifted the glasses to his eyes. "Well, look here, Peanut. We might be having company real soon." Kelly saw a large steamer coming around Cottonwood Island. He took one last look at the steamer blowing black smoke from her stack like a forest fire because she was moving against the Stikine River spring flow. Sticking the glasses back into his saddlebag, Kelly mounted Peanut and urged him quickly down the slope back to camp.

Seeing Kelly coming at a gallop toward the camp, Fisher yelled at Payuk, "Kelly's coming hell-bent for leather."

Hearing Fisher, Payuk started setting harness on the teams as he yelled at Fisher, "Get in here and help me set the harness."

Reaching the camp, Kelly dismounted and started saddling the other two riding horses. Speaking loud enough for all to hear, Kelly reiterated their plan. "We'll tether one horse on the rear of the front wagon and the other two on the rear of the last wagon. Remember, Fisher, we changed our driving positions. You drive the front wagon, and Payuk and I will be riding on the rear wagon. You be sure and wave, smile, and act like nothing is different or wrong. We'll be right behind you. Payuk and Fisher, you will take care of the deckhand in the wagon area. I will be making my way up to the wheelhouse to put the captain under my control. If you have to shoot, shot to wound, but if there is not time, shot to kill. Remember to have a couple of lengths of small rope with you for tying crewmen up and taking them out of action."

Watching Payuk and Fisher getting the harnesses and double trees hooked up to the wagons, Kelly hurried to put two rifles in the rear wagon and one rifle in the front wagon.

Payuk hailed to Kelly, "How long do you think it will be before they signal?"

Stopping and standing up straight, Kelly admitted, "I don't know. I'm not even sure it is the riverboat we are waiting for, but it is the only large one that has come up the river today, and there are not that many of the big riverboats coming up the river anytime."

Soon Kelly, Payuk, and Fisher were checking loaded rifles, checking harness, and generally talking about the plan.

Suddenly the noise they had been waiting for finally charged the whole canyon with a billowing blast from its foghorn.

"OK, Payuk," Kelly instructed, "Wait for a minute and then fire two quick shots into the air for our signal that we are here and coming. We don't want to seem to be in any great hurry. Everything has to seem very routine."

Payuk pulled his rifle hammer back and fired one round, then levered another round into the chamber and fired the second shot.

"Fisher, get aboard your wagon and lead out nice and slow. We will be right behind you."

Leaving the camp clean, the fire out, and the bear carcass skinned and ready for the animals to eat when the camp area was abandoned, the teams and wagons moved toward the Stikine River.

Plugging along at a slow pace, Fisher signaled he could see the riverboat. Turning backward, Fisher advised, "The riverboat crew is setting out the stable poles for the riverboat to stabilize the movement of the craft. Once the stable poles are set, the boat crew will then let down the ramp to drive the team into the lower level of the boat. I see only two deckhands, but I'd bet there is another inside the lower level."

Turning back forward, Fisher kept a slow and steady pace to the riverboat.

Reaching close to the riverboat, Fisher waved and waited until the ramp was lowered on the riverboat to set on the stable river bank.

Looking closely, Kelly asked Payuk, "Are there two people in the wheelhouse?"

Straining to see, Payuk answered, "Yes, I think there are."

"Huh," Kelly muttered. "That could make it interesting. I will have to change my plan to take control of the riverboat."

Remembering he never chambered another round into his rifle's chamber, Payuk slowly chambered a round into the rifle's chamber.

Kelly saw what he was doing. "Good thing to do right now."

Finally one of the riverboat crewmen signaled for the teams to be driven onto the ramp into the riverboat.

Easing his team ahead with a soft slap of the reins on the horse's backs, Fisher led the way into the riverboat. He pulled to the left and made room for Kelly to drive his team inside the riverboat.

There was only one man inside the wagon staging area and Fisher jumped off his wagon seat and hit the surprised riverboat crewman with the butt of his rifle and drug him to the side, out of the way, and quickly tied his hands behind him as the crewman lay on his stomach out cold.

At the same time, Kelly jumped from the wagon seat and ran toward a ladder that led up to the wheelhouse. Entering a small hallway, Kelly had not been challenged. Pausing for a second and taking a deep breath, Kelly kicked the door open and the two men in the wheelhouse looked shocked. Kelly immediately hit the younger man in the face with his rifle butt and quickly aimed his rifle at the older man, ordering, "Take your coat off."

Immediately the older man yelled at Kelly, "What the hell do you think you are doing? This is my boat."

Not seeing any weapon on the older man, Kelly ordered, "Get on the floor and stay there. The younger man was bleeding from his nose and mouth as he lay there moaning and groaning, and Kelly advised him, "Use your shirt to stop the bleeding." Looking at the older man on the floor, Kelly asked, "Are you the captain?"

"Yes, I'm Captain Charles Weber. You are on the *Blue Sea* riverboat, a ferry and freight out of Seattle, Washington. She is a one-hundred-and-twenty-foot, powerful, single-screw steamer with three decks: wheelhouse deck, quarters and mess hall deck, and livestock and freight deck."

Payuk quickly grabbed Fisher. "Stand on the inside side of that door," he said, and pointed. "Just inside so the two crewmen can't see. I'll stand on this side, and when they come in we'll surprise them and tie them up."

Seeing the crewmen coming back from the stability poles to use the ramp to enter the riverboat, Payuk grabbed one man as Fisher grabbed the other, and both Payuk and Fisher stuck the rifles up under each man's chin. Payuk cautioned them, "You want to live, don't be a hero—no funny tricks." Once the men understood, Payuk ordered, "Lie down on the floor, on your stomach."

"What the hell are you doing?" yelled one of the men. "We didn't do anything to you. You wait till the captain finds out about this."

"Shut up," Fisher demanded as he hit his man in the back of the head with his rifle butt.

Getting the men secured to separate upright deck supports, Payuk told Fisher, "You stay here and don't let these guys get loose. Also watch the first guy you hit. He may be waking up about now."

Quickly making his way toward the wheelhouse, he found Kelly well in control. "What can I do, Kelly?"

Nodding his head, Kelly instructed, "You need to go crank the ramp up so it is standing vertical or straight up and down, and then lock the wheel so the ramp cannot fall down going down the Stikine River."

"I don't know much about cranks," Payuk reasoned.

"OK, Payuk, you stay here and I'll be back in just a minute. Keep an eye on that guy over in the corner. Keep him lying down. This guy here," Kelly motioned with his rifle, "is the captain. By the way, before I leave, Captain, I want you to make yourself comfortable on the floor and don't move."

Soon Kelly returned to the wheelhouse and instructed Payuk, "Take this man," he pointed to the man he had smashed in the face with the rifle butt, "and take him below with the rest of the crewmen."

"What are you doing with my crew? You better not be beating them like you did to my chief mate."

"What is the chief mate's name?" asked Kelly. And, addressing Payuk, "Keep him away from the rest of the crew. I don't want anyone talking among themselves."

"Hartford Harrison," Captain Weber replied.

"OK, Payuk, take Harrison down to lower deck. Don't do anything with the riverboat crew. I need to talk with the captain about the estuary and tides."

"We'll keep a good eye on them, Kelly, you can count on that."

As Payuk took Chief Mate Harrison to the lower level to be tied, Kelly turned to Captain Weber. "Stand up."

"What are you going to do with my vessel?" inquired Captain Weber.

Captain Weber, I am Kelly O'Brien. I work for the Department of Agriculture out of Wrangell. My supervisor is James Kincaid. I and my fellow employee, Payuk, have come from the Twin Forks Mining operation at the intersection of the Iskut and Snippaker Rivers. Did you know that the wagons in your lower deck are filled with poached animal skins and body parts?" Raising his hand for Captain Weber not to respond, he continued. "I realize that we are operating in British Columbia, but we have been given direction to enforce laws by the Providence of British Columbian authority. We wish you and your crew no harm, at least not lasting harm. We do not wish to confiscate your *Blue Sea*, unless you are part of the smuggling operation. There is gold aboard the wagons, but we have not really looked for it. That will be the responsibility of the officials in Wrangell. My responsibility at this point is to get the *Blue Sea* to Wrangell in one piece. At Wrangell, you will be questioned by our legal staff and the local sheriff. While the interrogation is proceeding, your vessel will be searched, but not harmed. If you satisfy our legal staff that you are nothing but a transporter of goods for Twin Forks Mining, you and your crew will probably be released."

"To answer your question, I did know there were skins, but I was told not to concern myself with the cargo—that I was being paid to transport and nothing else."

Nodding, Kelly advised him, "Captain Weber, the poaching took place in British Columbia and they are being transported through Alaskan waters. The Twin Forks Mining people figured they would

138

not get checked going through Alaskan waters with British Columbian cargo posted on your flag staff."

"How long will this investigation take in Wrangell?" asked Captain Weber.

Shrugging, Kelly responded, "I don't know. Another subject we need to talk about is getting back to Wrangell. You undoubtedly came through the estuary at high tide. When is the next high tide we can take to get back to Wrangell?"

Captain Weber motioned toward a cabinet behind Kelly. "I need to get in that cabinet for my charts." Kelly moved as the captain reached in the cabinet and laid the charts on his navigation table and turned several pages. He scanned down one page and jokingly advised, "We could do it at 2030 hours this evening, but I would not recommend it. It looks like the next best time to hit that estuary is tomorrow morning early, about 0500 hours in the morning. We would have to get to the estuary at that time. I think we will have enough light to unset the stabilizer logs with the vessel's lights."

"OK, then, Captain Weber," Kelly decided, "I want to get things ready to go and I want to hit that estuary at five o'clock tomorrow morning." Pausing and looking around the wheelhouse, Kelly muttered, "Now what am I going to do with you?" He looked at the captain. "You know, Captain Weber, if you were to help me get the *Blue Sea* back to Wrangell, I'm sure my boss would take all that into consideration." Scratching the side of his face, Kelly advised, "Of course, the Department of Agriculture will confiscate the wagons, the teams, the skins, and any gold. I don't have a lot of control of that, but I can put in a good word for you to my boss, James Kincaid."

Captain Weber smiled. "Kelly, you say your boss's name like you really trust his decisions, and I really do respect that. Son, don't worry about me. I won't cause you any problems. I'm no criminal. I'm just concerned about my four crew members, and of course myself. You hit Chief Mate Harrison pretty hard with that rifle you are holding."

"Yeah, I did, and I will apologize to him for that. But I really did not have too much time to introduce myself."

"Don't worry about getting to Wrangell tomorrow. For me and the crew it will be nothing more than a routine trip to another port."

"I know, Captain Weber, but your men will not be much help to you. They will be tied up for security purposes."

"Well, Kelly, I need them to Mark Twain on the port and starboard sides of the vessel as we are going downriver, and especially as we are going through the estuary, and I need one man in the engine room," explained Captain Weber.

Shaking his head, Kelly asked, "Is it necessary for you to be in the wheelhouse right now?"

"No. What have you got in mind?"

"First, before we do what I have in mind, I want to ask you a few questions about the *Blue Sea*. What are the main details to take into consideration when you are sitting like this along the shoreline?"

Taking a deep breath and looking out the forward wheelhouse window at the Stikine River flowing by, Captain Weber crossed his arms and lifted his chest and explained, "There are several tasks that need to be taken care of while we are at anchor." He waved his hand to the starboard side. "Not that we are at anchor, but rather stabilized along the shore. The main one is keep the fire box stoked, not necessarily hot like underway, but just keep a fire going in it. We have lots of wood because we made a wood stop in Ketchikan. The next thing to do before we sail is to block in the freight wagons so they don't start rolling around. Then we need to secure the horses to the railing alongside of the bulkhead." Stopping to think, Captain Weber continued. "The last thing, maybe, is checking the stabilizer poles. They are bolted to the vessel, but are tied to posts that are driven into the ground."

Nodding slightly, Kelly said, "We are now going down to see your crew and my two men. I'm going to explain what, who, and when, before the journey, during the journey, and arriving at Wrangell. How long will it take for the *Blue Sea* to reach Wrangell from here?"

Shrugging, Captain Weber estimated, "About four to five hours, maybe less."

"Before we go talk to the other members of this vessel, do you have anything else you want me to mention?"

"No, not right now, but I might think of something when we are down on the livestock and freight deck."

Motioning Captain Weber down the stairs to the second deck and then down to the lower deck, Kelly followed closely behind him. Reaching the livestock and freight deck, Kelly quietly said to Captain Weber, "OK, hold up right here." Looking for the best place for himself and the captain to address the crew and Payuk and Fisher, Kelly pointed with his rifle, and Captain Weber led off in that direction.

"OK, Captain Weber," Kelly said. He spoke loudly to be heard over the noise of the water hitting the boat and the squeaking of the wooden hull. Kelly got everybody's attention with, "Listen up. Captain Weber and I have something to say to all of you. Tomorrow morning we will be leaving to go back to Wrangell." Kelly looked to Captain Weber for input.

Captain Weber quickly responded. "We want to be crossing over into the estuary about 0500 hours. That means we all get up early, meaning about 0200 hours. We need to loosen the post stabilizers right after breakfast. Mike, I want you in the kitchen getting coffee and pancakes ready at 0200 hours. Everyone will have a quick opportunity to gobble down a pancake and drink a quick cup of coffee. Paul and Stan, I want you two guys out on those post stabilizers no later than 0230 hours. The boat lights will be on so it will not be dark while getting the post stabilizers out and the post back on board. The fire box will be kept hot during the night by whoever is on watch. Paul, you and Stan make sure the ramps are secure. Are there any questions?"

Chief Mate Harrison asked, "What happens when we get to Wrangell?"

Captain Weber stepped back and let Kelly answer, "Good question, Harrison. By the way, I'm sorry for hitting you so hard. I did not mean to do that, but I did not have a lot of time for introductions. Now, what happens to you in Wrangell? The Department of Agriculture is not interested in arresting you as Captain Weber has explained to me that your *Blue Sea* was used for transport and had nothing to do with the operations of Twin Forks Mining. We'll probably moor somewhere in the bay next to Wrangell. I believe you will be held in Wrangell for a while so our legal people can talk with you. I don't think you have anything to worry about. You will probably be put up in the jail with the doors unlocked. The local sheriff is an alright guy and he won't screw with you."

Stepping forward, Captain Weber asked, "Could they stay on board if the crew chose to?"

Shrugging, Kelly answered, "Hell, I don't know why not. You can sure ask and I'll help you. You got to remember James Kincaid is a fair man. Are there any more questions once we get to Wrangell?"

Paul asked, "I don't have any money—how do we eat and live?"

142

Captain Weber spoke up. "I have some money on the boat in my cabin. It will be enough for us to survive on till we can leave Wrangell."

Mike whined, "When the hell do we get untied?"

Everybody laughed.

"For supper, you will be untied one at a time and you will always have either Payuk or Fisher right with you with either their side arm or their rifle pointed at you. The same goes for breakfast in the morning. Even when you take care of the stabilizers, there will be either Payuk or Fisher with you. Once we get under way you will not be tied anymore."

Captain Weber jumped in. "Chief Harrison, I know you are having a problem with this, but we are not the criminals here and Kelly knows it. He just needs to have you available when the time comes. Let's not make a problem for the Department of Agriculture. It will go a lot easier for us if we play along. Incidentally, when we start down the Stikine River we will be under full lights for night running. Chief Harrison will be in the wheelhouse operating the spotlight from shore to shore. Paul and Stan will be doing Mark Twains, and Mike, you will take care of the fire box."

Captain Weber looked to his crew and saw all of them tied to support posts and motioned to Kelly. "Come over here for a minute." Waiting for Kelly to get close to him out of earshot from his crew, he shook his head. "I hate to see my crew tied up like this." Gently laying his hand on Kelly's shoulder, Captain Weber emphasized, "Son, I will give you my word that if you let my crew be free of being tied that they will not give you any problems and they will go about their jobs like any other trip and actually help you get the *Blue Sea* into Wrangell without a hitch. They have been with me for several years and they are all good lads and loyal to me. You have my word on it."

Shaking his head in disbelief, Kelly looked at the captain and quietly responded, "You are a fair man and I can sense that you are a good person. Only a fair-minded and good person would have laid his own reputation on the line. I want you to tell your crew because you are the captain."

Shaking Kelly's shoulder before he let it go, Captain Weber stepped back into earshot of his crew and stated, "Mr. O'Brien and I have come to an agreement. He has decided to release all of you on your own good behavior. I have given my word to Mr. O'Brien that none of my crew will do anything to stop the *Blue Sea* from getting to Wrangell. You are to go about your business as always, taking care of the vessel's needs, and Kelly's men will even help you if you ask."

Immediately Captain Weber turned and shook hands with Kelly, which sealed the deal and everybody saw that happening and knew the captain and Kelly trusted each other.

"OK, Payuk, you and Fisher cut them loose." Pulling his pocket watch from his pocket, Kelly inquired of the captain, "When is supper usually taken on board the *Blue Sea*?"

"What time is it now, Kelly?" Captain Weber asked.

"It is about six o'clock. Fisher can help whoever in the kitchen to make supper if you want," Kelly answered.

"Paul, will you come over here?" Captain Weber called. When Paul got closer, Captain Weber explained, "I want you to work with Fisher in the kitchen to get supper fixed."

"Aye, Captain. We'll have it ready in about a half hour or so from now." Turning to face everybody, Paul hailed, "I believe there is hot coffee in the kitchen if anybody wants any."

144

Turning away from Kelly, Captain Weber muttered quietly to Kelly, "Yeah, this will work. I know my crew is happy."

"So are we, Captain Weber."

CHAPTER TWELVE

Next morning James stretched and uncovered from his bedroll. Thinking, *I'm glad Moaka and Janet set up the tent while I was walking around last evening because it rained during the night.*

They had moved the saddles and gear inside the tent to keep dry and Janet had her own little tent that she and Runback slept in.

Getting breakfast over with—fried potatoes, salt pork, biscuits, and coffee—Janet jumped to the task of cleaning up.

"Thanks for cleaning up, Miss Moore. Moaka and I do not like that job. We like to cook and eat, but not the cleanup part."

"Oh that's alright, Mr. Kincaid. My dad always had me do the cleanup part. How long are you going to be gone today?" Janet asked.

Finishing their coffee, James and Moaka saddled the horses, leaving the packhorse for Janet to care for. "I don't know how long we're going to be gone." Stopping in his tracks, James looked at Moaka...

Moaka spied Kincaid looking at him, and he asked, "What say, Kincaid?"

Excitedly he said, "You ever heard of a water flume, Moaka?"

"No."

"By the damn," James expounded. "It is a wooden trough to carry water in over rough ground or over gorges. It normally sits on top of a structure that makes the flume have some flow toward where the water needs to go. I think a wooden flume is just what we need to solve this problem. Listen," James leaned close to Moaka, "I don't want you to tell anybody about this. I want to see if the group we have will think of such a thing as a flume. If they think of it they will own it, and it will mean more. If you or I tell them about the flume, they may not accept the hard work that will be needed to build it."

"No say, Kincaid."

Before mounting, James walked over to the fire and asked Moaka, who was rounding up the edges of the fire, "You got anything else we need to talk about at the meeting?"

As he finished pushing the fire together some, Moaka instructed Janet, "Keep fire close." He motioned with his hands to keep it together.

"Yes, I will, Moaka. Thank you for the advice."

"OK, Kincaid, ready go."

As James and Moaka slowly made their way up the slope of the mountain, Moaka advised, "Baxter no own land, he squatter."

"I know, Moaka. That's what makes the problem more unsolvable by normal legal channels. And I'll bet Ferrell Jones knows that Neil Baxter does not own the ground."

"Can stop mine tailings go down all over hill?"

Not answering right away, James thought, *I don't want to stop the sluice tailings from going down the slope, but rather channel the tailings into a ditch or flume so they don't spread all over the slope and destroy habitat.*

Reining up Red, James explained, "Moaka, it is not that we don't want to stop the sluice tailing, but we need to control the flow so the tailings don't scatter all over the slope."

"Baxter want stop."

"Well, Moaka, that will never happen. Undoubtedly Ferrell Jones probably has a free flow clause in his claim."

"Can't ask how much gold."

"You're right, Moaka. How much gold is not an issue at this time, and it is really none of our business."

Letting Red slowly make his way up the brushy slope, James could see several people standing in the trees ahead of him. "Moaka, we have company."

"Yesterday they say want meet before see Jones."

Reaching the group of five men that were dismounted, James met each one and explained his and Moaka's position. "Moaka and I are employees of the Department of Agriculture out of Wrangell. One problem is I don't have absolute authority over this entire situation." Shaking his head, he sighed. "As far as the lands, I have jurisdiction, but over the mining I'm a little short on the legal status of certain things. All in all, I hoped to have this meeting to solve a problem. For Stone Mountain Mining and Ferrell Jones it's not a problem, but for folks like you it is a major problem. I'm sure you can recognize the solution could be difficult. Are there any questions?" Right away a hand was raised, and James recognized.

"Mr. Kincaid, I'm Ted Wells, and I live about a half mile south of here toward Hoqur Cove. I built a cabin there about ten years ago and I've lived there ever since. I sold out my fish store business and my local newspaper business down below in a town called Astoria, Oregon, and moved up here. My wife and I had one son, ten years old, when we moved here, and now he is a newspaperman in Seattle. We have made a good living selling firewood to steamers coming up the channel. Also, my wife sells art pieces she does from natural stuff in the forest. Actually she has built a good business selling the art articles to the lower forty-eight folks." He hesitated and then blurted out, "And I don't want things to change. We like it just like it has always been."

Breathing out, James give Moaka a quick glance and then responded, "Mr. Wells, I'm sure all of you," James pointed to the group as a whole, "have a lot of good stories about settling here, but right now we need to concentrate on finding a solution to the problem at hand. What are we going to do with the sluice tailings that are spoiling the landscape and threatening to do damage to some structures?"

Another hand showed as Archie Bench introduced himself and complained, "The sluice tailings are ruining the fishing in this area."

"Mr. Bench, I understand you may see dirt in the shoreline water at times, but because of the high tides in this area, that does not seem to be a problem because during the next cycle of high and low tides, the dirty water is all washed away. No, we must concentrate on the sluice tailings destroying or at least damaging the environment, whether it be washing gutters into the land or covering up new growth."

"Mr. Kincaid," Tim Cord asked, "what do the Indians around here think about such mining operations?"

James stepped back and let Moaka speak: "Mr. Cord, Tlingit feel least bother nature to be good. Nature is Tlingit entire life. Tlingit would never destroy nature with mining."

"Well, there you go, Kincaid," Jud Dillan blurted out, "hire a bunch of Indians and burn the damn mining people out."

Holding his hands into the air, James called for calm, as the group nodded their heads in approval. "Now come on, you guys, that is not a solution to this problem and you know it."

"What do you suggest, Kincaid?" came a question from the group.

"I thought about taking Moaka with me, and we would just go home and declare this situation not our problem." James smiled and winked to the group. Clearing his throat and sniffing, James continued. "Then I thought about digging a trench from the mining sight to water's edge, but it would be almost impossible to keep the sluice tailings from loading up the trench and the tailings would again flow all over the place."

"Who would dig this trench you are talking about?" asked Roger Ray.

Quickly and in an irritated voice, James answered, "Forget about the trench, it will not work for the reason I gave you."

"So what are we going to do? Just walk up there and ask Jones to stop mining?" Ted Wells declared sarcastically.

Looking up the slope, Moaka noticed Ferrell Jones standing on a large rock and looking down the slope at the meeting of the cabin owners. "Kincaid," Moaka pointed up the slope, "Jones see us meet."

Looking to where Moaka was pointing, James stopped all conversation and advised, "We better get up the slope to the mining camp. We are a little late already."

Leading the way, James and Moaka led their horses up to the mining camp, with the rest of the men following in single file.

Seeing more cabin people coming to the meeting than he expected, Ferrell Jones had a man cut more short logs for the men to sit on for the meeting. Motioning to the men to take a short log to sit on, Ferrell Jones remarked to Kincaid, "More people here than I thought." Seeing all the men settled in a circle, Ferrell Jones motioned to James and said, "OK, Mr. Kincaid, let's see what you have to say."

Removing his lightweight gray Stetson hat, James rubbed the back of his head, and replaced his hat. Taking a deep breath, James looked at Ferrell Jones and to the other men in the group. All of a sudden, the weight of the world was on his shoulders. James thought, *All of a sudden, these men are waiting on me to come up with a good plan to solve their problem.* He nodded his head. *How did this become my problem? I guess it comes with the job.*

"Well, Kincaid, you gonna say something or not?" Jones asked harshly.

Quickly Archie Bench spoke up, "Be quiet, Jones, and let him speak."

"Shut up, you," Ferrell Jones said, pointing his finger at Archie Bench.

"Be quiet, you guys. Let's start this meeting with everybody introducing themselves and where they live."

"Good idea," chimed in Archie Bench.

"OK," James stated, "I'm James Kincaid and I work for the Department of Agriculture out of Wrangell." Then each man stated his name and where he lived, including Moaka.

Having the introductions bought James some time to think. *OK, I need to talk about the 'A' in the hole when the time comes.*

Crossing his heavy arms across his large chest, Ferrell Jones asked again, "Go ahead, Kincaid. We are listening."

"The problem for the cabin owners is that the sluice tailings are raising hell with the environment—mainly the undergrowth and small trees trying to get started, also the small animals are being evicted from their burrows. Another reason the cabin owners want the sluice tailings controlled is that it promotes erosion of the slope and any other structure that may be in the way. An additional problem is that the sluice tailings make the area look dirty and unsightly."

Hearing James give all the reasons for the mining sluice tailings to be controlled, Ferrell Jones looked around the group of men and asked, "Do all of you believe what this man," he pointed to James, "has just said?"

James sat quietly as he noticed all the cabin owners nodded in the affirmative.

"Well," Ferrell Jones retorted, "I've got a claim that states I have free flow from the mining operation to water's edge. It does not talk about routes, structures, or environment." Then he stood up and hastily said, "I'll be right back."

While he was gone, James said to Moaka, "I'll bet he's going after the claim contract."

No sooner had James spoken, than Ferrell Jones came out of his hut and presented the claim contract. "I want you to turn to page twelve and read what the contract says about free flow."

"Here, Mr. Jones," James called. "Let me have the contract and I will read it so all can get the same meaning."

"Good idea." Ferrell Jones handed the paperwork to James.

As James began to read, he would occasionally look up at the group, and as he read he could sense frustration in the cabin owners. Finishing the paragraph concerning the free flow opinion of the mining claim, James concluded, "You heard me read it; it is legal, straight from the Alaska Mining Council in Juneau." Nodding with the group, James admitted, "Mr. Jones, you are surely legal. Now, is there anything anybody can think of to solve the problem we have with the sluice tailings messing things up?"

Tim Cord stood from his cut log stool and faced down the slope toward the water's edge. "There has to be a way to control the sluice tailings so they don't run all over the slope." Turning to look at James, he reiterated, "Mr. Kincaid says a ditch won't work...what else?"

Roger Ray lifted his hand and began to speak. "When I was a young boy we used to float down an old flume for a long ways. The flume was built up on stilt-looking things to keep it almost flat. We floated in that thing many years and it probably is still there. I don't know what kind of wood they used, but it held up for many years."

"Are you suggesting I build a flume all the way down to water's edge to carry the sluice tailings?" Ferrell Jones sarcastically inquired.

James immediately jumped in. "Why not, Mr. Jones. How long is your contract for on this mining claim?"

Stammering, Ferrell Jones finally blurted, "Five years...why?"

"Well," James explained, "that means you have four more years to go. If the flume is built, your problems and the cabin owners' problems will go away."

"I don't have a contract to cut lumber," Ferrell Jones explained. "We had one for the building of our buildings, through Tongass National Forest, but it is expired now."

Nodding, James stated, "Don't worry about that. I can take care of any timber permits."

"Who in the hell do you think is going to build this stupid flume as you call it?" Ferrell Jones exclaimed.

Sensing the conversation was happening between him and Ferrell Jones, James looked to the five cabin owners and asked, "Are you guys willing to help build the flume? I don't mean come down from your cabins once in a while, but rather eat and sleep this project until finished. Also there are other cabin owners not here. Are they willing to sacrifice part of their lives to this project? Are you willing to donate some money for bolts, screws, and other things that are needed to build this structure? You can't just sit around and expect someone else to do the job for your benefit. You're in all the way or you're not."

"I'll have about half of my miners working on the flume if that is what we decide on. That will be about ten guys, Kincaid. How far from the mining works down to water's edge?"

"I was just thinking of that," James informed him. "I have walked up and down this slope several times since I have been here and I would estimate about one hundred and fifty yards, or about four hundred fifty feet." Standing from his stool, James lifted his shoulders and commented, "We need a good plane saw. All the saw needs to do is cut flat boards."

"Hell, I got one of those. Where do you think the lumber came from to build those buildings?" Ferrell Jones said as he pointed to them. "Only thing is, it will only take ten- to twelve-inch logs no more than ten feet long. It is diesel, so there will be some expense operating the machine, but it saves a whole lot of work."

Jud Dillan jumped into the conversation. "I can help there. I used to run one of those things in the lower."

Sitting back down, James spread his hands out. "OK, the next step is to find out how many men can show up from the cabin owners. I want to have a meeting here, if that will be alright with you, Mr. Jones, in the morning at about ten o'clock. Go see your neighbors and get them to commit to this project. Bring them up here tomorrow if they want to come. We have a golden opportunity to get this flume built and the mess cleaned up; let's not screw it up with personal objections."

Slowly the men stood and started talking among themselves, and James heard them talking about a lot of work and expense that might not be necessary. Then Neil Baxter walked over to James and quietly said, "We'll be here, don't worry—we'll be here."

...

Next morning, James and Moaka had breakfast with Janet Moore. As soon as the meal was over, Janet jumped to the task of cleaning up.

"Thank you for cleaning, it good not to do," Moaka praised.

"Keep track of the packhorse, Miss Moore, if you let him graze, and keep the fire low. If you get a chance, and if you want, you can catch some trout for supper."

Saddling up and starting up the slope to the mining camp, James heard Miss Moore call. Reining in Red, James turned to see her coming toward him. She had a couple of small rocks in her hands. When she got close, Janet showed Moaka and James two colors she had made from natural materials. "See, I told you I could make natural color. I'm sorry I stopped you, but I forgot to show you at breakfast." In a bubbly voice she announced, as she turned to go back to camp, "OK, you can go now."

Moaka looked at James and James looked at Moaka. They shook their heads and turned the horses toward the mining camp.

Arriving at the mining camp just before ten o'clock, James and Moaka dismounted and sat on their original stools. James opened his notebook and started reviewing a few notes from yesterday and going over some of the things he wanted to cover in today's meeting. "Moaka, did you get the feeling that some of the cabin owners did not want to get involved with the building of the flume?"

"I think want to stop sluice tailings from making mess, no want to help in big job. They want mining company do all work."

"What happens if the cabin owners decide not to build the flume?" James suggested.

"I go home," he said and smiled. "I no build flume."

Slightly laughing, James muttered, "You got a point. Well, I'll be damned; look, Moaka, there have to be twenty people riding up."

Not noticing Ferrell Jones coming up behind them, James was startled when he greeted, "Good morning, you two." As Jones looked beyond James and Moaka, he commented, "Looks like you brought your army with you."

Shaking his head, James responded, "It's not my army, Mr. Jones, but I'm glad to see them all here. It must mean either hell yes or hell no." He laughed and was joined by Ferrell Jones.

"Well, they will just have to sit on the ground or stand. I'm not cutting any more stools."

"That's alright, Mr. Jones, they will make do," James assured him.

Leading the line of men in single file coming up the slope was Neil Baxter.

James stood and extended his hand and Neil Baxter accepted. "Kincaid, seems like everyone wants to have a say in this project. Not everybody is in favor of the flume idea. I'm afraid we need to do some fancy talking to bring folks along." Quickly looking back, Neil Baxter quietly stated, "They don't like to be dedicated too much and they don't want to spend any money."

"We'll just have to build a fire under them." James smiled.

CHAPTER THIRTEEN

Sitting at the supper table, everyone felt a solid, hard bump to the vessel's river side. Quickly jumping up from the table, Captain Weber and Chief Mate Harrison dashed for the port side. Hastily they looked over the side of the railings, looking for damage to the *Blue Sea*. As the rest of the men came rushing out of the mess hall, Captain Weber shouted instructions: "Look for holes or something sticking out of the side of the hull." Leaning toward Chief Mate Harrison, Captain Weber instructed, "Get a lantern and go below and check for damage. Take one of the men with you."

"Aye, Captain."

As Kelly came close to Captain Weber he asked, "What in the world was that noise and hard bump?"

Shaking his head, Captain Weber explained, "It was a big log floating down the Stikine River. It must have been a big log because it shook the whole hull. When we are under steam, logs and debris are only some of the many dangers we look for constantly. Chief Mate Harrison helps me do that all the time."

Looking around, Kelly inquired, "Where is Chief Mate Harrison?"

"I sent him down below decks to check for damage to the hull and bulkheads." As Captain Weber kept looking for damage, he ordered Paul, "Go check the stabilizer poles."

"Aye, aye, sir."

"Is there anything we can do, Captain?" Kelly asked. He leaned over the railing as far he could to check for damage to the outer hull.

"Yes, Kelly, take one of your men and check to see that the wagons are still stable, and check the blocks under the wheels. Also you might settle down the horses if they are jumping around any."

"Aye, aye, sir," Kelly hailed, which brought a second look from Captain Weber and a smile from Kelly's lips.

"Payuk," Kelly called, "come with me to check the wagons and horses." Seeing Fisher wondering what to do, Kelly yelled, "Fisher, come with us."

Instantly a large smile came across Fisher's face, being happy to be involved.

Hurrying to the stock deck, Kelly, Payuk, and Fisher found that several of the wagons had pushed the wheel blocks away and several of the wagons were moving back and forth between the blocks. Readjusting all the wheel blocks, the wagons seemed stable. Moving to the horses, Kelly instructed, "Gently go to the front of them and pet their neck and talk slowly and calmly to them."

Finding everything in order, Captain Weber hailed on the loudspeaker for everyone to come back to the mess hall. As everyone was returning to the mess hall, the chief mate returned from below decks and reported, "Captain, the bulkheads are still anchored well, and the hull does not seem to be damaged, but we sure took a hard hit."

The captain stood and addressed the men. "I'm assuming that everybody got their fill before the ruckus with the log happened? What needs to happen now—this is for the benefit of Kelly and his men—is to set for night. My crew will fill the lanterns and place them, and when it gets about dark we will light the lanterns for the night. Next, the post stabilizers will need to be checked and tightened if need be. The kitchen will be cleaned and readied for the morning. The horses will be watered and the wagons checked. All upper doors and windows will be closed. All ramps will be pulled in and secured." He sighed. "I don't know, there may be more, but right now we need to set watch. I believe Chief Mate Harrison has that set up for the night. Oh, and by the way, there should be hot coffee on the stove during the watches."

"Yes, sir." Looking at his pocket watch, Chief Mate Harrison began. "Right now it is 1800 hours. Watch will start at 2000 hours for two hours with Payuk and Stan, then 2200 hours with Fisher and Paul for two hours, then to finish out before wake-up call, Mike and I. Wake up calls go at 0200 hours. I've tried to put one of our crew with one of Kelly's men. The watch will consist of checking the horses, wagons, and lanterns—sometimes the lanterns have a habit of burning out, so you have to check them—checking the outside of the stock deck for anything coming loose, and checking in the wheelhouse for all being secure. Other than that, just keep the vessel's fire box warm and be aware of anything hanging around that is not supposed to be there. Are there any questions?"

"How many of these lanterns are there?" Fisher asked.

Chief Mate Harrison blinked and squinted. "Fisher, that is a good question. I've never really counted them, but you won't have any problem seeing them."

Payuk leaned over to Kelly. "Where sleep, Kelly?"

The captain cleared his throat and addressed Payuk's question. "You can bring your bedroll up to one of the rooms on the second floor and lay it on one of the canvas cots. Remember when you select a room, there is a little slot on the door you open that says TAKEN."

The chief mate waited until the captain was finished and asked again, "Are there any more questions?" Not hearing any comments, Chief Mate Harrison advised, "OK, the first watch starts at 2000 hours. See you in the morning if not before." Quickly stopping and turning, Chief Mate Harrison advised, "Find out where your relief is sleeping." He laughed. "We don't want someone woke up that is not his watch."

159

As the men started leaving the mess hall, the captain asked Stan, "Is the personnel ramp still down?"

"Yes, I believe it is, Captain. I'll pull it up right away."

Waving his hand slightly in the air, the captain replied, "No, don't. I want to take a walk before I retire for the night."

Hearing the captain's intent to take a walk, Kelly asked, "Can I join you, Captain Weber?"

Captain Weber looked back at Kelly. "Sure, I will enjoy the company. Chief Mate Harrison, will you please be so good as to go get my belt and pistol in the wheelhouse?"

Quickly Kelly snapped a look at Captain Weber. Shaking his head, he muttered, "You had it all the time."

"Yes, Kelly," the captain answered, "One never leaves himself entirely open." And both men laughed.

"Fisher," Paul addressed the young man. "I guess we have watch together. Show me where you will be sleeping tonight so I can come and get you."

Both men went to the second floor where the state rooms were and Fisher pointed to the first room. "I'll be in here," he said as he opened the door. Walking inside, Fisher was amazed at the room. It had three cots, a dressing table with a large bowl for water, a large pitcher for getting water, and a small mirror above the dressing table. The room was small, but very comfortable. "I didn't know you carried passengers on the *Blue Sea*."

"Oh yeah," Paul responded, "usually between some of the bigger towns and Seattle and sometimes to Portland if we are steaming that far south." Sitting on one of the canvas cots, Paul excitedly asked Fisher, "Did you look for the gold? There has to be gold on those wagons somewhere."

"I never looked for it. My job was just drive the team down the Iskut River to the riverboat on the Stikine River. Believe me, I've thought about the gold, but I wouldn't dare look for it. My boss would kill me if I touch the gold or even thought about it." Pausing, Fisher shook his head. "Too much of a risk."

Getting off the canvas cot, Paul headed for the open door. "OK, Fisher, I was just asking, curious more than anything else."

"Wait," Fisher said, "I'm going down to the stock deck to get my bedroll and gear."

"Don't worry, I'll wake you at 2200 hours," Paul advised as they disappeared through the doorway.

Kelly followed Captain Weber across the personnel ramp until they both stood on firm ground. "I think I've heard of your James Kincaid," Captain Weber explained. "Isn't he the guy that stopped a lot of poaching around the southeast part of Alaska?"

Looking surprised, Kelly responded, "Yeah, he has built himself a reputation that he does not want. He is just a regular guy. He is married to a wonderful person and she is a school teacher at the school in Wrangell, and they have two children. He is an educated man with a degree in Wildlife Management, and he knows how to address problems with people, offenses against the law, and the bureaucrats."

"I'm rather looking forward to meeting such a person, Kelly. How old is he?"

Shaking his head, he answered, "I don't know for sure, but about forty or forty-one. He is starting to show a little gray, but I would not mention it if I were you."

"Well..." Captain Weber smiled. He surmised, "He'll know right from wrong."

Soon Captain Weber and Kelly returned to the *Blue Sea* just in time to see the crew lighting the lanterns. Seeing Mike, Captain Weber instructed, "Mike, will you get some help and crank the personnel ramp in for the night."

"Aye, Captain."

Bidding Captain Weber good night, Kelly headed to pick up his bedroll and select a cabin for the night.

"Kelly, make sure you open the slot that says TAKEN, when you decide what room."

As the night wore on, Payuk and Stan paced the vessel checking lanterns, keeping the small fire in the kitchen stove burning to keep the coffee hot for the next watch, and keeping a small fire in the fire box in the engine room. Stan poured him a cup of coffee and offered one to Payuk, but Payuk waved it off.

"Are you a Tlinkit Indian, Payuk?" Stan inquired.

"Yes. My native tribe has lived around Wrangell for more than a thousand years. I'm not sure how long, but at least that long. It is a good place and we try to take care of the wildlife, streams, and nature's ground. Where are you from, Stan?"

"Oh…" Stan sighed. "I guess my main family came to the United States in the late sixties, right after the Civil War. They came from Poland. My dad was a shoemaker and my mother did nothing but raise kids. I have four brothers and three sisters. Eventually, my father opened his own shop in Boston and he did very well in that small shoe shop. He sold and repaired shoes. Both of my parents died years ago, and I only know where two of my brothers are living and only one sister. Kind of a shame not knowing where more are located, but time has separated us."

"That's the good thing about staying in one place with the family like the Tlingit. We always have connection to our family and ancestry."

"Yep, sounds good to me, Payuk. Let's make a round before we wake up the next watch."

Not sleeping very soundly, Fisher heard the knock on the door and replied, "OK, I'll meet you at the mess hall." Pushing his bedroll down, Fisher slipped into his trousers and put his boots on. Stomping down on his boots, he thought, *I'm glad I've got good boots that fit. I know some guys that their shoes or boots did not fit and they could not walk very well or for very far because of their feet hurting.*

Meeting Paul in the kitchen, they both had a quick cup of coffee.

"So what do we do, Paul," Fisher asked.

"You just follow me around for one time and then we will go our separate ways for a while."

Soon Paul had taken Fisher around the loop that covered the vessel for night watch. "Just remember, Fisher, look for anything out of order, or a lantern that is not lighted. Now you stay on the same route we just went and you will be fine. Be careful walking on the outside walk. I've got to go up to the wheelhouse and enter some information into the log and check the ship's boiler. I'll catch up to you in just a bit."

Seeing Fisher disappear outside to walk around the outside walk, Paul grabbed a lantern and headed for one of the wagons that was loaded with skins. Climbing into the wagon and holding the lantern high so he could see, Paul threw back the tarp to expose the skins. Thinking, *Now, where would the gold be hid?* he lifted up a few layers of skins, but all he saw was more skins. *There has to be a cash box or safe looking thing somewhere.* Digging farther into the skins,

Paul was losing patience. Resting back against some skins he thought, *The cash box might be in the other wagon.*

Straightening the skins to lie flat, Paul covered up the skins with the tarp just like they were before he got there.

Going to the next wagon, Paul climbed into the wagon as he held the lantern high. Throwing the tarp back, he began laying skins back as he searched for the evasive cash box.

Suddenly Paul was looking into the face of Fisher. Jumping back like he had been shot, he said, "My God, Fisher, you scared the hell out of me! Why didn't you say something?"

"I thought I would climb up here and see if you had found the gold. Did you find any?"

"Hell, no," Paul blurted out. "I thought they were mining gold where you work."

"They are and I've seen lots of it. I just can't figure out how they get it out of the mining area down to Seattle."

Sitting on the skins and sighing, Paul crossed his arms. "Well, I'll be damned if I know. There is no other way. The *Blue Sea* has an exclusive contract to transfer goods both coming and going from Twin Forks Mining. Damn it, Fisher, that gold has to be on or in these wagons somewhere. Is there a false bottom to these wagons? Here, hold this lantern, Fisher." Paul straightened the skins and covered them with the tarp like the other wagon.

"What are you doing, Paul?" Fisher asked.

Jumping down from the wagon bed, Paul slipped under the wagon and said, "Give me that lantern."

Fisher stood silently watching in all directions so they would not get caught. Hearing Paul hitting the bottom of the wagon, Fisher asked stressfully, "What are you doing? You are going to wake the dead. Get out from underneath there. There is no gold under there."

164

And with frustration in his voice, Fisher demanded, "Get out of there."

Finally Paul slowly slid out from underneath the wagon and hung the lantern back where he got it. "Do not say a word about this to anyone. If Captain Weber were to find out about this he would put me off at the next stop, and I like this job so don't say a word."

"Yeah, I understand. Paul, I won't."

"OK, you go up and put a few small sticks into the cookstove and I'll go stoke up the ship's fire box. I'll meet you right back here in ten minutes," Paul instructed.

Moving past the wagons for the last time on their watch, Paul shook his head. "That gold is in there—I know it, I know it."

Fisher smiled. "Maybe we will find it in Wrangell."

Paul and Fisher were making their last round on their watch, and Paul advised, "You can go on back to bed for a while, and I'm going to wake Mike and the chief mate for the last watch."

At 0130 Chief Mate Harrison gently shook the captain. "Captain, it is time. Mike is in the kitchen, preparing pancakes and coffee for the crew. I will wake the crew at 0200."

"Wake them now, Chief. Let's get this thing underway."

"Aye, aye, sir," Chief Mate Harrison pertly replied.

Knocking on doors and calling, "Reveille, reveille, breakfast is on. Let's go, we are headed to Wrangell this morning."

As the men drug themselves into the mess hall after a short night's sleep, they walked into the large room that was well-lighted. The lanterns were out and the steam-powered generator was turned on. Mike was at the stove cooking pancakes and the crew got their own coffee.

Clearing his throat, Captain Weber announced, "Stan and Paul, as soon as you are finished eating go stand by the post stabilizers. Chief

Mate Harrison will shine the lights toward you so you can see, and wait till I give a short blow on the horn before you start unlashing the posts. Make sure you secure the post on deck and pull up the personnel ramp before you give me the all clear. By that time, Mike will have the steam up and we can be in control of the *Blue Sea*. When we get under way, Stan will take the port side and Paul will take the starboard side for Mark Twain. Chief Mate Harrison will try to keep the ship's lights forward into the water or wherever you two might point. Mike, you clean up the kitchen and man the ship's boiler." Looking toward Kelly, he added, "I would like Fisher to help in the kitchen for a short while, and then Mike will send him back to you. I would like you and your men to take care of the wagons and horses. It should not be that rough until we hit the estuary. Sometimes when the current is still coming in from the ocean, it causes some strange currents. I'll try and hold a steady course. Are there any questions?"

"When will it get light?" Fisher asked.

The captain pulled his watch from his breast pocket. "It is 0215 hours right now. It should be getting light about 0430 hours. That's just about the time we'll enter into the estuary. OK, let's get underway."

Without any further urging, the crew quickly left the mess hall and undertook their assigned duties.

Kelly, Payuk, and Fisher spread out among the horses and wagons to keep check on any movement by the wagons or horses that might get anxious as the boat might be rolling and jumping around, especially during the estuary crossing.

Speaking loud enough for the other two men to hear, Kelly advised, "Take a walk around your area and just make sure things are secure. I don't remember the estuary being too rough, but Captain Weber seems to know what he is talking about."

The noise of the steam engine starting to turn the propeller reverberated throughout the *Blue Sea* as Stan and Paul were securing the stabilizer post on deck. As the *Blue Sea* turned into the open river to the port, Stan and Paul slammed the personnel ramp up into place and headed for their positions port and starboard for Mark Twain readings. As Stan flew by Payuk he yelled, "Hang on, it could be a rough one, the river is really high and rolling."

Feeling Captain Weber increasing power to the propeller, the vessel came around to head straight down the Stikine River.

Kelly lightly held onto one of the upright supports and called to Payuk, "How are you doing?"

Nodding his head, Payuk replied, "OK," as he stood braced next to the outside hull. "It seems to be rougher than I expected."

Yelling, Kelly hailed Fisher, "Hey, Fisher, how are you doing?"

Fisher hollered back in response, "Me and this horse are holding each other up, other than that, everything is fine over here."

Suddenly the vessel stopped shifting to one side and then the other, and the ride became somewhat smooth. Kelly thought, *We must have gotten out into the main channel. We should have smooth steaming until the estuary.*

Hearing Chief Mate Harrison announcing on the ship's loudspeaker, "We are just crossing over into the United States," made Kelly smile. He thought, *Just about home.*

Soon Payuk came over to Kelly and slapped him on the back and admitted, "I never thought we could have pulled it off, but here we are taking this riverboat down the Stikine to Wrangell." Smiling, Payuk joked, "Kincaid is going to be amazed if he doesn't put us in jail for hijacking." Payuk looked and pointed at the wagons, saying,

"Kelly, look at those freight wagons. Look at how they are built. They must have thought the mine was going to haul the whole mountain down the river, the way those things are built. I've never seen a wagon for freight built quite that heavy. And look at that pipe railing along each side; I guess they are there to support the sides."

Nodding, Kelly agreed. "Big and tough."

After several hours of traveling, Captain Weber announced on the ship's loudspeaker, "Estuary coming up; it looks OK, but hold on just in case."

Kelly walked forward and unlocked and opened a small wooden door to peek at the estuary ahead. Just as he unlocked the small door, the force of the wind on the door swung it open violently, hitting Kelly with enough force to push him backward. Stepping forward, Kelly stood off to the side of the opening to stay out of the direct wind flow rushing through. Looking downriver he could see the estuary, and he thought, *There's just enough light that the estuary can be seen. I hope we don't have any problems with this, because beyond the estuary is open sea to Wrangell.*

As Kelly walked past Payuk, Payuk asked, "How does it look? Is there a wave coming in?"

Shaking his head slightly, he answered, "I could not see one, but the light is not real good right now. I would not worry about the tidal wave into the mouth of the Stikine. The river is running pretty high. We are a little ahead of schedule because the *Blue Sea* had to steam a little faster for guidance in the river currents." As Kelly continued on to his area, he declared, "I think it will be just fine. The *Blue Sea* is big enough and powerful enough to power its way through any tide wave that would be coming up the Stikine River."

Suddenly the captain's voice came over the loudspeaker: "Hang on."

Instantly, the *Blue Sea* lurched to the right and the bow lifted out of the water, then as the bow came down onto the foamy water that came cascading over the bow, the vessel listed back to the left. All the crew knew that the *Blue Sea* had just smashed into the tide wave and had survived, save maybe Fisher.

As the *Blue Sea* rolled through the wave, all the crew cheered because all knew the next stop was going to be Wrangell, with fair winds.

Kelly hailed to Payuk and Fisher, "I'm going up to the wheelhouse."

Payuk waved his acknowledgement.

Climbing the steps up to the second deck, then onto the wheelhouse, Kelly opened the door and saw Captain Weber and Chief Mate Harrison putting maps, charts, and weather tables in drawers below the map desk. "Hi, Captain Weber. Looks like you guys are getting ready to port."

"Oh hi, Kelly. How was the ride on the stock deck?" Captain Weber inquired.

Smiling, Kelly answered, "One rough spot at the estuary, but other than that, it was smooth enough. There were no problems with the wagons or stock."

"Chief, step outside and make sure the Canadian flag is flying on our staff. I don't need any revenuers getting on board from Wrangell just to check things out."

Seeing the captain relaxing as the trip would be over shortly, Kelly asked, "Why don't you have a dog on board as a mascot?"

Laughing lightly, Captain Weber remarked, "Well, I've thought about getting a dog, but haven't—"

"Pardon me, Captain," Chief Mate Harrison said, "What do you want to do with your belt and pistol?"

"Just put it under the counter desk in the third drawer," the captain answered as he turned his attention back to Kelly. "Anyway, I haven't really looked for one. I favor a Husky or a good, strong Labrador. Actually I prefer a Lab because that breed of dog is friendlier to everyone and they like to be around water."

Instantly Kelly started thinking, *Sam Boren's black Labrador bitch had a litter of pups about two months ago. I wonder if they are old enough to sell or give away.*

Looking out the forward window of the wheelhouse, Kelly could see they were just passing Kadin Island on the right and soon would be passing Deadman's Island on the left, then into Wrangell Harbor. Smiling, Kelly informed Captain Weber, "We need to all go into Wrangell and check in with Sheriff Marlin."

Showing some concern, Chief Mate Harrison quickly inquired, "Are we all going to jail?"

"No!" Kelly exclaimed. "This move is just an administrative action for the Department of Agriculture. Captain Weber, if you will pull the *Blue Sea* into the beach, and drop the front ramp, we'll have the teams pull the wagons off the *Blue Sea* onto land. Then the wagons, horse teams, and extra horses can be taken to our local livery stable for safe keeping and care of the stock. Then we can take care of the legal requirements after you anchor in the bay."

"Kelly," the captain quietly mentioned, "I must keep one man on board at all times. There is a sea law—well so say some that it's a law—but anyway, if I don't keep a man on this ship who is assigned to this ship, anybody can come on board the vessel and take command as an abandoned vessel, especially when we are flying foreign colors. Do you understand?"

"Yes, Captain Weber, that will not be a problem. I'm sure everyone in town will know this vessel belongs to you."

"Another thing, Kelly…after we unload the wagons and extra horses, and anchor in the harbor, we have a small skiff we use for times like this to go back and forth between ship to shore. Is there any particular place I need to anchor for several days?"

Cocking his head to one side, Kelly said, "No, I don't know of any place special. I guess just out of the way. And, yes sir, Captain Weber, that is a great idea having a small skiff. I know you won't try to make a run for it, because there is a Navy ship stationed at Sitka, and you know you can't outrun that steel-hull, double-rotary gunboat."

Smiling, Captain Weber joked, "You are right, Kelly, and I would not even try. I really don't have any reason to try to escape…do I? Where do I meet you when we get on shore?"

"Go directly to the Deputy Sheriff's office. Ask anybody in town and they will direct you." Looking straight into Captain Weber's eyes, Kelly confessed, as he shook his head and sighed, "I sure hope not. I'm going to do my best to keep you out of hot water. You and your crew have made this trip down the Stikine River possible." Pausing for a moment, he added, "Yes, let's dock, get rid of the wagons and teams, anchor in the harbor, and then you come back on shore to do the legal stuff."

"OK—Chief, summon the crew up here so I can explain what we are going to do. Kelly, you get your guys and get the teams hooked up ready to move at a moment's notice."

"Yes sir…rather, aye, aye sir," Kelly said, smiling at Captain Weber.

"Get out of here," Captain Weber joked with Kelly.

As Kelly, Payuk, and Fisher mounted harness and hooked the teams up to two of the wagons getting ready to drive the teams off

171

the *Blue Sea*, they could feel Captain Weber maneuvering the vessel so as the teams could be driven off the forward ramp.

Suddenly Stan slid down the railing of the stairs, and quickly moved toward the front of the vessel and called, "Payuk come and help me get the forward ramp down."

Quickly, Payuk glanced at Kelly, and Kelly nodded his consent.

Kelly watched as Stan and Payuk opened a large door and slowly lowered the front ramp down with a crank that loosened a cable that lowered or raised the ramp.

Hearing the front end sliding onto the shore, Stan and Payuk finished letting the ramp down to set firmly on the beach. "OK," Stan hailed Kelly, "Let's get the first wagons off."

Urging the teams ahead slowly by gently slapping the reins on their backs, Kelly and Fisher drove the two teams and the first two wagons out the large opening and across the forward ramp, and onto the beach up to level, firm ground. Payuk had quickly followed the teams as Kelly had motioned to him. "Payuk, you drive this second team to Keller's Livery and tell Jeffery or Keller we have two more wagons and several horses besides the two teams coming his way."

"OK, Kelly," Payuk hailed back.

"Also, Payuk, stop by on the way back, and let Deputy Sheriff Marlin know he is going to have some business."

Waving his understanding, Payuk urged the team onto the dirt street of Wrangell on the way to the livery stable with Fisher following.

When Fisher and Payuk returned from Keller's Livery, Kelly helped them quickly hook up the two teams to the last two wagons. Kelly kept hearing the engine of the *Blue Sea* roaring as Captain Weber kept the *Blue Sea* tight against the shore with the forward ramp. Slapping the reins on the horse's backs, Fisher and Payuk drove the third and fourth wagon off the *Blue Sea*. Following the wagon out, Kelly helped Stan haze the extra horses out of the vessel, with Kelly hanging onto their hackamore leads. Standing on the shore, Kelly waved to Stan as Stan eased the front ramp up into place.

"See you later," Kelly hailed to Stan.

Stan hurriedly hailed back, "Now I've got to let the captain know we can back off this beach before it damages the keel."

Nodding, Kelly watched and thought, *Well, damn, we got it done. Now I have to get everybody to see Deputy Sheriff Marlin.* Then he saw the *Blue Sea* surge backward, the bow dropped down, and she was again afloat.

CHAPTER FOURTEEN

Neil Baxter was the first one of his group to the meeting place that had several stools cut. "I'm sorry we don't have chairs, but there are several blocks to sit on, or the ground. I would recommend you find a comfortable spot on the ground because this meeting could take a while."

"Come on up, everyone. Let's make a closed circle for better eye-to-eye communication," James encouraged.

"This better not take damn long," one of the cabin owners declared. "I have to get back to my wood cutting."

Listening to several cabin owners grumbling about the mining destroying the landscape, and seeing everybody settled, James started the meeting. "OK, everyone, I believe you all know why this meeting was called. I'm James Kincaid and that gentleman over there," he motioned toward Moaka, "is Moaka. We both work for the Department of Agriculture and our office is in Wrangell. The boss of the mining operation is Mr. Ferrell Jones. I, Moaka, Mr. Jones, and all of you," James motioned around the group, "have come together to solve a common problem. The meeting will be non-structured and that means anybody can be recognized by me to have their say. I will make a few opening statements and then I will throw the floor open for questions or discussions. I want to thank each and every one of you for coming to this important meeting. It demonstrates the interest in the matter at hand.

"Mr. Jones," James motioned toward him, "has a legal permit to sluice mine on this slope. The permit was issued to him by the Alaska Mining Council in Juneau, and the claim is for five years. He has broken no laws and has stayed within his border claim. Some—"

Interrupting James, a hand went up and the man started talking before James could react. "Baxter," the cabin owner gruffly asked, "Is that the claim you read yesterday?"

Looking back at the man, Baxter answered, "Yes, Arnes, several of us that were here read it."

James let Baxter answer, then continued, "Let me finish, then we can discuss things all we want. As I was saying, some of you read the claim and found it to be legal for the mining operation to have free flow from the mine down to water's edge. Herein lays the problem. The sluice tailings are causing a few problems like destruction of new growth, laying down a hard base enabling erosion to occur more rapidly, destroying small animal populations, and the sluice tailings are unsightly. Mr. Jones," James motioned toward him, "has acknowledged these are problems and is willing to work with the cabin owners to solve the problem." Pausing, James looked down at his notes, which was a blank sheet of paper, wanting the group to think about what he had just said before he mentioned the flume. "It has been suggested that a flume be built from the mining area to water's edge to carry the sluice tailings so as not to disturb the ground or ground cover. Now are there any questions that I or Mr. Jones can answer for you?"

Standing, Baxter began, "I want to say a few words before the discussion starts. Jones has volunteered eight or nine men for this project. He has also said he would make his diesel-powered flat saw available for the job, and you know how much work that will save. Mr. Kincaid has said that he could arrange for cutting of trees without going through the governmental works trying to get a timber-cutting permit." He paused for a moment. "Now we have the timber, we have the saw, and we have some labor from the mine operation. All we as cabin owners have to do is obligate some folks to help build the flume. It will take some funds for diesel and bolts and other hardware, which can be divided up between us." Baxter sighed and walked to where his stool was and muttered, "I've said my say."

One of the cabin owners stood and said, "I'm Wilbur Nelson. I live down around Hoqur Cove and I can't see that this is any of my problem. I don't have time to be obligating any of my time to this crazy project, and I damn sure ain't gonna give you any money for it."

No sooner than Nelson returned to his place seated on the ground than another cabin owner stood and remarked, "My name is Fred Brass. I live a short ways from here toward Hoqur Cove and I realize the sluice tailings make a mess, but they always do. That's part of sluice mining. Why does this mining operation surprise anybody? I can see Baxter's concern because it is right next door to him, but most of us are away from the sluice tailing."

Hearing grumbling from the cabin owners who agreed with Nelson and Brass, James was getting the feeling he was on the losing side of this argument.

Suddenly a voice came from the back of the circle. "I would like to speak." James's heart came up in his throat, and at the same time he heard Moaka groan. James turned to Mr. Jones and Mr. Baxter. "OK with you guys?"

Both men shrugged their shoulder as if saying OK.

"OK, gentlemen, this is Janet Moore. She and her father have lived around these parts for many years as they fished, hunted, and trapped for a living. "OK, Miss Moore, you have the floor." James motioned her to speak.

"I have come to this meeting today because I have heard Mr. Kincaid and Moaka talking in our camp. We are close to water's edge, not too far away from where the sluice tailings are pouring into the water and then at low water pouring onto the beach. To say the least it is an unsightly sight. I agree with the arguments that the sluice tailings are destroying the small growth of trees and underbrush, that the sluice tailings are making it harder for small animals to survive, and that the sluice tailings are making the mountain slope more susceptible to erosion. Moreover, the mining operation does not make a good impression of this beautiful area. Mining itself does not give a good impression because of all the ground that it consumes and destroys. All of these things I have mentioned this morning are true."

Turning slightly to look around the circle of men, Janet continued, "Why do you think the Territory of Alaska issues permits for fishing, hunting, trapping, mining, timber harvest, and whatever else? They believe the territory will grow and they need to control activities to nurture the lands and wildlife. Where the laws are not doing their job of caring for the land and animals, there must be other controls, or other mechanisms put in place by the public."

Stepping to the edge of the circle of men, Janet picked up a sack and carried it to the center of the meeting. "Here, take a look at these drawings." She dumped the rocks and bark on the ground. "I have done these in this very area you say you are not concerned with. I sell these to people from the lower forty-eight or to everyone that likes nice art of land, water, and animals." Handing them out, Janet was glad they were impressed. "Now, as you look at these drawings I want you to just imagine these lands being destroyed by careless men who did not care what they were doing to the land or game, but rather they took what they wanted and left a mess for Mother Nature to take many, many years to repair. If we do not take a stand and employ other measures to save our way of life and the reason you came here, it will someday be destroyed. Sure, Mr. Baxter may be the only one that has a problem now, but what about next year? Another mining operation could come to Hoqur Cove and at least one of you is from there and if we don't figure out what to do here at Terrace Point, the problem starts all over again. I think it behooves us all to really get behind this flume idea. It sounds like it could work if constructed properly, and I know there are men here who know how to do the job. You have moved here and built your cabins in a wonderful place to live and raise children—don't let this opportunity slip by to save all of that." Gathering up her samples and putting them in the sack, Janet returned to where she had been seated before she spoke.

One man started clapping and the entire group clapped for Janet and her speech. When the clapping stopped, the same man raised his hand and said, "Young lady, I don't know about the flume, but my wife sure would like a couple of those drawings to hang on her walls in the cabin."

Everyone laughed as one man chided, "Hell, Mel, she will probably teach your wife how to draw. If she can draw as good as she talks, she's got my vote on the flume thing."

Another man hailed, "Will the Stone Mountain Mining meet their obligation of what they said they would do?"

Ferrell Jones stepped up and declared, "Absolutely, and more if we have to. We don't want to make a mess of things around here. All we need is the logs cut to size and skidded to the saw station and my men will do the flat cutting. I have a good idea how many and what size of timbers we will need. I figure it will take about three weeks to complete, once the timbers have been cut. In the meantime some of you can be making the dowels we'll need for fasteners. We have the drill and bits for hole drilling for the dowels. The structure will last

178

much longer with dowels holding most of the loads together. We will need a few nails and bolts and nuts, but not too many. Along with the cost of the diesel, there should not be too much out-of-pocket expense."

"Thanks, Mr. Jones. Is there any more discussion on the flume job?" James waited for several moments and nobody came forward with any more discussion points, so he explained, "OK, we will have a vote. I will pass around a sheet of paper and it will have two columns. One column will be marked 'YES' and the other column will be for 'NO.'" Marking the paper and showing it to everyone so all would understand, James advised, "Don't worry about having to write anything. What we need is for you to just mark on the yes column for the flume or on the no column for not wanting the flume. Are there any questions before I start this paper around?"

James sensed that the group was tense with the vote coming. He knew that there were some who did not really want to do this job, but it did make sense when Janet had her say...*What a kid,* James thought.

Calmly, James handed the paper to Mr. Baxter, who made the first mark and then passed it on to the next cabin owner.

As the cabin owners quietly checked yes or no on the paper Baxter had passed around, James and Moaka sat silently.

As the last cabin owner checked the paper, he handed the paper to Jones. Jones looked at the paper without expression and marked the sheet. Handing the paper to James, Jones commented, "Well, that's done."

James considered the vote, and as he looked up, he smiled and pointed to all the cabin owners, and excitedly advised, "You're going to build a flume!"

Instantly, everyone started clapping and cheering. Baxter stood and faced the group, "This will be an easy job with Mr. Jones doing all the flat cutting for the timbers. Before everybody leaves, we need to speak with everybody about the jobs that need to be done, either short or long range." Glancing toward Jones, Baxter asked, "Mr. Jones, can you make yourself available for some of that discussion?"

Nodding, he responded, "Yes, of course. That way I can explain some details I need everybody to know."

"Mr. Baxter," James said and attained his attention, "could Moaka and I sit in on the planning meeting you're going to have?"

"Yes, of course."

James nodded and thought, *That Baxter, yesterday he looked like a bum, and today he is shaved with clean clothes, he even combed his hair.*

James walked back down the slope to Red and placed some paperwork into his saddlebags as Moaka came up behind him and commented, "Miss make good talk."

Turning slightly, James agreed. "Yeah, Moaka, she seems to be well-versed in making her opinion known."

James and Moaka stood with the group of cabin owners as Baxter explained the jobs that would need to be done before actual construction began. "We need to skid the logs to the flat saw. Mr. Jones has already given us the dimensions of the log the flat saw will accommodate. We need two or three of you to make dowels." Looking to Jones, Baxter asked, "How big a diameter of dowels will be needed?"

"I have two sizes of drill bits that will work: one-inch and three-quarter-inch. The dowels can be close to those dimensions because we will drive them in using quaking aspen sap. The dowels need to be fairly uniform in size, but as long as you can make them, then we can cut the length we need at the site. A good spoke shave will save a lot of time."

Nodding, Baxter continued, "We need to take up a collection soon for some hardware and diesel. How much should we start with on the collection, Mr. Jones?"

Shaking his head, he answered, "I'm not sure, but probably about ten dollars. That will cover the diesel for a while and some bolts, nuts, and washers to start. Those supplies can be gotten in Wrangell."

"OK," Baxter declared. "When do we want to start getting the logs to the flat saw and," looking at James, "where can we cut logs from for this project?"

Shaking his head, James replied, "Anywhere you want; just no clear cutting. I will label this harvest as a thinning cut, that way you can pretty much get the trees anywhere."

"Good," remarked Baxter. "Now, when do we start?"

Fred Brass spoke up. "Well, today is Tuesday. For me I have a couple of things I need to do, but I could start falling next Monday."

Quickly, several other cabin owners spoke up and volunteered to fall, bump limbs, or skid.

Jones advised, "I'll keep a log of what comes in and how many more logs will be needed. My men will do all the flat sawing and stack the timbers tight. Did we agree that red cedar would be the best wood for the job?"

Baxter nodded his head. "Yes, Mr. Jones, I think that was the thought. OK," Baxter reiterated, "We'll start next Monday with the trees and dowels. How many can made dowels and bring them here to the site...Oh, also wrap them tight so they won't warp so bad."

Several hands went up as one cabin owner asked, "How many dowels do we need?"

Mr. Jones quickly stated, "Let's start with about two hundred about two-feet long."

Holding his hands in the air, Baxter cheered, "Well, by golly we are going to get this job done. As this job goes along, we will need other things, so be ready to move in any new direction."

Cheering, the cabin owners started shaking hands and vowing to get the job done.

James looked at Baxter and Jones and nodded. "Well, by the damn, Mr. Baxter and Mr. Jones, I think you are on your way to getting the flume built. Moaka and I will be in our camp down below here for the night, but tomorrow morning we will be leaving to go back to Wrangell. Don't concern yourself with the timber permit; I'll take care of that for you. If I don't see you again for a while," he and Moaka extended their hands, "be careful." The men shook hands and Moaka and James left the camp.

James pointed to a group of men that surrounded Janet Moore. "What they do?" Moaka asked.

"I can't quite get it all, but it sounds like they are congratulating her for her speech and looking at some of the drawings she has made."

"She speak good," Moaka added.

Waving at Janet, James hailed, "We'll meet you at camp."

Janet waved back to signal she heard James.

. . .

"Moaka, before we go back to camp, I want to ride up and around the mining camp. I want to check on the supply of suitable red cedar they are going to need for this flume."

Riding to the north and heading above the mining camp, James was pleasantly surprised to see so much red cedar about ten to twelve inches in diameter. "Moaka, these trees are perfect. Cut them down, bump the limbs off, and use horses to skid the logs to the saw."

"All not far away. How many trees needed for flume?"

Shrugging, James responded, "Heck, I don't know. I don't even have any idea. Mr. Jones said he would keep track of the timbers and I trust him. Besides, why would a mining outfit care about harvesting timber."

"Tree need be thinned. Too many try to grow."

Reining up Red, James agreed, "Yeah, Moaka, this country could stand a good tree trimming. Only thing is, the timber outfits don't make much money thinning forests, they want the big logs. Well, let's get back to the camp; Miss Moore should be back there by now."

"She want to go Wrangell. She say maybe good opportunity for her."

"She's probably right, Moaka."

Arriving back at the camp, James and Moaka found Janet making coffee on a freshly built fire. "What kept you guys?"

James smiled. "The way those cabin owners were around you, I thought you might be there for a while. How did they like your drawings?"

Shaking her head, Janet answered, "I could not believe it; they were very happy to pay good money for something I have been throwing into the fire for years. Yes!" exclaimed Janet. "They did like them, and digging into her pocket, she dug out several dollars. "See," and in a disbelieving tone she continued. "I can't believe it. This is the most money I've had for years."

"Kincaid say picture drawing sell good," Moaka expressed.

"And he was right, Moaka. Isn't it wonderful?"

After a supper of salt pork, biscuits, and flour gravy, Janet jumped to the job of cleaning up.

"I help," Moaka volunteered.

"If you want to be of help, you could go pick some berries for in the morning, and I'll show you the best pancakes you've ever eaten," Janet bragged.

Pouring a cup of coffee, James wandered off toward the beach. *I hope Baxter and Jones don't let this flume thing get dropped because of some stupid reason. I purposely let them have the lead so the rest of the cabin owners would feel like the Department was not pushing them. Hell, I don't have a lot of controls over environmental issues anyway.*

Sighing as he walked along the beach enjoying his coffee, he spied Moaka scrambling among the bushes picking berries for tomorrow's pancakes. He smiled. *I wonder when Moaka will want to go north to Barrow.* Kicking a stick out of the way from where he was walking, he kept thinking about it. *He will probably want to go pretty soon, I should think. That will be fine. I know Payuk wants to go to work for the Department of Agriculture as the Native American Liaison that Moaka is now. Moaka does a fine job in that capacity, but I believe Payuk could relate to the Native Tribes better because he is part of the tribes. Oh well, we'll see, soon I hope.*

"Here, missy," Moaka said as he handed a metal bowl full of berries to Janet.

"Oh, thank you, Moaka," she said as she examined them. "These will be just perfect."

Walking over to the fire, Moaka picked up the coffeepot, poured a steaming hot cup of coffee, and sat down next to the fire. "Where Kincaid?"

"He got a cup of coffee and walked off toward the beach."

"He be back; it get dark soon."

"And I'm back already." James flipped the dregs of his coffee into the fire as the fire sizzled with the moisture. He perched on his stool that Moaka had made for him out of a short log and sighed, and nodded with contentment.

Moaka lifted his head and looked at Kincaid. "We sit at many fire. With Anore and Bray sitting at our side. Will Kincaid come to Barrow?"

Smiling at Moaka and folding his hands together, James responded, "You are a true friend and I would never abandon you. I will come to Barrow."

Both men looked back into the fire as the flames gently lifted into the darkness of the night.

. . .

Next morning, James and Moaka woke up to the surprise of Janet preparing pancakes and hot coffee perking beside the warm fire. "It's about time you guys got up. Runback and I have been up since daylight. There is warm water in that bucket," she pointed, "to wash your face and hands before breakfast. I have not started to cook yet, so if you want to shave before breakfast you can."

Moaka felt his face. "No shave."

James did the same, and decided to shave. "Since we are going back to Wrangell today I think I will shave this morning. Will breakfast wait, Miss Moore?"

"Yes, but don't tarry."

"Miss Moore, I have not heard that word for a long time. How do you know such a word?"

"I read everything I get my hands on. My father always said you have to be good with words and sums."

Later, setting the jar of jam down away from the fire, Moaka commented, "I eat one more pancake. Missy, you make good pancake. Need water horses before we leave."

"I've had enough," James admitted, "but they sure were good with the berries in them and the jam," and he set the metal plate down next to the fire.

"Just leave the plates and utensils by the fire, and I'll take care of them while you guys break camp. Mr. Kincaid, you said we will get back to Wrangell today. What about my boat?"

"Miss Moore," James sympathized, "the boat you have is in bad need of repair, and I'm not sure it can be repaired at all. The wood is badly rotted in several places. I believe it has seen better days. Why don't you leave it here and have good memories."

Sighing and kneeing down to clean the plate and utensils that Moaka just handed her, she confessed, "It does leak a lot, and it kept me busy dipping the water out of it." Shrugging, Janet admitted, "Yeah, I guess it is about time to move on to a better boat."

Getting the tent down and folded, the fire doused, the bedrolls rolled up, including Janet's, and the food and cooking pans and utensils cleaned, everything was mounted on the cross bucks of the packhorse Moaka had brought.

Looking the campsite over, James mentioned, "Miss Moore, you can ride up behind me." He lifted his boot from the stirrup. "Here, Miss Moore, put your foot in the stirrup and grab the back of the saddle and come on up."

Handing Runback to James, she moved in one graceful motion and settled herself behind James as he handed her Runback.

James hailed to Moaka, "You ready?"

"I ready, Kincaid."

Walking the horses at a steady pace, James, Moaka, and Janet reached a good stopping point to take a break. "OK," James called, "let's give the horses a break and let's rest our butts also."

Right away, Janet rushed to the shore as Runback found a bush. She gazed intensely. "What a wonderful place to stop. Do either of you know this place?"

Moaka looked at James and just shrugged, and James answered, "It looks like an old fishing wharf. There are a lot of them scattered around Wrangell Island. Most of them were established by the early settlers to Wrangell Island in the 1870s, soon after the purchase of Alaska from Russia. Some of them might even be Russian originals."

As Janet was riding up behind James, she asked, "Can I ask you about Wrangell?"

"Sure, go ahead."

"Are you married, and if so what does your wife do?"

"Yes, I'm married, and my wife is a school teacher and we have two children and an old dog."

"How big is Wrangell?"

Sighing, James estimated, "I think about three thousand or so. Sometimes it varies from season to season."

"Are people nice?"

Quickly turning half around in the saddle, James stammered, "Nice?" And shrugging, he continued. "I guess they are. They seem to be average folks to me."

"Is it a good place to settle down?"

"Yes." James nodded. "I think it is a good place to settle down."

And the questions went on and on...finally they reached Wrangell late in the afternoon.

James headed straight for the office to get rid of his personnel gear. The front door was locked and Moaka unlocked the door so the gear could be put in the office for the next morning. James grabbed his personnel pack as he told Janet, "Miss Moore, take anything you want for the night because you will not be back here this evening. You will be spending the night at Mrs. Mackly's Parker Boarding House."

Locking the door to the Department of Agriculture, James, Janet, and Moaka headed for Shane Keller's Livery. Letting Janet slide off, James dismounted. Janet let Runback down and he started watering posts. Jeffery came walking out and saw who it was and declared, "Boy, are you a sight for sore eyes. You would not believe what Payuk and Kelly have pulled off."

"Where is Shane?" James asked.

Jeffery waved his hand like it didn't matter, "Well after this morning and afternoon we got a little slow so he went home for the day. I think he got tired out some with all the new horses." Shaking his head, Jeffery remarked again, "You won't believe it."

Feeling a little tired after his ride from Terrace Point, James advised Jeffery, "Well, take care of the horses, and I'll see Shane in the morning." Pausing, James asked, "What in the devil are you smiling at?"

"You ain't going to believe it."

"Well, take care of the horses...oh, by the way, this is Janet Moore. She will be living around here for a while. Miss Moore this is Jeffery Maxwell, he works at the livery for Shane Keller."

"Nice meeting you, Janet. I hope to see you around our little town, and welcome to Wrangell."

"Moaka, I'll see you in the morning. Miss Moore, let's you and I walk over to Mrs. Mackly. She is the sweetest gal you will ever meet,

188

and I'm sure she will be glad to get the help you can give her in the boarding house."

Calling Runback, she exclaimed, "Hey, what do I do with Runback?"

Breathing out quickly, James hollered at Jeffery, "Jeffery, have you got a place for this dog for tonight?"

"Sure, Mr. Kincaid. I'll put him in one of the rabbit cages. They are pretty big and it won't take much room for that little guy. I'll even give him some scraps form the Steak and Stack."

As James and Janet were walking away, Janet looked back at Jeffery holding Runback. "Take good care of him."

"Oh, I will, Janet. I like animals."

"Don't worry about that dog, Janet. Jeffery will take good care of him," James added.

Walking up the wooden steps that led into the front of Parker Boarding House, James opened the screen door and let Janet walk in first. "Turn in here, Miss Moore," he said as he pointed to the right.

As Janet entered the kitchen, she paused and looked intently. Turning back to James she gleefully noted, "What a wonderful cookstove. It has four burners, two warming ovens, and a large baking oven. What a great stove."

Hearing the conversation, Mrs. Mackly came into the kitchen, surprised. "James, what are you doing here at this time of day?"

"I know it is late, Mrs. Mackly, but I have a problem. Or rather we have a problem." He motioned toward Janet. "Mrs. Mackly, I would like you to meet Janet Moore; Janet Moore, this is Mrs. Mackly. She owns and operates this establishment."

"So what is your problem, James, and how can I help?"

189

"When I was at Terrace Point, this young girl," James nodded toward Janet, "came wandering into our camp. Her father had been killed by a bear a while back and she was living out in the woods alone, eating whatever she could find."

Without warning, Janet jumped into the conversation, "Oh, we— my dog, Runback, and I—had lots to eat. We had fish, roots, berries, and an occasional squirrel I would shoot or trap."

Shaking his head, James continued. "Well, Mrs. Mackly, she needs a place to live and a job. I thought maybe you could use her around here for cooking, cleaning, and general work and give her one of the old back rooms for board."

"Hold your hands out, Janet. Turn them over. How old are you, Janet?"

"I'm eighteen, and I can read well and do sums. I would work real hard, Mrs. Mackly, and you won't be sorry if you hire me."

Mrs. Mackly looked at James. "She just wandered into your camp?"

"Yes."

"I have a small dog and his name is Runback, but he will not cause you any problems. He minds good and will eat table scraps."

"Can you cook?"

"Yes, Mrs. Mackly. I can cook and I enjoy doing it."

"There are beds to change almost every day, floors to clean, windows to clean, laundry to be done. I serve a meal in the morning and in the evening for my guests. There is a lot of work here—are you still interested in working here?"

"Oh yes, Mrs. Mackly."

"OK," Mrs. Mackly looked at James, "I will solve your problem. She can try the job and if she does well I'll keep her on permanent."

"Thanks, Mrs. Mackly. I figured I could count on you. Now I need to get home before Suzette sends out a hunting party for me."

As James started for the front door, Janet ran to him and gave him a hug, and muttered, "Oh thank you, Mr. Kincaid. You don't know how I appreciate this."

Hearing the screen door slam, Mrs. Mackly waved to Janet. "Follow me and I'll show you where you will sleep."

Walking from the dining room and kitchen down to the end of the hallway, Mrs. Mackly unlocked a wooden door and walked in, leaving the door open. "I did not put the new power light in this room because up to this point it has been a storage room. You will have to use a lantern. The privy is right out the back door. There is a good single bed for you to sleep on and a water bowl and pitcher with a mirror on the chest." Pausing and looking at Janet, she continued. "We have to do something about your clothes. Look in that big box over there," Mrs. Mackly pointed, "and you will find some very good women's clothes. The clothes were left in the rooms from folks down below. You are about normal size so you should find plenty to wear. As far as I'm concerned, you can have anything you want in there if you stay working here. Are there any questions?"

"Yes, Mrs. Mackly...was wondering what time I need to get up to start cooking breakfast. I mean I need to start a fire and all."

"In the morning I will get you up in plenty of time. Tomorrow I'll get you a lantern and an alarm clock. You can tie your dog up right outside the door so he won't bother anybody. You've got to remember that a lot of folks come here and they don't all love dogs."

"Can I keep him in the room at night? He won't piddle on the floor."

Nodding OK, Mrs. Mackly responded, "Just keep him quiet. Turning to go out the door, Mrs. Mackly advised, "Put clean clothes on in the morning, wash your face and hands, and comb your hair. I'll see you in the morning."

As Mrs. Mackly went out she left the door slightly open so the light in the hallway could penetrate into the room slightly.

Janet stood in the faintly lit room and started to cry. Walking over to the door she silently closed the door and walked toward the bed. The window let a small amount of light in the room from the street as she lay down on the soft mattress and fell asleep.

CHAPTER FIFTEEN

Stomping his feet off on the wooden porch deck below the back door, Bray slowly came out of his dog house and yawned. James walked over to Bray and quietly spoke. "Yeah, I know, Father Time is taking its toll on you, old boy." James reached down and petted Bray's head lightly. "Yeah, your old buddy, Anore, had to go and so will you. Hell, we all will." James sighed. Noticing that Bray hadn't eaten all his supper that Thomas had fed him, James shook his head. "Damn, I hate to see you go."

Opening the back door, Sadie came running to greet her father. Kneeling down, James picked up Sadie and playfully patted her butt. "How's my little girl been?"

"Thomas went to the doctor."

Looking surprised, James said, "Well, did he come home or did he stay with the doctor?"

Using one of her tiny fingers, Sadie pointed. "He is in his room."

James grabbed her tiny hand and kissed it before setting her on the floor to run into the living room yelling, "Daddy is home!"

Suzette set her darning down. "How was the trip to Terrace Point? Don't worry about Thomas, he fell off one of the high bars at school and put a gash in the back of his head; he'll be just fine."

Standing close together, James wrapped his arms around Suzette and spoke quietly. He murmured, "You feel good," as he kissed her gently.

Breaking their embrace, Suzette asked, "Are you hungry—have you had supper yet?"

"Yes, I am hungry. Had to stop over at Mrs. Mackly's Parker Boarding House on the way back from the livery, to deliver Janet Moore."

"Who is Janet Moore?" questioned Suzette, as she began getting some leftovers out of the icebox.

"She's a young girl that came into Moaka's and my camp one night...her and that damn dog. She was dirty, hungry, and her clothes were a mess.

"Where's a towel?" James asked as he had just washed his face and hands.

"Here." Suzette threw him a towel.

Drying his face and hands, James continued, "Yeah, she just wandered into our camp. I had to laugh when her little dog came charging through the camp barking and squealing. Moaka quickly put his rifle up to his shoulder and was going to shoot the poor dog before I yelled at him."

Laughing, Suzette quickly replied, "I would've liked to be there for that."

"Yes, it was funny." James shook his head. "Anyway, she and her father had lived out in the open for some time hunting, fishing, picking berries, and eating squirrels. Then her father was killed by a bear and she was alone. She seems to be quite smart; she reads well and knows her sums. Her dad made sure of that before he got killed. Oh, and she is a fine speaker. You should have heard her give those cabin owners 'what for' when they were not really in favor of the flume that needed to be built." He shook his head. "She sure got after them."

Suzette set some warmed-up leftover soup, some ham, and bread on the table. "When you get finished, I would like for you to come into the living room; I have something to tell you."

"OK, Suzette." James thought, *Now what in the world does she have to say to me? Both kids seem to be alright. I hope everything is alright at the school. We aren't going anywhere. I don't know, I guess I'll find out.* Finishing his supper, he asked, "Have we got any coffee?"

"Yes, and I think it's still hot."

Pouring a cup of coffee, James retired to the living room and sat in his favorite chair and commented, "OK, Suzette, what is on your mind?"

Smiling at James from behind her darning basket, Suzette announced, "You are going to be a father again."

Smiling, James rocked in his chair. "It's a good thing. Three is what we wanted, so now we will have that many. Do you have a name picked out?"

"Oh, don't be silly. I just found out that I was pregnant today. I have suspected it for a while."

Standing up from his chair, James walked over to Suzette, and leaning down gently kissed her on the cheek. "You are a fine wife and I love you very much, and thanks for supper. I am going to bed. We'll talk some more in the morning, but right now I'm too tired."

Next morning James was up early. Apparently Kelly and Payuk had gotten back from Twin Forks Mining, and James had not been in any mood to listen to Jeffery last night because he had to get Janet Moore set up with Mrs. Mackly.

Shaving and eating a quick breakfast of hot cereal and toast that Suzette fixed for him and the kids, James left the house early. Stepping from the back step, James looked at Bray, still lying next to his house. James walked over to him and knelt down and rubbed Bray on the back of his neck, "Good old boy, how you doing this morning?" Looking down at Bray, who didn't get up, James said, "I'm going to miss you, old boy."

Walking to the office of the Department of Agriculture, James was met by Moaka before they reached the office, and Moaka asked, "Can leave soon?"

"Yes, Moaka, as soon as I can get the letter mailed to Sid Bonner and he returns it with his approval. I know he will approve your transfer. That will take about two weeks or so. Will that be soon enough?"

Nodding, Moaka said, "Yes, I want go."

"Good morning," Sara greeted James and Moaka. "Kelly and Payuk are in Kelly's office with another man. They are waiting for you."

James went to his office and took a seat behind his desk and opened the day's log. And Moaka went to his office.

"Good morning, James," Kelly and Payuk said as they came into James's office. Kelly immediately advised him, "Payuk and I have a person you will want to talk to." Letting Captain Weber come forward, Kelly introduced him: "This is Captain Charles Weber of the *Blue Sea*. The *Blue Sea* is the large, three-decker vessel anchored in the harbor. And Captain Weber, this is James Kincaid, the manager around here for the Department of Agriculture."

Captain Weber stepped forward and extended his hand, and James stood behind his desk and rigorously shook hands with the him. James motioned for the captain to have a chair, as Kelly and Payuk did. "Sara," James called, "You got any coffee made yet?"

"Yes sir, Mr. Kincaid. I'll be right in with it."

James sat back in his chair just as Sara entered the room with a tray of four cups of coffee. Handing James's cup to him, she put the tray down on a small table for the other men to take their own cup. "Thank you, Sara," everyone said.

"Oh and Sara will you get your pad and come in here and take some notes on this meeting we are going to have? Also tell Moaka I would like him in on this meeting."

"Yes, Mr. Kincaid, I'll tell Moaka and be right back."

Resting back in his chair, James looked at Captain Weber. "How long have you been the skipper of the *Blue Sea*, Captain Weber?" Before the captain could answer, James interrupted him. "Excuse me, Captain Weber, but I want you to meet another member of my staff. This gentleman is Moaka...don't worry about his last name, you could not say it anyway. Moaka this is Captain Charles Weber of the *Blue Sea* vessel that is anchored in the harbor." Moaka and the captain shook hands and Moaka found a chair for the meeting.

"Now Captain Weber, go ahead," James said.

Smiling, Captain Weber said, "Just call me Charles. Sometimes I like to feel like I'm off the vessel. I have been on the *Blue Sea* for about eleven years." Taking a drink of his coffee, he continued. "I was skipper on another small craft for the company for about eight years before they gave me the *Blue Sea*. She is a fine, sturdy craft."

"What company do you work for?" James inquired.

"The company name is Braddock Shipping out of Seattle and Portland. It is a large company with twenty or so vessels under their flag."

"The *Blue Sea* looks to be quite large as I see from the shore. What is her capacity?"

"She's 450 tons structure and freight at 130 feet long. She has three decks with one lower hole deck. In open water she'll do 14 knots. She was built in Seattle in 1898 and is still holding strong."

"That's quite a job sailing that big a vessel up the Stikine River," James commented.

197

"Yeah, we did not want to do it, but the Twin Forks Mining and Dredging Company paid the company well and made the risk worthwhile. I don't like fooling around with the estuary."

"How long have you been shipping for Twin Forks Mining?"

"This is our second season. My crew of four men rather like the idea about river travel because the ocean gets pretty boring after a while. Course we don't go way out in the ocean, but rather just in the channels."

"What kind of freight do you normally haul?"

"The *Blue Sea* will haul most anything. Bulk, stakes, containers, and we haul a lot of livestock from Seattle and Portland to outlying areas. I've even hauled stock up to your livery here at Wrangell. Mostly horses and a few cows, but pigs and sheep also."

Instantly Sara gasped, "You've hauled stock for my husband; he owns the livery. His name is Shane Keller."

Nodding, Charles confirmed, "Yes, I think that was the man's name."

Everyone smiled as Sara collected herself. "I'm sorry, Mr. Kincaid, I spoke up out of turn."

Laughing, James exclaimed, "Yes, you did Sara!" And I want you to do it again whenever you feel the urge."

Everyone laughed.

"Charles, what do you haul for Twin Forks Mining?" James inquired.

Smiling, Charles looked at Kelly then to Payuk. "Well, these two fellows know for sure. Braddock Shipping contracted with Twin Forks to haul gold and animal skins and animal body parts from the convergence of the Iskut River into the Stikine River to Seattle. The contract also included hauling mining supplies and other food and general supplies back to the convergence."

"Did they seem to care if they got caught?"

"Funny thing about that," Charles submitted. "By being in Canada and being able to hoist Canada's flag, we were able to steam right on by inspections by Customs Enforcement by the United States. I guess there is so much freight coming and going up and down the Stikine River that United States Customs don't bother with them too much unless they have a reported problem with a certain shipping company."

Looking at Kelly, James asked, "How many skins are in this shipment?"

Sighing, Kelly shrugged. "We didn't get a good count yet, but there are elk, deer, muskrat, beaver, and even several wolf pelts. Payuk and I estimated probably around two hundred pelts all together."

"Charles, you said you freight gold for Twin Forks Mining. Have you got a strong box or a safe to carry the gold in for transport?"

"Huh." Charles smiled as he sipped his coffee. "I have never seen even an ounce of gold come out of that mining operation. I've only saw piles of hides going to Seattle tanneries."

"James..." Kelly jumped into the conversation. "Payuk and I have searched those wagons from tip to toe. We never found anything that even looked like gold. No hidden walls, no double bottoms, no compartments under the driver's seat...nothing."

Clearing his throat, James asked Kelly, "Have you notified Deputy Sheriff Marlin?"

"Yes," Kelly responded. "He made out the report that will be turned over to customs when we give him the word. I told him not to turn over the reports to customs until you approved them."

"Good." James nodded. "OK, gentlemen," he said as he scanned the men in his office, "where do we go from here?"

Kelly shrugged. "Well, I told Captain Weber that if he helped Payuk and me get the *Blue Sea* down the Stikine River into harbor at Wrangell that he and his men would be thought better of and they would have some consideration for their cooperation."

Crossing his arms and rolling back and forth in his chair, James looked at Charles and explained, "I think we can keep you and your men out of jail, but Braddock Shipping has some questions to answer from U.S. Customs here in Wrangell. Where are your men now, Charles?"

"Kelly told us they could stay aboard ship."

"Wait, James." Kelly held up his hand. "We are forgetting someone. He's the one who really helped us get on the boat with the wagons. His name is Fisher Minnow."

"What!" James exclaimed. "Fisher Minnow..." He shook his head. "OK, Kelly, go ahead."

"Well," Kelly explained, "He has helped us a lot and is willing to help more if we need him. He's important because he knows the full layout of the mining operation. He was one of the original drivers of the freight wagons; I had to kill the other one. I did not want to, but he came at me."

Payuk mumbled, "He was not the only one."

"Where is Fisher Minnow now, Kelly?" James asked.

"Right now he is sitting in Deputy Sheriff Marlin's jail with the door unlocked...well that's not quite right, Marlin has him cleaning the jail, washing floors, and cleaning windows. He doesn't mind because he has nowhere to go and he's living off the Borough of Wrangell. A place to sleep and three squares a day."

"What did Payuk mean just then when he said, he was not the only one?"

Glancing at Payuk, Kelly sighed deeply. "When we were talking to the bookkeeper of the Twin Forks Mines, this guy named Simmons came into the office firing a rifle everywhere claiming that we, Department of Agriculture people, killed his brother in a poaching raid. He shot Payuk," Payuk showed James where he'd been shot, "and I shot him with my .38 as fast as I could."

Moaka smiled. "Sound like you, Kincaid."

"Never you mind, Moaka." James smiled and shook his head.

"Also, just for the record," Kelly explained, "the bookkeeper, Jesse Holmes, has offered to help us if we want to build a case against Twin Forks Mining and Dredging Company."

"We'll talk about all that later, Kelly.

"Damn," James cursed as he leaned back in his chair. "I don't know. Charles, I think the best thing for you to do is contact, by letter, your legal department in Seattle. Let them know what is happening here, and have them advise you of what action you should take. Tell them that you and your men are not under any arrest and will probably be set free because of your cooperation with the local Department of Agriculture. Let them know that the shipping line is being charged with shipping illegal goods...skins and animal parts. You might also advise them that a legal staff needs to be at Wrangell as soon as possible."

"How long will that take, for a letter to get to Seattle?" Charles inquired.

"I will allow one of your men to act as an official currier for the Department of Agriculture to Braddock Shipping. I will give him all the necessary papers to clear all hurdles to get to Seattle as soon as possible. If he leaves today," James leaned back to check his calendar, "the letter should be in the hands of Braddock Shipping in two days."

James nodded toward Kelly. "Kelly will help Charles's man get a ticket and get on a ferry that goes straight through from Wrangell to Seattle. Is there anything else right now we need to take care of?"

Kelly spoke up. "There were four freight wagons on the *Blue Sea*. They are now at Keller's Livery as are the four teams of two horses. Two wagons have the furs and pelts and the other two have equipment and supplies for the mine. Keller put the horses in the corral and the freight wagons are in the barn behind Keller's Livery."

"OK, Kelly, you go get the man that is going to Seattle."

"Ah, wait," Kelly retorted. "Captain Weber, who do I get to go to Seattle?"

"That will be Chief Mate Hartford Harrison, but don't worry about that; I'm going with you to the *Blue Sea* to write a letter before he goes with you."

James pointed to Payuk. "I want you to go and check on the horses and wagons. I don't want anybody monkeying around with the wagons or stock. Tell Shane he can bill the Department of Agriculture for the feed for the horses."

Everybody left the room except Moaka and Sara. "Sara, I would like a draft of this meeting by tomorrow morning if possible."

"I'll take care of it, Mr. Kincaid. It should not be a problem."

"OK, Moaka. Hell, we don't have any problems with Terrace Point compared to what is going on up the Iskut River. What in the world are we going to do about the poaching, and how are we going to do it?"

"Kelly say he have help from bookkeeper and Minnow. That be good."

"You sure you want to go back to Barrow and leave all this behind?"

"You can handle it, Kincaid," Moaka mused and smiled.

"Have you decided when you want to go?"

"Maybe two week. Need sell house. Maybe Jeffery want. I give him good price."

"OK, Moaka, I want you to keep track of the Terrace Point problem and get back to me if there are any more problems. If I don't see you every day, just scribble down some notes for me to read and put them on my desk to read about the progress of Stone Mountain Mining and the cabin owners." Pausing, James nodded. "Yeah, you should go as soon as I get the paperwork back from Sid Bonner." He was thinking, *That should work out just about right.*

Quickly James stood from behind his desk. He left Moaka sitting in his office, and walked faster than normal by Sara, who was at her desk. and explained, "I'll be back in a minute." Hurrying after Kelly and Captain Weber, James hailed them.

Kelly heard James call his name and turned and waved, saying, "We'll wait."

As James got to Kelly and Captain Weber, he explained, "Charles, I need your man to take a letter to the Department's home office in Seattle to a man named Sid Bonner."

Nodding, Captain Weber agreed, "Sure, he will do that. My chief mate is a responsible man. He won't let you down."

"OK, Kelly, I'm going back to the office to write the letter; make sure the chief mate has it before you put him on the ferry."

"Sure thing, James, I won't forget."

"And Kelly," James advised, "I think that ferry you want to catch leaves Wrangell at four o'clock p.m."

Kelly said he understood, and he and the captain headed for the skiff for the *Blue Sea*.

Returning to his office, James asked Sara, "I know you're busy, but could you please come in my office and take a letter?"

203

James got settled behind his desk with his note pad and pencil, and Sara came right in. "OK, Mr. Kincaid, I'm ready."

James dictated the letter explaining Moaka's leaving and all situations pertaining to the move, like being on contract, living in Barrow, traveling from Barrow to Teshpuk, then north to the coast and back to Barrow. James also included the duties that Moaka would be responsible for, and outlined about buying dogs for his dog team, paying rent, buying food and clothing for him and the children, and general supplies for his duties. Finishing the dictation, James asked Sara, "Could I possibly have this letter in one hour?"

She smiled. "Yes, Mr. Kincaid. I know it's important so I will be sure to have it in one hour or less. I will also have the outside envelope addressed to Sid Bonner, Department of Agriculture, with the proper address for the person to follow. Also I've got the letter to Jacob Perkins ready to go, and I can mail it today when you sign it. That letter to the British Columbia Mining Office in Victoria is also ready for your signature."

"That would be just fine, Sara. I'll sign them now. After that I'm going over to Deputy Sheriff Marlin's office to meet this Fisher Minnow." Shaking his head, he smiled and mumbled, "Fisher Minnow."

Walking into Deputy Sheriff Marlin's office, James spied a young man on his hands and knees scouring the wooden floor. Walking over to a chair that was out of the way of the young man, James watched the skinny, brown-haired fellow working very hard to get the floor clean.

Fisher Minnow noticed James sitting across the room, but never stopped scouring the floor.

Clearing his throat, James asked, "Where is Deputy Marlin?"

Stopping for an instant, Fisher looked at James and replied, "I think he went to the mayor's office."

"What is your name?" James asked.

"My name is Fisher Minnow."

"Are you supposed to be in jail, Fisher Minnow?"

"Nah, I'm just staying here for a while so the Deputy Sheriff put me to work. I don't mind because I would rather be doing something than just sitting around. When I get finished with the front office floor, I'll go back and do all the jail cell floors."

"Did you come in on the *Blue Sea* earlier today?"

"Yes. I used to work for Twin Forks Mining, but I quit them. Kelly—he works for some guy named James Kincaid at the Department of Agriculture—told me because I helped get the wagons onto the *Blue Sea* and other work that he would talk to this James Kincaid to see if something could be worked out because I was only a driver for the freight wagons. Kelly said he knew several people in Seattle that would be glad to hire me on his recommendation."

Standing and walking to the door, James turned back to say, "You keep scouring, young man. It looks like you are doing a good job."

Stepping out into the street, James saw Deputy Sheriff Marlin walking down the street with papers in his hands. Quickly walking toward him, James put his finger to his lips, for the signal to be quiet. Turning Marlin around to walk the other way, he said, "I don't want that young man in your office to know who I am right now. Did you get the paperwork filled out for customs?"

"Yeah, what a job. I just had the mayor sign all the copies and we're ready for the customs folks to kinda take over from here."

"Did you fill out paperwork on Fisher Minnow?"

"No, Kelly said to hold up on the kid until you had a chance to evaluate what was going to happen to him, if anything."

"Good," James replied. "Let's let it be for now. He was only a driver for the mines. I'm not sure that is a crime."

Nodding, Deputy Sheriff Marlin sarcastically asked, "So what the hell am I supposed to do with him? He can't stay in the jail like it's a boarding house. Right now he has a private room, clean clothes, and three squares a day."

"I don't know; keep him busy working for Keller or cleaning all the Borough of Wrangell's offices. He seems quite innocent. I don't think you need to worry about him for a while. I'll get back with you soon enough." Patting Marlin's shoulder, he added, "Thanks, Oliver, now I've got to get over to the livery and check out the wagons and teams."

"Dammit, Kincaid, I told you not to call me that in public."

Smiling, James waved good-bye. "See you later, and keep young Minnow busy."

Standing at the corral at Keller's Livery with one foot hitched on one of the lower rails, James looked at the horses that were used for pulling the freight wagons down the Iskut River to the *Blue Sea* in the Stikine River. Rubbing his chin, James thought, *Those are fine horses. Someone took good care of them.*

When he saw Shane Keller, James climbed through the corral railing and hailed, "I see you got your horses back from Twin Forks Mining."

Laughing, Shane Keller waved back at the horses. "I even got some extra. What do I do with the extra horses? Do I bill the Department of Agriculture or keep billing Twin Forks Mining? I hear you got the goods on them for poaching and illegal shipping from Alaskan waters."

Sighing deeply, James explained, "I think we got them for poaching because British Columbian officials asked us to check on permits and other activities. The Canadians might have a case for hydraulic mining. I think Canada outlawed large hydraulic mining operations several years ago because of the environmental destruction it causes to the landscape. As far as the gold being shipped, I think they are legal, only thing is no one can find any gold on or in the wagons. The charge of shipping out of Alaskan water is pretty gray. They were mining in Canada and the ship sailed under Canadian colors. All they really did was pass through Alaskan waters."

"Well, James, I'm sure you can get them on something, if nothing else they owe me a bunch of money for horse rental or they can just give me the extra horses for the rental fee...which I'd really rather have. Motioning toward the big barn behind the livery, Shane asked, "Do you want to go see those freight wagons? I have never seen anything like them. They were built to last...mighty sturdy and heavy."

Walking up to one of the wagons, James placed his hands on one of the wheels and pushed and pulled as hard as he could...nothing moved. He looked at Shane. "Hell, these things could carry several tons each. What is in these wagons?"

"I can answer that for you, James," Payuk advised. "Those two wagons over there," Payuk pointed at them, "Have the skins and body parts that have been kenched. These two have the supplies that were ordered on the previous trip. Actually, it works pretty well. Ship the skins and gold out, ship the supplies in." Looking at the wagons, Payuk shook his head. "These wagons can carry a lot of weight, and that's why they needed two teams of horses for each wagon."

"Did you and Kelly check out the loads?" James asked.

"We just checked the two wagons with the skins in them, and we could not find anything except hides and animal body parts...we checked pretty close."

"Payuk, I want you to inventory the supplies' wagons. I want to know what they were ordering from shipment to shipment. U.S. Customs will want to know."

"OK, James, I'll have that list for you in the morning. It will probably take me the rest of today to unload the wagon and then reload."

"I got a better idea. I'm going to have Deputy Sheriff Marlin send Fisher Minnow down here to help you, Payuk. When you get finished, make sure Fisher goes back to the jail." He smiled. We would not want to disappoint our sheriff. Shane, where's Jeffery?"

"Jeffery!" Shane yelled.

"I'll be there in a moment."

Before Jeffery got to Shane, James asked Shane, "Can Jeffery go get Fisher Minnow at the jail?"

"Sure," Shane answered.

Putting his hand on Jeffery's shoulder, Shane asked, "Can you go get Fisher Minnow at the jail and bring him down here to help Payuk?"

"Yes sir, Mr. Keller. I'll be right back."

Quickly James asked, "Does he know Fisher Minnow?"

Shane nodded. "Yeah, they met when Fisher drove one of the teams here from the docks."

"Payuk, I want you to notify the tribal leaders that there are a bunch of skins that need to be distributed among the clans and lodges for their use. Make sure you keep a real good inventory of the skins and body parts because the U.S. Customs will want to know for sure, and probably the Canadian authorities too once they have been notified. The sooner we get these skins in the right hands, the sooner they will be used for good purposes. We just can't let them sit here and rot or deteriorate."

"Thanks, James, my people will enjoy getting these."

Soon Jeffery returned to the livery, and reported, "Fisher Minnow will be here pretty quick—as a matter of fact, here he comes now."

Climbing through the corral fence and making his way to James, Fisher said, "What can I do for you or whoever sent for me? I was told to help Payuk."

"I would like you to help Payuk unpack the supplies wagons and inventory them, and then repack them back up," James explained.

"Wow!" Fisher exclaimed. "That's going to take a while; they are usually jam-packed with a little bit of everything. By the way, who is this guy James Kincaid? I hear his name all over the place, like buildings."

"You just talked to him," Shane piped up.

Looking at Payuk, James advised him, "Take care of it, Payuk, and get back to me in the morning or as soon as you can. If you find anything that will go bad or spoil, let me know as soon as you can."

"OK, James, we'll get right to it."

"I'm sorry, Mr. Kincaid, but I did not know you."

"That's alright, son, I like to be buildings." Motioning to Shane to follow him, with a head motion, James said, "Let's go over there. I have something I want to talk to you about."

"Sure," Shane said and quickly followed James. "What is it I can do for you?"

"Shane, you know Bray. He is an old dog and I got a feeling he is in real pain. He whines when he gets up and down and he is not really eating a lot of food. When I take him to the beach, which he always loved to do, all he does is just slowly walk around and soon he is heading for home."

"How old is Bray?"

"He is about thirteen years, and that is a lot for a Husky."

"Well, James, you know about as much about animals as I do. What do you want to do?"

"I don't know, Shane; I thought you might take a look at him for a final analysis."

"Yes, I will take a look at him, but James, you and I both know what is coming and it sounds like it will be sooner rather than later."

"If you can, Shane, come by this evening. I need to know as soon as possible."

He nodded OK. "I'll be there on my way home."

Parting from Shane, James made his way back to the office to check on the letter to Sid in Seattle. As he entered the large day room of the office, Sara handed James the letter he had dictated not long before. "Oh thanks, Sara. This makes it easy. By the way, I really don't need that meeting letter tomorrow; that was just a reference."

"I'm glad, Mr. Kincaid, but I'll have it as soon as possible."

As James walked into his office with the letter to Sid Bonner, he remarked, "Good job, Sara."

James sat behind his desk rocking in his chair, and he thought, *Moaka will be very happy in Barrow. Hell, he's going back home.* Fidgeting with paperwork, James thought about something else that was bothering him. *Where could that gold be in those wagons? Fisher said he never saw any gold. They aren't using gold mining for a cover for poaching...nah, that would be stupid.* His thoughts interrupted, James heard Kelley enter the office and ask, "Is James in?"

"I'm in here, Kelly."

Quickly appearing around the corner, Kelly found a chair and informed James, "OK, the chief mate is getting his stuff together. He has Captain Weber's letter and I need to get the letter to Sid if it's ready."

Both men heard Sara remark, "It's ready—what did you think?"

Smiling, Kelly hailed in return, "OK, Sara, I knew it would be, but just checking."

James handed Kelly the letter in the addressed envelope. "I hope the captain's guy will get it delivered."

"Oh, don't worry about that. Captain Weber made it clear to Harrison that he would like an answer to his letter before Harrison left Seattle, and Mr. Kincaid would also like an answer to his letter if possible."

"Where do you think that gold is hidden on those wagons?" James asked.

Shaking his head, Kelly frowned. "Damned if I know, but we aren't finished looking yet."

"OK, Kelly, get that letter to the chief mate and start your report on your trip to Twin Forks Mining and Dredging Company. You might want to get Payuk's input for some details. I'll see you in the morning...maybe things will look different."

CHAPTER SIXTEEN

As James walked toward home all he could think about was Bray. *Shane is coming to our house after while and he will probably tell me what I already know. Bray's time has come, just like Moaka had to put Anore down, I'm going to have to do the same to Bray.* Slowly walking around to the back of his home, James saw Bray lying half in and half out of the house. As he approached Bray, James's partner in life got up slowly and whined a little as the pain was in his joints. James knelt down and brushed some grass from Bray's back and patted him on his side. Bray's coat was not in the best of condition, being dry and thin.

"How is he doing, James?" Shane Keller appeared around the corner of the house.

"Oh, I don't know. He is hurting. You can tell by the bloodshot eyes and he whines every time he gets up and down. I see you even brought your stethoscope you use on stock."

Leaning over Bray, Shane felt under his legs and along his stomach. Lifting one of Bray's front feet, Bray whined, and Shane instantly put the paw down gently as he used his stethoscope to check Bray's heartbeat. "Well, James, he has really bad bone spurs, arthritis has set into his joints, and his heart sounds like an out-of-rhythm drummer. There is nothing you can do about it other than give him some pain medicine, but that will only prolong the agony. You need to bring yourself to do what has to be done. Several years ago I had the same conversation with Moaka about Anore. I know of an operation to remove some of the bone spurs, but he is too old to go through that, and besides it would be temporary at best. Yeah, you need to get it done as soon as you can. I know it will be hard...it's just like losing a kid."

Standing beside Bray, James offered, "Well, thanks for the advice. I was afraid you would say just what you said, but I appreciate you coming over and taking a look. Thanks, Shane."

I'll ask you this question just once and then I'll let it be: "Do you want someone else to take care of Bray?"

Quickly glancing at Shane, James shook his head. "No, I'll do it. I owe Bray that much."

Seeing Shane disappear around the corner of the house on his way home after work, James thought, *I know I've got a good friend in Shane and he'd always be honest about things like this.*

Reaching down and petting Bray on top of his head, Bray looked up at James with his bloodshot eyes and his gray-haired face.

"Go get in your house, Bray. I'll bring your supper out to you soon." Looking at Bray's food bowl, James shook his head. "Hell, he didn't eat much of his breakfast."

Walking into the house, he saw that Suzette was not home yet, but Thomas was in his room shooting his dart gun at the wooden target James had made for him. "Make sure you hit the target so you won't put holes in the walls."

"I got it, Dad," was Thomas's reply.

Looking in the icebox, James picked up a small piece of cured fish to snack on before supper. Closing the icebox, James leaned on the cabinet as he looked out the window at Bray. *Poor old dog, he deserves better than being shot in the head.*

Suddenly the front door flung open as Sadie ran to James and wrapped her arms around his leg. "Daddy home."

Bending down, James scooped her up and hugged her. "How's my girl today?"

Pointing back toward Suzette with her small hand, she said, "Mommy not happy."

Looking beyond Sadie, James questioned, "Not happy, why?"

"Thomas, get in here," Suzette demanded.

James quickly looked at Sadie with raised eyebrows. "Thomas in trouble?"

Nodding swiftly, Sadie squeaked, "Yes. Mommy not happy."

Thomas instantly showed out of his room into the kitchen.

"What have you got to say for yourself, young man?" She shook her head, looking at James. "You know what your son did today at school?"

James shook his head. "No, what?"

"He and two other misbehavers were caught throwing spit-wads in class. And they were made to sit outside the classroom in the hall, on the floor, reading, which they probably never did. Did you?" she questioned sarcastically.

"Yes, we did," Thomas fired back.

"Go wash up for supper, young man; we'll talk about this later," Suzette scolded.

Sitting Sadie down, James got a clean dog bowl and went outside to get some choice meat parts for Bray's supper. As James lifted the heavy insulated lid to the meat storage, he noticed that the ice was about gone. Selecting several pieces, he placed them in the bowl and closed the lid. Walking over to Bray, James set the new meal down and picked up the breakfast bowl that still had food in it.

"Here, Bray, the best the house has got. Chow down."

Not looking back, James entered the house and quickly looked out the kitchen window to see if Bray was eating, and he had not moved a muscle. "Bray is in pretty bad shape," he mentioned to Suzette. "I had Shane come over earlier today to check Bray out, and he agrees that Bray's days are limited."

"So what are you going to do?" She pushed by him with hot meatloaf and mashed potatoes that she had prepared the night before. "Get the bread on the table, will you?"

James moved for the bread as Suzette asked again, "What are you going to do?"

"I don't know."

"Get in here for supper, young man."

"Coming, Mom."

"James, get Sadie up to the table."

After supper James walked out the front door and stood looking out over the bay, thinking, *Wrangell is a great place to raise kids. It's also a place where folks can get good jobs.* He shrugged. *Bray had his turn at life. He had a good life with Anore as his buddy for all those years.*

Turning to leave as the sun set into the ocean, James entered the house, not saying anything, and picked up a magazine and sat in his favorite chair.

"What are you going to do?" Suzette asked again.

Shaking his head, James repeated, "I don't know. I really can't see myself putting him down."

Thomas came into the living room and quietly asked James, "Is Bray going to die like Anore?"

Sighing, James looked at Thomas. "I think so, son. He is very old and he is in bad pain. Besides that, Shane Keller said his heart was not beating right."

Looking out the front window, James noticed it was getting dark. "Oh, Thomas, has your mom spoken to you about today's little misbehavior stunt?"

"No," said Suzette, coming out of the kitchen. "What do you think, James?"

215

"I don't know. Maybe ground him at home for a week."

"No!" Thomas exclaimed. Me and Henry are going fishing tomorrow. We got the worms and everything," Thomas pleaded.

"Yes, I think that is a good idea your father had. That's it then...one week grounded to the house—to school and right back home for a week."

Suddenly Bray started to howl in a very bad voice for him. James jumped out of his chair and exclaimed, "What in the world is wrong with that dog?"

Rushing outside, James saw Bray standing up and howling at the darkened sky. Walking over to him, James started patting him on his back and head. Sitting down beside him, Bray stopped howling and turned around a couple of times and lay down beside James with his head lying on James's lap.

James instantly heard Bray's breathing was stressed...he was having a very hard time breathing. James started stroking him slowly and gently around his neck and ears as he looked up at James.

The night had come upon Wrangell, but the lights from the kitchen gave James enough light to see Bray's face. Speaking quietly aloud, James talked to Bray. "Old man, you are such a good friend. You have fought polar bears to save me as well as cougars and wolves with no thought of your own safety. I remember when you and Anore led our teams across the tundra at breakneck speed and loved every minute...you were born to pull. I remember many times we would huddle together in the cold to say warm." Suddenly James heard Bray take a deep breath and then nothing. Listening for more breathing, he knew Bray had breathed his last.

Tears were running down James's cheeks when Suzette came out to see about Bray. She saw James weeping and knew it was all over.

Sitting down beside James and Bray, she started to weep as well. "I can remember when I first saw Bray. He was a magnificent animal. Large, strong, and he almost knocked me down."

Both James and Suzette laughed between their tears and held each other's hand for support.

Stammering, James said, "Well, it is over. I'm just glad I was here for him at the last. The last thing he saw was me looking down at him." Wiping the tears from his eyes, James commented, "A man never had a better friend."

Unhooking his collar, James quietly reflected, "Let his spirit be free." Getting up and helping Suzette up, James said, "Just let him be for tonight. He loved the night and his freedom."

. . .

Next morning James was up before light getting ready for work. There were several very important issues to be handled today, but the first issue was taking care of Bray.

He was putting on his jacket when Suzette came out of the bedroom. "Where are you going so early?"

"I'm going to the livery to get a buckboard from Shane and take Bray out in the woods and bury him. That's where he would have wanted to be buried."

"Are you coming back for breakfast?"

"No, I'll grab some toast and coffee from the Steak and Stack. Then I'll go on to work. I've got a lot on my plate today." Opening the back door, James waved. "I'll see you this evening." Stopping, James quickly turned around and approached Suzette for a quick good-bye kiss.

"I was wondering if you had forgotten."

Shaking his head, he said, "Well, I'm not that busy," as he exited the back door.

Stopping on the porch, there was just enough light for James to look toward Bray lying there as peaceful as ever, just like nothing was wrong. "Lie still, big boy, I'll be back to get you real soon."

Getting to the Keller's Livery at the same time Shane did, James waved. "Well, Bray called it a day last night. He howled two or three times and laid his head in my lap and breathed a few times and then it was silence. He went real easy, and I was glad I could be with him for the last. I was the last thing he saw as he closed his eyes for the last time. Suzette and I cried our eyes out as we laughed about some of the stuff that Bray used to do."

"Good, James, I am glad it was that easy for you, Suzette, and Bray. You are lucky; it could have been very much the other way."

"OK, Shane. I need to borrow a buckboard to haul Bray off to bury him in the trees. He liked the forest and all the animals in the forest, even the predators."

"Sure, James, but take that little surrey just inside the door. One horse does a good job on that one. You can put Bray behind the seat on the flat surface. Also here are a couple of seed bags you can cover him with."

"Oh thanks, Shane. I would have never thought of them."

Shane helped James get a horse harnessed and hooked up to the surrey and James headed home to get Bray. Gently loading Bray into the surrey, James could tell Bray was not well. He weighed less than half his normal weight. Getting Bray loaded, James grabbed a shovel and headed for a good spot that he knew Bray would like to have as his resting place.

Arriving at the location, about three miles from Wrangell, James dug a suitable hole and lifted Bray into the hole and stood standing over the hole looking at Bray lying comfortably. He immediately started to weep. Tears cascaded down his cheeks like rainwater. Wiping the tears from his eyes, he covered Bray with the seed bags and sifted small amounts of soil over him. Unable to stop weeping, James continued to cover his friend until the grave was filled with love and soil. Mounding the soil up slightly, James walked on the grave to compact the soil and then gathered leaves and sticks to cover the soil. Stepping back, James knew within a short period of time the grave would not be visible any longer.

Taking the surrey back to Keller's Livery, Shane met him coming in. "Here, James, let me take care of the horse and surrey."

"Thanks, Shane, you're a help."

Getting back to the office, Sara stopped James. She told him, "Suzette came by here early this morning and told me what happened. I'm so sorry, Mr. Kincaid. It is tough losing an old friend."

He nodded his appreciation and continued walking into his office and closed the door. Standing with his back against the door, James thought, *I've got to stop this. I have work to do and I must be at my best. Bray is gone...that's it.*

Walking over to his desk, he sat down and took a deep breath and started shuffling papers.

Soon there was a soft knock on the door and James answered, "Come in."

The door open slightly and Sara asked, "Would you like a cup of fresh coffee?"

Shaking his head, James responded, "Boy, would I."

"OK, I'll be right back."

As Sara brought in the coffee, James asked, "Will you leave the door open?"

"Yes sir."

Taking a sip of the hot coffee, James rested back in his chair and smiled, and thought, *Who says they don't have a soul?*

CHAPTER SEVENTEEN

"Sara," James called, "has Moaka come in yet this morning?"

"No, Mr. Kincaid. I haven't seen Kelly or Payuk yet either."

James busied himself catching up on his Departmental readings from Seattle and other places having to do with policy changes, new laws being made, and requests from different organizations for legal advice from the Department of Agriculture concerning timber rights and timber permits. Putting down the paperwork, James thought, *Ever since the Tongass National Forest has been turned over to the main operating body of the Forest Service, I have had less and less to do with timber contracts. Someday, I hope soon, they will be doing all the timber rights and permits stuff.*

Seemingly sudden, Kelly popped into the doorway office of James's office. "Good morning."

Startled, James jumped and scolded Kelly. "Don't you knock?"

"I'm sorry, James; I did not mean to startle you."

Smiling, James confessed, "I was many miles from here. Come in and sit for a minute. I want to run something by you: I want you to contact Captain Weber and let him know that I would like to speak with him privately at his earliest convenience."

"That will be easy; he is ashore now doing some shopping for supplies for the *Blue Sea*."

"I only want to speak with the captain at this point."

"OK, James, I'll give him the message. Any special time?"

"As soon as it is at his earliest convenience."

Standing and starting to leave, Kelly turned back, "Oh, by the way, Payuk and Fisher are still inventorying the two supply wagons this morning. They should be finished by noon or so."

"Have you started on the report for Twin Forks yet?"

"Yes. I kinda worked on it at home last night. Just made a few notes so I could get my head around all the stuff that happened."

"Well, I appreciate it, Kelly, but that's not necessary. That is why we come to work."

"OK, James, I'll go find Captain Weber, and then I'll return to the office to work on the report, but I'd like to stop by and check out what Payuk and Fisher are doing."

Kelly disappeared and James heard the front door open. He heard Moaka's voice, "Good morning."

"Oh, good morning," Sara said. "Mr. Kincaid is waiting for you, Moaka. Oh, Kelly, will you please mail these for me...now don't forget."

"I'll do it right now, Sara."

Moaka walked over to James's office and advised, "Be back."

"OK, Moaka, I'm in no hurry."

Soon Moaka returned to James's office with a cup of tea and found his normal chair.

"Good morning, Kincaid. I sorry for you and Bray. Keller say Bray die last night. Had go livery this morning, get map out saddlebag. Left them there last night when got back from Terrace Point.

"Bray die quiet?"

Smiling, James looked at Moaka. "Yes, Moaka, he died quiet. His head was in my lap and the last thing he saw was my face."

Nodding, Moaka commented, "Good, fine dog." He took a sip of his tea and asked, "Missy OK, this morning?"

Quickly looking up at Moaka from reading a complaint, James looked out the window. "I don't know, Moaka. I took her to Mrs. Mackly last night and Mrs. Mackly said she would give Janet Moore a try on the job. I guess she is still there."

"Think Jeffery buy my house? I make good price."

"Do you need all cash or can he make payments to you?"

"He can make payments...bank can do this?"

"Yes, Moaka, the bank will make all the arrangements if he can make a payment every month."

"I want go Barrow soon. Make dog team before bad weather."

"Yeah, I know, Moaka, but it is only May now." Nodding his head, James commented, "Yeah, I know you want to go soon, and I'm working on it right now. A letter is already on the way to Sid and we should have the final answer from him in about three to four days. If I were you, I would get with Jeffery soon and see if he is interested in buying your house and how much. The bank will tell you how much your house is worth. In the meantime, I need you to go over to Woronkofski Island and talk to the tribal leader over there and see what his problem is about fishing rights. He claims in this letter, that someone wrote for him, that men are fishing in the tribes' sacred fishing grounds." Sighing, James leaned back in his chair. "Moaka, we have been up and down this ladder many times. Why can't the Tlingit get it through their heads they can't run everybody off from fishing in an open stream? As long as the fishermen are obeying the laws for fishing, they can fish in the stream. It is only when the laws are broken, like over-limit, fishing at night, or netting where it is not legal, that we can stop the fishermen from fishing in the streams that the Tlingit feel are their sacred fishing streams." He shook his head. "Moaka, I know we must be sympathetic to the Tlingit for their sacred streams, but they must understand the laws have been changed so all can fish anywhere they want, as long as it is legal."

"Can wait until tomorrow to go?"

"Yes, Moaka. Talk to Jeffery and then both of you go to the bank to see what can be worked out financially. How long will you be at Woronkofski Island?"

"Maybe two day."

Sitting up in his chair, James added, "I want you to go by the Terrace Point gang and see how they are doing. Take a packhorse with you because you will probably be gone for several days. If you need to stay at each place a little longer to ensure issues are settled, that will be fine.

"OK, Moaka, get out of here and get your house sold." James laughed and Moaka smiled.

"OK, Kincaid. You come see Moaka at Barrow?"

"Of course, Moaka,"...and with a wave of his hand, "get out of here."

Hearing Moaka going out the front door, saying good-bye to Sara, James thought, *He is happy. He will do well in Barrow. A job absolutely made for him.* Quickly jerking around in his chair, James scanned the calendar. *Damn, I've got that mayor meeting this afternoon.* Quickly pulling his pocket watch out of its place, James sighed. *Good two hours till the meeting. I still got time to talk with Captain Weber if he gets here.*

As if by clockwork, Sara appeared at James's office door. "There is a Captain Weber to see you. He said you would be expecting him."

"Yes, Sara, show him in."

Standing, James met Captain Weber with a firm handshake and asked, "Do you need coffee or tea?"

"No thanks, James, I'm fine."

James motioned toward a chair. "Have a seat, Charles. I need to talk with you for a while about the situation of the *Blue Sea* knowingly shipping illegally. I might have a solution to all of our problems, including Braddock Shipping's." Shuffling through some papers on his desk, James finally grabbed the one he was looking for and explained, "Here is a letter from the Department of Mining in Victoria addressed to Department of Agriculture in Wrangell. Among other things it asks the Department of Agriculture to travel up the Iskut River and check mining permits, especially the Twin Forks Mining and Dredging Company and see that they are complying with the contract's requirements. Apparently the mining company is supposed to be hydraulic mining for a maximum of fifteen percent of their mining operation, but we have found they are hydraulic mining for one hundred percent of their mining activities. Also the letter states that if any activities are sited as being unnatural or illegal, a full report will be made and sent back to them in Victoria. The letter also states that the Department of Agriculture, Wrangell, has the authority to stand down and arrest persons involved in illegal activities." Standing away from his desk, James walked to the large window in his office and continued, "And, Charles, both of us know they are poaching the hell out of anything they can shoot and skin, let alone the shipping of animal parts that is also illegal."

"OK, James, you haven't told me anything I don't know already. What is your idea?"

"Charles, we can have our cake and eat it too. We just need to be smart about this situation. First off, if you decide to throw in with us, the Department of Agriculture will pay all your bills like wood for your fire box, food for your crew, and any other incidental costs you have running the *Blue Sea* during this operation."

"I think I would like to have that cup of coffee now, James."

"Sara, would you please bring in two cups of coffee for Charles and me."

"Sure thing—does Captain Weber need sugar?"

James looked at Charles, who waved no.

"No, Sara. We will both take it black."

"Well, James, you make a good offer...now what does the *Blue Sea* have to do to earn all this attention?"

Smiling, James explained, "Take the wagons and teams back to the Iskut River and set them ashore so they can be taken back up the Iskut River to the Snippaker River to Twin Forks Mining. Then wait at the Iskut River for anything that will happen." James continued, still smiling. "Hopefully bringing the boss of Twin Forks back to Wrangell for preliminary processing for illegal mining and poaching for British Columbia."

"How long will I be standing ground at the mouth of the Iskut River?"

Shaking his head, James said, "I don't know, Charles: I haven't got that far yet."

"Here is your coffee." Sara said as she set the tray with two coffees on a table next to James's desk. "Will there be anything else?"

"No thanks, Sara." James handed one of the hot cups of coffee to Charles.

"Yeah, that is a good question I haven't worked out yet. It is going to take several people doing several things to get this thing to jell together. One thing though, you and your men will not come under any danger. You will be a lot of help on the shipping end of the deal, but you will also be helping us catch an illegal mining and illegal poaching operation. Which I know the United States and Canadian governments will appreciate greatly."

"So when does all this start?" Captain Weber asked.

"Actually, it has already started. Payuk and Fisher are inventorying the supply wagons and as soon as they get the inventory to me we can load the wagons onto the *Blue Sea*. Payuk has already informed the local clans to get the animal parts and skins for their use out of the wagons that were going to be shipped to Seattle. But first we must get our forces together. I have two men and Fisher available for the job. Also I think I can get another man for our operation. I will fit into the mesh as I see fit. You and your crew will stand by on the *Blue Sea* at the mouth of the Iskut River until Kelly and his men return from the mining camp."

Captain Weber shrugged his broad shoulders. "When do you want to have a planning meeting? I would like all my crew in on all aspects of the raid, even though they will not be going to the mining camp." Hesitating for a moment, he added, "The *Blue Sea* should not have to stand ground at the mouth of the Iskut River for too long."

"With any luck, I'm guessing not more than five or six days." James explained further, "It depends on what we run into at the camp. All that will be covered at the planning meeting. I would like to have the planning meeting tomorrow morning, if possible, say about nine a.m., but just now I have to go to another meeting with the mayor and other Wrangell officials."

Standing, Captain Weber stressed, "My crew will be intent on this assignment. They are just used to floating around and loading and unloading freight. It will be different for them. OK, James, I and my crew will see you in the morning...Oh, by the way, from time to time I am not going to leave someone on board the *Blue Sea*. I hope she is not confiscated." He smiled.

"Don't worry about that, I think everybody in town, by now, knows who that boat belongs to. OK, Charles, I've got to go."

With that, Captain Weber and James left the office, going their different ways.

By the time James returned from the town meeting with the mayor, the only one in the office was Kelly. "What are you doing, Kelly?" James said, stepping into his office.

Smiling, Kelly relaxed in his chair and took a deep breath. "I was just finishing a few notes. I should be finished with the report maybe tomorrow."

Shaking his head, James advised, "Don't count on it. I'm having a planning meeting with all involved people attending, even Captain Weber and his crew. You, Payuk, and Fisher will be there, but Moaka will not. He has to leave for Woronkofski Island in the morning to settle a fishing claim and then go over to Terrace Point to check on the flume building project."

Leaving the office to Kelly, James cautioned, "Don't spend the night here, Nancy may come looking for you."

Walking to Keller's Livery, James saw Jeffery cleaning down one of the horses and currying the horse's mane. "You take good care of the horses, Jeffery."

"Oh hi, Mr. Kincaid. Well, that's what Mr. Keller pays me for."

"Where is Shane?"

"Looking over the back of the horse, Jeffery pointed. "I think over that way."

"Thanks, Jeffery."

Finding Shane, James approached him. "I have a favor to ask you."

"Ask away. I'm full of favors as long as they don't cost me anything."

"I need to borrow Jeffery for a few days. He knows how to drive a team and I need someone that knows how to drive a team of four. Kelly and Payuk know how, but I can't use them to do that on this job. I got Fisher and he knows, but I need another."

228

"I was requested to meet Moaka and Jeffery at the bank this afternoon," Shane mentioned. "Apparently Jeffery is going to buy Moaka's home. Where in the hell is he going? Someone said something about Barrow."

Shaking his head, James asked, "Don't be passing that around right now."

Laughing, Shane told James, "Are you kidding?" Moaka and Jeffery were telling everybody. I guess Jeffery makes enough money here at the livery, with his down payment, to make payments to Moaka's account. It's a nice small house with a great view of the bay."

"Yeah, Jeffery will like it there. Moaka will be leaving soon, maybe as little as a week or so. He wants to get up there and get a dog team trained some before bad weather."

"Will he still be working for the Department of Agriculture?"

"Yes, but on contract, I think, as of now. His duties will be wildlife surveillance, wildlife counts, and making trips to villages checking on animals being killed for meat and skins. Course he will always be looking for poaching."

"Well, damn, I bet he is looking forward to that, back up to his old stomping grounds."

"Yes, Shane, he is excited. Now, what about using Jeffery for about a week or so, maybe less?"

Shane waved his hand in the air. "Of course, James, on one condition."

Shaking his head, James mumbled, "Here it comes."

"No, here is the condition. I want you to buy that red roan you like to ride. If you don't buy the horse, I have to let others ride the animal and that may not be the best thing for the roan. He is only four years old, sturdy, well-built, and has a good personality. He is a good horse. The monthly keep you can charge to the Department like you did the other horse. It isn't much anyway."

Nodding, James replied, "OK. I hope you don't charge me too much for the horse, saddle, and tack."

Laying his hand on James's shoulder, Shane said, "Ah, I wouldn't worry too much about that."

"Mr. Keller, I've got that horse ready for the customer tomorrow morning. If that will be it, I'll be shoving off for the day."

"Wait, Jeffery. I believe Mr. Kincaid wants to speak with you for a moment."

Turning to face James, Jeffery responded, "Yes sir, Mr. Kincaid."

"Jeffery, I want you to help the Department of Agriculture out with a project we've got going. I've asked Shane if I could borrow you for a week or so and he has agreed. Can you drive a four-team harness?"

Smiling, Jeffery replied quickly, "Sure. Where do you want me to go with the team?"

Nodding, James looked at Shane. "Can Jeffery be at a meeting we are having in my office at nine a.m. in the morning?"

"Sure, I'll make sure he is there."

"OK, thanks guys," James concluded. "Oh, by the way, Jeffery, congratulations on buying Moaka's home. You will like it. It's small, but very cozy with a good view."

As James walked home from Keller's Livery he thought about what he was going to say to start the meeting off. *What the Twin Forks Mining Company has done on the mining front is wrong and against the law, and what they did on the poaching front is defiantly unlawful. Besides, the company was using the Canadian colors to cover their shipping out of Alaskan waters. I don't know if that's against the law, but it was sure a good cover for illegal shipping.*

Turning the corner on his street, James saw Suzette and the kids going into the house. Smiling, he thought, *I wonder if Thomas behaved himself today in school.*

Walking around to the back of the house, James looked to where Bray would have been lying or jumping around wanting to be let into the house to be with the rest of the family. Shaking his head, James turned and walked up the wooden steps to the porch and opened the back door.

Instantly Sadie yelled, as she ran toward James, "Daddy's home."

James reached down and swooped her up in his arms. "How's my little girl? Were you good today?"

"Thomas, come in here," Suzette called. "Here, take this milk jar and go get it filled from Mrs. Harris and come right back with the milk."

With Thomas heading out the door, Sadie asked, "Did Bray die?"

James nodded. "Yes, Sadie, Bray died last night. He went to a dog heaven."

Setting Sadie down, James hugged Suzette and asked, "How are you feeling?"

"Oh, James, I'll be fine for a few months; don't you remember the last two times?"

"Yeah, I guess so. I want to eat soon because I want you and I to go over to Mrs. Mackly's, and I want you to meet Janet Moore."

"Let's eat as soon as I can get it on the table and get the kitchen cleaned up, then we can go. I really don't want to be there very long; I need to get back and get Sadie to bed."

"OK, I'll get the kindling in for tomorrow. Thomas," James hailed, "get the wood in."

Being May, the sun was still high in the sky when James and family strolled over to Mrs. Mackly's Parker Boarding House. On the way over, James explained, "Now, Mrs. Mackly probably gave Janet some clothes to wear so don't expect too much. Janet is a hard worker, I know that."

Opening the squeaky screen door, James let Suzette and the children go in ahead of him. Janet was bent over wiping the tables from supper and when she heard the squeaky screen door she turned around to see James coming in the front door.

"Oh hi, Mr. Kincaid. Can I get you and—"

"Janet, you look wonderful! Did Mrs. Mackly give those clothes to you?"

"Yes, all I did was a little hemming and cutting to make them fit and now you see the results."

"Janet, this is Suzette, my wife, and these are Thomas and Sadie, and this is Janet Moore."

"Here, Mrs. Kincaid, we have a high stool for Sadie to sit up to the table."

"Oh, thank you," Suzette expressed, as she sat Sadie on the stool.

"Can I get you guys any coffee or tea?"

"Yes, Janet, get me a cup of coffee, and...".

"You can get me a cup of tea," Suzette added, "and get the children a glass of water, please."

"What in the world are you two doing here this time of day?" Mrs. Mackly inquired, as she walked in the dinner room from the kitchen. "I heard voices out here and thought Janet had started talking to herself." Everybody laughed.

Janet quickly returned to the dining room with the coffee, tea, and water for the children.

Suzette offered, "Thanks, Janet, this is nice."

"OK, Kincaids, what can I do for you, or is this a social visit?"

"I wanted Suzette and the children to meet Janet Moore," James said to Mrs. Mackly. And looking at Janet, James continued, "Well I see you've still got a job here."

Smiling, Janet joked, "Yeah, I'm still hanging in there."

"Oh, don't believe that, she is doing just fine. All of my guests like her and her carvings, besides the good work she does around here. Look at those clothes. When I gave them to her they looked like something you would steal off from someone's clothesline. She actually remade the garments. I'm going to have her redo some of my clothes."

"Oh, Mrs. Mackly, it was nothing," Janet insisted.

Suzette picked up a carving from the table and asked, "Where did you get this, Mrs. Mackly?"

"From that young lady right there." Mrs. Mackly pointed to Janet. "She's good at carving and drawing, and several of the guests from down below want to buy some selected carvings and drawings and take them back to wherever for souvenirs from Wrangell, Alaska."

"My word, young lady," Suzette admired, "You have talent. Where did you learn to do the carvings and drawings?"

"From my father. He got killed by a grizzly bear a while back, but before that he was a miner. He also taught me my sums and reading. Mr. Kincaid said that you were a school teacher. What do you teach in the school?"

"Yes," Suzette explained, "I teach phonics, reading, writing, and sometimes English skills when needed."

"Wow!" Janet declared, "that is a lot. I bet that keeps you busy?"

"Yes, I really do enjoy it, and I do keep busy."

Standing up away from the table, James sipped down his last bit of coffee and announced, "We better get to going. We don't want to be a bother. I know you both have more work to do," and, looking at Janet, "you keep getting along with the guests and you'll be just fine."

"Yes, and nice meeting you, Janet. You have talent so make it work for you."

As James and family were leaving, Mrs. Mackly commented, "Yeah, she is getting along fine with the guests, especially that Jeffery Maxwell."

Holding the screen door open, James advised, "He is a good, hard-working person."

"I know he is; he has stayed here at the Parker Boarding House for several years."

With that, James closed the screen door and hurried to catch Suzette and the children.

CHAPTER EIGHTEEN

James arrived at the office early the next morning. He needed to check his notes for the meeting before everybody began to come in. He had told Kelly to drop by the Steak and Stack and pick up a dozen of the sweet rolls they made every morning. He was thinking, *Suzette does not like me to buy them; she says they're not healthy...too much sugar.*

Standing from his desk, James walked into Moaka's office, but apparently he had already left for Woronkofski Island because his side arm and pack were gone. *He must have had to catch an early boat over to the Island.*

Standing at his map case, James had spread the map out on top of the desk that would show all aspects of the terrain and distances the teams would have to be dealing with. Shaking his head, he thought, *A helluva lot of ground to cover. How in the world are we going to have communications between groups? Fisher is a key person in this operation. If he performs as he should, and this thing is a success, Kelly won't need to get him a job, I'll get him the best damn job he ever had...working for the Department of Agriculture, somewhere.*

Hearing the door open and close, James looked out his office door to see who it was. "Hi, Sara. Good morning. Did you get the letters sent to Jacob Perkins and the British Columbia Mining Office?"

"Oh hi, Mr. Kincaid; yes, they went out yesterday."

"Better have the coffee going real steady this morning. You know we are having the planning meeting here at nine a.m."

Suddenly something hit the front door and it opened slightly as Kelly pushed it open all the way rather forcefully. "I damn near dropped all these sweet rolls. I guess I'll set them on the table," he said as he motioned toward the table in the middle of the reception room of the office.

Smirking, James teased, "Having a hard time this morning, Kelly?"

"Well, I carried those stupid sweet rolls all the way down here from Steak and Stack and I get to the door and damn near dropped every one of them." Shaking his head, he said, "It better get better."

James waved to Kelly. "Come on in my office after you've put your stuff away. I need to talk with you before the others get here."

Getting notes set up for the meeting, Kelly soon arrived in James's office. Sitting down and taking a deep breath, Kelly expounded, "OK, I'm ready for the meeting. You know, James, we have a lot on the line with this one. I guess you have communicated by letter to Sid and British Columbia people. On this one I should think we are going to be turning a lot of evidence over to both parties."

James nodded. "You're right on that one, Kelly. This meeting has to be orderly and to the point. I can't let it get bogged down with opinions and what ifs." Lifting a page of notes up, James asked, "What is the name of the guy that works for Twin Forks that said he would help us if we were going to press charges?"

"His name is Jesse Holmes. He's the bookkeeper for Henry Wilson; Wilson is the boss for the mining company."

"Why does he want to help us and destroy his job?"

Kelly smiled. "Because he's afraid he's going to get caught falsifying documents for the company. Henry Wilson tells him what to put in the reports and that may not necessarily be the truth."

"Have you set up some signal with him?"

"No, but he'll know something is wrong when the wagons don't show up on time coming back with the supplies. I asked him what they would do when the wagons never showed up at the mining camp, and he just said they would blame the boat being late. Apparently that has happened before."

"Have you got something worked out for an excuse why the other team driver never shows up, but rather some other guy?"

"Fisher just said, 'I'll tell them he did not want to return and this other guy decided to drive the team up the Iskut River to the mining camp for the adventure and a little better pay.'"

"How are you going to contact this...this Jesse Holmes?"

"I need to talk to you about that."

James leaned back in his chair, then stood, and walked to the window. "Why can't you go to his cabin in the middle of the night, on the day the supply wagons get to the mining camp? You said you know where he sleeps, and let him know what we intend to do the next night?" Turning back toward Kelly, "Go to his cabin at say one a.m. the first night and set the plan, and quietly leave until designated time on the next night to put the plan into effect. We will tell Fisher and Jeffery—"

"Jeffery, Jeffery Maxwell?" Kelly was surprised.

"Yes, Jeffery is going to drive the other team into the mining camp from the *Blue Sea* that will be anchored on the Stikine River at the mouth of the Iskut River." Pausing, James asked, "You have a problem with that?"

Kelly shook his head. "No, it was just a surprise."

"Anyway, we will tell Fisher and Jeffery the plan will go into effect the second night after they get there and they are not to make contact with Jesse Holmes because he will know that you and Payuk are going to be there the second night to work the plan. During the planning meeting this morning, we will talk about tying and gagging Henry Wilson and getting him out of the camp, also stampeding their horses off so they can't follow us real soon."

"Yeah, we need to really have a tight schedule set for this to work," Kelly added. "Oh and, by the way, just for information, Jesse Holmes sleeps in the main or administration building."

"OK, now, let's get these chairs in my office out into the reception room, and get the chairs in your office and Moaka's office. Counting the chairs already in the reception room, that should be enough chairs."

Seeing Kelly and James carrying chairs, Sara offered, "Can I help?"

"No Sara, we can do this, but thanks," James acknowledged.

The chairs were all set up in the reception room just in time because Captain Weber arrived with his crew. After introductions to Sara, the crew of the *Blue Sea* got their coffee and seated themselves.

"Sara?" James asked. "Can you get me the charts for tides for the next couple of days?"

"Oh James," Captain Weber exclaimed, "I have a copy right here in my satchel."

"Great." James nodded.

Just then Fisher and Payuk came into the office and were surprised at the gathering in the reception room. Spreading his hands out wide, Payuk commented, "What a group. This meeting better be important with all these important people in the room."

Everybody laughed as James responded, "Get yourself some coffee and have a seat..." James paused his statement when Jeffery came rushing through the door. "I hope I'm not late. Had to help Mr. Keller deliver a colt."

"Get some coffee and have a seat. You are not late. Everybody, this is Jeffery Maxwell, he will be driving the other team up the Iskut River to the mining camp along with Fisher Minnow." Quickly turning away from the group, James smiled to himself...*Minnow*...

"Sara," he asked, "Will you please take minutes of this meeting and if there is anything you don't understand, ask us to stop and I'll try to explain."

"Yes sir, Mr. Kincaid."

Standing next to Sara's desk, James announced, "Everyone is here. Captain Weber will you introduce your crew?"

"Sure, James. My chief mate is Hartford Harrison," and as he pointed to each man, "this is Paul, Stan, and Mike."

James pointed to Payuk.

"Oh, I'm Payuk and I work with Kelly."

Next, Kelly waved and stated, "I'm Kelly O'Brien. I'm sometimes James's left-hand man," and the group snickered, knowing what he meant.

"I'm Fisher Minnow. I used to work for Twin Forks Mining. and I will drive one of the wagons up to the mining camp."

"James already introduced me, but I'm Jeffery Maxwell. I will be driving the other wagon to the mining camp. I work for Mr. Keller who owns the livery here in Wrangell. Oh, and, by the way, Kelly, your gift will be here soon from Mr. Boren."

James quickly inquired, "What gift?"

Waving his hand slightly, Kelly explained, "It has nothing to do with this meeting, you'll all see when it happens."

Still standing beside Sara's desk, James suggested, "Let's just use first names in this meeting; it will make things a little easier. OK, and finally, I'm James Kincaid. I have worked for the Department of Agriculture for about fourteen years here at Wrangell. I don't want to bore you with all the things the Department or I am responsible for, but understand this: I and this organization are dedicated to justice for all peoples and protection of wildlife. Justice for all peoples means, miners, forest workers, recreationalists, hunters, fishermen, and over all general travelers. Protection of wildlife means lawful hunting and fishing, habitat protection, and animals to view and enjoy at a distance."

"Now—"

There came a knock on the door, and Kelly jumped up to answer, knowing who it would be. "Come on in, Mr. Boren. We have been expecting you."

Mr. Boren slowly walked into the large reception room with a box held in front of him, and asked, "Who wanted to look at these ten-week-old black Labradors?"

Hearing Charles give a big sigh, Harrison looked to him and asked, "Did you finally decide to get a Lab?"

Charles quickly looked at Kelly. "You don't miss much, do you, young man. Let me see the pups." He reached in the box. Holding one of the pups up into the air, he smiled. "I'll take both of them. How much do they cost?"

"There is no charge. They are the end of my Suzie's litter. She is a good mother and they are house broke. If you want, I can take them back to the livery and you can pick them up there at your convenience."

"That would be just fine, thank you. By the way, what is your name?"

Looking around the room like everyone knew his name, he responded, "Of course, my name is Sam Boren. I own and operate the Mercantile here in Wrangell."

"Well, thank you very much, Sam. I appreciate your bringing them to me to look at."

After Sam Boren left the office, Sara asked, "Do you want me to put that in the minutes?"

James shook his head and smiled as everyone laughed. Looking at Sara, James pointed at her. "I'm going to tell Shane on you."

Everybody laughed again as James cleared his throat. "OK, thank you, Kelly. What I'm going to talk about now is what is going to happen over the next few days. Remember what is going to happen, not necessarily how it is going to happen. I will not be on station with you, but rather Kelly will act in my capacity. I will be here in this office or close by to tend to the latest developments in this event or other duties I have."

Charles raised his hand and asked, "What if the *Blue Sea* is shore grounded at the Iskut River and the company's legal staff we sent for gets here?"

"Yeah, that will be one of the things I will have to deal with. I'm sure they will understand the importance of you and your crew helping capture the boss of the Twin Forks Mining and Dredging Company, especially with what Braddock Shipping is being charged with."

Charles nodded his head. "Good point."

Picking up his cup of coffee and going to his chair, James slowly sat down as he began to explain. "Charles, will you look on your charts and see when it's the best time to hit that estuary tomorrow morning?"

Unfolding his chart, Charles followed his finger down a column, "OK, it looks like the best time to sail the estuary is at about ten a.m. tomorrow."

"Perfect," James exclaimed. "That will give us lots of time to load the teams and wagons, load wood on the *Blue Sea*, and get your riding horses loaded with pack animals. The estuary is only about thirty minutes from Wrangell. Payuk and Fisher I want you two to see to the loading of firewood onto the *Blue Sea* this afternoon. Have

241

them bill the Department. They will have to haul the wood out on a barge because the *Blue Sea* will not move from anchorage until in the morning. Kelly and Jeffery, you guys take care of the wagons and horses. Just make sure the wagons are ready and the horses are harnessed by eight a.m. in the morning. Charles, I will need you to have the *Blue Sea* ready for the teams just after seven a.m. That will give us plenty of time to load teams, wagons, riding and packhorses, and supplies on the *Blue Sea* and still be at the estuary by ten a.m."

Charles, make sure you have proper provisions for your crew for a waiting time of about five to six days on the river waiting for Kelly to get back to you from the mining camp. You can charge your provisions to the Department. You just met the man you will be dealing with for provisions. If you need anything special, make sure you contact Kelly or me before you buy the item. Is there anything special you think you will need?"

"We are running low on flares," Harrison advised Charles.

"OK. Kelly, get some extra white and red flares for Charles and his crew when you buy the dynamite. Also get them a few red and green smoke bombs when you get the ones we will need. Is there anything else, Charles?"

Shaking his head, Charles waved off, no.

"Well, Charles, I think that does it for you and your crew. Get your supplies and stand ready to help the wood haulers if you would. Oh, by the way, on your way out grab one of those sweet rolls just made at the Steak and Stack—they are delicious."

"You bet, James; we'll give them a hand with the wood."

Charles and his crew grabbed a sweet roll each as they left the office, and Charles looked back at James. "I'll be in touch if I need anything else," and he waved going out the door.

"OK, the four of you, listen and listen close. Kelly and Payuk will be shadowing you from the ridgeline south of the river. They will not try to contact you at any time. The first night Fisher and Jeffery are in camp is for Kelly and Payuk to talk with Holmes to set up the next night. The first night Fisher and Jeffery will do as the rest of the mining crew does or take work assignments for the next day." Pausing, James looked at Kelly. "You said you know where Holmes sleeps?"

"Yes," Kelly answered, "He sleeps in the main office."

"The next night will be all hell breaking loose at about...what time, Fisher, would be best?"

Thinking for just a second, Fisher answered, "The best time would be at one a.m. The watch changes at twelve midnight."

"OK, Fisher, you and Jeffery have to take out the guard on the second night right after he takes over, or before twelve-thirty a.m. You don't have to kill him, just tie him up really good and gag him. That should be easy; he will know you, Fisher. Once the guard is out of the picture, make arrangements for four riding horses saddled and ready, two for you two, one for Henry Wilson, and one for Jesse Holmes. Before the fireworks start, Kelly and Payuk will find you in the corrals, and find out where Henry Wilson sleeps...Oh," James exclaimed, "How many guards are there?"

Fisher quickly answered, "One, that's all there ever is and he mostly wanders around the camp."

"Kelly, you and Payuk will be the only ones throwing any explosives or any smoke bombs or flares. Fisher and Jeffery will immediately go get Henry Wilson. Gag him and tie him up tight. Take some small rope along with you so you don't have to try and find something to tie him with. I don't care how tight, but he must not get away. What I would do is hit him over the head with your

243

pistol butt. You may not knock him out, but he won't give you any problems after that. Then get him on a horse and let Jeffery start taking him downriver right then and there. Also you will need to tie Wilson on that horse and I do mean across the saddle. Up to this point all is quiet. Jeffery you walk those horses out of camp real quiet and slow...no noise of galloping horses. Payuk, you will have to hang onto the four horses that are saddled and ready to go. When Jeffery gets on his way, then you, Fisher, will take over hanging onto horses.

"What do we do with our horses," asked Kelly?

Shaking his head, James considered. "Give them to Fisher. You will have to hang on to four horses: yours, Holmes's, Payuk's and Kelly's."

"OK, once you have Jeffery and Wilson down the trail to the *Blue Sea* the action really starts. I want smoke bombs lit off, flares shot off, and dynamite thrown in all directions. Kelly when you get that dynamite, get the one-inch diameter ones that are about eight inches long. You will need about twelve of them. Take a pencil and make a hole in the end about four inches deep into the dynamite. That is to slide the cap and fuse into the dynamite. Once you have the cap and fuse stuck into the dynamite, pinch the hole together around the fuse so it won't come out when you throw the dynamite. Make sure you keep the box of caps away from the dynamite. Have Payuk carry the caps. The inside of the box with the caps is padded so there is not much danger of getting bumped.

Just before dark, before you go to the mining camp, crimp one cap onto one fuse that should be about six inches long. Wrap each cap and fuse in some cloth and when it's time to throw the dynamite, stick the cap and fuse into the dynamite, pinch it tight, light, and throw. Payuk will have the caps and you will have the dynamite. I know it sounds crazy, but that is the only way you can keep from blowing yourself and everybody around you into little pieces. Kelly and Payuk, now be damn careful. Only take one stick out of your bag at a time and light it, and throw. Make sure you have plenty of matches. I want at least two dozen smoke bombs thrown into the entire camp area. The darkness will make it twice as hard to see anything. With the flares being shot off pointed away from camp, it will make seeing that much harder. Fisher and Payuk, you guys make sure all the miner's horses are all stampeded out and way from the corral. Hopefully they might head down the river after Jeffery and Wilson."

"Do I throw the dynamite into the buildings?"

"Not into the building, but close. I want you to destroy as much as possible with that explosive. I don't want to kill anybody if the job can be done without that, but I can't do anything about it if it happens. Just don't stay too long and get captured. Once you have Jeffery and Wilson on the way, hit hard and often, and then get the hell out. If you do it right, you will look like twenty people throwing explosives."

"Won't they come after us once they have got their stock rounded up?" Payuk asked.

"Payuk, I'm sorry I could not tell you. A lot of times the least amount of people that know certain pieces of information the better. Moaka set it up with Kiviaq to cover your retreat down the Iskut River to the Stikine River to the *Blue Sea*. There will be about fifteen men of your clan that will be just above the camp on the mountain side just south of the camp across the canyon. They will be able to see if the miners the next morning take out after you, and they will stop them from going down the Iskut River by staging an Indian attack. They will be able to hold them there indefinitely. It rather goes without saying; there will be no stopping for the forty miles or so from the mining camp to the *Blue Sea*. Resting a short period, and watering of horses, and that is it. You can eat when you get on the *Blue Sea*. If you need to, take some jerky with you in your packs."

Walking over to the sweet roll table, James sneaked one out of the pile and commenced to chow down. He smiled with his first bite. "Damn good...

"By the way, Jeffery, you don't wait on Kelly, Payuk, and Fisher. They will probably catch up with you soon enough. Don't be in a hurry with Wilson over the saddle: we don't want to kill him by shaking him to death. After a couple of hours you can stop and sit him up straight if you feel comfortable doing that; if not, just wait until Kelly catches up to you."

"Wow!" Jeffery declared. "I didn't realize this stuff could get dangerous. I'm going to have a sweet roll and some more coffee if that would be alright." He looked at James.

Motioning with his hand that he still had a sweet roll in, James encouraged him. "Sure, go ahead, and then we have to get busy getting things in motion. Before all you guys get out of here, I want you to put the chairs back where they belong."

Soon the office was empty except for James and Sara, and Sara looked around. "Boy, we had quite a group in here. I hope this works for you guys. Everybody seems to understand what they need to do. I like the idea of Kiviaq and the tribal members stopping the mining crew from coming after Kelly and the other men as they are trying to get to the *Blue Sea*. Is the *Blue Sea* a nice boat?"

He shrugged his shoulders. "Sure, I guess so. It carries passengers and most anything else. It is a large vessel with lots of power."

"Is there anything else I need to put in the minutes before I start typing the report?"

"No, I don't think so." Pausing for a moment, he shook his head. "There always seems to be something we leave out or didn't cover well enough."

"That's why you put Kelly in charge when you are staying here."

Sighing, he agreed. "Yeah, you're right. He is quite able to be the leader in the field."

"Do you think Payuk knows Moaka is leaving to go to Barrow?"

"Sara, I would bet on it. Apparently Jeffery and Moaka told everybody they knew about Moaka leaving and Jeffery had bought his house."

"Listen, Sara, I'm going to go down to the livery to check a couple of things. I should be back in a while."

As James walked slowly toward the livery he thought, *That gold has to be somewhere on that wagon. Nobody so far has found it, but I'm going to get that smithy that works for Shane and see if he could lend a hand in locating the gold.* Seeing Shane work a horse in the corral, James hailed, "Where is your smithy at?"

Shane pointed and said, "Over there in the metal shop."

Walking around the corral, James walked into the metal shop and interrupted the smithy. "Can I bother you from hammering on that steel for a minute?"

"Yes sir, Mr. Kincaid—just a moment, I need to get it straightened out before it cools too much."

Raising his hand, James stepped back and watched the smithy hammer the piece of flat metal on the anvil until it seemed straight.

Laying his hammer and the piece of flat metal down on the anvil, he smiled and asked, "What can I do for you?"

Extending his hand, James apologized. "I'm sorry; I have forgotten your name."

Taking James's firm handshake, the man replied, "My name is Fred Bingham."

"Well, Fred, I want you to come with me over to the wagons and let's look for some gold."

"Mr. Kincaid," Fred said and smiled, "you are about the tenth person to check out those wagons, but let's go over and look again."

"OK, Fred. I'll follow you."

Fred led the way to the large warehouse behind the livery, opened the large wooden double doors, and pointed to the two empty freight wagons. Pointing to the other two wagons loaded with supplies for the mine, Fred commented, "I guess you guys are taking these supply wagons out tomorrow morning."

"Yes, that's right, Fred. Now let's take a good look at these empty wagons. Well, they sure as hell look empty to me." Looking back at Fred he said, "No false bottoms or false side panels?"

"Not that I can see, Mr. Kincaid. These wagons are built hell for stout."

James grabbed one of the metal side braces that was attached to the side of one of the wagons and jerked as hard as he could. To both men's surprise, one of the bolts holding the brace to the wagon gave way. Quickly glancing at Fred, James said, "Get hold on this thing. Let's see if we can jerk it off the wagon mounts."

Getting a firm grip and a good stance, both men jerked at the same time and the brace came completely off the side of the freight wagon. Both men fell backward with the brace across their bodies.

Getting up, Fred gave James a hand to get up. "Well, I guess we did that in good shape." He smiled.

After closer examination of the inside of the freight wagon, Fred and James discovered the bolts that were pulled through the wagon side boards were sunk in with wooden plugs over them to hide the bolt heads.

James bent down and motioned to Fred. "Pick up the other end and let's carry this thing into your metal shop."

Picking up the other end, Fred remarked, "This brace should not be this heavy."

Laying the half-round brace across two benches, James looked at Fred. "I'll bet you a week's wages there is gold inside of the brass brace. It's a half-round brass brace that weighs twice as much as it should—you taking any bets?"

Smiling, Fred shook his head. "No sir. I agree with you."

Turning it over and over, James asked, "How do we get into the brace?"

Going to the end of the eight-foot brace, Fred waved James over to take a look. "I think I can take a chisel and hammer and knock the end right off. Here, get back and let me try." Holding the chisel at the right angle, Fred gave the chisel a good, solid strike with his five-pound hammer...Clang, the hammer sounded as it struck the chisel, and the end of the brace flew off across the metal shop. Fred quickly looked at James as James looked at Fred, and they both tried to look into the brace and banged their heads together in their haste to see inside.

James slowly pinched a cloth that was just inside the brass brace between his fingers and pulled out a sack of gold just sized around to put into the brace, and about eight inches long. Holding up the bag, James shook his head. "By the damn, the lost is found."

Instantly, Fred glanced around outside and then came back into the metal shop. In absolute wonder, he asked James, "What are we going to do with all this gold? There must be a lot more of these bags in the other three braces."

James held up his hand. "Go get Shane. Don't say why, just get him here now."

Soon Shane walked into the metal shop with Fred, and instantly knew James and Fred had found the gold.

Shane approached James as James handed Shane the first bag of gold. "My hell, that is heavy," Shane commented. "What are we going to do with it?"

"OK, Shane, I want you to go get the bank president and one other man from the bank. Bring them back here right away. In the meantime, Fred and I will empty this one brace."

"OK, I'll be right back." And looking back as he left, Shane smiled. "Now don't let any of that gold get lost before I get back."

Holding the sack of gold up that was about two inches around and about eight inches long, James stated, "I did not realize gold was so heavy. OK, let's see how many are in this brace."

Going to the closed end, Fred put his large, strong body to good use as Fred picked up the closed end of the brace, and seven bags slid out the open end.

Soon Keith Mason showed up with one of his bank employees, Tom Marks, and they heard the story of how the gold was found and that the Department of Agriculture wanted the bank to hold the gold until it had been decided what was to be done with it.

Keith asked, "How much gold is there all together?"

"We don't know," advised James. "We need to take the rest of the wagon braces off and see."

"Just a minute, James," Fred observed. "We don't have to take the other braces off. I'm sure they didn't. All we need to do is knock the ends off the braces and push the gold out one end or the other."

Everybody shook their heads OK, and Fred advised, "I can do that in no time at all."

"OK," Keith announced, "I'm going to leave Tom here," he pointed toward Tom, "as a witness as you salvage the gold out of the other three braces. When you get all the braces empty, someone come and get me, and I'll certify the amount of gold to be deposited in the Wrangell Bank." Pausing, Keith glanced at Tom. "You stay with the gold."

"Yes sir, I will."

Shane stepped in and calmly said, "Well, let's get the rest of the gold and get rich," which brought a look from Keith Mason. "I was only joking, Keith."

James watched as Fred methodically used his chisel and hammer the same as before and knocked the ends off the half-round braces.

Shane used a snare rope handle to push the bags of gold out one end, and James caught the gold out the other end.

Finally, after getting all the bags of gold stacked on the steel shop bench, there were twenty-eight bags of gold. Tom counted them carefully and Fred went to get Keith from the bank.

When Keith arrived and certified the amount, Shane volunteered, "Fred and I will put the gold in some freight boxes and use my buckboard to haul the gold to the bank."

"That will work just fine, Shane, and Tom, you stay with the gold," Keith instructed. "I'm going back to the bank to find room in the vault."

James shrugged. "Well, I guess I'm done here. Thanks, Fred, for your help. Shane, do you need me here anymore?"

"No, James. I think we got it. I knew you could not let that gold issue be unsettled. I told Sara last night that I bet Kincaid isn't sleeping tonight just thinking where that gold is."

251

Everybody laughed. "You're right, Shane, it was bothering me some."

Waving to everybody, James started back to the office. As James slowly walked to the office, he thought, "Now that we have the gold, who does it belong to? I guess I'll have to wait until all parties are here and represented.'

James walked in the office and Sara quietly said, "Captain Weber is in your office."

Nodding to Sara, James continued into his office. As soon as Captain Weber saw James he stood and announced, "We are ready to go in the morning. Boy, that Kelly is a real hotshot. He seems to know most everything there is to do. We got the wood on, supplies bought and stowed, and the stock deck set up for the two teams and supply wagons."

James slid behind his desk and sat as he shook his head. "Yeah, he is a good man. One more thing, do you have any rifles on board the *Blue Sea*?"

"Yes, we have one as far as I know, and it usually stays in my quarters. I have my sidearm and so does Chief Mate Harrison. We never needed anything else."

Opening one of this desk drawers, James started to write a message to Deputy Sheriff Marlin on Department letterhead. "What I'm writing here is a message for you to take to Deputy Sheriff Marlin asking him to loan you five rifles and two hundred rounds of ammunition. If you take it to him now, he is in his office; he will do as I ask, but you have to return them." He smiled at Captain Weber.

"Why do I and my men need rifles? Do you expect bears to attack us while we wait on the Stikine River?"

Shaking his head, James replied, "No, Charles, something much more serious. If things do not go the way they should with our plan, you and your men may have to give Kelly and his men covering fire till they get on the *Blue Sea*."

Getting serious, Captain Weber apologized for being light about the subject. "Do you think it will come to that, James?"

"I don't know, just covering all bases."

"OK, James, I'll be on my way to see the sheriff, and I'll see you in the morning... about what time?"

"You need to have the *Blue Sea* ready to take on the teams and wagons at seven a.m. Then we can start our operation forward."

"OK, James, I'm out of here." He waved good-bye.

Hearing Charles saying good-bye to Sara, James sat back in his chair and began rocking slowly and smiled as he thought, *I wonder how this will all end? Kelly better be paying attention. I think I'm going to call this operation, OPERATION BRAY.*

CHAPTER NINETEEN

Kelly slowly walked home from a very busy and trying day. Laughing to himself, he thought, *Old Captain Weber was so happy with those dogs he took both of them. Well, that's good; Boren finally got rid of the last of his litter.*

It was later than normal so Nancy would have already fed Sidney. Opening the back door, Kelly cleaned his shoes off and walked into the kitchen. "Nancy, are you home?"

Instantly, Sidney came charging out of his bedroom. "Hi, Daddy."

Leaning down, Kelly picked him up and asked, "Where is your mom?"

Hearing the back door open, Kelly sat Sidney down, and he ran back to his room. "What are you doing outside, it's almost dark."

"Oh, I had to go over to Mrs. Raymore's," Nancy replied. "Her son, Jerry, is having a real hard time with his reading so I gave her a small book of phonics. Her husband works for one of those fishing companies and he's not home a lot to help. I asked Suzette, and she said of course and she said give Mr. Raymore a beginning book of phonics and it will help him. Anyway, why are you so late tonight?"

"Just getting ready for tomorrow." Walking over to Nancy, Kelly leaned over and kissed her gently on the cheek. "How was school today?"

"You need a shave." She give Kelly a quick hug. "School was fine. We have received some new books that the school just got for next year. I got a chance to look at some of them and they stress math and reading as a basis for a good education."

"That sounds about right. Although I never was a good reader."

"Oh Kelly, you are a good reader. You have the ability to scan well."

"I'm late tonight because we had to go over the last minute details with everybody before the operation starts, and Kincaid wanted to talk more about this job. I need to pack my pack tonight with a few things I'll need because I will be gone for a few days."

"How many few days, Kelly?" Nancy asked in a frustrated voice. "You told me that we were going to make a trip to Seattle this spring. Is that going to happen?

"Are you hungry? If you are, I'll warm up the noodles and pork."

"Yeah, I could eat something. Has Sidney eaten yet?"

"Yes, he likes to eat earlier in the evening."

"Yes, we will make that trip to Seattle. I want to buy Sidney a small pony to ride and some good tack."

"Did you hear that Moaka is leaving Wrangell to work in Barrow?" Nancy asked. "I can't imagine anybody wanting to go there, at least on a permanent basis."

"Well, the way I hear it, Moaka wants to raise his children Inuit." He smirked slightly. "Yeah, he wants to raise his children Inuit, but he wants them to have a good education—he promised that to Tess before she died. I think he's really looking forward to getting up there before bad weather so he can get his dog team built or at least assembled. No one told me that, but I just assumed that."

"Get washed up...the noodles will be ready pretty quick."

"I had to laugh at James the other day. When James and Moaka were at Terrace Point, this young lady came into their camp. Apparently she was hungry, cold, and had a small dog. She came to the camp rowing an old wooden boat her and her father had. He'd gotten killed by a bear some time ago."

"Here, sit down and have your noodles and pork. What did he do with her?"

255

Shaking his head, he continued. "Well, he took her to Mrs. Mackly and wanted Mrs. Mackly to give her a job, and I guess she did. Now she works for Mrs. Mackly in the Parker Boarding House: cooking, cleaning, or anything that needs to be done."

"What time do you want me to get you up in the morning?"

"Well, I don't know...get me up at five a.m. That will give me time to pack the packhorse and my saddlebags for the trip."

"Where are you going to be gone so long?" Nancy questioned.

"We're going to get on the *Blue Sea* steamer and ride up the Stikine River to the Iskut River, then offload and travel alongside the Iskut River till we get to Twin Forks Mining camp."

"Is that the large steamboat that is anchored in the bay? I don't even know where those places are located. Are they in Alaska or Canada?"

"Yes, that's the steamboat, and it is a nice vessel. Most of the travel will be in Canada, but James has been asked to take a look at some of the mining claims in the upper Iskut River area for the British Columbia folks, and also our office here in Wrangell is taking a close look at that mining outfit for poaching."

"Sidney, come in here and say good night to your dad. You won't see him for a few days."

"Thanks for the noodles and pork. That is always a good supper." And standing away from the table after finishing his supper, Kelly stretched and commented, "I've got to get packed and hit the sack. It will be an early and busy morning." Bending down and hugging Sidney, Kelly told him, "Now you mind your mom when I'm gone. Now go to bed, and I'll see you when I get back."

. . .

James tried to unlock the office door, but it was already unlocked. Opening the door, he was not surprised to see Kelly packing ammunition, wet gear, and a warm cap into his personal pack he had brought from home.

"Getting ready pretty early."

"Yes, I have to meet Payuk at Boren's soon to pack the packhorses. He is going to have the packhorses at the horse railing at six a.m. We will fill the cross buck saddles with our supplies and a few extra just in case. Oh, and by the way, can I take that small windbreaker tent with us? It's small, but it will keep the wind and rain off of us."

"Sure, Kelly, take what you think you need. Just remember, you and Payuk need to stay out of sight. You're taking two packhorses?"

"Yes. With taking the small windbreaker tent there will be lots of room for supplies on two packhorses. We also have our personal packs and our own saddlebags. I think there will be plenty of room for supplies and gear."

James noticed Kelly had his side arm on. Pointing to the piece, James advised, "Keep that thing close, you never know."

As Kelly closed his pack, he shook his head. "You bet. Always makes me feel a lot safer when I have my pistol close. Well, I'll see you at the loading. I've got to go meet Payuk at Boren's to load the packhorse."

"Wait, Kelly," James advised. "You have to be very careful out there. There are many things out there that can kill you or put you on a stretcher. When crowded, be calm; don't get in a hurry to make a bad decision. What you decide may save someone's life. Just think before you jump."

Knowing that James was concerned for everyone on this operation, Kelly shook his head. "I understand. I will do my best."

"OK, get out of here." James smiled. "Have a good trip."

Getting the packhorses loaded, getting their saddlebags loaded, and quickly stopping by the Steak and Stack for a stack of pancakes and bag of corn dodgers, Kelly and Payuk headed to the livery to help Fisher and Jeffery get the wagons to the loading area where the *Blue Sea* would let down the front ramp for loading. Following the wagons being driven by Fisher and Jeffery, Kelly and Payuk checked to see that the wagons were pulling straight and the horses were pulling evenly. It was seven forty-five a.m. as Paul and Stan slowly lowered the front ramp.

Fisher was leading the way and he heard Captain Weber hailing, "Come aboard."

Slashing the reins down on the backs of the four-horse team, the first wagon eased onto the ramp and slowly entered the stock deck of the *Blue Sea.*

As soon as Fisher was inside the *Blue Sea*, Captain Weber hailed again to Jeffery as he waved, "Come aboard."

Smiling, Jeffery waved back and was excited to be part of the operation. Thinking to himself, *What an experience. Something to tell my grandkids...if I have any.* Bringing his attention back to his driving, he moved the team inside the *Blue Sea* without any problems.

As soon as the teams were in, Kelly and Payuk led their horses and packhorses into the *Blue Sea.*

Paul signaled that all the stock was inside and Captain Weber motioned to close the ramp. Stan and Paul started cranking the front ramp up into position and locked it in place. And at the same time, Captain Weber eased the *Blue Sea* out into the bay.

Feeling the vessel stop, Paul instructed, "OK, you guys, we need to get the horses tethered to the bulkheads: leave the harnesses on, unhook the teams from the wagons. Make sure to lock down the wheels of the wagons so they can't move."

Kelly handed Peanut's reins to Payuk and said, "I'm going up to see the captain. I'll be back in a bit."

"OK, Kelly."

Opening the door to the wheelhouse, Kelly was surprised to see a large wooden box with two black Lab puppies lying on soft blankets. Smirking, Kelly teased Captain Weber, "You are going to spoil those dogs right away, and I can see it now."

Chief Mate Harrison chimed in: "You can't have them lying on the hard floor, can you?"

"I guess not," Kelly answered. "Captain Weber, would you let me drive this thing, if that is what you call operating it?"

Quickly looking at Kelly, he replied, "Sure, Kelly." He looked at Chief Mate Harrison and they both smiled. "Just let me get the old gal moving out in the open seas, and you can take over."

As soon as the *Blue Sea* passed around Wrangell Point, Captain Weber stepped back and motioned to Kelly. "The helm is yours. This is the wheel for navigation and this handle is the Chadburn or Engine Order Telegraph. We just call it the E.O.T. It lets the engine room, or Mike in this case, know you want to stop, increase or decrease speed, or go in reverse."

Kelly quickly rubbed his sweaty hands together. "I want to go faster."

Captain Weber slowly touched the Chadburn. "Take hold of this and move to whatever position you want for what speed you want. Remember, this is called the Chadburn or E.O.T."

Taking a deep breath, Kelly lightly moved the Chadburn handle, and a loud bell sounded, making Kelly jump.

Captain Weber calmly spoke. "Move the pointer to SLOW AHEAD."

Kelly moved the pointer to the position on the Chadburn that showed SLOW AHEAD. "Like that?" Kelly quickly asked.

"Yes. Now keep both hands on the wheel as you steer the *Blue Sea* toward the estuary."

Captain Weber explained, "Now we are going to use visual guidance. Paul and Stan are standing by to do their Mark Twain when we get close to the estuary. When we are out in the ocean away from shore, we use that—" Captain Weber pointed to the compass. "We have to follow compass reading so we don't get lost."

Turning the wheel slightly, Kelly could feel the *Blue Sea* shifting slightly to the right, and as he turned the wheel to the original position, he could feel the *Blue Sea* shifting back. Smiling, he said, "Well, thank you very much, Captain Weber. That was exciting."

As Kelly stepped back, Captain Weber took the wheel and instructed Harrison, "Signal Paul and Mike to start Mark Twain. I think we are alright for now, but I want them on the spot. I think we are a little early, but I believe it will be just fine for the depth."

"Aye, aye, sir." He stepped out of the wheelhouse and flagged both men. Paul was starboard and Stan was standing port.

Kneeling down to pet the Labs, Kelly said, "I'm going down to the stock deck to help with the stock while we are going through the estuary. Thanks again, Captain Weber."

Getting to the stock deck, Kelly checked Peanut and the packhorse. Walking over to Payuk, he said, "Did those rifles get on board for the *Blue Sea*'s crew?"

"Yes, I saw the chief mate carry them on board with the ammunition."

Nodding, Kelly approached Jeffery and Fisher. "Everything OK here?"

"You bet, Kelly," Jeffery answered.

Suddenly the *Blue Sea* shifted hard to the right as the horses struggled to stand, but Kelly was glad the wagons did not break loose. Hurrying to the bow, Kelly opened the small door and saw that the estuary was very turbulent because of the spring run-off crashing into the tidal wave. "Hang on," Kelly yelled, "here comes another one!"

Just as Kelly warned, the *Blue Sea* shifted hard to the left and seemingly turned sideways a small amount, then instantly straightened back out to head straight up the estuary. Continuing to peer out the small door, Kelly was amazed as he thought, *Look at all that water coming down the Stikine River.* And, unexpectedly, Kelly had to grab an upright to keep from falling.

"Kelly," Payuk yelled, "Need some help with a horse that is down."

Slamming the door closed, Kelly ran to help Jeffery and Fisher stand a horse back up that had slipped and gone down. Finally the horse got its footing and stood as the three men balanced the animal for him to get his footing. "Here," Kelly said. "Let's get the harness straightened out."

Jeffery had to unbuckle a couple of clips because the horse had stepped through one of the traces. "OK," Jeffery called, "he's clear, and buckle him up again."

As soon as the horses were calmed down, the *Blue Sea* began to run smoothly over the water.

"We must be out of the estuary." Fisher opened one of the side doors.

"Damn good thing!" Kelly exclaimed. "I wouldn't want much more of what we just had," and everybody laughed. "Now we've got a while before we debark at the Iskut River."

From time to time, everybody could hear the steam engine roar with power, then ease back as power was not needed. Visually, Kelly could see Captain Weber in the wheelhouse manning the helm and turning the wheel and adjusting the Chadburn for slower or for more speed. Smiling, Kelly thought, *It's a good plan and I'm satisfied that the plan James and I made, with the others' help, has a good chance of working—as long as everybody does as they're supposed to do at the right time.*

Digging into his saddlebags, Payuk got out his glass to see along the back. Adjusting the glass, he called Kelly, "Come over here."

Kelly eased over to where Payuk was, trying to keep his balance. "What is it that you want?"

Handing the glass to Kelly, Payuk pointed. "Look along the shoreline. What do you see?"

As Kelly looked through the glass, he smiled. "Looks like Kiviaq taking his warriors up the river, getting ready to give ground cover for us if we need it. Course, they will be way up the Iskut River just a couple of miles downstream from the mining camp. They will stay on the back side of the ridge to stay hidden until they're needed. Once they see you, Fisher, and I going downriver, two or three will stay even with us in case we have any problems, and the rest will hold position to stop the miners if they come after us."

Looking at Kelly in amazement, Payuk noted, "You and Kincaid must have stayed up late planning all this stuff."

"Actually it was James, Moaka, and I. You don't think for one minute James would have planned this without the input of Moaka. Moaka is just like James's right hand everything. They act alike, think alike, and live life to the fullest. They are very good friends. Years from now, if one of their children needed help, the other would be there instantly, no questions asked."

Nodding, Payuk agreed. "Yes, they are very close. That is something to have someone that close to you." Sighing, Payuk announced, "I think I will go up to the wheelhouse and see what the river looks like from higher up."

"Sure." Kelly motioned to him to go. "I'll stay here while you're gone. I suspect the river won't be very rough from here on out."

Watching Payuk walk away from him and up the steel stairs, Kelly thought, *Payuk is a good man. I bet he was very sorry when his family died. I wonder if he will ever remarry.* Looking out the small window next to him, he could just barely see Kiviaq traveling in the trees upstream of the Stikine River. *Kiviaq will turn east before he runs into the Iskut River, to stay behind the south ridge.*

Slowly opening the door to the wheelhouse, Captain Weber and Chief Mate Harrison greeted him, "Come on in, Payuk. Take a look up here. It looks a lot different than at the water's level."

"That's what I wanted to see. I hope I'm not bothering anything."

"Of course not," Captain Weber commented. "I'm just standing here watching the river go by and paying attention to Stan and Paul, who give me Mark Twains once in a while or when I ask for them. And the chief mate is checking charts and scanning the river ahead for logs and sand islands that show up every once in a while. We'll be crossing over into Canada pretty soon. Actually, you can't even tell the difference; the river sure doesn't look any different. You want the helm?" Captain Weber offered the wheel to Payuk.

Holding his hands up, Payuk shook his head quickly. "No, no, I could not do that. I just want to be here for a minute longer to look at the shore, the waves, and the river moving fast." Looking down to the dogs in their bed, he pointed. "They sure are cute; only thing, they grow up into big dogs."

Both the chief mate and the captain laughed as the captain boasted, "That's what we what them to do."

Waving, Payuk said, "Thanks for letting me up here. It was a real treat. I guess I'll get back to the stock deck in case someone needs some help."

Getting back down on the stock deck, Payuk saw Kelly leaning against the outside bulkhead more or less dreaming as he watched the river flow by, with small pieces of wood, moss, and occasional birds floating by.

"What are you thinking about, Kelly?"

Being startled, Kelly jumped. "What the hell...Damn, Payuk, I was a thousand miles away from here. I was thinking about home in Pennsylvania."

Not too long after Payuk came back from the wheelhouse, Captain Weber got on the speaker and announced, "Crossing into Canada. We have about six miles before Iskut River. Don't hook up yet, but keep the animals calm until we get stopped and locked into shore."

Tightening the cinch straps of the riding horses' saddles and on the packhorses' cross bucks, Kelly and Payuk checked their gear and packs. Jeffery and Fischer made sure the harness was straightened out and laid up on the teams' backs in readiness to hook up to the double trees.

Feeling sure everything was OK, Kelly instructed Fisher and Payuk, "You guys might have to help Stan and Paul with the stabilizing poles."

Kelly looked out the starboard side window and saw that the *Blue Sea* was moving close to shore.

Captain Weber pointed to a small cove as Chief Mate Harrison nodded. "Looks good. We can get good stabilization there from each end."

"OK," Captain Weber instructed, "go let Paul and Stan know we want to be stabilized into that cove as best we can. You might have one or two of them other fellows help."

"Aye, aye, sir." Chief Mate Harrison quickly exited the wheelhouse.

Captain Weber slowly moved the Chadburn to the SLOW AHEAD position as he quickly turned the wheel to turn the bow of the *Blue Sea* into the bank, and then quickly moved the Chadburn to SLOW BACK position as he turned the wheel the opposite direction to push the aft over to the bank. Once that maneuver was made, he moved the Chadburn to the ALL STOP position. Knowing that Mike would not leave the control room until the Chadburn was moved to the FINISHED WITH ENGINES position, Captain Weber waited for Chief Mate Harrison to report back for it being a suitable place to ground to shore for a few days.

Soon Chief Mate Harrison appeared on the forward deck and waved. "It is just fine, sir. We can set the stabilizer pole into firm ground."

Nodding his head, Captain Weber looked down the starboard side and saw Paul and Stan on the bank with ropes. Smiling, he was thinking, *Good men. They know what they are doing.* Moving the Chadburn to the FINISHED WITH ENGINE position, Captain Weber secured the wheel so it would not turn and bent down to pet his newly found friends.

Chief Mate Harrison enlisted Fisher and Payuk to give Stan and Paul a hand installing the stabilizing poles. And soon the *Blue Sea* was firmly anchored to the shore and was out of the Stikine's main river flow and away from large logs floating down the river. Captain Weber came down to the stock deck and commented to Chief Mate Harrison, "Being in this little cove gives us a lot of protection from the river debris, and the *Blue Sea* will not be constantly rocking with the river surges."

Kelly helped lower the side stock ramp from the *Blue Sea* to the shore, and Stan and Paul set the cables so the weight of the ramp would be on the ground.

Stepping back, Captain Weber sighed. "I think we are about ready to take the teams off. But before you do, I want someone leading the team off the *Blue Sea* and someone driving the team. OK, get the teams hooked up and lay to it."

As Fisher drove the first team off, Jeffery led the teams to help settle them as they started to cross on the wooden ramp. As the first wagon slowly rolled onto shore, Fisher went to drive the second team as Jeffery led as before. Once the teams were off the *Blue Sea*, Kelly and Payuk took their horses and packhorses to shore.

Getting all the teams and horses onto shore, Kelly walked back to Captain Weber, "By golly, we did it." Shaking his head, Kelly continued, "It is easy with the help of people that know what they're doing."

"OK, Kelly." Captain Weber commented. "You are on your own. We have finished our job so far."

"Yes, you have, Captain Weber. Have you got those rifles and ammunition handy, just in case?"

"Yes. When will we know that you need rifle cover?"

Nodding, Kelly answered, "Don't worry about that...you will know."

"It's about one p.m. Are you going to leave right now?"

"Yes, I don't want to lose any time hanging around here. We need to get these wagons to the mining camp as soon as we can."

Extending his hand, Captain Weber said, "Godspeed, young fellow." As he raised his voice, he hailed to the others, "Be careful up there. Mr. Kincaid seemed to think it could be quite dangerous."

Mounting Peanut, Kelly shifted to one side to center the saddle. "Thanks again, Captain Weber, and the rest of your crew." He looked around and saw none of the crew. "Where is your crew, Captain Weber?"

"Oh, they all have jobs to do right after we anchor anywhere. We'll all be waiting for you—hurry back." Captain Weber waved as he turned to enter the *Blue Sea*.

Kelly rode up to check with Fisher. "Follow down the wagon road for a short distance to get out of eyesight of the *Blue Sea*. When we stop, I'll be giving last minute instructions."

Soon Fisher reined up his teams and Jeffery followed suit. Setting the brake and tying the reins off, Fisher climbed down off the freight wagon as Jeffery did the same.

Riding up on Peanut with Payuk and the packhorses right behind, Kelly dismounted and called for everyone to gather around.

Looking to both sides of the canyon, Kelly observed, "What a beautiful valley." Shaking his head, he continued. "Anyway, this is how it is supposed to go. Fisher, you and Jeffery follow the road to the mining camp. You will probably be on the trail for two nights...does that sound about right?" He nodded toward Fisher.

"Yes. By leaving this late in the day it will be two nights on the road."

Kelly pointed to the south ridge. "Payuk and I will be just on the other side. We will keep you in our sights all the time. Be careful of wash-outs, deep ruts, and generally a rough wagon road. If a horse falls lame, kill it." Pausing, Kelly asked Fisher, "Have you guys got plenty of supplies and grub?"

Both Fisher and Jeffery nodded yes, and Jeffery added, "We have a rifle each."

"If you have any problems...Payuk, get me that red flag out of my saddlebags." As Payuk handed Kelly the red material, Kelly explained, "Use this for signaling if you can't keep moving. If Payuk and I don't see this flag, we won't see you until the second night at the mining camp. Remember, Kiviaq and his men will be covering our retreat down the Iskut River to the *Blue Sea*. Are there any questions about what is going to happen at the mine? Does anybody have any questions about what James explained in his office?"

Fisher and Jeffery both shook their heads no, and everybody shook each other's hands and wished good luck.

As Kelly and Payuk mounted, Kelly warned, "Be careful," as he slowly rode away up the slope toward the south rim of the valley.

And Payuk, from on top of his horse, smiled and looked down at both men. "You guys are the key to this operation, but don't try to be heroes."

CHAPTER TWENTY

School was dismissed as the teachers met in the meeting room of the Wrangell School. Ted Bean, the principal, sat the chairs in a circle so all the teachers could equally participate. Soon the teachers came in with notes for the meeting as required by Ted.

Listening to conversations around the circle of teachers about the day's activities, Ted called, "Let's get started."

Each teacher was required to review their classroom activities and any problems they were having with certain students; whether it was a problem with behavior or a problem with learning, both were discussed. And finally Ted informed the teachers of the financial standing of the school.

With the required information covered by each teacher, the floor was opened for discussion on any subject that could or would be for the betterment of the school or individual teacher and class.

There were discussions about field trips, testing, and promotions of certain students to the next higher level, for next year.

Standing to close the meeting with a prayer, Ted was interrupted by the math/science teacher, Simon Middleton. "When is the last day of school this year?"

"Oh yeah, I forgot to mention that." Ted sat back down. "The school year will end the day before Decoration Day, May 30th. Is there any more discussion?"

"Yes," Suzette spoke up. "There is a young lady that has just moved into our community that works at Parker Boarding House for Mrs. Mackly. She has an unusual talent that should be brought forth to the children for summertime activities. She is an excellent artist and painter. I would like for her to come to school one afternoon when scheduling would allow and have her give a short demonstration of her works. She actually uses almost all natural paints and draws and paints on natural materials like bark, rocks, or driftwood. She is a very good artist."

"OK." Ted asked, "Everyone look at your calendar you have with you...give me a day we can schedule this person." He looked at Suzette. "Name?"

"Oh yes, I'm sorry. Her name is Janet Moore. I'm sure she could get away from work anytime for a short demonstration of her skills."

Nancy O'Brien, geography/history teacher noted, "The 28th of May will work, I think, for most of us, because we are having our promotion meetings with the students that day."

Ted looked around the circle of teachers. "OK with you, Maggie," the English/Literature teacher, "for that day? How about you, Simon and Suzette, will that work for you also?"

Nodding, both Simon and Suzette agreed on May 28 for Janet to come and do her demonstrations of drawings and paintings.

"Are you, Suzette, going to contact Janet Moore and ask her if she could be here about two p.m. on May 28th?"

She nodded. "Yes, I'll do that right away."

"OK, if there's nothing else..." Ted stood and gave the closing prayer and the meeting was closed.

As Suzette made her way back to her classroom, she stopped Nancy. "Would you like to come with me this evening after supper to see Janet Moore?"

Pausing before she went into her classroom, Nancy nodded. "Yes, that would be fine. Kelly mentioned her last night before he left."

"Good." Suzette smiled. "I'll see you at Parker's Boarding House about seven p.m., after supper."

Just at seven o'clock both Suzette and Nancy opened the squeaky screen door and walked into the main day room. Looking beyond the day room, Suzette motioned that they had to go farther back to the dining room.

Coming out of the kitchen, Mrs. Mackly was surprised. "Mrs. Kincaid, what a surprise, and if memory serves me right, this is Nancy, Kelly's better half."

Feeling embarrassed, Nancy acknowledged, "Yes."

"OK, what can I do for you ladies? Can I get you anything to drink?"

"No thanks, Mrs. Mackly. We actually need to see Janet, if you don't mind, and if she is not too busy."

"Sure, we just got the kitchen cleaned up from supper." She disappeared, and Janet soon appeared from the kitchen.

"Oh hi, Mrs. Kincaid. Mrs. Mackly said you wanted to talk with me."

"Janet, this is Nancy O'Brien. She is also a teacher at the school. And this, Nancy, is Janet Moore, the artist."

"Hi, Janet. I've heard a lot about you from Suzette."

"If you could sit down for a minute, Janet, we would like to ask you for a favor, if you want to do it." Suzette asked.

"Sure," Janet accepted.

"When James and I and the kids were in here last evening you showed me some of your work. Could you bring a couple of samples out for Nancy to see?"

"Sure. Just sit tight and I'll be right back. I have to go to my room to get them."

Soon Janet returned with several paintings on bark, driftwood, and rocks. Also she had carvings on bark and wood slabs. Some were colored, some were not.

Looking at the artwork, Nancy praised her. "My word, Janet, where did you learn to do this art?"

"My father taught me a lot, but I kinda taught myself some of it. There seems to be no limit to what can happen when you let yourself go."

"Well," Suzette asked, "the teachers would like you to come to the school and make a short presentation of your work. Maybe some of the students will want some lessons during the summer and that could be source of income. Granted it may not be much, but every little bit helps. Anyway, the principal approved your coming for the presentation so you are good to come if you desire. We would like to have you come on the twenty-eighth of May about two in the afternoon for about an hour or so. Would you like to do something like that?"

"Of course," Janet gleefully responded. "That sounds like it will be fun for me and for the students. You can count on me to be there. Mrs. Mackly won't mind at all. She is very, very nice about such things."

"OK, then. Until the twenty-eighth, at two p.m." Suzette stood to leave.

"Nice meeting you, Janet. We'll be seeing each other around Wrangell, I'm sure."

As Suzette and Nancy left, Mrs. Mackly came out of the kitchen. "Those two women are highly rated in this town, and at least you're rubbing shoulders with the right people. I would like you to do more of your artwork. It sells good for you and with the 20/80 split for showing them in the boarding house, I can make a little also." Tapping Janet on the shoulder, she said, "You have an amazing talent, young lady."

...

Next morning, Moaka reined up in front of the lodge house of the Island Clan of the Tlingit Tribe. Keeping his packhorse tied to the back of his saddle, Moaka dismounted and let the reins fall to the ground for the horse to stay. Looking to the sky Moaka thought, *The Island of Woronkofski is always wet and damp. If it is not raining, it has just stopped.*

Moaka did not know the clan chief's name, but from past experience, he knew he liked to be called Many Fish. Many Fish could speak some English, but he always had a younger person with him to interpret. His English was just about as good as Moaka's knowledge of the Tlingit language.

Moaka waited patiently for someone to come out of the lodge or come to the lodge so he could be introduced as he entered.

By and by a young man came walking up to the lodge and asked, "You want enter?"

"Yes," Moaka replied as he stepped aside. "I am Moaka from Department of Agriculture."

"Who want see?"

"Many Fish."

"I tell to him." The young man entered the lodge.

Soon Many Fish came to the door and opened it wide and the man he had with him stated, "Thank you for coming to our lodge. You are welcome."

"Tell the chief that I am honored to be in his lodge for talk."

"Come in, Moaka," he said as the chief nodded.

Leading Moaka to a spot in the lodge where the chief stationed himself so he could see all activities in the lodge, the chief motioned, and commanded, "Sit."

Adjusting his side arm, Moaka sat on the soft woven mat that was made from the bark of a red cedar tree.

Looking around the room, he saw there were small children playing with homemade toys, young girls making ornaments and baskets from natural materials such as reeds and long thick dried grass, and at one end of the lodge an old man was telling stories to young men, probably about hunting and fishing by their grandfathers. Smiling, Moaka thought, *This is much like the Inuit way, passing on skills and stories to young people of the tribe.*

Soon Many Fish returned and a young woman behind him was carrying a hot liquid to drink while they talked. Moaka reached up to take the cup that the young woman handed him and he nodded and said, "*Gunalche'esh tlein*" (thank you).

"Oh, and thank you, Moaka, for coming," she replied in perfect English. "This man," she pointed to the interpreter, "his name is Kaare."

"Trip good?" Chief Many Fish asked.

"Yes, Many Fish, some rain."

"How Kincaid?"

"He busy Many Fish."

"Can stay night? You stay here," and Many Fish pointed to the inside of the lodge.

"Yes, I can. I want see what I can do for sacred fishing stream."

"Kaare can show." He drank most of his drink.

"*Wa'asa' iyatee,*" (how are you doing) Moaka asked.

"K'el wook'ei," (feel good) Many Fish replied.

"Want go see problem at sacred stream today."

Many Fish touched Karre's arm and pointed and Karre stood and addressed Moaka. "Are you ready to go? Many Fish will talk with you when we return."

Standing, Moaka bid Many Fish farewell and exited the lodge with Karre. Outside, Moaka inquired, "Do we ride or walk?"

"We can walk, it is not far."

Walking over to his horse, Moaka loosened the cinch straps on the saddle and the cross buck cinch on the packhorse.

Karre warned several children that were playing around the lodge, "Leave the horses alone or wood pile."

"What say Karre...wood pile?"

"Yes, Moaka, working on the wood pile is punishment for disobeying elders."

After walking for a distance, Moaka asked, "What is biggest problem with intruders? Karre, it legal for non-native people can fish in streams that are your people's sacred fishing grounds as long as they obey law of government. Non-native peoples can no set fish traps, fish with net, only catch certain limit, they only fish certain times of year. If they within law it legal them fish anywhere in territory of Alaska. This is United States of America they have law must be followed. Your tribe fish anywhere, anytime, anyway, for food and living. Other people must stay to law I just say to you."

Stopping, Karre asked, "How do we stop intruders from fishing in our sacred streams if they do break the law?"

"That why I here." Continuing to walk toward the stream, Moaka advised Karre, "Kincaid knows problems with intruders. He help how he can. Now I need see situation it is now."

Stopping on a small ridge, Karre pointed toward the stream in the bottom of the small valley. "See the fish trap they have installed. They have also installed nets in the stream. They get many salmon and trout. There are men in a small village not far south from Woronkofski Island that buys as many fish as they bring to them. They are gone from their camp taking their catch to those men south of here. They will be back this evening to harvest their catch tomorrow morning. The same every day. How do we stop them without killing?"

"Don't do that. Tribe have lot problem if start killing people. Let's go see fish trap. Good time look because they gone. How long fish trap and net been in stream?"

"About two weeks. They have harvested many fish from the stream."

Holding his hand up, Moaka pleaded, "I know, Karre, I know. They need be stopped and they break law with fish trap and nets in stream." Standing on the stream bank, Moaka looked around and saw their camp. The camp was well organized with fire pit, nice tent, and firewood cut for fire. "How big boat do they have?"

"They have two boats. One small boat for stream work and the other larger for the ocean travel. They know what they are doing."

"You are right, Karre. I want walk downstream for while, see what else they do. The ocean no far from here, I like look at smaller boat."

Walking a short distance, Moaka and Karre saw where the stream flowed into the ocean. Moaka started walking faster in his excitement. Looking at the boat at ocean's edge, that was drawn up on the narrow beach and tied off on a small tree, Moaka removed his cap and scratched his head and then replaced his cap. "Karre, they use good equipment, this boat made strong." Gazing out into the ocean, looking southward, Moaka could see a small island and pointed to it. "What island name?"

"It is called Hat Island."

"How many men in intruder party?"

"There are three men in their party. They shot a deer two days ago. Some of it is still hanging in a tree covered up with a bag."

"How big boat for ocean travel?"

Karre thought for a moment. "I think about thirty foot long with power engine and propeller. I don't know much about boats, but I think that is what it is."

"Where they from?"

"I think I heard one say something about Ketchikan."

Sighing and shrugging his shoulders from a chill, he said, "Why Woronkofski Island always wet?"

Smiling, Karre looked to the sky and raised his hands. "Because it rains all the time."

Both men laughed as Moaka and Karre headed back up the stream to the intruder's camp. Arriving at their camp, Moaka looked closer at their fish trap. "It well made. They plan be here all summer."

"Yes, Moaka. That is what we think also. That is why the letter was written to James Kincaid. We did not know what to do to keep them from fishing with a fish trap and nets on our sacred stream. They are taking a lot of fish from this stream."

Moaka walked over to the tent and untied one of the tent flap strings and opened it enough to peek inside. Nodding, he thought to himself, *Three beds, stove, extra wood, three boxes for food and clothes, shovels, axes, and rope.* "They come ready for stay," Moaka advised. Closing the tent flap and retying the flap string back, Moaka suggested, "Let's go back to lodge."

Arriving back at the lodge area, Moaka asked, "Can I put horse in shed?" as he pointed to an old wooden building with poles across an opening to keep the horses inside the building for the night.

"Yes," Karre replied, "and you can give them some hay from the small stack outside. We just need to cover the hay up when we give them some, to keep the hay dry."

Taking the saddle off his horse and removing the cross buck off from the packhorse, Moaka noticed that Karre had gotten some hay for both horses.

"Thanks for hay, Karre. They won't eat much."

That evening, Moaka was treated to supper of fine salmon, cooked mushrooms, and berry jam on fry bread.

When supper was finished, Karre sat next to Moaka and explained that he talked to Many Fish about what they had done that day and Many Fish was pleased.

Nodding his head, Moaka replied, "Thanks Karre. That helps a lot. My Tlingit is not too good. Did he have any suggestions what might help?"

Shaking his head, Karre replied, "No, he is leaving it up to you to fix the problem with the intruders."

Moaka rested back against a large pad made from red cedar bark. As he watched the young girls dancing, he asked Karre, "Why are they dancing all together?"

Karre pointed toward them. "You see that old man in front of them. He is their teacher. He has taught them the dance for the potlatch that is coming up soon. During the potlatch there is much dancing and giving, old arguments between tribal leaders are settled, and much food is eaten that is brought by everyone. It is one of the biggest celebrations of the year."

"Sounds like it will be fun," Moaka said. "When does this potlatch occur for our tribes?"

"This year it will be next month. We are all happy about the potlatch."

As Karre explained when the potlatch was going to be, Moaka thought, *I will be in Barrow by then making my dog team and getting my children settled for school. Kalli is really excited, but Kasha does not understand; she will like being with her own kind.*

As the evening continued, Moaka noticed that the lodge was getting very quiet as people were getting ready for bed. Standing, Moaka went outside to relieve himself before turning in. When he returned, Karre escorted him to his place of sleeping. "This is where you will sleep tonight and here are several blankets for you."

"*Gunalche'esh tlein*, (thank you) Karre."

Next morning after having a breakfast of fish eggs, berries, and venison, Moaka stretched. "I ate too much," he said, and rubbing his stomach he belched quietly.

"Are you ready to go see the intruders?" asked Karre.

Moaka stood and stretched his arms above his head, "Yes, I need to talk with them."

Just as Moaka was starting to step toward the door, he felt a tug on his arm. Looking to see what is was, Moaka saw Many Fish. "You do good."

Moaka smiled, and replied, "Yes, Chief, I will try."

Walking back over the small hill to the intruder's camp, Moaka and Karre were undetected as they watched the men from a distance. They were unloading the fish trap and several nets and they were pulling out many large fish. The fish were dipped from the fish trap, and the fish from the nets had to be untangled from the gill net.

Moaka slowly eased his .38 pistol from its holster and checked to make sure it was loaded and then slid it gently back into the holster.

"You going to shoot someone, Moaka?" Karre questioned.

"No," Moaka replied, as he felt for his knife. "Karre, stay little behind me." Instantly, Moaka stood and started walking toward the men pulling fish out of the stream, as Karre stayed close.

Walking down the easy slope to the stream, Moaka hailed, as he approached the men, "Where you from?"

All three men jerked up from their work as they never saw Moaka and Karre approaching. "Who the hell are you?" one man asked.

Stepping close to the man that spoke, Moaka identified himself and Karre. "I am Moaka from the Department of Agriculture and this," Moaka motioned toward Karre, "is Karre, chief interpreter Chief Many Fish of Shx' at Kwa'an Tlingit Tribe. You fish in stream illegally, using fish trap and fish net."

"Illegally, my ass." The man mocked Moaka. "This is free and open water to all."

Having patience, Moaka explained, "Yes, open water to all, not fish trap and net. These used by Tlingit tribes."

Waving his hand at Moaka, the response was, "Who the hell are you? You look just like any other Indian around here. Just like that idiot behind you."

Moaka instantly kicked the man on his knee and the man fell to the ground grasping his knee in pain. "You have broken my leg, you stupid Indian!"

Instantly, Moaka was atop the man with his eight-inch blade lying next to the man's neck. "You men, get out of water! Lie on ground."

"We ain't going to do that," one of the men screamed as the other man in the water yelled, "You have no right to do this!"

"Get out water and lie on ground." Not seeing the men obeying, Moaka pushed his knife in the man's neck until blood oozed onto the knife blade. He showed the man, and said, "This your blood; want see more?"

Feverishly, the man on the ground shook his head. "No, no. You guys get out of the damn water and get on the ground. This guy is a madman."

After seeing the blood on Moaka's knife, the men in the water crawled up the bank and out of the water and lay on the ground.

Moaka noticed they had knives in their sheaths so he told Karre to get the knives from the men and throw them a distance away, but notice where they landed. "When you finished, Karre, go inside tent, get rope lying on ground, bring to me."

Hurrying, Karre ran to the tent, got the rope, and brought it to Moaka. "Take rope, tie his feet together tight." Seeing movement from one of the other men lying on the ground, Moaka drew his pistol and fired one round near the man's head. "Lie still, no move," Moaka commanded.

Once Karre had tied the man's feet together, Moaka instructed, "Grab rope and drag him to tree there with strong limb hanging out over ground." Moaka put his knife back into its sheath and stood when Karre drug the man to the tree.

Pointing the .38 pistol at the two men on the ground near the stream, Moaka ordered, "You crawl to tree. No walk, crawl."

Once the three men were close to the tree, Moaka instructed Karre, "Throw rope over limb—"

After hearing Moaka telling Karre to throw the rope over the limb, one of the men started screaming, "He's going to hang us all."

"Shut up," Moaka yelled at the man. "You no hung yet." Addressing the man that was yelling, Moaka told him to help Karre. "Karre, you pull rope over limb till man's head four feet off ground."

The man instantly jumped to help Karre lift the man off the ground and as soon as Moaka waved his hand to stop, Karre and the other man tied off the rope around the tree trunk. "Now get back on ground with partner," Moaka ordered.

Wiping the pitch from his hands, Karre asked, "What do we do now?"

Smiling, Moaka bragged, "He look funny upside-down."

Standing over the two men on the ground, Moaka asked Karre, "Go into tent and get heavy hammer and axe, bring them to me."

"Sure, Moaka." Quickly, Karre returned with the tools.

"Karre, carry tools over to the fish trap. I going cut off long piece of this rope we used for hanging this man," he pointed to the man hanging in the tree, "and you men on ground, you crawl over fish trap."

As the two men crawled over to the bank of the stream next to the fish trap, Moaka stated, "Now take tools Karre brought over here and tear down fish trap."

From behind him Moaka heard the hanging man say, "You can't do that. That fish trap is private property."

Moaka turned back to the man that was hanging. "Your private property doing illegal task." And turning back to the men at the stream, he ordered, "Cut up and haul to fire pit for burning." Handing Karre the pistol, he said, "Make sure fish trap all out of the water, destroyed, and hauled to fire pit, and at same time make sure fish net is taken out and hauled to fire pit. I question man hanging."

Walking over to the man hanging upside down, Moaka began his questioning. "I asked once where came from; you did not answer, now answer."

"I'm not going to answer any of your stupid questions."

Turning to Karre, Moaka instructed, "Burn their boat."

"Oh wait," the hanging man stammered. Frustration in his voice, he said, "That is not our boat. It belongs to someone else where we live."

"Burn boat, Karre," Moaka ordered again.

"No, no, wait," the man screamed. "We are from Ketchikan."

"You haul fish to Ketchikan?"

"No, no," the man shook his head as his hair dangled down toward the ground. "We load the small boat with fish and in the afternoon we take the fish out to our larger boat and off-load it onto the larger boat. We deliver the fish to a small camp on Hat Island, and then return with larger boat. We use the small boat to come up the stream to the fish trap and nets. You can see the larger boat in the bay at anchor waiting for us."

"Who sell fish to?"

"They are from Ketchikan. They get deliveries from several fishermen like us and when they get a load they head for Ketchikan."

"How often go Ketchikan?"

"I don't know...every three or four days...I'm not sure. They have a large fishing crawler. Cut me down. I think all the blood is going to my head."

"You be fine. Be quiet."

Walking over to where the fish trap was being torn out and destroyed, Moaka patted Karre on the shoulder. "You doing good job. Make sure get all fish net out of the stream."

Karre turned to Moaka, smiling. "The chief was right—he said, 'Moaka will know what to do.'"

Shaking his head, Moaka muttered, "I hope so." Walking into the tent, Moaka dragged one of the boxes out into the light to examine the contents. In this particular box there were clothes, an extra pair of boots, and some food. In the others, the contents were about the same, except for the last one. Finding what he was looking for, Moaka closed the box that was sitting outside the tent, where he'd pulled it for better light. Then he sat on the box and began reading a book with names, dates, fish count, and company names that were buying the fish and shipping to Ketchikan.

Taking the ledger book over to the man hanging in the tree, Moaka stated, "You keep good records. I will take these records from you. Tell companies you sell fish that their business is finished. When Department of Agriculture get hold of information, you have no job anymore and you could go jail for long time."

Shaking his head, the man said, "Hey, mister, we only get the fish for a price, 'go jail' the big guys that make all the money."

Nodding his head, Moaka replied, "We will. Your name in book?"

"No, I don't think so. We are just the little guys."

"Karre," Moaka called, "send me one man here. Make him crawl here."

Soon the man came crawling over to Moaka, "Why in the hell do we have to crawl everywhere?"

Moaka looked at the man with disdain. "Because you have dishonored Tlingit tribe by fishing in their stream illegally. Fish in this stream, but must obey law, you did not."

"What the hell do we know about Indian laws?"

"Law you have to follow not Indian law, white man law."

"Yeah, you would stick up for the dirty Indians see'en how you are one of them."

Instantly, Moaka got up off his stump perch and kicked the man in the face. He rolled over with blood oozing from his face from Moaka's boot.

"Now crawl back here. Want ask you few questions."

Spitting blood, the man sputtered, "I'm not going to answer any questions for you."

"My hell, Arnold," the man hanging in the tree yelled, "answer the man's questions or he will burn the small boat."

"Want know your name and where live."

Looking at the man in the tree, he said, "They aren't going to like this one bit. My name is Arnold Smith, and I live in Ketchikan."

"What name of other man working on fish trap?"

"His name is Harry Brooks, and he lives in Ketchikan also."

"What is name of man in tree?"

Arnold looked up at the man in the tree hanging upside down, and as he shook his head, he continued, "This fishing thing didn't turn out right. His name is Ben Shaper from Seattle."

Sighing and resting back on the stump, Moaka ordered Arnold, "Crawl back, work on fish trap and fish net."

"You don't have anything on us," screamed Harry, who had crawled up from working on the fish trap.

Instantly, Moaka jumped up and placed his knife across Harry's throat and quietly said, "You make much noise. Stop yelling or I let blood out of you."

Slowly Moaka sat back down on his stump and quietly explained, "Yes, Department of Agriculture can charge you with illegal fishing practices and transporting fish out of Alaskan waters without permit. Both are jail time offense if judge decide that way."

"So what are you going to do with us now?" Harry demanded.

Moaka ignored his question and sent both men crawling back to their job on the stream.

Sometime later, Moaka hailed Karre. "When are men going be finish removing fish trap and net?"

"Soon. They have the nets out and are just about finished with hauling the wood over to the fire pit."

Turning to look downstream, Moaka could see small pieces of wood floating downstream of what was left of the fish trap. Staring, Moaka thought, *Fish trap out, fish nets out, I have record book and names, and I have witness to what went on here.*

Out of the corner of his eye, Moaka detected quick movement and turned just in time to see Harry throw a piece of wood at Karre and Arnold jumped on him, trying to get the pistol.

Karre yelled, "Moaka, get the gun," as Karre had enough quickness to throw the pistol toward Moaka.

Moaka quickly ran and dived for the pistol that was lying in the grass. Just then Harry jumped on Moaka and the pistol fired. Harry rolled off from Moaka holding his guts. Quickly, Moaka looked to Arnold, who had stopped in his tracks when he saw what happened as he was coming to help Harry take Moaka.

Pointing the pistol toward Arnold, Moaka frowned at him. "Don't move or I kill you."

Backing up and holding his hands in the air, Arnold pleaded, "Don't shoot," and then he sat on the ground.

"How are you, Karre?" Moaka called.

"I'm OK; the wood hit my side, but didn't hurt me."

Moaka got up and examined Harry, who was dead. Apparently the bullet went into his stomach and punctured his heart, and he died almost instantly. Looking at Arnold, Moaka ordered, "Get shovel and bury him over there." Moaka pointed at a burial spot.

Moaka walked over to Karre, who was brushing himself off and who shyly said, "Sorry for the commotion. I should have been paying more attention."

"Did good, throwing me pistol. How you feel?"

"Oh I'm fine, Moaka, don't worry about me."

Turning and walking toward Ben Shaper in the tree, Moaka explained, "Now I will answer question what happen now. What happen now is you and Arnold going tear down tent and load belonging in boat and return Ketchikan, never return this stream. Tell your company you work for I have names of men, name of company, and fish count in record book. I turn record book over to Department of Agriculture when I return Wrangell."

Seeing Karre fooling around with the fire and trying to get the wet wood to start burning, Moaka called, "No worry about fire right now. It dry and later you come back and burn wood. Now I want you come and get pistol and help me guard these men till they get in boat and go down the stream."

Watching Arnold roll Harry into a hastily dug grave, Moaka glanced at Ben. "How long you been doing this kind fishing on small streams that fish are from ocean?"

"Will you please," Ben emphasized, "cut me down so we can get the hell out of here before someone else gets killed?"

"No be stupid and nobody get hurt," Moaka stressed.

Seeing Arnold pat the dirt down on the grave, Moaka instructed him, "OK, Arnold, come over here and grab onto your partner when I cut him down."

Seeing Arnold walking slowly, Ben yelled, "Hurry up, Arnold, get me out of this tree."

"Harry and I have known each other for years," and pointing to Moaka, "you better watch your step. We'll meet again someday when you don't have a gun pointed at me."

"Shut up, Arnold; what's done is done. You can't change that; now get me out of this tree."

As Moaka walked over to the tree trunk, he told Arnold, "Grab him because I'm cutting rope now."

Arnold barely grabbed Ben as he dropped to the ground. "Untie me and let's get the gear in the boat and get the hell out of here."

Standing back, Moaka and Karre watched the two men tear down the tent and quickly fold it, haul the boxes to the boat, and pick up all the tools and equipment and haul them to the stream bank.

Putting all the belongings into the boat, Arnold warned, "We'll meet again, Indian," addressing Moaka, and Ben pushed off from shore into the stream.

Moaka and Karre watched the boat wind and turn in the stream flow until the boat disappeared around a sharp bend. "Thank you, Moaka. Chief Many Fish will be very pleased."

Arriving back at the lodge just about suppertime, Moaka enjoyed another evening with the Tlingit people. They were dancing and singing in celebration of getting rid of the intruders. Once in a while he watched Karre explaining what happened today and Chief Many Fish laughed and slapped Karre on the shoulder and nodded his head in approval. Toward the end of the evening, Moaka started thinking about his move to Barrow. He was really happy inside and looked forward to getting there and building his own dog team again. He was also happy that Kincaid said he would come and see him in Barrow.

Suddenly Chief Many Fish was sitting beside him, with Karre next to the chief. "The chief wants to give you a gift for what you have done today. You have honored the chief and he is appreciative of your work."

Holding a small fish carved from birch wood, Chief Many Fish said, "You have power, Moaka," and handed Moaka the carved fish.

Nodding his head, Moaka replied, "Chief Many Fish is great leader. Will tell Kincaid your decision let me handle intruders with help of one of your warriors."

Without a word, Chief Many Fish stood and walked back to his station in the lodge, and Karre escorted Moaka to his sleeping place.

The next morning, Moaka was up before the lodge was awake, and as he was saddling his horse and loading the cross buck on the packhorse, Karre come from the lodge and again thanked Moaka for coming.

"If have any more problem like this one," Moaka assured him, "Be sure contact Kincaid for help. He understand your situation. Need get to dock get picked up for Wrangell Island. Need go Terrace Point check on other project for Kincaid. I make full report for Kincaid so he understand what went on at Woronkofski Island."

As Moaka mounted, Karre hailed one more time, "Thank you, Moaka."

Moaka waved and disappeared through the trees, headed for the docks to get a boat ride back to Wrangell Island.

Catching a small ferry coming back from a fishing village, the skipper agreed to take Moaka and his horses to Terrace Point on Wrangell Island and charge the Department of Agriculture for the fee. He was dropped off at Hoqur Cove, just south of Terrace Point. Moaka thanked the skipper and made his way north to the Stone Mountain Mining camp.

As Moaka approached the camp, he heard the cracking of trees being felled. Dismounting and tying his horse to a small tree with the packhorse tied to his saddle, Moaka walked up the short way to the flat saw that was owned by the mining company.

"Oh, there you are!" exclaimed Ferrell Jones. "We thought we might see you coming by to check on the progress. Well, as you can see the landowners are falling the trees and skidding them by mule and horse right up to my doorstep. They are doing a good job of bumping off the knots and the trees are the right size. Probably tomorrow my men will start cutting planks for the flume. I want to thank you, Moaka, and James Kincaid for helping solve the problem. I can't tell you how much pressure that took off the miners. Now it seems that everything is OK, and everybody is satisfied with the situation."

"Glad you are happy and will start saw plank tomorrow."

"Oh, by the way," Ferrell added, "tell Kincaid that my mining engineer designed the flume. Are you going to stay for a while?"

"No need, Mr. Jones. You have job going well. I will report to Kincaid about what you are doing and that the flume designed by your man."

Nodding, Ferrell walked forward and extended his strong hand. "Thanks for everything."

Excepting Ferrell's handshake, Moaka replied, "Kincaid will be back soon to check again if you are having any problems."

"OK, Moaka, have a good trip back to Wrangell," and he turned to go back to the flat saw.

Turning to look down the slope where the flume was going to be built, Moaka thought, *It will be a good thing for all.*

Remounting, Moaka shifted the saddle for center and pushed forward toward Wrangell. It was early in the day, and Moaka needed to stop and eat something, but he thought, *I'll stop along the way. It is only about twenty-five miles to Wrangell. I'll be there before dark.*

Moaka dismounted in front of the Department office earlier than he thought he would be in Wrangell. Walking into the office, he saw that Sara was just getting ready to leave the office for the day. "Hi, Sara," Moaka greeted her.

"Oh hi, Moaka...Mr. Kincaid is still in his office and I bet he would like to talk with you."

Leaning into James's office door, Moaka stated, "Be back in minute..."

"By the damn, Moaka, you're a sight for sore eyes. How did everything go at Woronkofski Island?"

"Go to office. Be right back."

Later, settling himself in a chair next to James's desk, Moaka smiled and replied, "Everything go good at Woronkofski Island and Terrace Point. Chief Many Fish happy."

"Good, Moaka, good. It is late now so why don't we finish this conversation tomorrow morning over fresh coffee?"

"Sound good to me," and Moaka went back to his office. Hearing the front door close he knew Kincaid was glad to see him by his greeting, and Moaka thought, *I will miss James Kincaid. He is good friend.*

CHAPTER TWENTY-ONE

Looking through the glasses, Payuk scanned the canyon below and up the Iskut River east toward the mining camp. "Kelly!"

"What?"

"Come and look at this."

Kelly slowly walked over to Payuk as Payuk handed him the glasses. "What am I looking at?"

"Look at what Fisher and Jeffery are doing."

Adjusting the glasses, Kelly finally focused in Fisher and Jeffery. Laughing, Kelly stammered, "They are swimming. I'll be damned. They don't seem to be too worried about tomorrow when they get to the mining camp."

"Why should they be?" The plan is all laid out and they know what they have to do. Why not have some enjoyment."

Handing the glasses back to Payuk, "We had better have a small fire tonight...I mean a damn small fire. We have been lucky with the good weather we are having so far."

"Where do we want to hold up tomorrow when they go into camp?"

"Good question, Payuk. We'll just have to look around and find a good place to hide until we can get into that camp tomorrow night."

Looking back to the west, Payuk commented, "Sun will be down over the mountains pretty soon. Do we stay here tonight?"

Shrugging and visually checking the spot out, Kelly replied, "I guess this is as good as any. One thing we have to be aware of tomorrow is the lookout that Henry Wilson sends out every morning. I'm really not sure where he goes to be the lookout. I'd think he would be somewhere he could see the entire camp and some of the Iskut River canyon. Yeah, let's stay here tonight."

Unsaddling the horses and hobbling them, they set up the windbreaker tent.

"Kelly, what do you want to eat after a while?" He asked and again started watching the canyon and Fisher and Jeffery.

"I don't know, Payuk. I'm not very hungry right now. Noticing the horses grazing on new grasses, he grabbed two buckets and announced, "I'm going down to that stream just below here and get two buckets of water for the horses."

Taking the glasses away from his eyes, Payuk asked, "Why don't you just walk the horses down to the stream? That would make more sense to me."

"I don't know. I haven't done a thing all day except ride Peanut, and I need to get a little exercise."

"Exercise?" Payuk questioned. "That is one thing about you white people. I don't know any tribal person that even considers exercise important. We get a lot of exercise walking and running when we are hunting. Very few Tlingit ride horses when they are hunting. They haven't for thousands of years, so they feel why should I now?"

"Are you through lecturing me for now, Payuk?"

Smiling and waving Kelly down the slope, Payuk answered, "Yes, you are excused to go pack water for the horses."

Soon Kelly returned up the slope packing two full buckets of water for the horses to drink.

"Wait," Payuk hailed, "I want to fill my canteen before you let the horses drink."

Stopping and looking at Payuk, Kelly said, "How much are you going to pay me for my trouble? The horses carry us and the gear; what are you going to do?"

"I will cook supper."

He thought for a second. "OK, then, come and get some water."

293

As Payuk watched Fisher and Jeffery build a small fire and cook supper, he commented, "They are eating late tonight. They were swimming late, I guess. Well, it's starting to get dark even on top of this mountain. I'm going to turn in for the night. Do we need to do anything about the horses?"

Kelly stood and looked to the west. "No, Payuk, I've hobbled them again and they are all tethered to small trees. They had a lot of time for grazing and they got their last drink a while back. They will be just fine until morning." Adding a small piece of firewood to the fire, Kelly expounded, "It is way past eleven p.m. and I can still see light coming over the west mountains, but I'll bet it is darker than a burnt skillet down where Fisher and Jeffery are staying tonight."

"Turn in, Kelly. It is up early tomorrow. If you remember yesterday morning, Jeffery and Fisher were rolling just before light."

"Yeah, you're right, Payuk. I still haven't figured out where we are going to be tomorrow, waiting for tomorrow night. Reaching high into the sky as he stretched, Kelly shook his head. "I guess we'll figure that out tomorrow." Looking over to Payuk, he looked to be sound asleep..."Well, I guess it's time."

Next morning, Kelly and Payuk did not make a fire for breakfast; instead, they had some dried fish, jerky, and corn dodgers. Loading up the packhorses and saddling the other two, they made ready to follow Jeffry and Fisher, who were just hooking up the teams.

Looking through the glasses, Kelly stood back off the ridgeline but just up high enough so he could see over the crest. "Payuk, I think I see a good place to hold up if it will be close enough to the mining camp. We'll know more about it as we get closer to the spot."

Watching Jeffery and Fisher drive the teams alongside the Iskut River toward the mining camp, suddenly Kelly dismounted from Peanut and grabbed the glasses from his saddlebags and signaled

Payuk to come to him. "Look, I can see smoke coming from the camp. We are really close. Let's get down off from this ridge to the back side of this slope. I see the place that I looked at before through the glasses, but I didn't realize it was so close to the camp. It will be just perfect. No one can see us unless they come looking for us."

Payuk took the glasses and scanned the area that Kelly was pointing at for the day's hold-up. "It looks good. Good, easy access to the camp, especially at night."

Carefully and slowly making their way down the slope, not making any dust for the camp lookout to see and get suspicious, Kelly and Payuk finally reached a small but thickly covered grove of aspen trees.

"This should do it, Payuk. Let's unload and hobble the horses so they can graze. As Kelly dismounted, he noticed a small stream. "Look, Payuk, I won't have to haul water for the horses."

They both laughed as they began setting up camp.

After the camp was set up, Kelly mentioned, "I think I'll take a walk over around that hog's back and see if I can see the camp. I want you to stay with the horses. When I get back, I want you to take that same walk so you will have some insight on where we are going to travel tonight."

"Good idea, Kelly. In the meantime, I'll set a small fire for some coffee. There are plenty of dry sticks around here for a fire with no smoke."

After both men took their turn in scouting out the route for tonight's travel to the mining camp, they settled down to an almost cold supper of jerky, smoked salmon, fry bread, and coffee.

Seeing Kelly relax against his saddle, Payuk asked, "What are you thinking about, Kelly?"

"Hmm, you would not believe. As soon as school is out, Nancy and I are going on a trip to Seattle for a short vacation. She wants to go see some of her friends she went to college with, and I'm going to buy Sidney a pony and tack."

"What kind of pony, Kelly?"

Shaking his head and sliding his brown felt hat over his eyes as he slid down on his saddle, he said, "I don't know right now. Wake me up in two hours, and then I'll let you sleep until we go at about midnight. I would like to get to the camp about twelve-thirty p.m. or maybe a little later."

"OK, Kelly. That will work for me."

Waking Payuk gently by touching his shoulder, Kelly spoke low, "Time to go Payuk. I have seen to the horses, they should be alright while we are gone."

Slipping his boots on, Payuk put on his side arm and made sure he had his knife in the scabbard. "OK, Kelly, I'm ready."

Looking up into the sky, Kelly mentioned, "We have a clear sky with a half-moon shining to help us see. I wonder why that mining camp does not have a dog. I meant to ask Fisher about that, but forgot."

Making their way around the hog's back and across the Snippaker River, Kelly and Payuk were very near the camp. Their progress was slow, but the clear night and moon gave enough light for travel without falling over things on the ground. There were a few lanterns hanging around to show some dim light for the camp. They could see the guard sitting by the fire poking the fire with a stick.

Kelly pointed and whispered, "Let's go to the left and stay out of the light of the fire. Then we can come in from the back to the office building where Jesse Holmes sleeps. That way the guard will never know we have been there."

Kelly moved slowly and steadily, and they paused from time to time, checking for noises or anything that sounded out of character for the night.

Payuk touched Kelly's arm. "Kelly, the guard is up and moving toward us."

Kelly and Payuk quickly lay down in the tall grass as the guard walked within twenty feet of them. Not hearing the guard walking, Kelly rose up slightly and saw him headed over toward the corrals to check the stock.

"OK, Kelly," Payuk cautioned, "this is our chance to get around back of the office building."

Kelly eased up and started walking low as he led the way to behind the office building. Leaning back to speak into Payuk's ear, Kelly whispered, "Stay outside and I'll try this door."

Kelly slowly turned the knob of the door handle and it opened the door without any noise. Sliding inside he could see some light and shadows from the camp lanterns shining light into the building through the windows. Crawling to a dark spot, Kelly let his eyes get used to the light and shadows in the room. Finally he was able to spot the door that led to Holmes's bedroom. Crawling over to the door, Kelly turned the knob slightly and the door opened. He could hear Holmes breathing deeply, in a sound sleep. Crawling over to the edge of Holmes's bed, Kelly quickly placed his hand over Holmes' mouth and whispered, "Don't yell out. This is Kelly O'Brien. I need to talk with you. Nod your head if you understand."

Holmes instantly nodded as he patted Kelly hand to remove it from his mouth. Whispering, Holmes stated, "I knew something was up when Fisher came back with another driver and they were so late getting back to the camp. What is the plan?"

Talking in low voices, Kelly explained to Jesse Holmes what was going to happen tomorrow night at about twelve-thirty. Then Kelly asked, "Do you have any questions?"

"No Kelly, I'm ready to make this move out of here, away from this mining business."

"OK, just remember, you head for the corral when you hear the fireworks get started. Take what you have to but don't load yourself down. You will be moving fast. Don't worry about food or water that will be taken care of for you, just get to that corral."

"OK, Kelly, I got it."

Patting Holmes on the shoulder, Kelly crawled back to the bedroom door and then out through the main room to the outside back door where Payuk was waiting. "OK, Payuk," Kelly whispered, "Let's go. I saw Holmes and he understands for tomorrow night."

Suddenly a shot sprang from the darkness as someone yelled, "Stop, you dirty Indians!" Then another shot was heard by Kelly and Payuk as it ricocheted through the grasses next to them. "Run," Kelly whispered, "I'm right behind you."

As Payuk started to run he screamed as loud as he could, "*Wooch Kanax wutuda.aadi; Wooch Kanax wutuda.aadi*" (we are together).

Running as fast as they could, Kelly and Payuk faded fast into the darkness. Reaching the shallow Snippaker River they crossed hurriedly, not going to the bridge. Arriving back at their camp, Kelly advised, "Let's move the camp farther up into the canyon, just in case they want to make a circle in the morning to check things out."

Getting the camp packed up and the fire put out, Kelly said, "I'll lead Peanut and you can follow close with your horse and the packhorses tethered in back of your horse."

Moving up the canyon, the light was going away as the half-moon was dropping below the horizon of the mountain ridge. "OK, Payuk, this should be alright for tonight. Let's strip the saddles off the horses and try and get some shut-eye before morning. Where is that medicine kit we brought with us?"

"Are you sick, Kelly?"

"No, the first round that the guard fired gave me a pretty bad flesh wound on my side."

Payuk jumped to see Kelly's wound, but he could not see much because the moonlight had all but vanished. "Let me get a small fire started so we can take a look. I thought we got away clean."

Getting a small fire started, Kelly and Payuk could see the blood-soaked shirt. Payuk cut a small hole in the shirt and breathed out, "Wow, what a mess," and handed Kelly a clean rag. "Sit down and keep holding the rag to the wound. It does not look bad, but we have to clean it up and get it wrapped."

"Get me a drink of water, Payuk. I'm so thirsty."

"Yes. That is a natural reaction from getting shot...a person gets thirsty."

Warming some water in a small pan, Payuk bathed the wound and was finally able to see the damage the bullet made to Kelly's side. "It is not bad at all, Kelly. You are lucky; the bullet just grazed your side. Let me get this thing cleaned up and I'll wrap a bandage around you to hold the gauze bandage in place. Lift your shirt up so I can wrap around you." Putting infection cream on the wound, Payuk laid a piece of gauze over the wound and wrapped a bandage around Kelly's middle to hold the gauze in place. "OK, Kelly, put your shirt down. That will hold you until we look at it again tomorrow. Does it hurt much? You haven't lost much blood."

"Not bad. I think that cream has some numbness in the mix."

Seeing Kelly trying to stand, Payuk helped him. "What do you want, Kelly?"

"I want my bedroll. I need to lie down and sleep."

...

Early next morning, Henry Wilson stood before his entire crew and announced that for those that did not know it, the camp had some visitors last night.

"Jake," Henry pointed to him, "said they showed up around one a.m. last night. Some of you heard the two shots that he fired at the intruders. We suspect them to be Indians. Jake thinks so because he heard one of them yell something like...well, you try and say the words, Jake."

Clearing his throat, Jake tried his best to mimic the sound he heard last night.

Laughing, Jeffery raised his hand. "Mr. Wilson, I can speak some Tlingit and it sounds like the man, or whoever it was speaking, was saying something about being together."

Shaking his head, Henry said, "Damn those Indians. They will steal you blind if you don't watch them. I remember at another location we were mining and the local Indians stole blankets, food, and a couple of horses before we realized they were doing it."

"Did they steal anything last night?" came a question from the men.

Henry looked at Jake for an answer.

"I don't think so, Mr. Wilson. They sure hightailed it out of here when I shot at them. It was dark and I don't think I hit any of them. I think there were about three or four, but I can't be sure."

Henry raised his hands in the air, and said, "Jesse, I want you to double the guard. Have the times the same, but just double the guard. Now listen, you guys, when you are on guard duty, don't be hanging around the fire all the time. Get out and move around and check things out...Alright, back to work."

"OK, everybody," Jesse raised his voice so all the men could hear, "I will post the night watch list on the bulletin board for you at noon."

At noon Fisher looked at the watch list and was not surprised that he and Jeffery were on the twelve p.m. to two a.m. shift. Smiling, he quietly walked away, and thought, *Yeah, Kelly got to Jesse in good shape. What a good break for us.*

As the sun was first shedding its light up and down the canyon walls, Payuk watched Kelly deeply sleeping. Payuk thought, *No sense waking him, I'll let him rest. Even though the wound is not serious, Kelly needs his rest.*

Tending the horses and making himself a few biscuits so he could at least have some biscuits and jam while he waited for Kelly to wake up, Payuk thought, *I figure the plan is still going to work. Maybe better.*

Finished eating his biscuits and jam, Payuk sat down and leaned against his saddle and relaxed waiting for Kelly to wake up.

Payuk closed his eyes and daydreamed about this land being Tlingit land for many generations. *The tribe could go and come as they pleased without asking permission of anyone. The clans were free to be who they wanted to be as long as tradition was followed. The hunting and fishing rights were established within the clans and had nothing to do with the white man. Times were easy for the tribe back then with the ocean on one side and the friendly tribes of the Tahltan to the east. The Tahltan are like a brother tribe in*

301

many ways. The Tlingit and Tahltan traded goods and food often, and I know many Tahltan because of the many times we trade goods.

Hearing Kelly moan, Payuk woke from his half-sleep daydreaming and quickly crawled over to Kelly. Seeing Kelly's eyes open, he said, "You had a good sleep. That is good for your body to rest after getting shot."

"Oh hi, Payuk. What time is it?"

"It is about eleven a.m. You had a good, long sleep. Do you want to try and sit up for a cup of coffee?"

"Yes. Help me sit up." Kelly reached out for Payuk's arm.

"Ouch!" came the instant complaint from Kelly. "That hurts like hell."

"Actually, Kelly, you would be a lot more comfortable sitting on that log over there next to the fire. Let me help you up so you can walk over there and sit up straighter."

"OK, let's do it," Kelly confirmed.

After getting his tall frame to sit on the log, Kelly acknowledged, "Yes, this is much more comfortable. Thanks, Payuk."

Handing Kelly a cup of hot coffee, Payuk asked, "Are you hungry yet?"

Raising his hand, Kelly answered, "No, not yet. Just let me sit here for a while and drink this coffee and I'll see how I feel."

Looking around the campsite, Kelly commented, "Well, we didn't do too bad a job selecting another campsite in the middle of the night. I still think we should go ahead with the plan that is in place. By you yelling all that Tlingit as we ran away, I think everybody in the camp except three people thought it was Indians."

"I think we can keep the plan and move on it come twelve-thirty a.m. tonight. Now I need to take a look at your side and redress the wound."

"Alright, Payuk, let me finish this coffee and let me stand and move around for a minute. I just want to see how it feels."

"You want some fried salt pork and biscuits and jam for breakfast when you're ready and after we have changed the bandage?"

"Yes, Payuk, that really sounds good right now. Come over here and help me stand."

Standing, Kelly turned from the waist up one way and then the next. Looking at Payuk, he said, "Doesn't seem to hurt too much. The wound is above my belt line so that helps."

Getting the bandage changed and breakfast over with, Kelly mentioned, "Payuk, I think I'll ride up to the ridgeline above us and see if anything is going on that seems to be different at the mining camp. I'll be back in an hour or so...why don't you take a nap while I'm gone. I know you didn't get as much sleep as I got."

"That would be fine with me, Kelly. I could use a good nap right now."

Saddling Peanut, Kelly made sure the glasses were in his saddlebags and started up the slope.

"Don't get too busy and open that wound again. It is a small wound, but we don't need you getting infection in it."

Smiling back at Payuk, Kelly said, "Yes, Mother."

Letting Peanut find his own way back and forth up the slope to the ridge crest, Kelly dismounted and got the glasses out of his saddlebags. Standing beside a large cedar, Kelly could see the entire mining camp. Everything seemed to be quite normal with blasts every once in a while. Hanging the glasses up on a broken limb on the tree with the neck strap, Kelly stepped back to get a drink of water from his canteen.

Being frightened out of his wits, he jerked around and realized Kiviaq had touched his shoulder.

Kiviaq started to laugh as another Tlingit came seemingly out of the woodwork. "I did not mean to startle you, Kelly. We heard you set up camp last night and we heard gunshots from the camp. Your camp is only a short distance from ours. Our camp is farther up the canyon. Tomorrow morning early we will be on the ridgeline downriver some, to stop any miners from coming after you."

Kelly nodded. "That is the plan. Just make sure none of your warriors get captured."

Noticing Kelly's bloody shirt, he asked, "Did you get wounded?"

"Yes, a small wound, but Payuk took care of it, and it hardly hurts anymore. When are you going to move your camp to the west?" Kelly asked.

He nodded. "We are now in the process of moving it farther downstream of the Iskut. We are too close to the mine right now."

"OK, Kiviaq, you guys be careful, no heroes."

"Yes, Kelly, that is the last thing Moaka told me." Smiling, Kiviaq and his partner disappeared into the forest.

Going back to his tree, Kelly scanned the mining camp, looking for something different, thinking, *What could possibly go wrong...horse falls and someone gets captured, somebody gets killed, Kiviaq can't keep the miners from catching us...oh, what the hell.* He put the glasses back into their leather carrier. Mounting Peanut, Kelly rode west down the ridgeline for about a mile or so. Dismounting, he grabbed the glasses and scanned the valley floor, as the river continued to run fast and deep. Suddenly he saw movement on this side of the river. It was Kiviaq and his men setting up the ambush on the slope about halfway up to the ridge in heavy brush and trees. He smiled. *The miners will never see them and they will never know what hit them.*

Remounting Peanut, Kelly slowly made his way back to Payuk and his camp. Arriving at the camp, he saw that Payuk was still asleep on his blanket. It was a warm day with the sun shining brightly, but the camp was in the shade of the aspens, which was comfortable. Dismounting Peanut, Kelly led Peanut into the camp and removed the bridle to let Peanut graze close to camp.

Kelly touched the coffeepot that was sitting next to the fire and it was still warm. Pouring himself a cup of lukewarm coffee, Kelly sat on his log and enjoyed the day, waiting for Payuk to wake up. Stretching, Kelly could feel the wound, but it hurt very little.

As he waited, Kelly tended the horses...tied a hackamore onto two at a time and led them to a small stream not far from camp. After getting the horses watered, he let them graze again close to camp.

Finally Payuk woke up, and as he sat up asked, "Is there any coffee left?"

Laughing, Kelly replied, "Sure. I had to make a fresh pot just for you."

"Good. Can you pour me a cup?"

"Sure, Payuk."

Looking up into the sky, Payuk asked, "What time is it, Kelly?"

"It's about four p.m. We'll have something to eat after a while and then wait till it is time to go. While we are waiting, I want us to get the dynamite and other smoke bombs and flares in our packs."

The evening meal finished, Kelly and Payuk started sorting out the dynamite and the rest of the explosives. Payuk had the smoke bombs and flares and Kelly had the dynamite in special heavy canvas bags that had a leather strap that went over the shoulder.

Kelly and Payuk crimped the caps onto the four-inch fuses and wrapped them in small pieces of cloth.

"Where do we want to tether the packhorses on our way downriver?"

"I know a good place," Kelly answered, "if I can find it in the dark. It is right along the side of the wagon road. We can pick them up as we make our escape."

"Do we still want to leave at the same time as planned, or because of the packhorses being tethered maybe take a little more time?"

Thinking, Kelly replied, "Yes. Instead of leaving at midnight, let's leave at eleven-thirty."

Kelly held his watch toward the fire and sighed a big breath. "Well, it is now or never." He kicked out the fire, and suddenly it was very dark. The clouded sky covered over the moon most of the time, making it hardly visible. Standing still next to Peanut and letting his eyes get used to the darkness, he quietly commented, "Not a better night for a raid." Stepping into the stirrups, both men's cold leather saddles creaked as they mounted.

Payuk said, "You're right there, Kelly. Good luck to you."

"And good luck to you, Payuk."

CHAPTER TWENTY-TWO

Riding slowly over known ground, they came to the Snippaker River and then turned west to go down the Iskut River and tie off the packhorses. Riding a short distance, Kelly stopped and dismounted. Walking back to Payuk, he pointed to a large willow tree on the left side of the wagon trail. "Let's tether the packhorses under that willow tree."

"Good choice, Kelly; the canopy of the tree will give the horses some cover when the fireworks start."

"Got your pack animal tied tight and short?" Kelly asked.

"Yes, I'm ready."

Seeing the lights of the mining camp through the misty night, Kelly and Payuk made their way back to the Snippaker River and crossed the shallow river. After crossing the river, Kelly pointed. "Can you see the wooden bridge over the Snippaker River? That is where we will be heading for after we get finished with the dynamite and other flares and smoke bombs. If I can I'm going to save one stick of dynamite and blow that bridge right after we cross." Dismounting, Kelly checked his side arm and dynamite bag. Barely able to make out what Payuk was doing, Kelly asked, "Are you ready to go?"

Payuk stepped next to Kelly. "Yes, I'm ready. Are we going to lead the horses? I have the fuses in a bag and I can hand them to you one at a time."

"I think it would be better to lead them. Yeah, I will need them handed to me one at a time. What time is it?"

Payuk fetched his watch out of his side pocket and angled it toward the dim light from the mining camp. "Twelve-fifteen."

"OK, let's wait until twelve-thirty before we go in from the back side."

Kneeling down and waiting for the time to pass, Payuk asked, "Does the Department of Agriculture give medals of honor for being wounded at work?"

Quickly looking at Payuk, he answered, "No, I don't think so. I know that Nancy will be upset and want me to quit this job. She thinks it is crazy for me to be running around looking for poachers and law breakers. She always tells me that I'm not a lawman."

"I wonder what Kincaid will say?"

"James will not say much. He has been wounded at least three times that I know of."

Hesitating for a second, Kelly motioned to move forward. Staying in the darkness and out of the shadows, Payuk followed Kelly, leading his horse as Kelly was doing. Stopping once in a while to listen, they would move forward a bit farther. Finally reaching the back of the office building, Kelly squatted down. "Payuk, you stay here. If I'm not back in two minutes, head for the hills as fast as you can because the plan has gone to hell in a handbasket. Here, hold Peanut."

Sneaking around the side of the building, he saw two men in the corral putting saddles on horses. Shaking his head, Kelly muttered, "What in the hell is going on?" Moving closer, he could recognize Jeffery. Moving closer, Kelly hissed, and both men turned and rushed to meet him. "What are you two doing? Where's the guard?"

As Kelly saw a smile come over each man's face, Fisher whispered, "We are the guard. Jesse was told by Wilson to double the guard, and he put us on the midnight to two a.m. shift."

"Stay right here, I'll be right back." After going to get Payuk, both men arrived at the corral as Fisher and Jeffery were saddling the last two horses that were needed for the getaway.

"Jeffrey, you and Fisher go get Wilson right now. We will wait right here in case you need some help." Quickly, Fisher and Jeffery headed for Wilson's sleeping quarters. Jeffery signaled Fisher to open the door...and as soon as Fisher opened the door, Jeffery jumped through the door and hit Wilson on the head with his pistol butt. Wilson groaned, and Jeffery hit him again and then there was silence. Tying Wilson up and gagging him, Fisher and Wilson carried him to the corral and put Wilson across a horse and tied him securely.

Kelly stepped into the corral and looked at Wilson. "How many times did you hit him?"

"I hit him twice. I did not want any problems with him. He's a big guy."

"OK, Jeffery, get on your horse and start down the Iskut River nice and slow until you get out of camp...go right now. Fisher, you hang onto your horse and Holmes when he gets here, along with mine and Payuk's horses, and make sure these horses in the corral," Kelly pointed, "are run out of the corral. I don't think you'll have to haze them too much when we start with the dynamite. Now get to it. Where is Holmes?"

"I'm right behind you, Kelly. I've been watching you ever since you and Payuk got here."

"Here..." Kelly handed Holmes his horse's reins. "You and Fisher are going to ride out of here on my signal. You probably will catch up to Jeffery soon. OK, take the poles down that close the corral and get out of the way, and make sure you hang onto your mounts because there's going to be a lot of noise real soon." Noticing a large canvas bag that Holmes was carrying, he asked, "What in the world is in that bag?"

Smiling, Holmes patted the canvas bag. "This is the evidence the courts will need to stop this operation."

"Is everybody ready?" Kelly removed the first stick of dynamite from his bag. "Get ready to run these horses out of the corral."

Kelly looked to Payuk, "We ready to dance?"

Payuk smiled. "Start the music."

As Payuk handed the first stick of dynamite to Kelly, Kelly stuck the cap and fuse into the hole in the dynamite and squeezed the dynamite around the fuse and lit the first stick and threw it as far as he could, and Payuk fired off his first flare into the air. As soon as the loud noises started, the horses in the corral lit out into the darkness, hopefully down the wagon road and across the bridge.

Seeing Fisher hanging onto the horses and hazing the few horses left in the corral, the air in and around the camp suddenly became thick and heavy from the smoke bombs and gun powder. Kelly saw Fisher and Holmes mounting and waiting for Kelly's signal to go, as Fisher was hanging onto Kelly's and Payuk's horses.

"Payuk, come with me," Kelly called. As they moved their position closer to the building, Kelly started lobbing dynamite toward the building and the men tried to come out, but the dynamite blasts were holding them inside. By moving, Kelly could finally get close enough to the building to blast the roofs off from them. There was utter confusion with men running every direction and not knowing what in the world was happening. Men were yelling, running, and cursing, trying to make sense out of what was happening. Several men kept yelling for Wilson and Holmes, but their yells were not being answered. In the meantime, Kelly and Payuk were still throwing dynamite and firing off flares into the smoky sky.

"Payuk, I only have two sticks of dynamite left. I'm going to throw one more and then mount and ride like hell to the bridge across the Snippaker River and stop and blow the bridge. You keep on going; I'll catch up with you."

Kelly realized that he and Payuk had been spotted as men were firing rifles at them and rounds were hitting the ground around them. Kelly turned to Payuk in time to see Payuk fall to the ground. "Kelly, go on! I have been hit badly."

When Payuk fell to the ground Kelly instantly grabbed Payuk and lifted him over Peanut's saddle and Kelly put his foot in the stirrup and landed behind Payuk as Kelly yelled, "Fisher, bring Payuk's horse and let's get the hell out of here."

Stopping at the bridge so suddenly, Kelly had to grab Payuk to keep him from sliding off Peanut. Sliding backward to dismount, Kelly lit the last stick of dynamite and tossed it onto the bridge. Not wasting time to mount, Kelly started running all out while leading Peanut away from the coming blast.

After about six seconds of hard running, Kelly heard the explosion that took out the bridge. Stopping, Kelly lifted Payuk head. "How are we doing?"

"I won't die, but the shot went right through my upper right leg. I'm losing a lot of blood. We need to hold up soon and stop the bleeding if we can."

"When we get to the packhorses, we'll stop and take care of business." Looking back at the mining camp, Kelly thought, *It's as if it's burning to the ground. Most of the buildings are on fire and smoke is close to the ground so visibility is terrible for the men in the camp. It'll be morning before they discover the total loss.* Smiling, he wondered if they would figure out why Wilson and

Holmes were gone, and also Fisher and the new man, Jeffery, were gone.

Reaching the large willow tree where the packhorses were tethered, Kelly discovered that some of the horses had stopped under the tree to be with their packhorses.

"I hope they don't come after us tonight," Payuk groaned.

"I wouldn't worry about that. That mining camp is in complete disarray."

"Help me down, Kelly. We need to dress this wound and get the bleeding to stop."

Helping Payuk down, Kelly tied a large rag around Payuk's leg to stop the bleeding. "Payuk, let me help you on one of these horses. We need to ride a bit to get away from the mining camp. Then we can build a small fire to see your leg better." Kelly quickly looped a rope around one of the corral horses and led him behind Peanut.

"Alright, Kelly, whatever you say."

After riding for a short while, Kelly halted Peanut and helped Payuk off his horse and sat him on a small log for comfort. Dropping the reins to the ground of Peanut and Payuk's horse, he left the packhorses tethered to Peanut with Payuk's horse tethered to the last packhorse. The other corral horses came one behind the other in the darkness.

Riding for a short distance more, Kelly announced, "We should be far enough away to build a fire to check out your wound. Quickly finding a few small sticks, Kelly lit a small fire, and then put larger wood on the fire as he was able to see better.

"Hold still, Payuk," Kelly said as he cut the trouser leg to inspect the wound. "Wow!" Kelly exclaimed. "The bullet went right through the underside of your leg. Actually, it's not a bad wound, it just bled a lot. Let me get the medical stuff off the packhorses and I'll be right back."

"Better put some more wood on the fire when you get back and bring me my canteen." And as he smiled, Payuk said jokingly, "I get thirsty too."

Soon Kelly returned with the medical supplies and set them next to Payuk as he gathered more firewood for the fire. "OK, let's look at that leg." Using cool water and a soft rag, Kelly wiped the blood away from both sides of the leg where the bullet went in and came out. Once the wound was clean, Kelly massaged cream into the wound and around the outside edges. Once the cream was worked in, Kelly placed gauze on both sides of the leg and wrapped a bandage around the leg to hold the gauze in place. "I think that will do it for now. We'll take a look at it tomorrow morning when we've got better light."

After getting the medicine bag put away, helping Payuk get mounted on the unsaddled corral horse, and checking the tethering of the packhorses to Payuk's horse, Kelly kicked the fire out and mounted Peanut. "How does that leg feel, Payuk?"

"It does not hurt unless I move it. That cream is good stuff."

"Well, hang in there the best you can. We'll see how things are come daylight."

Riding though the rest of the night without stopping, at first light Kelly stopped and dismounted and walked back to Payuk. He was burning up with fire. "Payuk, how do you feel?"

"Oh, Kelly, I'm not going to make it. I'm burning up with fever and I know infection has set in inside the wound."

Taking a deep breath, Kelly helped Payuk off his horse and laid him flat on the ground. "You lie still. I'm going to try and get us some help."

Going back to the first packhorse, Kelly dug out a large piece of red cloth and found a long stick to mount the red cloth on. Removing his revolver, Kelly fired three rounds into the air and waved the red cloth high into the air.

Grabbing his pack from his horse, Kelly put it under Payuk's head. "Let me take another look at this thing."

As Kelly tried to remove the pant material, Payuk hissed, "Kelly, that is very sore."

Building a small fire, Kelly got the coffeepot and started some coffee...thinking, *I don't know how long before help will be coming, if any.*

"Kelly," Payuk moaned, "Try firing more shots and waving the red cloth again."

"OK, Payuk, I will right now, and I'll push the stick into the ground so the cloth is waving in the breeze."

Soon the coffee started cooking as Kelly attempted to unwrap the bandage and remove the gauze. Each time Kelly touched somewhere close to either wound, Payuk would cringe with pain.

Suddenly three shots were heard from the crest of the ridge. Kelly jumped up from Payuk and ran and grabbed the cloth and waved it as high as he could. Within a short period of time, Kiviaq and two of his warriors were hurrying their horses toward Payuk and Kelly.

Standing, Kelly greeted Kiviaq, "I'm glad to see you. Payuk got shot in the leg. I tried to doctor it some, but riding on the horse just raised hell with the wound. Now Payuk has a fever and is not doing well."

Kneeling down to face Payuk, Kiviaq uttered several sentences in Tlingit to Payuk and to each one Payuk nodded yes. Placing his hand on Payuk's forehead, Kiviaq shook his head and stood. "We must take Payuk with us. Leave us his horse for the travois and you can be on your way."

"Will he be alright?" Kelly desperately asked.

"Yes, Kelly, but he needs some certain medicines that you do not have. We will keep Payuk with us and deliver him back to you in Wrangell, if that will be alright?"

Turning his head from side to side, stretching his neck muscles, Kelly said, "I can't see why not. We should not need him anymore." Kelly motioned toward Payuk. "He isn't much use to us now. Yeah, I think that would be a good plan. Take him with you, Kiviaq." Walking over to Payuk who was lying on the ground, he said softly, "I hate to lose you, Payuk, but it will be better if you go with Kiviaq." Kelly patted him on the shoulder. "Do you need anything off the packhorses, Kiviaq?"

"Yes," Kiviaq quickly replied, "we need some small rope to build the travois easier."

Kelly was getting the small rope while the two warriors lifted Payuk up onto his unsaddled horse, and everyone heard Payuk's painful gasp. "Don't worry, Kelly. We will build him a travois as soon as we can get over the ridge crest. He needs to just get off that horse, which is rubbing the wound. We will treat his wound as soon as we get over the ridge crest where we cannot be seen. The others of my party are maintaining a lookout on the wagon trail from the mine."

"OK, Kiviaq. If you can't hold them for any reason, you need to send one of your warriors ahead to find us and let us know the miners are coming behind us."

Kiviaq, nodding his head, said, "I will do that, Kelly, but I think my warriors can stop them."

As Kiviaq mounted, Kelly advised him, "Take good care of him."

Turning his horse, Kiviaq waved and they headed up the slope.

Watching them until they were into the trees and out of sight, Kelly sighed. *OK, Peanut, it's you and me again. We should be able to overtake those other guys pretty soon.*

Tethering the packhorses one behind the other, Kelly started down the Iskut River on the wagon trail as the corral horses followed along behind. Enjoying the great scenery of the river valley, Kelly thought, *I wonder what Nancy is doing. She's probably teaching some kid to read or something. I wonder what Kincaid is doing right now. I got to get Sidney a pony. Not too small because I want him to ride the horse for a number of years. If he has to get on a corral rail to get into the saddle, he will grow. Jeffery will always help him saddle and unsaddle the horse. What am I going to do while Nancy is visiting all her friends in Seattle? I guess I could go see Sid Bonner for a while. I could buy a new hat...nah, I got too many already.*

Being shaken out of his dream world as Peanut misstepped into a shallow hole in the trail, Kelly realized he was getting hungry and the horses were probably getting thirsty. Stopping near a small stream that crossed the wagon trail, Kelly watered the horses and let them graze on the new grasses. While the horses were grazing, Kelly dug into one of the pack animal's load and got out several pieces of jerky and several corn dodgers.

Finishing up his lunch, Kelly remounted and continued along his way toward the *Blue Sea*, which was anchored in the Stikine River waiting for everyone to get back from the mine.

Pushing Peanut to a faster pace, Kelly knew he was going to overtake the other members of his team. He remembered Kincaid's directions—no long stops getting back to the *Blue Sea*, eat and sleep when you get to the *Blue Sea*. Moving around in the saddle, Kelly thought, *Damn, it's starting to get dark. When the hell am I going to catch up with the other guys? I hope Payuk will be alright. He will be a good addition to Kincaid crew, if that works out. Damn this saddle is hard. Need to stop and water these horses.*

Having to slow down because of the night, Kelly thought, *I didn't hear any firing all day. That could mean that the mining crews never took out after us.*

Suddenly Kelly came upon two unbridled and unsaddled horses. *They didn't seem to shy away from me. I'll just let them follow like the others. Maybe I'll find more of the miner's horses.*

Slowly trudging on through the night, Kelly made slow time. Stopping once in a while to check the other horses, Kelly was amazed how tame they were. *There must have been a good horse tender working for Henry Wilson.*

Hearing talking, Kelly immediately became more alert. Pushing Peanut forward, he stopped and called out, "Who is on the wagon trail?"

The return call was, "Who in the hell wants to know?"

Smiling, Kelly recognized Jeffery's voice. Leading his horse train, Kelly walked to where Jeffery, Fisher, and Holmes were standing, while Henry Wilson stood off by himself. "You guys taking a break?" Kelly asked.

"Yeah, our prisoner was complaining so much we let him sit in the saddle a ways back, and we even tied his hands in front to him, but we tied his feet together under the horse...he's not going anywhere," Jeffery explained.

Kelly addressed Jesse Holmes. "Mr. Holmes, how does it feel to be a free man away from the mining industry?"

"Good, Kelly. I'm not worried about getting another job. I know a few people who can get me a good job in Seattle or Portland; at least I'll stay out of jail."

Walking over to Mr. Wilson, Kelly patted him on his shoulder. "How're you doing on this trip? We have been given instructions by our boss to keep pushing for the *Blue Sea* that's anchored in the Stikine River waiting for us."

He turned to face Kelly. "You'll never get away with this trick. The mining commission for British Columbia will be all over this in no time at all."

Shrugging, Kelly replied, "We'll see.

"OK, let's load up and get down the trail. Did you see any of the mining horses along the way? I picked up three on the trail some ways back."

"You know," Fisher unsurely answered, "I think we did see two more of these horses, or what looked to be elk to us in the dark, but I bet they were horses now that I think about it."

"Well, keep an eye out. The horses did come down this wagon trail, but we just need to see them and take them back to Keller's Livery. OK, let's go." Kelly mounted and brought up the rear.

Looking up at the stream of horses and men in front of him, Kelly could see forms and not necessarily people. *What a beautiful night. The only noise is the chipping of the horse's hoofs on the ground. Tomorrow night we should be getting close to the Blue Sea.*

Riding the rest of the night, morning finally showed up with the sun's rays beaming over the east mountain of the Iskut River canyon. Continuing for another hour, Kelly saw a small stream that crossed the wagon trail and he yelled to Jeffery, "Hold up. We need to give the horses a rest and water."

Listening to the men groan as they dismounted, Kelly encouraged, "One more day of this and we can get off these horses. Let the horses drink and we will have something to eat. What I mean to eat is jerky, dried salmon, corn dodgers, and berries if we have any left. No cooking, just eat up and we're on our way again."

"These horses aren't going to last the way you have been pushing them, O'Brien," Henry Wilson complained.

Smiling, Kelly replied, "These horses will be just fine. Don't complain about them for your own shortcomings. Beside I know more about horses than you ever will. Don't concern yourself with hoping your men will come after you. Now let's everybody eat up. This will be the last stop until noon or so to water the horses and we take a quick break off these saddles. How are you doing, Mr. Holmes?"

Smiling slightly, Jesse commented, "The saddle is a little hard to get used to when you don't ride much."

"It is hard to get used to anytime when you travel as hard as we have," chimed in Jeffery.

"OK, Jeffery, lead us out. Keep some distance between horses everybody," Kelly advised.

After a quick stop for watering the horses and a quick bite to eat, the caravan stopped again just before dark.

Suddenly Fisher informed Kelly in an excited voice, "Kelly, we are only about two miles from the *Blue Sea*. See that rock pile across the river? I remember it, and it was close to the *Blue Sea*. I'd bet we could be to the *Blue Sea* in about fifteen minutes from now."

"OK, everybody, up and on them, we are just about home."

Fisher was right. The caravan reached the *Blue Sea* in about fifteen minutes, and Kelly fired three shots off and waited for a response.

Suddenly all the lights on the *Blue Sea* were turned on all at once. It was like daylight. The side ramp door was opened, the ramp was let down, and the horses were led in and stripped of saddles and cross buck packs. Kelly pointed toward the bow and said, "There are water buckets and hay in the bow. Let's take care of the horses first."

Suddenly Captain Weber was right behind Kelly. "How was your excursion? If you have noticed, we have five extra horses that showed up earlier today. I don't know where they came from, but we ran them in here. They seemed to be well-behaved so we fed them some hay and gave them water. We wrapped some rope around their necks and they're tied in the back, out of the way."

Kelly smiled as he thought about this. *Keller is going to love this. Kincaid said Keller could have all the horses we get from the mining outfit for the back rent that the mine owed him.*

"Oh thanks, Captain Weber. We picked up a couple of extra ourselves along the way. What we need is a bath, food, and a place to sleep for a week." Both men laughed. "Oh, and by the way, could one of your men watch our prisoner? See that man over there, the big guy in the red shirt...we will need one of your men to watch him when we get some shuteye."

"You bet, Kelly. We can help you out with that. I've already got Paul and Mike in the kitchen. You and your men can eat, take a bath, and then we will assign each one of you to a room for a good night's sleep. How long has it been since you guys have slept?"

Shrugging his shoulders, Kelly replied, "About three days, and we're about done in, as are the horses."

"Where is that Indian you had with you?"

Slowly shaking his head, Kelly replied, "He got shot in the leg, and we had to leave him with the Tlingit that were covering our retreat. I also got shot in the side, but it was not a bad wound. Which reminds me, we have about used up our supply of bandages, could you have someone bandage my side after I take a bath?"

320

"You bet, Kelly. I'll have Chief Mate Harrison take care of that. He is our doctor on board. And after breakfast in the morning we will start for Wrangell," Captain Weber advised Kelly.

Once Kelly and his group, including Henry Wilson, ate a large delicious meal of elk steak, mashed potatoes, bread, and a large piece of cake that Chief Mate Harrison had made himself, the men bathed, and they were assigned a room for the night.

Next morning, Kelly was awakened to the noise of the engines revving up power to move into the Stikine River. Quickly getting dressed, he made his way to the wheelhouse. Opening the wheelhouse door, Kelly asked, "Are we leaving right now?"

"No," Captain Weber said loudly, "we are just getting the power up so when it's time, we can pull out into the river at full power. We'll have breakfast first if that will be alright?"

Nodding his head, Kelly answered back, "OK. I'll go back and shave before breakfast."

Captain Weber turned his large frame toward Kelly and nodded as Kelly left the wheelhouse.

While everyone was eating, except the captain and the chief mate, Captain Weber entered the mess and announced, "It is 0930 hours and we need to leave here by 1030 hours to hit the estuary at a good time. Kelly, that gives you and your crew about an hour to finish eating and check the horses before Paul and Stan pull stabilization poles. I would like two of your men to help out with that detail if it would be alright?"

"Yes sir, Captain," Kelly responded, as everybody laughed. "We can take care of that. Oh, and by the way, what do you want us to do with the dirty linen on the beds?"

Captain Weber waved his hand toward Kelly. "Don't concern yourself about that. Well take care of that once we get back to Wrangell."

"Thanks, Captain. We all sure did appreciate the beds last night." The other men chimed in with thanks.

Smirking slightly, Captain Weber shook his head. "You guys looked like death warmed over when you got in here. It must have been the lack of sleep. Anyway, one hour, Kelly," and Captain Weber left the mess.

"OK, let's eat up and check the stock. There are a lot of extra horses we need to check. Jeffery and Fisher, I want you to help out with the stabilization poles. Mr. Holmes, you might try to give us a hand with the horses. Mr. Wilson, when we get finished eating, I will retie your hands, and I want you in my sight at all times. If I move you move, got it?"

"I'm not some kid you can order around, Kelly, whoever you are," Henry Wilson said sarcastically.

"Mr. Wilson, if you don't cooperate with me, I will shoot you in one of your knees, and you will never walk right again. You know I will do it. You have seen me pull the trigger before." Then, looking from Henry Wilson to his crew, he continued. "When we pull out into the Stikine River, I want everybody standing by watching for problems with the horses. Now, if there are no more questions, let's get to it."

With the help of Fisher and Jeffery, Stan and Paul got the stabilizer poles brought in, and at the same time Captain Weber signaled down to Mike on the Chadburn, FULL SPEED AHEAD. Captain Weber mumbled under his breath, "Give'r to me, Mikey Boy." And the engine roared as the *Blue Sea* entered the full flow of the Stikine River current. Stan and Paul immediately took their stations on the forward port and starboard, getting ready to do their Mark Twain just in case the captain wanted some depths.

Feeling the *Blue Sea* heave high into the water, Kelly yelled, "Hold on."

Jeffery and Fisher were standing steady with the horses, as the *Blue Sea* settled down in the river current. Jesse was even helping to hold and steady the horses.

Captain Weber's voice came over the loudspeaker. "Alright gents, we got about two hours before we hit the estuary. Relax and get some coffee."

Out of the corner of his eye, Kelly saw Henry Wilson trying to coach Jesse over to talk to him, but Jesse turned away and went to the mess for a cup of coffee. Kelly followed him to speak to him about what was going to happen when they got to Wrangell. After some conversation, Kelly ended with, "Whatever happens, you don't talk to him. I don't want him to be able to say anything you might have said offhand."

"I understand, Kelly, I won't."

Arriving back down to the stock deck, he waved over Fisher and Jeffery. "Give me a hand sorting some stuff out while we've got some time. What I want to do is get all the food stuff onto one packhorse and all the rest of the equipment and gear onto the other packhorse. Then, Jeffery, when it becomes convenient, I want you to take the packhorse with the food over to Payuk's lodge and give it to his tribe over there. Do you know its location?"

"Yes, I do."

"Fisher, the other packhorse and Payuk's horse goes to Keller's Livery. The Department has a small storage room behind the large barn that the equipment goes into. All the horses will be run into Keller's front corral for him to decide what to do with them. I'm going to take Mr. Wilson and Jesse Holmes to see Deputy Sheriff Marlin. Then probably I'll see if James is in his office."

Getting the packhorse's loads organized, Kelly looked to Wilson to make sure he was staying within his eyesight. Waving Jesse over to him, Kelly explained, "When we get to Wrangell, you and I have to go to the Deputy Sheriff's office with Mr. Wilson and that satchel full of records and notations about the Twin Forks Mining and Dredging Company."

"OK, everybody," Kelly raised his voice, "everybody knows what to do when we get to Wrangell. I'm going to talk with the captain now for final instructions for him and his crew."

Slowly opening the door, Kelly noticed the two Lab pups right off. They were sleeping in their box just as before.

Closing the door, Kelly asked, "I'd like a word with you, Captain."

"Sure thing, Kelly, what can I do for you?"

"OK, when we get into Wrangell Harbor, I need you to situate the *Blue Sea* so you can drop the front ramp for us to unload the horses. Once we get the horses unloaded, I'll need you to anchor like you did before and sit tight until we get word to you."

"Would it be permissible for me or my men to go into town?"

"Sure, Captain Weber. You or your men are not under arrest. We just need you here for witnesses. It's just that it will take a while to get our ducks in a row on shore. I have to talk to the Deputy Sheriff and James Kincaid and let them know how things stand as of now. There will be a helluva legal battle brewing, but not in Wrangell. It will probably be in Seattle or somewhere like that."

Again the captain's voice sounded on the speaker. "Getting near the estuary, but it does not look bad."

Feeling a small roll in the *Blue Sea*, everyone sighed in relief at being through the estuary without any problems.

Going to the bow of the *Blue Sea*, Kelly and Holmes looked at a calm sight. "Well, Jesse, here is where you start your new life. I think you will have to hang around here for a couple of days, but eventually I think the judge will cut you loose, especially after he looks at your bookkeeping."

The *Blue Sea* was coming into shore, and the bow ramp was ready to slowly drop, then the *Blue Sea* finally stopped and the bow ramp went down. "OK, you guys, you know what you have to do. Mr. Wilson, you stay with me and Holmes."

When the *Blue Sea* stopped moving, Kelly led the way for Holmes and Mr. Wilson to debark the vessel. Waving back to the captain, who was in the wheelhouse, Kelly was glad to be back in Wrangell.

Making his way through town to Deputy Sheriff Marlin's office, he was being greeted by folks. Opening the sheriff's office door, he saw that Deputy Sheriff Marlin was cleaning his rifles that he kept in the office.

"I'll be damned. They haven't killed you off yet."

"I have one prisoner for you to lock up, and I have one witness I will take over to Mrs. Mackly's. "Right now," Kelly reached over and cut the small ropes that tied Mr. Wilson's hands, "I need you to lock this guy up for safe keeping."

"Who is he, Kelly?"

"Just lock him up first and then we'll get to the details."

Waiting for the jail cell to lock, Marlin came back into his office, "OK, it better be good."

"This man's name is—"

"Wait, wait, Kelly. I have to get the right paperwork...Now, go ahead."

"This man's name is Henry Wilson. He is the manager of the Twin Forks Mining and Dredging Company out of Seattle, Washington.

He is charged with poaching, illegal shipping, and illegal mining procedures. Is Judge W. G. Thomas around this week?"

Nodding, Marlin replied, "Yeah, I think so."

"OK, thanks, Deputy Sheriff Marlin. We'll be talking again real soon. Right now I'm going over to the Department of Agriculture office to check in with James. By the way," Kelly pointed at Jesse, "this is Jesse Holmes; he is part of this mad circle."

"Boy, James is going to be glad to see you. He has been running around here like an old mother hen. Maybe now he will settle down."

"OK, I'll see you later."

CHAPTER TWENTY-THREE

Opening the large wooden door, he saw Sara staring right at him, and Kelly put his finger up to his lips, to be quiet. He and Jesse walked into the reception room, leaning close to Sara. "Is James in?"

Nodding yes, and speaking in a very low voice, she answered, "He has been worried sick for you guys."

Smiling, Kelly spoke loudly, "I got shot, Payuk got shot, but we made it back."

Instantly, shuffling could be heard as James came tearing out of his office. "Both of you got shot...bad?"

Shaking James's outreached hand, Kelly replied, "No, not bad."

"Who is this?" James asked.

"This man is going to be our prime witness. This is Jesse Holmes, the bookkeeper of Twin Forks Mining."

"Come on in, you two. Sara, get some coffee. Kelly, quickly fill me in on the big picture."

Finding a seat and relaxing, Kelly invited Jesse to sit down. "I stopped on the way from the *Blue Sea* and had our prime suspect, Henry Wilson, locked up in Deputy Sheriff Marlin's jail, and I made the charges."

"Damn," James exclaimed, "I wish I'd have been there with you guys.

"Jesse," James addressed the bookkeeper, "Do you have any proof of Twin Forks operations other than your say-so?"

Jesse smiled and handed James a canvas satchel. "Inside are all the sales, receipts, skins counts that were shipped, and all the gold that was shipped. I have also taken the liberty of making a few margin notes along the way, after Henry Wilson approved and signed the reports. The papers in that satchel will show many things that were being done contrary to the contract with the British Columbia Mining Office in Victoria."

Nodding, James explained to Jesse, "Yes, I received a letter from the British Columbia Mining Council in Vancouver, British Columbia, requesting we check into Twin Forks's activities. They also requested us to stop any existing activities that seemed not to stay within contract boundaries, or something like that. You have to be a lawyer to read and understand a lot of that kind of language. Oh, and by the way, Kelly, I sent for Wilbur Johnson—you've met him—he will be here tomorrow to start getting affidavits from everybody involved." James quickly glanced at Jesse. "Wilbur Johnson is the legal staff for the Department of Agriculture in this region."

"So what happens now?" Jesse asked.

Sighing deeply, James thought for a second before he answered, "By the damn, I don't know for sure." Shrugging, he continued. "I think it will go something like this. Tomorrow, Wilbur Johnson will interview you, Kelly, for all the pertinent players and how they were involved. Then I think Johnson will start getting affidavits from all the players about what they knew and when they knew it. By that time, I'm thinking that a representative from the British Columbia Mining Council will be here to try and collaborate stories with Wilbur Johnson. Somewhere along the way, there will be a lawyer showing up for Henry Wilson from the Twin Forks Mining and Dredging Company out of Seattle, Washington. Once all the affidavits and preliminary questions have been taken care of, Judge W. G. Thomas will review and send the whole event probably to Victoria or Vancouver for trial."

Shaking his head, Jesse showed some concern about living expenses. "My money is in a bank in Seattle."

"The best thing I can suggest is go see the banker here and talk to the bank president and see if you can work out a deal to get money from your Seattle bank. But before you get too worried, you have just come under the jurisdiction of the Territory of Alaska. When it is all transferred as a trial, or whatever is going to happen is transferred to Victoria or Vancouver, you will be the ward of British Columbia." Smiling, he said, "Jesse, you are the prime witness on this case and the governments are going to take care of you."

"Well, that makes me feel better."

"I spoke with Judge Thomas about the gold that is in the bank safe. I asked him if some of that gold could be used for expenses for the *Blue Sea* or any other expense needed for the witnesses. His answer was not only no, but hell no! All expenses will be paid by the Territory of Alaska like any other case."

Kelly shifted in his seat. "James, you were assuming a lot about what was going to happen at the mining camp."

Smiling, he answered, "No, I wasn't, Kelly; I knew who I had put in charge."

And everybody laughed.

"Jesse, can I put that satchel in my safe here in the office? I would feel a whole lot better about that evidence being in my safe."

Jesse handed the satchel to James, who immediately took the satchel to his safe and opened the door, put the satchel in, and closed the door that automatically locked. Standing to address Kelly and Jesse, he said, "That makes me feel a whole lot better. Kelly, why don't you take Jesse over to the Mercantile for some new clothes or whatever he needs and then take him to Mrs. Mackly's Parker Boarding House and get him settled?"

"Right away, James," Kelly replied as he and Jesse rose and exited James office. "Oh, by the way, Sara, this is Jesse Holmes, in case you missed it before. Jesse, this is Sara; she runs the outfit sometimes."

"Oh, get out of here, you two. Nice to meet you, Jesse. If you have any questions you can always come here to get some of your answers."

"Thanks, Sara, nice to meet you also."

Getting Jesse some new clothes, boots, and a new hat, Kelly headed for Parker's Boarding House.

"Mrs. Mackly," Kelly said when they arrived. "This is Jesse Holmes. He will need a place to stay for at least four or five days. Just send the bill to the Department of Agriculture."

"Good," Mrs. Mackly replied.

Before Mrs. Mackly started reading off the rules, meal times, and the other rules Kelly waved good-bye. "Listen, I've got to go. Jesse, I'll see you tomorrow."

Leaving the boarding house, Kelly thought, *I hope all this legal stuff works out like James described to me and Jesse. I think James will talk to Captain Weber tomorrow. Right now I have to get Fisher put back in jail before I go home.*

Coming to the livery, Kelly was surprised to see Janet standing very close to Jeffery. He smiled. *I wonder...*

"Fisher," Kelly called, "what are you doing—currycombing those horses out?"

"Oh hi, Kelly. Well, before we went to the mining camp I was told by Sheriff Marlin to help Keller and work at the livery. I guess he didn't want me hanging around the jail."

"Well, that's great, Fisher. Just make sure you're in jail by meal time or you might not get fed."

"I'll sure do that, Kelly." He said as he waved to Kelly.

330

Walking over to Jeffery and Janet, Kelly commented, "Nice to see you out and about, Janet."

"I just would not be happy with myself before I came down here and saw for myself how Jeff survived the raid you guys went on. Something like that was very dangerous."

"Yes, it was, Janet," Kelly agreed.

Hugging Jeffery one more time, Janet advised, "I've got to get back to work before the evening meal. I'll see you tonight, Jeff."

Nodding, he replied, "Yes, you will, Janet."

Waving back to both men, Janet hailed, "I'll see you guys later."

Letting Janet get out of hearing range, Kelly jokingly said, "Jeff, Jeffy...what's this?"

"Oh shut up, Kelly, it's nothing."

"Well, it doesn't sound like nothing. Anyway, make sure Fisher gets back to the jail before meal time or he may not get fed."

"He's in jail!" Jeffery exclaimed. "I thought that was all over with."

"Well, he never really was, but I put him in there just for a place for him to spend his nights. When James talked with Deputy Sheriff Marlin about Fisher, he told the deputy that Fisher could come to work for Keller in the daytime."

"Oh, that really makes me feel good. I would have not liked to see Fisher in jail after what we have all been through together."

"Right now, I have to get on home. I'll see you in the morning." Kelly waved and walked away.

"Janet and I are just friends," Jeffery stressed.

Nodding his head without looking back, Kelly said, "Must be really good friends."

Opening the door to the Mercantile, James saw Sam Boron waiting on a customer, so he stood by. He was amazed at all the stuff Sam had managed to cram into his store to sell.

"What can I do for you, James?" Sam asked.

Digging two pieces of paper from his shirt pocket, James handed them to Sam and explained, "Here is a list of people that are authorized to buy certain goods from you, and I would like you to charge the Territory of Alaska. You can give the charge tickets to Judge Thomas. The names are there and a list of only certain goods. I don't need to tell you, Sam, that the payment might be coming a little slow, but eventually you will get paid."

Nodding, Sam said, "Yeah, I have to deal with the mines and fishing contractors about the same way, so it's nothing new. Yeah, I can do this, James, not to worry."

As James was walking home, he happened to see one of Payuk's companions and he stopped to ask him, "Have you heard anything about Payuk yet?"

"No, Mr. Kincaid, but it should not be too long. Kiviaq is a good, reliable warrior."

"I'm sure he is. Thank you for your help."

Entering the house from the back door as always, he saw that Suzette was in the kitchen getting ready to feed Thomas and Sadie. Suzette said, "Boy, have you and your guys made a stir around town. Everybody is talking about how Payuk almost got killed and Kelly was also shot in the side. And several of the Tlingit boys at school are talking about getting a lot of skins and body parts for their lodge."

"Yeah, Kelly and the guys really did a good job." He paused. "That Kelly, he's just like me. A good deed well done justifies the means."

"Oh, you don't believe that, and I don't think Kelly believes it either," Suzette countered.

"No we don't, but sometimes you have to stretch the bounds to make your point."

"Get washed up, we're having mutton tonight."

"Good. I like mutton. A lot of people don't, but it's a good change from pork, beef, and fish."

"Too bad Moaka is not here tonight. Mutton is his favorite meal."

Finishing supper, James helped Suzette get the children ready for bed, while Suzette cleaned up the kitchen.

"Do you miss Bray, James?"

"Yes, but it's hit and miss. I think of him, and then somehow those thoughts just seem to go away. He was a good friend to the entire family. I don't plan on getting another dog, at least not right away."

"Have you heard from Sid Bonner about Moaka's transfer yet?"

"No, and that bothers me some. Course things take time. I know that, but Moaka is really anxious to know. Oh, he'll go to Barrow alright, but there is a chance of some other stuff working in Moaka's favor for this job. We just need to hear from Sid."

"Did you hear that Janet is going to be working at the Steak and Stack part-time? Mrs. Mackly give her the OK, because Mrs. Mackly said she does not need Janet full time at the boarding house."

Shaking his head, he said, "Yeah, she's a go-getter. She'll do well around here."

"How do you think the legal proceeding will go for Wilbur Johnson?"

Smiling, James nodded. "He'll be in his glory. This kind of stuff is what he lives for. Kelly is going to make it real easy for Wilbur to get people aligned with what they did in the whole process." He picked up the paper and then laid it back down in his lap. "You know, Suzette, I'm really not going to be a very big player in the case. Kelly is the guy that has all the information first hand. Anyway, Judge Thomas will be right on top of this until he sends it to a high court."

"Well, listen, James, I'm going to bed. I'm a little tired tonight."

"How are you feeling? Has the baby started moving yet?"

"Oh no, James. It's too early for that; good night."

"Good night, Suzette."

Next morning, James walked into the office and Sara was all smiles. "I have something for Mr. Kincaid." She handed James a large envelope. "It came on the night mail."

Smiling, James looked at the return address; it was from Sid Bonner. Holding it in his hand, he looked at Sara. "It's heavy. Has Moaka been in yet this morning?"

"Yes, he has. He asked me to tell you he would be back midmorning. He does not know about the letter. I figured you were the one to tell him everything."

"OK, thanks, Sara. In the meantime I need to go see Captain Weber. I want him to know that he and his men are not the object of this investigation, but he will have to stick around for a while for Johnson to visit with him and maybe a lawyer or two. Also I need to go over to Payuk's lodge and see if they have any news about Payuk. Kelly will most likely be busy with Wilbur Johnson when he gets here soon." Walking into his office, James sat down at his desk and thought, *This large envelope holds a man's destiny.* Shaking his head, James laid the envelope on his desk. *Of all the years Moaka and I have been together it came down to our parting with a note from some guy in Seattle. Moaka will be really happy in Barrow. Suzette and I are very happy for him.*

Letting the envelope rest on his desk, James pushed it around and around wondering what was in the wording of the instructions for Moaka. Looking out the window, James suddenly became sad because he was not going to have Moaka around. *Moaka was loyal to the point that he would follow me into hell, as long as I was leading the way. Employee loyalty like that just does not come around every day.* Picking up the envelope, James slowly opened the seal and removed the contents. There were forms that were to be signed concerning personnel, change of duty stations' forms, and most importantly, the letter explaining the circumstances under which Moaka would be transferred to Barrow.

Starting to read the letter, James could not read fast enough. He could not believe what he was reading. This was a complete turnaround from previous conversations James had with Sid when James was in Seattle. Putting the letter and forms back into the envelope, James placed it in his top desk drawer. He would share the information with Moaka when he returned to the office.

Just then, James heard Sara's voice. "Well, bless my heart, if it isn't Wilbur Johnson. Come on in and sit, I'll tell Mr. Kincaid you are here." Leaning into James's office, Sara quietly announced, "Mr. Johnson is here."

James stood and walked out into the reception room and eagerly welcomed Wilbur. "By golly, Wilbur, we haven't seen you for some time. How have you been? Let's go in my office and talk for just a bit about the situation here. Do you want any coffee or anything?"

"No, James, I'm fine."

James laid out the entire event as he understood it to be, but suggested strongly that Wilbur speak with Kelly O'Brien before he started questioning witnesses.

Listening carefully and taking a few notes, Wilbur asked, "Is there a place around here I can use as a private room for my interrogations?"

"Yes, Wilbur, I set up a room in the city office. It is secure and with a good heavy door. The mayor said you could use the room as long as you needed it."

"Can we go take a look at it? I've already checked into the Parker Boarding House." He smiled. "That Mrs. Mackly is still as happy as she ever was. Is the Steak and Stack still the best place to eat?"

"Wilbur, you have just hit the two best places in town. They both will make you happy."

Showing Wilbur the office he would use, James introduced Wilbur to the city clerk. "Listen, Wilbur, I've got to go see someone soon; is there anything I can do for you before I leave?"

"No, James, thanks. I'll just get my paperwork over here from the boarding house and then I can start setting up shop. Where is Kelly right now?" Wilbur asked.

Thinking for second, James responded, "He is just about getting back to the office."

"If it would be alright, I'd like to talk with him this afternoon and get things started."

"Sure, Wilbur. You can check at the office on your way to the boarding house because it's kinda on the way. Also, I will send him to you if I see him."

"That would be fine, James. Thanks."

"OK, Wilbur, I'm on my way. I'll catch up with you later."

About to catch a ride on a small boat to the *Blue Sea*, James jumped from the boat and pointed. "Here comes the man I was going to see," as Captain Weber was coming to shore with one of his crewmen. "Thanks for the lift anyway, Mace."

"Sure thing, Mr. Kincaid; anytime."

Meeting Captain Weber at the dock, James warmly greeted him. "Welcome to Wrangell again, Charles. I just wanted to speak with you a short time and let you know that you and your crewmembers' affidavits will be most helpful in closing this case against Twin Forks Mining. I want you to feel relaxed and not intimidated when the

Department of Agriculture's legal man, Wilbur Johnson, starts asking questions of you and your crew. Your company may have to pay a fine of some kind, but I have laid the groundwork for you and your crew to be spared in all this."

Smiling broadly, Captain Weber thanked James. "That makes us feel real good. You've already said that we will be staying here for a while, but that will give us a chance to do some repair work on the *Blue Sea*."

"By the way, all the food and clothing you will need while you are here can be charged to the Territory of Alaska. You are no longer a ward of the Department of Agriculture. You are now called prime witnesses to this case. You can do most of your business at Sam Boron's at the Mercantile. I've already talked to him about you and others."

Turning back to the man he had brought along, Captain Weber said, "Hear that, Mike? We are all prime witnesses. That will give you something to tell your grandkids. Thanks again, James. I guess we'll be seeing you around from time to time."

Shaking Charles's hand again, James turned and left Captain Weber and Mike on the dock tying up their dingy to the dock. James thought, *Going to be a lot of players in this case, but Wilbur Johnson is just the man to sort it all out.*

James knocked on the lodge door where Payuk lived, and a small, older maiden took James's hand and led him just inside the door and announced his presence.

"Thank you," James said and nodded to the old maiden. "Has Payuk returned to his home?"

Motioning him to follow her, she led the way to the back of the lodge where several people were gathered. Getting closer to the group, James could see Payuk lying on mats being attended to by the tribal doctor.

Being welcomed into the group, James knelt down and smiled. "I'm glad to see you back, Payuk. Are you feeling well?"

Smiling back at James, Payuk replied, "Yes, I feel fine. I can walk, but the tribal doctor wanted to check me out. I can be in the office in the morning. Kiviaq and his men really did a good job of taking care of me."

"If you feel good enough, I would like to talk with you in the morning."

"I will be there, Mr. Kincaid."

James stood and took one step back and turned away to leave the lodge. The lodge was busy with children dancing, old men telling stories, women cooking food, and men working on their bow and arrows and spears.

As James left the lodge he thought, *Yeah, Payuk is going to replace Moaka real good, in some ways better. He is young, eager to learn, and intelligent. Kelly swears by him when it comes to tribal issues. He seems to understand, course why would he not...he is Tlingit.*

When James returned to the office, Moaka was there catching up on some of his reading of regulations and laws. Shaking his head, James thought, *They are always changing.* Walking over to his office, James asked, "Moaka, have you got time to come to my office for a minute?"

"Sure, Kincaid."

Seeing Moaka following James into his office, Sara felt saddened. That sight would be gone very soon.

James sat in his chair behind his desk and instructed Moaka, "Have a seat." He handed Moaka the brown envelope. "Open it up and read what Sid Bonner had to say about you going to Barrow."

Slowly Moaka opened the envelope as he asked James, "Is good news?"

"Go ahead and read it, then you tell me."

Starting to read the letter, Moaka looked at James and shook his head. "I still work for you. No contract...transfer."

"That's right, Moaka. You will be just another employee, just like here except you will be working in Barrow. Same pay, same benefits, same everything."

"Kincaid can be right?"

"Oh, it is right, Moaka. Sid Bonner just felt like he wanted to hang on to you. You will be of great value in the tundra counting game and looking for poaching, dealing with the problems of the Inuit, and trying to make people understand about new laws for the Territory of Alaska. Yes, you will be of great help to the Department."

"When can leave, Kincaid?"

"Well, I need you to wrap up what you are working on and give me a final report. I'd say you could leave in a week or so, don't you?"

"That be good," Moaka voiced excitedly.

"Is there anything that I can do for you to help you get things wrapped up?"

"No, Kincaid, I do."

"Alright, Moaka, get out of here." James smiled. "Let me know if I can help in any way."

Later in the day as James was on the way home, he shrugged his shoulders and thought, *Things are as they should be as of right now, but who knows what will happen tomorrow?*

* * *

AND THE SAGA FOR JAMES
AND HIS FRIENDS CONTINUES ON . . .
A Note to My Readers

* * *

The author is busily working on another adventure story,
so stay tuned. Expect the new adventure
story to be published next year.
The author, Curtis D. Carney

About the Author

Being a native of Idaho, Curtis has always been close to wild game, good fishing, and high mountains. He traveled extensively throughout the world while serving in the Marines and later in life as a tourist, during his working years and after retirement. In each country he visited, his interest in the country's cultures and traditions were of the upmost importance. For many years, he has worked closely with the Idaho Fish and Game protecting and establishing wildlife habitat, and has given numerous presentations concerning best management practices of rivers and reservoirs. Alaska has always sparked his interest, especially during the period of time just after the initial purchase from Russia. Having traveled broadly in Alaska and being inquisitive about the ancient traditions of the Eskimo people, Curtis was driven to write about the opening of the new frontier.

www.ingramcontent.com/pod-product-compliance
Lightning Source LLC
Chambersburg PA
CBHW071202020726
47502CB00002B/504